M. I. Weller, Thomas Nichols

Asmodeus in New York

Asmodeus in New York

M. I. Weller, Thomas Nichols

Asmodeus in New York

ISBN/EAN: 9783743337626

Manufactured in Europe, USA, Canada, Australia, Japa

Cover: Foto ©Andreas Hilbeck / pixelio.de

Manufactured and distributed by brebook publishing software (www.brebook.com)

M. I. Weller, Thomas Nichols

Asmodeus in New York

ASMODEUS IN NEW-YORK.

M. I. Weller.

NEW-YORK:

LONGCHAMP & CO., PUBLISHERS.

1868.

CONTENTS.

CHAPTER IX.

CHAPTER X.

CHAPTER XI.

CHAPTER XII.

CHAPTER XIII.

CHAPTER XIV.

CHAPTER XV.

CHAPTER XVI.

CHAPTER XVII.

CHAPTER XVIII.

CHAPTER XIX.

CHAPTER XX.

CHAPTER XXI.

CHAPTER XXII.

CHAPTER XXIII.

CHAPTER XXIV.

Asmodeus in New-York.

—◆—

CHAPTER I.

WHICH IS SOMETHING LIKE A PREFACE.

WHOEVER has read the *Lame Devil*, from Le Sage,* has very likely wondered at the fancy of the novelist releasing a polite devil from his captivity in a vial, for the purpose of revealing to the world the mysteries of Spanish society.

The poets of the eighteenth century yearned in song for the good old time when people amused themselves with fairy tales; and in our own century we are even more inclined to consider as a mere fancy of the mind the interference of genii, either good or bad, in human affairs.

True, writers of olden times have more than once alluded to Asmodeus. In Tobit's book, for instance, he is made to bear a not very enviable character, being charged with the murder, one after another, of Sarah's seven husbands; and for that bloody performance, he was pointed out as the demon of divorce, or the evil genius of marriage. Tobit himself could only get rid of

---

* Born in 1668, died in 1747. His works, *Gil Blas* and the *Lame Devil*, are among the most popular novels up to this day.

this unwelcome visitor by dint of praying and fasting. It appears, also, that the great King Solomon got into difficulty with the same devil. According to the Talmud, he was expelled from his kingdom by Asmodeus ; and the author or compiler of that book is cautiously reticent of the causes which brought on this catastrophe, through an ill-disguised fear of Asmodeus, whom he calls, with every mark of respect, the chief or prince of demons.

Those who believe that Jewish legends emanated from God are, therefore, ill-qualified to discredit the existence of the personage we allude to, especially when we consider the remote times in which the momentous events we have briefly related occurred.   On the other hand, as the *Mercure Galant*, a French periodical, asserted, in 1707—the year the *Lame Devil* was printed—that Le Sage could never have written so charming a work but for the help of a supernatural genius, one is free to believe Asmodeus did really remove the roofs of the houses of Seville, to show to an eager public what was going on therein.

We admit, moreover that our hero has been seldom heard of, either in the Old or the New World, for one hundred and fifty years past ; the consequence being, that people have come to doubt whether he ever existed. What he did during that long period of time ; where he resided ; the services, good or bad, bestowed by him upon mankind, are circumstances involved in obscurity, and which I could not learn, though enjoying Asmodeus's friendship several days.

That friendship and how it happened are, after all, the points of interest for the reader ; for to this circumstance is due the present work. So, dropping all needless disquisition concerning the existence of the prince of demons, I will explain how I became acquainted with Asmodeus.

I had just arrived in the commercial metropolis of the
United States, not for the purpose of studying the manners
and institutions of that great country, (an enterprise which
had been so successfully done, it seems, a few years before
that it opened to two young writers the doors of the French
Academy,) but—and I state it plainly—only to make
money.　People want plenty of elbow-room in the Old
World ; and the New offers to merchants and operatives
facilities to be found nowhere else.　But with whatever energy he has been endowed, no man finds it easy to acquire wealth or achieve success in a foreign land.　Every
thing is against him.　He struggles among men whose traditions, habits, and laws are unknown to him.　He feels
his way in the dark, and often stumbles into pitfalls.
Guides for travelers have been published in every language, in both hemispheres ; but if any one be enlightened
as to the roads he has to follow and the stopping-places
where he may gratify his curiosity, he is, nevertheless, left
in the dark as regards the habits of the country he goes
through.　Their institutions themselves remain a dead letter for want of opportunity to see them in operation, as the
most ingenuous commentaries leave too often in unprejudiced minds false or exaggerated notions.　In our age, the
fight for a living is difficult everywhere ; a great deal more
so when carried on in a strange land, and against adversaries to whom a knowledge of their native country and its
wants secures, almost to a certainty, the prize.

Now, while I was thinking over the adventurous spirit
which drives, nowadays, so many young men from their
native land, and wishing to possess some magical power
through which I could detect the weak points of those
among whom I was destined to live, somebody knocked
at my door, and I saw coming in

ASMODEUS !

Such, at least, was the name by which the individual
who interrupted my meditations introduced himself ; and
on hearing this name, which has so conspicuously figured
in both ancient and modern literature, I stared with astonishment at the stranger.   He had all those peculiarities of
figure and countenance that tradition gives to Asmodeus—
a mocking smile, a small stature, and a queer though
tasteful dress.   He was leaning on a stick—a needful
companion, as I supposed, for his claudication.   He submitted awhile to my examination, and then said :

"I am Asmodeus—the same that conducted a favorite
novelist through the labyrinth of human passions.   European people and their vices have been so often depicted,
that in America only we may expect to find something new.
Yet, even here, new pictures of society are not easily taken,
as mankind is nearly the same everywhere.   Whatever
be its climate, we find the same passions, vices, and faults,
in every country.   The complexion changes, the blood is
more or less colored, but the passions that burn under our
mortal envelope are nearly identical, whether men live
near the frozen seas or by the banks of the Orinoco.   Still,
in spite of hundreds of books published at home and
abroad, the United States are little known, and no country, on account of its future greatness, deserves to be more
closely surveyed.   The task, I admit, is not an easy one ;
for American society likes to enshroud all its actions, good
or bad, in mystery, and it especially distrusts foreigners.
When Americans condescend to show themselves, it is
with the expectation that the observer will be favorably
impressed.   You wish to know something of the doings
and feelings of a people among whom you have resolved

to settle. Come along, then, with me; I will show them as naked as was Truth when emerging from the well. I care little whether I am pointed out as a good or bad spirit; I shall be satisfied if I succeed in amusing and teaching the reader. Such was the run for the book I suggested to Le Sage in the last century, that two young men fought a duel for the possession of the last copy. But it is not for me to promise you the same infatuation from the public for the work that will reflect, as in a trusty mirror, our strollings in New-York. The present generation is dull, and soon becomes tired of every new thing. I am well aware of it; and it remains to be seen how they will welcome the name of a devil whose mirth their forefathers so much enjoyed."

I eagerly availed myself of the proffered opportunity to become at once acquainted with the men and things of the New World; and as Asmodeus warned me we should visit the mansions of the wealthy, as well as the abodes of vice and misery, I hastily threw a cloak over my best clothes, and went out with my unexpected and obliging guide.

CHAPTER II.

"YOU are the Count of Montgomery," said Asmodeus, knocking at the door of a splendid residence situated in one of the principal avenues of New-York. "A title of nobility has a pleasant sound in this country, which boasts of democratic institutions. As for the name you assume, nobody will quarrel with you about it; for heraldic science is very limited among men unincumbered with a nobility; and besides, every body takes up, as a matter of course, whatever name suits him. Not a few even change that commodity as often as their linen. We have Washingtons and La Fayettes by the dozen, their number being quite as large as the innumerable Smiths and Browns. Another peculiarity of the American people deserves also to be noticed: many a father names his son, besides his Christian name, after either a friend, benefactor, or some great man, dead or living. When two or three generations have passed away, the family name is lost sight of, and the other, more pleasing or better known, holds its ground. It is in that way we have in the United States so many families who delight in the name of Washington—not to speak of other famous names—though in reality they have no blood relation with the founder of the great republic."

We entered. The lady of the house, richly attired in a

silver-brocaded dress and wearing a crown of diamonds, very kindly welcomed us, thanking Asmodeus for bringing in a distinguished stranger. The introduction over, we mingled with the crowd, and went through the rooms opened to the guests, while the lady led to an adjacent room a few female friends, to show them her necklaces, rings, bracelets, and other jewels.

" American ladies," said Asmodeus, " avail themselves of every opportunity to exhibit their treasures, down to their silver, china, and linen. They are fond of jewels, the most showy being especially in favor. But I would not warrant that all those gems that flash in the gaslight are genuine stones. There is such a demand now for California diamonds that, very likely, many sets now adorning the wives of lucky speculators are mingled with worthless imitations. Time is necessary to learn how to distinguish precious stones from spurious ones, and few persons can devote as much leisure as did yonder Jew banker in collecting pearls, the smallest of which in his possession is worth twenty thousand dollars. He recently gave to his wife a necklace made up of twenty of such pearls, and their number increases every year."

In the mean while, dancing had commenced in several spacious rooms ; in others, card-playing was being indulged in. Servants, wearing black garments and white neckties, were busy carrying refreshments around. Many persons, preferring the pleasures of eating to those of playing or dancing, were seated in another room at a table loaded with meats and delicacies. Next to this, another room, elegantly furnished, was crowded with young and old men, indulging in smoking. Boxes of cigars were piled up on elegant *étagères ;* and I noticed that many a smoker, besides the cigar he was smoking, filled his pocket with that

luxury.   While going through the several rooms opened to
the public, Asmodeus called my attention to their costly
furniture.   Some of these rooms were lined with fine *bro-
catel*, imported from France and Italy, China and Japan,
the latter conspicuous for their fantastical drawings and
patterns ; others with Persian and Indian cloths ; and the
several pieces of furniture were of unexceptionable taste.
Some were inlaid with gold, bronze, or China ; some were
made up of rosewood artistically carved.   Gems of art
and curiosities of every description were displayed upon
étagères ; and through the house, made bright as day by
hundreds of gaslights, one walked on soft, smooth carpets
of the best manufactures of Europe.   They alone were
worth a fortune.

Amazed at such luxury, exceeding that of many a patri-
cian family in Europe, I thought our Amphitryon was either
one of those wealthy merchants whose ships carry the
American flag over the broad ocean, or those manufacturers who build up enormous fortunes at the expense of the
public.

"You are mistaken," said Asmodeus.   "We will call, by
and by, on one of those merchant-princes you állude to.
For the present we are in the house of one of Juno's priestesses.   You are aware, Juno was called Lucina when she
superintended the birth of children.   But the lady who has
welcomed us so kindly is far from assisting in the birth of
children ; her calling, on the contrary, is to prevent it ; she
practices infanticide every day, and it is by carrying on
this business she has obtained the wealth she is making so
great a display of.   Every one of those window-shades, so
nicely arranged to ward off the rays of the sun, cost one
thousand dollars.   They were painted by our best artists,
none of them having declined to display his talent for the

benefit of Madame Killer—such is the name of the owner of this splendid residence. As there are thirty windows, you may easily figure up the cost of those gorgeous shades. That of all the furniture is in the same proportion: every piece of it, I dare say, has been purchased with the money received for the murder of a child."

Bewildered at these revelations, I thought Asmodeus was deceiving me. He quietly continued:

"That stout gentleman, going from one to another, and making himself affable with every body, who looks like a good-natured person, and whose unctuous manners remind one of a clergyman, is the husband of Madame Killer. He is an accomplished scholar, and has obtained his diploma from one of our best medical colleges. He might have obtained a competency by honest practice. But when Madame Killer, already enriched through her nefarious business, hinted that she was disposed to marry him, Bungling eagerly took the hint, and espoused this abortionist.

"Of course, after the marriage, Madame Killer retained her own name, as it was already a notorious one. Love, you may be sure, had nothing to do with this matrimonial transaction. Madame Killer married Bungling because his science might be of some service in many delicate circumstances—in about the same way a merchant takes in a partner when he has too much to do. The couple have been uniformly prosperous since they married, about ten years ago. True, they had two or three unpleasant misunderstandings with the police on account of a few poor creatures dying of ill-treatment at their hands; but they came out of all of them triumphantly."

"Must I infer from this that the laws of America do not punish infanticide?" said I, "that fearful crime of getting rid of children before or after their natural birth. Even

the unfortunate who stakes her life to conceal the consequences of a fault is amenable to law ; she is punished for
child-murder, as well as her accomplice, in every civilized
country."

"By and by," answered Asmodeus, "I will explain that
subject to you. I will content myself, for the present,
by saying that the laws of America are no less severe than
those of Europe, as regards the crimes of infanticide and
abortion. But in such cases, as well as in many others,
the law often remains a dead letter."

I longed to depart from the house. I fancied, after Asmodeus's frightful revelations, the very air we breathed
was impregnated with deadly miasma. Dancing had been
interrupted for a while ; and in a hall, connected with a
conservatory filled with rare and odoriferous plants, a
concert was beginning. Every note from a sonorous piano
sounded in my ear like the wailing of one of those poor
little beings the Amphitryons had brought to an untimely
death. And then, of what character were those women,
crowding the rooms, in spite of the crumpling of their
splendid dresses? Who were those men, who had either
accompanied or were courting them ?

"You are quite mistaken," said Asmodeus, "if you believe we are in the midst of a mixed crowd, such as that
denominated the *demi-monde* in the French capital, and not
tolerated, as yet, at private receptions here, or at places of
public resort. To be sure, what is called the social evil
unfortunately exists in New-York as in the large cities of
Europe ; but it keeps aloof from decent society. It is
true, that such is the discretion of corrupt females, it is
often impossible to distinguish an honest woman from one
who has lost her chastity. Of course, I do not speak of
those creatures so deeply fallen into habits of corruption

that they shrink no longer from exhibiting their degradation. Perhaps we shall have an opportunity of visiting
the backgrounds of our civilization, where those wretched
creatures live. For the present, I must set you right concerning the standing in society of the guests of this house.

" Most of those men, who so often appreciate the good
things served around by the waiters, are wealthy merchants,
lawyers, and physicians. I even recognize among them a
few magistrates and legislators. They have accompanied
their wives ; and some even have brought their daughters
to this dreadful house, where some unfortunate woman is,
perhaps, dying in the upper story, and paying with her life
the violation of nature's laws. Some guests have come
through curiosity, attracted by the splendors of a residence
opened for the first time to the gaze of strangers. Others
have availed themselves of the opportunity of gayly spending here a few idle hours, and do not trouble themselves
with the Amphitryons' respectability. Lastly, many guests
did not deem it safe to decline Madame Killer's invitation ; for that Thug of society holds in her hands the
honor of hundreds of families, and it would be dangerous
to arouse her resentment. A single word from her lips,
some well-concocted story, would bring on awful scandals.
She could, for instance, apprise yonder husband, so attentive to his wife, that the latter, during the two years he has
served his country abroad, has applied to Madame Killer's
art to remove the consequences of an adulterous intrigue.
That young man who has just inherited a large estate, and
seems so much enamoured of that light-haired young lady,
might learn to-morrow morning, through an anonymous
letter, that the fair beauty, instead of spending, as he believes she did, the summer months in the country, had
secreted herself in Madame Killer's hospitable house.

"Undoubtedly, the dread of some awful revelation has brought here many persons, as out of five hundred invited guests only a few do not attend Madame Killer's *soirée*. But I am far from believing that they would not have come under any circumstances, even had they been free from fear of personal consequences. Madame Killer is wealthy, and nobody cares about the way she has obtained her wealth. Whoever is worth one million dollars, no matter how acquired, honestly or dishonestly, is welcome everywhere, and his *soirées* and receptions are attended by the best society. I see, for instance, talking with Madame Killer, a merchandise broker, whose name was given to a ship launched this very morning, and who would be shut out of decent society in any other country. Three years ago, he failed to the amount of two or three millions of dollars. According to his balance-sheet, he could pay fifty cents on the dollar; but when his book-keeper joyfully informed his employer of such an unexpected result, 'Change it, by all means,' exclaimed the broker; 'my creditors do not expect even fifteen cents on the dollar, and were I to give them fifty, what benefit would I derive from my failure?' And he paid ten cents only on the dollar.

"Near that honest broker, who has become wealthy in consequence of that transaction, and at the same time a man of importance, being now a director of a trust company and other concerns, see that young man wearing side-whiskers, after the English fashion. His light hair and blue eyes denote his German origin. He is an exchange broker, and made two hundred thousand dollars last year in this quick way: Pretending to have realized large profits in stock-gambling, he succeeded in inspiring such confidence in the president of one of our most respectable banks, where he kept his account, that his checks were indiscriminately certified by that officer. One check for two hundred thousand dollars was in that way certified, and the money had just been paid out to a compeer, when the directors of the bank discovered the adventurer had but a small deposit in their hands. He failed the next day, and the president, who had rashly caused a heavy loss to the bank, blew out his own brains.

"The guest who is making his bow to the lady of the house was formerly secretary of one of our railroad companies. The stock had gone up one hundred per cent above par, on the strength of the managers' report, exhibiting the prosperous condition of the company's affairs, when an over-issue of stock, to the amount of two millions of dollars, was detected. To satisfy the public clamor, the secretary and another officer of the company were discharged. But all inquiry respecting this stupendous fraud was indefinitely postponed. The discharged employees of the company now live in high style, and give parties, which their former employers, the directors of the railroad concern, do not fail to attend.

"Next to him, that dandy who is talking with a gentleman whose beard, though he is a judge of the Supreme Court, might grace the chin of a musketeer, is a wealthy banker's son. . He is fresh from the State's prison ; and, strange indeed, the magistrate he is speaking to is the very one who sentenced him—perhaps, because of the pressure of public opinion, which must, after all, be taken into consideration. Our dandy, when his father retired, became sole manager of a banking-house, and attempted to double, in a few weeks, the wealth his father had toiled thirty years to accumulate. Discarding legitimate speculation, he gambled at the Stock Exchange, which soon swallowed up the money and other deposits confided to his keeping. Then he became almost crazy. To keep up his credit with our banks and procure resources, and led astray by the hope of realizing profits large enough to make up his losses, he became a forger. He imitated the signatures of his correspondents, his own friends—in fact, of every body in town ; and, one morning, the people were startled in reading in the newspapers that forged notes, amounting to several millions of dollars, were flooding the street. The young man was sentenced to prison for a term of five years—one for each forged million, as remarked the wag who is now talking with him."

"How is it he is out of prison ?"

"That is precisely a point of American law which deserves a passing notice. Most of the State governors are vésted with the pardoning power. When the exercise of such a prerogative devolves upon State legislatures, corrupting influences are less to be apprehended. A single individual may be coaxed to pardon by his political friends, or even bribed. But money and political connections are of little avail when one has to deal with one hundred legislators. In New-York State, the Legislature has no control over the pardoning power, which is vested exclusively in the governor. The family and friends of that youth represented his crime, stupendous as it was, as the first he had ever committed ; its enormity was represented as a proof of temporary insanity—the great argument, nowadays, of our lawyers—and he was set free by the governor, after remaining a few months in prison. He shows himself again among the wealthy classes, and is as kindly received by them as he would have been had he never forged notes to the amount of several millions of dollars—so deeply rooted in the American people is the feeling of tolerance, and especially when those who are the objects of it are millionaires, or in a fair way to become so.

" Among the fair sex here, many ladies really deserve that name from their decency—curiosity alone has attracted them ; but the dresses of many others, the most elegantly attired, have not been paid for by their husbands' money. How could it be otherwise, when most of them spend, in tinsel and jewels alone, the salary of those poor men, or the profits of their business? I firmly believe that out of the three hundred male guests, one half of them earn hardly two thousand dollars per annum—about the rent of the houses they live in ; and how they are enabled to face their other expenses is a problem which Euclid himself could not solve. I apprehend, also, that more than one of those fair young girls knows the way to those fashionable houses where foolish women, to satisfy their passion for luxury, jeopardize their chastity. Others have, through correspondence carried on in our newspapers, entered into some intrigue, the end of which, perhaps, will be an unpleasant confinement in this house. But, contrary to what takes place in many countries, where men complacently boast of their amours with the fair sex, affairs of love are kept here sedulously shrouded in mystery—a progress anyhow, as it is a homage paid by vice to virtue and decency. Lovelaces and Celadons are far from having free scope in America. Women, when their honor, whether justly or unjustly, has been assailed, do not shrink from any means to protect it and avenge themselves. Some cowhide the indiscreet suitor ; others seek even in his blood a retaliation for a real or imaginary insult.

" Public opinion ranges, in general, on the side of the fair sex, and the courts side with public opinion, when, in a case of seduction or of a breach of promise, the victims have recourse to them. Lovers are, therefore, affected with a salutary dumbness—being aware that their lives or for-. tunes are at stake, in case of any indiscretion. Add to this, that when an insulted wife, or a young girl whose prospects have been marred by a villain's treason, does not strive to vindicate her honor, her part is infallibly taken by a hus- band, a father, a brother, or even a cousin. The avenger provides himself with one of those pretty revolvers exhi- bited at all jewelers', and even in druggists' show-cases, and shoots down the defamer or seducer in broad daylight— even on the Sabbath-day, on the very steps of a church, as happened at the Federal capital a few years ago. True, the murderer is prosecuted ; but the jurors general- ly consider as justifiable murder the killing of a man for the above causes. And, in most cases, the man who has shed the blood of a fellow-creature reappears in society with an increase of popularity."

At this moment, we noticed some excitement among a few young ladies standing near a songstress who had just been rapturously applauded. A gentleman of command- ing appearance, but deadly pale, was speaking to her in a tone loud enough to be heard by those standing by. "You are certainly much indebted to Madame Killer," said the gentleman ; "but I wonder how you can sing in a house where you brought to an untimely death an innocent be- ing !" And bowing graciously to Madame Killer, he dis- appeared among the bewildered assembly.

"Ah !" said Asmodeus, with a sarcastic smile ; "the songstress's husband is dissatisfied with meeting her at Madame Killer's ; and this occurrence spoils that excel- lent person's party ! Let us go ; we can do nothing more here, and have time enough to visit one of those merchant princes, as we call here traders who become millionaires, whom you alluded to, a few moments ago. And I purpose, as we go along, to relate to you the history of the pair whose meeting has somewhat disturbed this party."

CHAPTER III.

IN WHICH ASMODEUS, AFTER ADVERTING TO SOME CON-
TRADICTIONS IN THE AMERICAN CHARACTER, BEGINS
HELENA RONFORT'S HISTORY.

"PEOPLE, as individuals," said Asmodeus, snuffing the bracing air of the street, "exhibit continual inconsistencies between their doings and their principles. Take, for instance, the Americans, who have inherited from the English a dignified prudery; who go to church every Sunday; and, service over, sing hymns at home the rest of the day; who prohibit traveling on Sunday, and close up inns and taverns for the sake of keeping the Sabbath, as that day of rest is called in Protestant countries. Again, were we to believe this young nation's panegyrists, all and every American family is a sanctum of purity; for whatever scandal or crime is served up to the public by the morning papers is invariably attributed to foreigners. Well, on reading those same dailies, one is struck at the audacity and nakedness of their advertisements; at the impudent transactions carried on through their columns. Were we to admit that style is the man himself, according to a profound thinker, might we not infer that the press is the mirror of a people's morals? It is customary with American journalists to speak contemptuously of the miserable condition of European populations; to deride their habits and traditions; to scoff at their corruption and moral decay. Still, in no country of Europe would newspapers dare to insert such indecent advertisements as those that disgrace the American. dailies; and from which it might be inferred that there is no true appreciation, in the United States, of decency; of reverence for law and religion; of those refining influences which govern human conduct elsewhere. Nowhere in the Old World would a quack doctress be allowed to inform the public that her profession consists in preventing the natural birth of children and thwarting the laws of nature. That such a nefarious business is profitable and extensive, is clearly shown by those very advertisements. Independently of the cause, common to all countries, which explains, though it does not justify, the crime of infanticide—I mean the desire to conceal the consequences of a fault—it seems that another has greatly contributed, within a few years past, to increase that fearful crime—I mean the fear of bringing up numerous children. In the New-England States, the number of children for each family, which was generally five before the War of Independence, is to-day but two. Many women, to satisfy their love of luxury, undoubtedly prefer to spend for finery the money that should go toward bringing up their little ones, and are thus led by degrees to silence their conscience, and, finally, to offend the laws of nature. They even boast of their skill and success in violating those laws, when exchanging confidences with their friends; which fact goes far to prove that the standard of morals is very low, at least in large cities.

"If I had any desire to dwell upon such a subject, what details could I give concerning many lying-in establishments, whose advertisements are a puzzle to those not initiated in the mysteries of the present age! When unsuspecting persons read, for instance, in the dailies, that infants are wanted for adoption, how could they imagine those benevolent advertisers are but debased creatures, whose business it is to bring slowly but surely to their graves innocent beings whose birth was a shame—whose bringing up would be a burden to their mothers?"

"Asmodeus," said I, "while you are thus indulging in this philanthropic dissertation, you forget that you promised me the songstress's history."

"I am coming to it. You will see, after all, this dissertation, as you are pleased to call my observations on conflicting notions in American character and morals, has some bearing on the following narrative.

HELENA RONFORT'S HISTORY.

"The name of the young lady whose singing was so abruptly interrupted at Madame Killer's is Helena. The gentleman who interrupted her is her husband, Edward Ronfort. Helena belongs to one of the most ancient families of New-York—if we may call ancient those families whose origin can not be traced beyond three or four generations. And it is so with all American families boasting of their antiquity. There are some who attempt to trace their origin beyond the settlement of the English colonies in North-America, and claim for their ancestors some of William the Conqueror's followers. But such pretensions can not stand a critical examination. The founders of the English colonies, with few exceptions, belonged to the needy and, in some cases, to the most dangerous classes of society; and it may be doubted whether any one among them, when coming over to find a new home, on a new continent, ever thought of providing himself with a pedigree or genealogical table.

"The origin of those American families the proudest of their birth is, therefore, of comparatively recent date, the aristocratic pretensions of Helena's parents to the contrary notwithstanding. They assert themselves to be upon an equality with the oldest stocks of the mother country, and they hold social intercourse only with the few descendants, most of them wealthy, of those Dutch colonists who settled in the State of New-York over two hundred years ago, with some Southern planters who contrived to save their fortunes through all political commotions, and with a few families whose members have occupied high offices in the Federal or State administration. They have formed out of these varied elements a small colony, a sort of China, in the midst of the New-Yorkers. They compose what is called, in the upper part of the city, the *crême de la crême* of society. As far as possible, they marry among themselves, after the Jewish fashion, and at their parties receive only foreigners of noble birth. Their servants are trained to wear a livery—a modest one, it is true ; for the American people would no more tolerate to-day than in the times of President Adams servants gorgeously and ridiculously liveried, as is customary with the English aristocracy and petty German potentates. It is the fashion with them to ridicule republican institutions, and in the secret of their hearts they long for those of monarchical Europe. They are, in fine, what may be termed American Bourbons.

"None among them shows more scorn and disdain for the working classes than Helena's father. He is fond of luxury, and his success in business permits him to keep his house in fine style. He is president of a wealthy bank ; and it was more than once surmised he uses the bank's

money for personal speculations. If so, he is only doing,
after all, what two thousand bank managers of the country,
who form a privileged class and fatten on immunities
detrimental to industry and commerce, have done before
him.

"The president's children were brought up in the way
the offsprings of wealthy families generally are in the United States—that is, in the midst of all the enjoyments wealth
can afford, and with the privileges of an unbounded freedom. European observers often wonder at the weakness
of paternal power in the United States, and at the loose-
ness of family ties. But they forget that a family's internal
discipline reflects everywhere a nation's political institutions. With the Romans, as long as institutions which
were republican but in name were in existence, the paternal power was unrestricted ; and such it remained, by the
force of tradition, even after the imperial form was sub-
stituted for an aristocratic republic. Wherever the Romans carried their flag, the paternal power knew no limit ;
and, as a matter of course, it was so during mediæval or
feudal times. In North-America, neither an aristocracy
nor an oligarchy was ever known. The first settlers
adopted everywhere a popular form of government ; and
at the time the war with the mother country took place,
the habits of the colonists were so imbued with democratic
principles that a republican constitution was the only one
the founders of the New World deemed practicable. In
every country where unbounded freedom exists, that freedom commences at the family threshold. The paternal
sceptre is wielded with mildness, parents being compelled
by public opinion to keep but slight control over their
children.

"As a consequence, young men choose the trade or profession they like, often dispensing with their parents' advice; and as soon as they are enabled so to do through their profits or salaries, they leave the paternal roof. Many, like birds that mount the air, as soon as their feathers are fully grown, emigrate to some distant territory or new State of the Union, in pursuit of a fortune, occasionally sending letters to the 'old folks,' as parents are usually termed in America.

"In virtue of the same principles and notions everywhere, girls go alone to private or public schools, to church, to parties—from time to time even paying visits to friends living in a neighboring city or State. On most occasions, they are neither accompanied by a duenna, as in Spain, nor by a chambermaid, as in France; but by a young man, a sort of *cavalier servante,* who seriously plays his part, lavishing marks of a disinterested and respectful attention. This knight is kept in office as long as the young miss is satisfied with his politeness and devotion. When he displeases, he is dismissed without ceremony, and his functions are transferred—I will not say to a rival, (for relations of this nature, though between persons of different sexes, do not savor of love,)—but to another party and companion. Such Platonic intercourse, or flirtations, as they are called in America, are looked upon by both parents and children as harmless pastime, or as a necessary preface or preliminary to matrimonial bonds. For this reason, the mutual privilege of separating from each other is well understood; and when exerted, neither resentment nor deception is manifested. It is a right the young man and the young girl undeniably have, in case one of them is satisfied they are ill-fitted to make the long journey of life together. In most cases, a candid explanation takes place, followed by a friendly separation; and pleasant recollections only grow out of such temporary relations."

"Are they always free of any sad consequence to the young girl?" said I, interrupting Asmodeus.

"*Always* and *never* are two bold words," replied my companion. "But young American ladies are not kept, as in Europe, in a state of complete ignorance as regards the relations between the sexes; and they know where to stop when danger commences. I am aware that purity of morals, especially in large cities, is fast passing away. Still, the freedom enjoyed by young girls in the United States is far from being exposed to the many dangers it would be in Europe. On the other hand, flirtation teaches cautiousness to young men; for, let any one either write a letter or do any thing that may be interpreted as an engagement, and he is infallibly caught in the snares laid by many an unscrupulous spinster, encouraged too often, in their hunt after husbands, by greedy lawyers and sympathetic jurors.

"Helena, fair and gracious, like most young American ladies, was 'trained for the world,' as say complacent mothers—meaning, I suppose, that the main object of education is to prepare the fair sex to adorn society; and so Helena was brought up a stranger to notions of a higher order concerning the part women ought to play in modern society.

"When eighteen, she could perform on the piano, embroider, sketch—in short, had a smattering of almost every thing. Above all, she was well posted on Parisian fashions. She learned to sing after her marriage, owing to the encouragement received from a foreign songstress, pleased with Helena's fine voice. Her marriage had been brought about in the way usual in similar circumstances. Helena introduced, one evening, a young

man to her father, and informed the old gentleman she
was engaged to him. The introduction over, Helena's
father asked the young man a few questions concerning
his prospects and family. Tea was brought in ; the 'old
folks' played whist with a few friends, and no further
notice was taken of or allusion made to the engagement.

"The young man she had chosen for her future husband
was handsome, and belonged to a family in good standing,
one of the relatives having recently served a term of two
years as Governor of the State of New-York. Though
passionately fond of Helena, Edward Ronfort discreetly
kept aloof, as other young men were also then paying their
attentions to her. When he discovered that he was the
most favored, he expressed his desire to accompany her
to parties and elsewhere, and a regular flirtation commenced—a means, as previously explained, to ascertain
whether strong sympathy exists between two persons of
different sexes. Between Ronfort and the banker's daughter this sympathy was not slow to show itself, maturing
into an engagement, which led to a wedding a few months
later.

"In many States of the Union, lads fifteen years old,
and girls ten years of age, may marry without the consent
of their parents. Magistrates, equally with clergymen, have
the right to solemnize marriage. The gentleman and lady
go to a magistrate or to a clergyman, and declare they have
resolved to marry. The ceremony is immediately proceeded with. When it is over, the magistrate or clergyman receives his fee, delivers a certificate of the transaction to
the bride and groom, when required, and, in less than ten
minutes, the act which is held by all civilized nations as
the most important in life is performed. No previous
publication is required ; all facilities are afforded by law

for conjugal unions, its main object being, one would think, to 'increase and multiply' the population of the vast continent of North-America.

"Sometimes, but very seldom, the bride's parents object to her marrying the man she has chosen. But public opinion is, in general, against them ; and they are constrained, in most cases, to soon relinquish all opposition. A few years ago, a young lady fell in love with her father's coachman. To prevent what was, in his judgment, an ill-assorted union, the father undertook to take his daughter abroad; but he was prevented from doing so by the officers of the law, and the young lady availed herself of her unrestrained liberty to marry her lover.

"Children care little for their parents' approbation when they are determined to marry, because they seldom receive a marriage portion or a dowry from them ; while in Europe, money in all conjugal unions is a consideration second to none in importance. The paternal power is intimately connected there with the power of money, and its necessary intervention is all-powerful. In America, young men marry the girls they love without troubling themselves about the marriage portion or dowry question. They know they will find in labor a means to support their family, and do not seek it in matrimonial speculations, to the detriment of feelings of manliness and personal dignity. They consult their hearts, and nothing else. Hence, it follows that unions are better assorted and, I think, more happy in the United States than in the Old World. A dowry or a marriage portion is no better than a bondage to European husbands. If scrupulous, they are incessantly under apprehensions of compromising what they consider as a trust confided to their keeping for their children. Should they be so unlucky as to squander the money they have received from their wives, they feel miserable the remainder of their life, vainly striving to retrieve their losses and reëstablish the trust in its entirety ; while, all the time, they are bound to keep up their house on a footing proportionate with the fortune brought by their wives. In the United States, a young husband ignores all those impediments and cares at the beginning of his career. His wife cheerfully shares his bad or good fortune, and in no case has any ground to complain. Sometimes foreigners of noble birth, but poor, or mere adventurers, hunt for heiresses, and, according to European tradition, stipulate for ready cash before marrying. Public contempt is their reward. All decent houses are shut against men making a mercantile transaction of an act which mutual sympathy only should control.

" Neither do sensible Americans admit that it is proper for a man, after toiling all his life to acquire a competency, to give it away for the benefit of his children—at the very moment, too, when old age and its infirmities make it the most needful. In their judgment, money given to children to secure their marriage, is a custom not to be thought of in the New, and should be left unreservedly to the Old World; as it proves to be, in most cases, a source of discord to the newly married pair, a burden to their parents, and, finally, an incentive to evil passions.

" Helena's father was too much imbued with the ideas prevailing with his countrymen, to either thwart the choice of his daughter, or to settle on her, at the time of her marriage, any money. Besides, Edward Ronfort, when he married, was in rather easy circumstances. His father, who died a few years before, left an income of five thousand dollars to each of his four children, and as much to his widow—the latter receiving, besides, a handsome residence situated on the sea-shore a short distance from New-York. On bequeathing that property to his widow, he had stipulated that all his children should reside there at pleasure, summer or winter, whether married or unmarried. That testamentary disposition proved fruitful of momentous consequences, as will be seen hereafter.

"Edward Ronfort and his wife spent there the summer months. During winter, they boarded in a fashionable hotel in New-York. Helena gave birth to two children, and their happiness, perhaps, would never have been disturbed but for the coming home, after a long absence, of Robert Ronfort, elder brother of Edward by two years.

"Robert had gone to California a few years before, in pursuit of a fortune. He was there at the time Edward married. After securing a competency in California, he had himself married there, but soon after lost his wife. Robert's mind was much depressed at his bereavement; and when he came to reside in the paternal mansion—as he had a right to do according to his father's will—his relatives and friends did their best to soothe his grief and remove his melancholy. Helena, in particular, showed a deep sympathy for her brother-in-law; and Robert, who was then about thirty-four years of age, gradually recovered his strength and cheerfulness.

"To keep himself busy and divert his mind, he established an evening school for the operatives of a factory near by, and also a Sunday-school for their children. Himself and Helena were the principal teachers of these schools; and while accomplishing this good work, an intimacy sprang up between them which proved a source of grief to two families, and added another chapter to the history of American domestic scandals.

"Seven years had now elapsed since Helena married

and two since Robert had returned from California, when Edward was obliged to go to the far West to take part in a law-suit in which important interests were involved. His love for his wife had so increased that he felt sorely grieved to leave her, and only did so on the assurance from his lawyers that his absence would last but a few weeks. But those weeks proved to be months; for, if law-suits in other countries require a long time and many tedious delays before they arrive at a conclusion, they are, in the United States, almost interminable. At last, after bringing his cause to a favorable issue, Edward wrote to his wife that he was coming home. But this piece of news, instead of filling all the members of his family with joy, struck terror into the hearts of two of them—his wife and his own brother.

" But," said Asmodeus, interrupting his narrative, "here is the house of the opulent merchant on whom we propose to call. I will tell you, at another time, the sequel of the domestic drama to which you have listened with so much interest."

CHAPTER IV.

IN WHICH THE READER MAKES THE ACQUAINTANCE OF
SOME ECCENTRIC CHARACTERS, AND IN WHICH ASMO-
DEUS DERIDES THE AMERICAN PEOPLE FOR A PREDOM-
INATING MANIA AND SUNDRY ODDITIES.

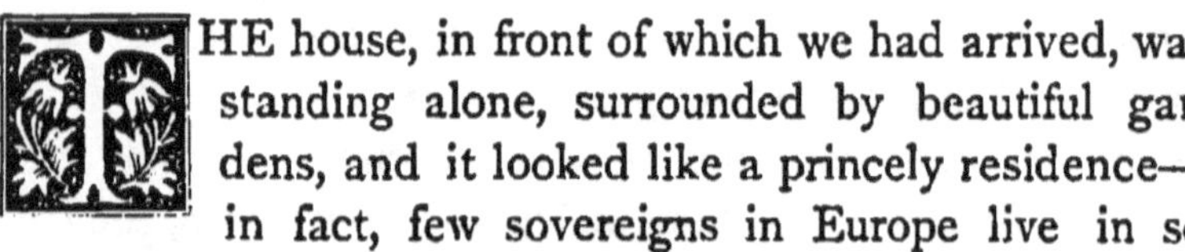

HE house, in front of which we had arrived, was standing alone, surrounded by beautiful gardens, and it looked like a princely residence—in fact, few sovereigns in Europe live in so splendid a palace as that of this merchant of the young Republic. Such was the thought that flashed through my mind as Asmodeus announced his name. That name operated like a talisman, for the doors were instantly thrown open. I had time, moreover, to observe the external appearance of the building. Entirely of white marble, it was of great size, and the architects of the New World had exhausted their ingenuity to make it a masterpiece. Every stone of the edifice was finely cut, and every ornament stamped with unquestionable taste.

The outside appearance foreshadowed the inside magnificence ; and I did not wonder at the number of jasper and rare marble pillars seen throughout the large halls and parlors. Masterpieces from every country in the world

adorned this spacious mansion, whose owner, a gentleman
of about sixty, kindly greeted us. He gave a party that
evening, and dancing was going on in a large conservatory
fitted up as a ball-room for the occasion. The society
seemed more refined than that we had just left, as the
men we mingled with looked more sedate, and the ladies
talked and laughed less loudly.

"You are not mistaken," said Asmodeus, to whom I
made this observation; "here may be found, excepting
those Bourbons I alluded to a few minutes ago, the best
people of New-York. Here are merchants worth millions
of dollars; manufacturers, magistrates, bankers, and some
distinguished foreigners. The Amphitryon seldom gives
parties, but he is particular about his guests. He has
not, as yet, forgotten an occurrence of a somewhat painful
nature which happened in the beginning of his mercantile
career. He had been extremely lucky in all his ventures;
so much so that he was nearly worth one million of dollars. Though living in a modest house, situated in a
modest street, he decided, one day, to give a large party
to his best customers, and, in consequence, invited the
wealthiest and oldest families of New-York. None of
them answered his invitation, and the party came off without any guests. After that, it is said, the future millionaire swore that he would astonish by his wealth and
luxury that proud mercantile aristocracy which he could
not win by kindness and urbanity; and uniting caution
with a rare perspicacity, he accumulated a fortune which
at the present time is one of the largest in the United
States.

"I must state that at the time this episode occurred, he
was not, like to-day, one of the largest importers of the
country; he was simply a retail merchant, and the thirst

for social distinction is so deeply rooted within certain classes of New-York society, that wholesale merchants and importers believe themselves to be far above retailers, whatever be the wealth of the latter. Down-town merchants look with disdain on the up-town retailers, the very men who purchase the goods they have imported. Again, our host was not born in the United States, a circumstance the import of which he was far from realizing when he tried to mingle with the picked society of New-York.

" Foreigners, even after residing half a century in this country, retain the mark of their birth, the natives persist· ing, even after aliens have become wealthy, to treat them as adventurers.

" You must also bear in mind, that the native Americans candidly believe themselves to be intellectually superior to foreigners. Hence, their way of speaking with pity and disdain of European people as no better than Indian Pariahs, or any other inferior race. They are not aware, perhaps, that the most illustrious men in the United States, in almost every branch of human labor, are foreigners. Not to speak of our host, whose business amounts to over one hundred millions of dollars per annum, the prominent bankers of New-York are either English, German, or French. The journalist whose energy gives an unparalleled development to the American press is a foreigner; the Union is, perhaps, indebted for her preservation to a foreigner; for, in the course of the late gigantic civil war, it was owing to the ingenuity of a Swedish gentleman that the navy of the Northern States escaped destruction, a catastrophe which would have very likely altered the issue of the struggle then going on.

" The learned men whom the American people most frequently boast of—Audubon, the celebrated ornithologist, and Agassiz—are foreigners ; the first, the son of a French admiral, was born in Louisiana before that country was purchased by the United States ; and the other, a Swiss by birth, was indebted to the natural phenomena of Switzerland for his first, and perhaps best, effort.

"The preëminence of foreigners in science, trade, and finance is not, after all, a fact of recent date in the history of the United States : it has been so since the American Republic first took rank among the nations of the world. Astor, whose name is known on both sides of the Atlantic, and who donated a valuable library to the city of New-York, was born in Germany ; Stephen Girard, who bequeathed two millions of dollars to Philadelphia for the establishment of a college which is a pattern for other philanthropic institutions, was a Frenchman ; and a Swiss— Gallatin—when the war for Independence was over, was intrusted with the duty of saving the public treasury from bankruptcy. But such is the pride of the American people, that when a foreigner residing in the United States becomes celebrated, either because of his talents or a useful discovery, they claim the illustrious man as an American, contending that he is indebted for his genius to his settling in this country.

"Now, if you wish to know the ordinary topics which absorb the American mind, mingle with the company and listen to their conversation."

Following the advice of my companion, I listened to the gentlemen who were idling through the rooms. Everywhere that word, "dollar," constantly repeated, struck upon my ear. All conversation had for its subject mercantile and financial transactions ; profits, either realized or to be realized by the speakers, or the general prospect of the market. Literature, art, science, the drama, all those topics which are discussed in polite European society, were not even alluded to. Another peculiarity I noticed—namely, the practice of self-commendation and praise. Egotism seemed to permeate the mind of every body. The word " I " was constantly on the lips of the speakers.

That maxim of good old Franklin, "Never speak of yourself," thought I, is quite obsolete here, as well as many others, perhaps, of the same philosopher. At any rate, the practice of making one's self of importance, of magnifying one's own achievements, seemed to me not less shocking than that burning thirst for money which, even in the midst of pleasure, preys upon the American mind.

I imparted my observations to Asmodeus, who said: " Many times I have heard experienced physicians and men of unquestionable science seriously contend that all Americans, without exception, are more or less demented ; for all are afflicted with that inveterate mania—money-making. Day and night, their minds are bent on the means of acquiring wealth ; all their thoughts, all their acts, converge to that one point.   It besets, it haunts them in their stores, at home, in the street, at the theatre, and in church. There is no room in their brains for any thought but that of making money.

"Well, a monomaniac is one who is preyed upon by a single or predominating idea ; and the love of money pushed to extremes, as it is in this country, having invaded all classes of society—males as well as females, old as well as young men—indeed, all alike—is a positive sign of mental derangement. Indeed, the American people have come to that point of weighing the worth of a man by the wealth he is possessed of, and thereby to proportion their estimation of him.

"In England, (I state a fact which I refrain from appreciating,) nobility or birth is alone looked upon as the true standard of merit.   In fact, England is nothing but an aristocratic hierarchy: at the head is the queen; next come the dukes; then the marquises and earls, viscounts and barons.   The government, in all its ramifications, from generation to generation, is transmitted to some noble family; and even in the servants' hall, an aristocratic hierarchy is still found: yellow-plush looks with disdain upon the cook, and the cook hardly condescends to hold converse with the hostler, who, in his turn, living in the stable of nobility, considers himself many degrees removed from the tillers of the land and workmen in the cotton-factories.

"Equality thus being out of the question in England, it is a positive fact that nobility, with but few exceptions, is considered the standard of merit.   It is true that men of eminence and popularity have sometimes been allowed to occupy stations of secondary importance in the English cabinet, notwithstanding they have sprung from the middle classes.   But a nobleman, like Russell, Palmerston, and my Lords Derby and Aberdeen could alone, up to our day, aspire to the premiership.   If ever a plebeian becomes a premier, the traditions of eight centuries will be put aside, the constitution of England imperiled—indeed it will be the signal for a momentous revolution in the habits, ideas, and social organization of feudal England.

"In Russia—it was so, at least,'not many years ago— the favor of the reigning prince was the standard of merit.   In all despotic states, favorites are all-powerful; neither birth nor talents has any thing to do with the qualification of men for public offices and public esteem;

and oftentimes the sovereign's favor rests with the most servile of his subjects.

"There is hardly any other country than France where the sole standard of merit is merit itself. Birth has nothing to do with Frenchmen; it occupies no room in their affections or prejudices. The aristocracy of France is rather nominal than real—a souvenir of the past—as an aristocracy without landed estates hardly deserves that name. In diplomatic or military affairs, in all branches of public administration, personal merit is the only available qualification for office-seekers or office-holders.

"In the United States, the masses are, very properly, indifferent to the prestige or claim of birth; but, at the same time, we find they entertain but a faint regard for personal preëminence and real talent.

"The standard of merit in the United States is money! An Englishman, when he desires to be informed about a stranger, propounds this question: 'Is he a man of good family—of birth?' With the Frenchman, the question would be: 'Is he a man of talent?' With an American, the question invariably is, 'How much is he worth?'—an expression certainly applicable to the value of a bag of corn, of a hog, or, in the palmy days of slavery, to a lively negro. Painful as it is to confess it, I repeat that the standard of merit in this democratic country is money. A learned man, if poor, is looked upon with scorn and pity. James Fenimore Cooper would have been shut out from every aristocratic house if his coat had been shabby. This aberration of mind is pushed so far that it gives birth to the most ludicrous distinctions in social life. For instance, I am worth, in the common parlance of the day, ten thousand dollars—my left-hand neighbor thinks he is worth fifteen thousand dollars; consequently, he declines

all acquaintance with me, and does not recognize me when
we pass each other in the street. But it happens that my
right-hand neighbor is possessed of about twenty thousand
dollars ; now, his wife would get excited if her lord showed
the slightest sign of recognition of the left-hand neighbor,
worth five thousand less !

" From a general point of view, the American people
may be divided into two classes, the poor and the rich—
the latter often harsh and indifferent to the former; for
poverty is one of the greatest known crimes in the United
States. You may now easily understand that those who
are not rich exhaust their ingenuity to make others believe
they are so; and thus the fortunes of many persons are
but superficial. Their houses are often heavily mortgaged,
and sometimes the dresses of their wives—of many, perhaps, of the ladies we see here—are worn out before paid
for. But as the people of no other country have more
regard for appearances, those who want credit resort, as
a necessity, to outside show. Why wonder, then, at the
many fitful changes in life here so frequent?

"The present generation resembles those governments
alluded to by an old philosopher, which, by dint of borrowing, keep themselves up in the same way that the body of
a man, just hung, is held up by a rope. The Americans,
as long as possible, pile expediency upon expediency to
keep up their credit, and often have recourse to means
that a tolerant public calls smart, but which, in any other
country, would be severely punished.

" The pursuit of gain has polluted private and public
morals, and corrupted political institutions; even patriotism
is made subservient to it. Most of our public men serve
their country with the hope, and the well-understood condition, of making money. In trade and industry, all

means are resorted to to obtain the golden prize; for it
is generally admitted that the end justifies the means,
whether honest or dishonest, and that, finally, the wealthiest man in the land is sure to be the greatest in the estimation of his countrymen.

"Some persons who have accumulated wealth by chi-
canery, build palatial residences in Madison or Fifth ave-.
nue, give balls and *soirées;* and the *élite* of society, holders of high public offices, ministers of the Gospel, and
generals of the army, all attend, because the glitter of
wealth has, upon the minds of the American people, the
fascinating influence reptiles have over beasts. And such
is the result of the generally accepted notion that the
worth of a man is in proportion to the bulk of his
purse.

"You have doubtless noticed that Americans admire
every thing they do, every thing they say, every thing that
transpires in their country—it is a weak point which never
escapes a foreign observer. They candidly believe their
country is the finest, their countrymen the most intelligent, and their countrywomen the handsomest on the face
of the earth. They also believe that the armies and
navies, arts and sciences, industry and commerce of
other nations can not be compared with their own. But
I would not find fault with this self-admiration were it not
so constantly conspicuous, especially when the hearers happen to be foreigners. This self-admiration has spread from
individuals to hamlets, cities, counties, and States. There
is hardly a State which does not believe itself superior, in
some respects, to its neighbor; not a city that does not assert its supremacy over others.

"But, after all, this harmless rivalry is an incentive to
progress. By the same reason, the Americans, with their

unbounded confidence in their own capacity and universal aptitude—any one among them being ready to be lawyer one day, physician the next, merchant, legislator, even President of the United States—would have achieved less wonders in the arts of peace were they lacking in self-reliance, like the effete nations of the Old World.

"Owing to this indomitable faith in their capacity, they ignore this feeling of envy so deeply rooted in the heart of the European masses. When he looks at the palatial residence of a New-York merchant, the workingman feels moved to make *his* way through the world, knowing that wealth lies within the reach of every óne who, in this country, displays sagacity and perseverance.

"What I can not consider as a weak point of a people entering national life is that disease, that scourge I have before spoken of, and which seems to catch hold of foreigners themselves after a few years' residence in this country. . Take, for instance, that wealthy merchant whose hospitality we now enjoy. He is one of our most respectable citizens, a man of refined mind, a scholar ; and still it may be asked whether there is any laudable purpose in his accumulating millions ; crushing young competitors, as he does, in the mercantile arena, failing to comprehend that, when they have become millionaires, merchants should, like soldiers after they have conquered, leave the field to others.

"The truth is, the worship of gold dims the intelligence and hardens the heart ; and those men who are now playing whist with our Amphitryon afford a striking proof of it. One of them—that one who gives himself many airs, and looks like an English snob—has made a large fortune by means of a combination which he carried through with the aid of some respectable banking-houses. He was director of a company whose regular dividends had amounted to twenty per cent for a couple of years, when he prevailed upon his brother directors to increase the capital stock of the company from ten to twenty millions of dollars. Our man subscribed for the new stock and sold it out before the public had any intelligence of the increase. The shares were worth three hundred dollars each before the watering-down of the stock; when it became known, they fell to one hundred dollars, and (a fact which shows a dreadful state of public morals) the honesty of the transaction, which put several millions of dollars into the pockets of the master-spirit of it and his accomplices, was hardly questioned by the community.

"To-day, this man plays Mæcenas; he imports from England his carriages, horses, even his servants, every one of whom is six feet high; and recently he was one of a committee of New-York capitalists who, taking upon themselves to suggest to the President of the United States some financial measures, prefaced their discourse with these words: 'Your Excellency will please notice there are ten of us here, worth altogether one hundred millions of dollars!'

"The other two players are avaricious men, who would beat Harpagon himself. One is an importer, who lives in a cold room in the third story of a modest house down-town. During winter he warms himself in the parlors of one of our hotels, which are properly the coffee-houses of the United States. You may see him every morning at the Custom-House, though he is sixty years of age, making his entries himself; he is his own bookkeeper, cashier, chief of correspondence, and even sweeps out his own office, I am told. His annual profits exceed one hundred thousand dollars. He is a bachelor, because he could never find time, as he asserts, to seek for a wife. On Sundays, as a diversion from his week's work, he rubs and brightens, one after another, the eagles he has received; for all his transactions are carried on in hard cash. That singular old man is worth several millions of dollars, and in spite of his fortune, he very seldom opens his purse for charitable purposes. 'Any gift of mine,' says he, to exculpate his stinginess, 'is attended with sad consequences to the recipient.' And then he relates that, a few years ago, a niece of his, the only relative he had, informed him of her approaching wedding, when, in an unaccountable fit of liberality, he sent her fifty thousand dollars as a dowry. The bride did not know her uncle was wealthy, and hence, when she received this handsome gift, lost her reason. 'And now you can understand,' invariably adds this miser, when he is asked for alms, 'the reason why I am decidedly averse to alms-giving.'

"The second player is also an old bachelor, who made large profits out of the frequent alterations in the tariff of duties on imported goods. When he invites a friend to dine at one of our fashionable restaurants, he is astonished to find that he has no money in his pocket-book, and his friend has to foot the bill. It is said he has gathered a voluminous library of fine books borrowed from his friends —of course, never to be returned. His only diversion is somewhat singular, and costs him every year a few thousand dollars. Fifteen years ago, he purchased a large property in France, a description of which he chanced to read in some newspaper. When the survey of that property was completed, he sent one of his clerks to manage it. The map of his domain is hanging up in his office, and every few weeks he resolves, on looking at it, to make some alteration. One day, a summer-house must be built ; the next, some material is ordered ; sometimes a wing has to be added to the main building ; again, the plan of the garden and walls is to be modified ; and all these improvements and alterations are carried on through correspondence with his clerk—for he has never visited his property, and will doubtless die without seeing it.

" Such eccentric characters are not very numerous, it is true, in America. Frugality is the exception, prodigality the general rule. Nobody thinks of to-morrow.

" A few years ago, some benevolent persons conceived the project of establishing an asylum for incapacitated and ruined merchants ; but they gave it up as completely impracticable when it was stated there were, in New-York alone, several thousand old merchants reduced to beggary. Among these were nearly one thousand who had been worth, in the course of their mercantile career, one hun dred thousand dollars each.

" If the American people were not as conspicuous for their prodigality as for their love of money, they would be a contemptible set of mortals. But it seems that Providence has always ready for every evil a remedy ; and on seeing the readiness of the Americans to spend money, one can not fail to wonder at their feverish anxiety to make it. At the same time, there is no people so easily misled by appearances, so liable to be deceived. They permit themselves to be cheated like children ; in fact, there is in their character too much puerile ingenuousness. They delight in relating to each other stories and anecdotes, which they applaud with enthusiasm, and on the hearing of which any European would soon grow weary. Indefatigable speakers, they nevertheless lack the talent of conversation—an attainment which is to be found only in old and polite society, and among people whose instruction is not superficial. It is principally in public meetings they exhibit their wonderful oratorical power: any one among them is ready to speak at any time and on any topic. He will keep his hearers attentive during several hours; but his sentences pass away like a fugitive noise; for extemporizers have few ideas, either in the New or the Old World.

"Concerning that other natural disposition of the Americans to be easily cheated, it is a singular feature in the character of men whose mercantile aptitude is so great and speculative power so acute. But the truth is, the United States are the cradle of 'humbug,' (an American word which has found its way into all spoken languages,) a paradise for charlatans. I recognize among this company three physicians, who have made enormous sums of money, not through the honest exercise of their profession, but simply by selling pills and other nostrums—infallible, of course, for all known diseases. One can hardly imagine the amount of their transactions and the number of workmen and agents they employ for the manipulation and sale of their panaceas.

"I lately visited one of those physicians' establishments. He showed me a department for the manufacture of pills and other medicines, another for their packing, another for their forwarding, another for the printing of circulars, pamphlets, and almanacs, with which the country is flooded, and many more of less importance.

"Four hundred operatives are employed in that factory, whose products are shipped to all the States of the Union. And what are they? Harmless waters or flour-pellets, for the most part, according to the candid confession of the owner of the factory.

"Said he: 'My remedies can never hurt any body, while

I am satisfied they cure many people, so powerful is the imagination as regards health!'

"Speaking of a favorite compound, he said he had in his possession thousands of certificates from most reliable individuals, stating that such and such compound promptly removed indigestion and symptoms of ague, cured the headache, soothed the nervous system, created a salutary perspiration, relieved rheumatism, purified and invigorated the blood, gave and increased appetite, cured marasmus, kept the brain clear and bright, and removed, without interrupting the ordinary occupation of the patient, all diseases the flesh is heir to.

"The American is always in a hurry. When he feels sick, he purchases, without waiting for a physician's advice, an already made-up remedy for his supposed disease. The profession of physician would not be very profitable did not the American ladies require, more often than the other sex, medical attendance."

In the mean while dancing was going on, to the strains of an excellent orchestra. After every quadrille, many young ladies patronized the richly laden sideboards and tables ; and I noticed their appetite might, without injustice, be compared to that of Albion's fair daughters. I also noticed the *soirée* was lacking in that warmth and animation conspicuous in like parties in Europe. There were many foreigners among the guests; and one could perceive that there was a marked coolness between them and the Americans. The latter were shy and reserved, did not seem exceedingly fond of intercourse with the former, and did not court it.

"I suspect," said Asmodeus, "though they often assure them of their sympathy, that Americans dislike foreigners ; ·

who, in their turn, if we are to believe the natives, do not like the Americans.

" It is an undoubted fact that, in the opinion of many, the continent of North-America ought to belong exclusively to those born on American soil ; and they see with feelings of sorrow thousands and thousands of Europeans landing every year, to compete with them for its possession. These persons have long considered, and perhaps consider to-day, as a national calamity, the homestead law which grants to every immigrant a farm of forty acres and over after the fulfillment of certain easy terms and conditions."

Among the ladies who seemed most interested in the dancing, and looked at it with feelings of undisguised gratification, I noticed one whose countenance interested me. One might have easily mistaken her for a marchioness of the old European aristocracy, so dignified was she, so kind and gracious were her manners.

" Ah !" said Asmodeus, "you are looking at a lady who will find, on her return, her home deserted. Some ten years ago she lost her husband, a general in the army, whose name had often occupied public attention during the war of 1812. When that war was over, he was appointed ambassador to Europe, and married, before leaving America, a lady of remarkable beauty and attainments. After several years spent in Europe, both returned to the United States. Here the general died, leaving a handsome fortune to his widow. She devoted herself to her children and grandchildren, giving them a good education ; for this lady has been a grandmother for twenty years, being now about sixty years old. A short time ago, a music-teacher—introduced into the family to teach her children—pleased the general's widow, and, to the surprise of her friends, she soon married the adventurer

By dint of coaxing and threatening, he contrived to have all the fortune of the old lady transferred to himself; and this very night he has taken passage for Europe, while his wife, whom he declined to accompany under pretense of indisposition, is enjoying herself at this party. To fill the measure of his villainy and ungratefulness, this man has eloped with the granddaughter of his wife, a child some sixteen years old!"

Here the fire-bells began striking at various points of the city, and several steam-engines rapidly passed in the street.

"Let us go to the fire," said Asmodeus; "such a spectacle will fitly terminate our adventures and observations for this night—or rather morning, as the dawn of day will soon break. There is, besides, in the mode of extinguishing fires, and also in their varied causes, an interesting subject for observation."

CHAPTER V.

E soon reached the fire. A large building, supported by pillars, and which looked like a church, was in flames. It was situated in one of the great thoroughfares of New-York, and occupied by a dry-goods firm. The sight was grand and awful. Flames were bursting from every side of the building, from the basement as well as from the upper stories—a fact easily accounted for, as the large warehouse was filled with dry-goods. The devouring element raged fiercely, and the superhuman efforts of the energetic and intelligent firemen were of little avail. Such was its intensity that they and the spectators were obliged to move some distance from it. Soon all hope was lost to save either the building or the goods stored therein ; and the firemen turned their attention to protecting the neighboring houses only.

"Were all the boxes full," said one of the lookers-on, "the fire could hardly make greater progress."

"Either full or empty," replied another, "the fire insurance companies will have to pay."

"Here are sagacious observers," said Asmodeus, "and

they plausibly explain the causes of this fire and its rapid
progress.   The merchants who owned that store often
gamble at the Stock Exchange, and have recently suf.
fered heavy losses.   Many of our merchants have abandoned old and sound traditions : they are no longer satis-
- fied with slow but sure profits, so great is their thirst for
money.   Fortunes may be rapidly made nowadays ; and
the Stock Exchange is the only field which offers a chance
for large gains.   Sudden reverses, it is true, are met with
in ninety-nine cases out of one hundred ; and inexperienced stock-gamblers are often led astray by delusive
hopes.   Such has been the fate of the partners of that
firm, whose books are now destroyed by fire—an accident
which will have for its result to conceal the true situation
of the concern from every body.   Their credit, to this day,
has not been impaired, because nobody but their stock-
broker knows how their resources have been squandered
away, and to-morrow they will stand on firmer ground than
before, when it is known that they have been fortunate enough to get rid of their goods at a satisfactory
price, with no apprehension of bad debts—their debtors
now being the fire insurance companies, bound by their
policies to promptly adjust their losses.   Should they suspect any thing regarding the origin of the fire, they will
keep their suspicions to themselves, as they are aware
that, though the law deals severely with the crime of arson,
a condemnation is next to impossible, because the jury
will not be disposed, unless some witnesses *de visu* are
produced by the State, to return a verdict of guilty.   Now,
it is obvious that, when a man sets fire to his own house,
he takes care nobody shall see him in the act."

"Then I apprehend that the business of fire insurance
companies, in the United States, is not a profitable one ?"

"You are mistaken ; with the exception of a few which are badly managed, nearly all distribute handsome dividends. Their premiums are proportioned to their risks. Admitting the latter to be ten times greater than in Europe, the premiums for insuring are simply increased in a corresponding ratio. In this case, as in many others, honest people suffer for the rascality of others. Besides, owing to frequent and serious fires, every body takes care to get insured. Hence, sound companies are relieved from the necessity of keeping, as in Europe, a staff of brokers and agents for the purpose of drumming up clients. The benefits of such institutions are so well appreciated by every American, that his first care is to insure his house and goods as soon as they are purchased. Some ill-natured people assert that the number of fires increases toward the end of every year—that is, at the time merchants balance their books and make inventories. I will not vouch for the correctness of this assertion, but I am quite satisfied the crime of arson is nowhere so frequent as here. Revenge, in some cases, and cupidity, in many others, are the incentives. But in every one the incendiaries act with the conviction that the law is powerless.

"To the above causes of fire, I must add the extreme imprudence of the American people, and the poor materials employed in the construction of houses. The devouring element has often free scope, and the firemen very seldom succeed in saving a building when once fully ablaze. The fire extends and increases as quick as lightning, and even stone itself makes but a poor show of resistance."

As if to confirm Asmodeus's assertions, the walls of the warehouse came down with a tremendous crash ; and soon

only the pillars which supported and adorned the front of
the fine edifice remained erect.

I noticed, during this magnificent scene, that policemen
had no trouble to maintain order in the street, and also
the excellent discipline displayed by the firemen.

" You must know," said Asmodeus, always disposed to
give information, " that such is the frequency of fires, the
people do not so much enjoy the fine sight."

" When the fire-bell rings, few persons leave their beds,
unless the fire threatens their own house.   Police-officers,
therefore, have very little difficulty to keep off spectators.
As a general thing, they know well how to maintain order.
If they were impudent and domineering, as they are in
many countries of Europe, their task, with such an excitable population as that of New-York, would be surrounded with difficulties; for at the slightest cause, and on any
occasion, bloody fights would take place between them
and the rough inhabitants of the lower wards ; for, as a
general rule, Americans are impatient of control, and
the show of too much authority is apt to excite their
worse feelings.   Policemen are, in reality, the citizens'
servants.   If you want any information, apply to a policeman ; in case you have lost your way, he will direct you
aright ; if you have any difficulty with a coachman—a
rough and insolent set of men in all countries—the nearest policeman will quietly, and in a gentlemanly way, settle it, to the satisfaction of both parties.   In case any
policeman intentionally forgets his duty—for no class of
men is free from fault—you have only to take down his
number, make the fact known to his superior officers, and
he will be made to apologize for his rudeness, besides receiving a severe reprimand.

" The costume of policemen, I think, exerts a salutary

influence on their behavior. Suppose, instead of a club, often concealed in a side-pocket, they carried a sword, and wore a three-cornered hat, it is quite certain they would soon lose all their present politeness ; they would gradually adopt the overbearing manners of military men, a class seldom urbane in time of war, and who become insufferable in time of peace.

"Concerning the good behavior and discipline of firemen, it is now a novelty, because of recent occurrence. It is owing to the fact that the extinguishment of fires now devolves on a body of paid men, while previously it was intrusted to volunteer companies. Of course, these volunteers were impatient of control, and had become quite a nuisance in this metropolis. If you wish to see the contrast between both systems, we have but to cross a narrow channel which divides New-York from a sister city—the third in the American Union, from the number of its inhabitants, but which, in reality, is a suburb of New-York, as most of its inhabitants transact their business here."

In spite of the late hour, I assented to the proposition, remarking, however, that perhaps no fire would be raging in the neighboring city, when we arrived there.

"Rest easy on that score," answered my companion ; "fires are just as extensive and frequent in Brooklyn as in other large cities of the Union. Besides, with the volunteer system, when the alarm-bell does not ring for a real fire, it does for a mock one, to give to rival companies an opportunity of settling some old quarrel. We are therefore sure to see, at all events, the mode of extinguishing fire as practiced throughout the States, with few exceptions."

Within five minutes' time, we were on the other side of the river—carried over by one of those spacious ferry-

boats which constantly ply between Brooklyn and New-
York, and which my guide, in his figurative language,
compared to a.street in motion.

As he had foretold, we heard, on landing, the alarm-
bell, and saw at a distance a glaring light, toward which
we hastened. The crowd increased the nearer we advanced ; company after company of men, wearing red flan-
nel shirts, ran in the middle of the streets, dragging with
fearful rapidity ponderous steam-engines, whose suffocating
smoke darkened the atmosphere. The shrieks of these
engines, and the wild yells of the firemen exciting each
other, as in a steeple-chase, imparted to the scene, in the
twilight, a wild, weird appearance. One might have easily
mistaken the firemen for a troop of Indian savages going
to a bloody festival, but for the thick smoke issuing from
the engines, and which rather reminded one of those ferocious Cyclops alluded to by Homer. One of the spectators, who failed to get out of the way in time, was crushed
by one of the engines ; while a fireman, stumbling, was
trampled under foot by his companions.

We soon arrived at the fire. From a dwelling wrapped
in flames, came fearful shrieks and lamentations. Many
families inhabited it, and a few of the inmates, unable to
escape by a single staircase, had taken refuge on the roof
of the house, there imploring help. The firemen made
a dreadful noise, running to and fro, and gesticulating like
maniacs. They failed to agree upon a plan of relief—that
suggested by some being rejected by others as impracticable. Amid this chaos, no trace of discipline could be
seen, and hence, no understanding as to the best way to
check the fire could be arrived at. Unfortunately, while
those of the inmates who had escaped to the roof were
becoming more and more enveloped by the flames, some

firemen noticed a bar-room at the corner of the burning building. Its doors were instantly burst open, and, no longer attending to the fire, they gave themselves up to carousal. Suddenly a dreadful crash was heard—the roof, with those upon it, had fallen into a perfect sea of flames; the main walls of the building began to oscillate like trees in a gale, and before they had time to escape from the bar-room, some firemen also were buried under the smoking ruins.

Horror-stricken, we left the scene, only to witness another sad sight. The fire had destroyed every thing, and as the services of the steam-engines were no longer required, every one of them was slowly driven away by the firemen.

"The engine-houses," said Asmodeus, "are, most of them, elegant buildings, and sometimes used as assembly or club-rooms. The young men who fill up the ranks of the volunteer companies are generally clerks and mechanics, who leave their desks, stores, or factories at the first stroke of the alarm-bell, and seldom return for the remainder of the day. They are not subject to any reduction of salary, as their absence from work is apparently justified by the requirements of public service. Besides, for obvious reasons, employers carefully refrain from exasperating such a dangerous set of men. The volunteers, in consequence, spend a part of their time in the engine-houses, enjoying themselves in every way, and giving, from time to time, sociables to their friends of the fair sex."

We were going the same way as one of the engines, and soon its drivers, at the intersection of two streets, met a rival company. All at once deafening shouts were uttered by the firemen, and they began hurling low epithets at each other. As with the warriors celebrated by Homer,

it was the prelude to a fierce struggle.   The firemen threw
stones at each other—indeed, any thing they could get hold
of, and revolvers, also, were soon brought into play.   The
fight threatened to be bloody, when a platoon of policemen made their appearance.   Brandishing their clubs,
they succeeded in separating the combatants ; but during
the fight one of the engines had been turned topsy-turvy,
and broken in many pieces.   The grief of the firemen to
whom it belonged—a grief so heartily felt that many almost
wept at sight of its ruin—would have provoked our risibles
but for the sad scene we had just witnessed, and the cries
of the many wounded volunteers.

"Volunteer firemen," said Asmodeus, "are a power in
the state.   The political party that secures their vote is
sure to win the day in local elections ; hence the reason
why this system is still kept in existence in many States.
These volunteers are active and influential canvassers,
and many public officers are indebted to them for the
situations they occupy.

"In spite of their name, volunteer firemen cost a city
much money, as they very frequently bleed the municipal
treasury ; for instance, for the purchase of new engines,
for repairs of old ones, building of engine-houses, and
indemnity for disabled members.   But withal there is
no question that some good emanates from this system.
Now, suppose a body of firemen to be as efficient as in
some countries of Europe, we should be deprived of a
powerful element of improvement in the United States.
Take, for example, New-York.   The frequent occurrence
of fires has entirely transformed that great metropolis,
and altered its outward appearance for the better.   Formerly, one could see, on the great commercial thoroughfares, main streets, and avenues, only ill-looking two-story

brick houses. In their place, white and brown-stone mansions, four stories high, with all the modern improvements, have been erected, also many warehouses, as spacious and handsome as palaces.

"To fires, undoubtedly, the city of New-York is indebted for such a thorough change within a few years. To them it is due that the Unied States possess the most regular and handsome cities in the world. At the same time, the art of building has remarkably advanced, and architecture has kept pace with the requiremens of the age. In short, as you see, you would be wrong in hastily condemning the volunteer system, which produces such valuable results."

While Asmodeus was thus talking, half-seriously, half-jocosely, we had arrived at the ferry, where a crowd attracted our attention. About a dozen men were in a state of great excitement.

"I recognize him," said one of them ; "I know him well ; I used to go to his saloon every evening."

"Let us hang the rogue !" exclaimed another "He is the cause of my brother being buried under the burning ruin."

"My father also has perished !" said a young man.

"And so has my poor baby !" added a woman, amid heart-rending sobs.

The man who was the object of this outburst of popular indignation was trembling from head to foot, and could utter only faint denials.

"You scoundrel !" shouted a man among the crowd, "you set fire to your house to swindle the insurance companies."

"No doubt of it," said another ; "and at the same time he wanted to cash the full amount of his policy,

after insuring to twenty times their value the poisonous
liquors he sells us."

At these words, an infuriated fellow, grasping the saloon-
keeper by the neck, commenced to beat him.　Soon others
kicked the wretch, and the crowd, which by this time had
considerably augmented since the beginning of this incident, shouted, to a man, " Hang him ! hang him !"

These savage threatenings, quite unexpectedly, were the
means of saving the bar-keeper's life.　A well-dressed
gentleman, very likely a lawyer—for, according to Asmodeus, lawyers always emerge from the ground at the
slightest sound of a riot or other disturbance—stepped
forward and exclaimed, in a stentorian voice, that the law
ought to follow its course ; that the bar-keeper, whether
innocent or guilty, was entitled to be judged by a jury of
free men.

" We are not," said he, " in Texas, or in a new territory,
where there is no other law save that of brutal force—no
other magistrate than Judge Lynch !　We have the honor
to be citizens of the first State, by its wealth and population, of the American Union ; and the citizens of a country unrivaled in the world must respect its laws.　Besides," said he, in winding up his harangue, " if you permit
yourselves to be led away by rashness, if you trample upon
the sacred rights vouchsafed to us all, you will be false to
your American origin.　Foreigners only—Irishmen only—
may be bold and unruly enough to deprive a citizen of the
benefit of the law in a free country !"

For fear of being mistaken for Irishmen, the rioters
gave up their project of hanging the bar-keeper, and he
was taken in charge by two policemen, who had just made
their appearance, when the crowd scattered in every direction.

CHAPTER VI.

IN WHICH ASMODEUS RELATES A SAD MISTAKE OF JUDGE LYNCH.

"WHO is this Judge Lynch?" said I to Asmodeus, when on board the ferry-boat.

"In Western wilds," said he, "and in territories not yet provided with regular forms of government, the rude pioneers know no other form of jurisdiction, no other form of proceeding, no other penalty, than those of Judge Lynch. Such was the name, it appears, of the settler who first advised the pioneers, in cases of murder and robbery, to take the law into their own hands, and to vindicate, in a summary manner, outraged justice and society. As there are no jails in those vast regions just redeemed from the red man, the settlers, not knowing what to do with evil-doers, deal with all of them in the same manner—that is, they hang them.

"However, the incident we have just witnessed reminds me of quite an interesting episode, which exhibits, in a sad and striking manner, the danger of these popular verdicts; and I have just time enough to relate it before the boat reaches the New-York side.

"A few months ago, on Christmas eve, Doctor Hamill, a friend of mine, invited me to spend that holiday with him—an anniversary always impatiently looked for and religiously observed in the United States. A particular circumstance made that festival, last year, doubly pleasant to the doctor. His father, an old gentleman of nearly eighty, had decided to celebrate his golden wedding—that is, having married fifty years before, he meant to make, according to American custom, the fiftieth anniversary of his marriage a great family reunion.

" I accepted the invitation, and we set out on our journey. The doctor's family resides about one hundred miles from New-York, and his dwelling is reached by means of one of the many railroads which connect the metropolis with the remotest parts of the State.

" When we arrived at a small place called Middletown, our journey was brought to a sudden stop. A snow-storm had been raging for two hours, and the locomotive was suddenly stopped by the huge mountains of snow which the wind had piled up in the valley where Middletown is situated. So we were obliged to stay there until the company's employees had made a pathway for us.

" Very luckily—a fact which no traveler in the United States will wonder at—we found a large and convenient hotel in Middletown ; and as we could not resume our journey until the next day, the young people among the travelers soon arranged to have a ball in the parlors of the hotel, and thus turned an unpleasant incident into a merry one.

" The sedate men of our party, (and I was one of them,) after enjoying a few moments the sight of the dancing, repaired to another room for the purpose of playing whist. While the waiters were bringing in tables and cards, Doctor Hamill offered us some genuine Havana segars, and related the following circumstance :

" 'I witnessed, many years ago,' said he, ' a never-to-be-forgotten drama in this very village of Middletown, where the snow-storm now detains us. It was, like to-day, Christmas eve, and I was on my way to the small town of Amenia, where my family resides, to spend with them the holidays. But a mishap prevented, as you will see, my joining them. At the time I speak of, Amenia was not connected by railway with New-York. An entire day and night—not a few hours, as to-day—were required to reach there. When we arrived at Middletown, the driver of a coach containing six seats, in which twelve travelers had been closely packed together, declined to go further. None of us insisted that he should take us that day to our destination, ten miles further, as night was coming on and a severe snow-storm had set in. We stopped at the only inn then in the village, and after warming our limbs by a wood fire, we repaired to the beds which had been prepared for us. At about midnight, we were awakened by the opening and shutting of doors and by terrific shrieks. We got out of bed at once, and inquired of some servants we met in the hall the meaning of the noise that had disturbed our sleep. The servants were so frightened they could hardly speak. At last, in answer to our inquiry, they pointed to a great light in an open space in front of the inn. We went out and saw a man hanging from a post over which our host placed a lantern every night. The unfortunate man was struggling in the last agonies of death! About fifty men, armed with rifles, surrounded him and kept the lookers-on at a distance. Some of these men had blackened their faces; others concealed theirs by the folds of their cloaks or broad-brimmed hats. A short distance from the post a fire was burning, and its red light, reflecting on the crowd, the wretch swinging in the air, and the snow-storm, then fiercely raging, made of the whole proceeding a scene of horror and desolation.   After a short time, the contortions of the wretched man ceased ; the rope holding him up was cut, and his body fell heavily to the ground.   Two men among the mob then threw it into a wagon and drove away at full speed, while others scattered the embers of the smouldering fire in every direction, and soon every thing was enveloped in darkness.

"We returned to the inn, none of us, as may be imagined, disposed to sleep again after the terrible scene we had witnessed.   We stood in the bar-room, and waited for the dawn of day ; indulging, from time to time in smoking, and drinking whisky-punches.   Neither did our host devote to sleep the rest of that eventful night.   He kept us company, and anticipating our desire, related the circumstances which had brought on the awful transaction we were talking about.

" The man who had just been hung, our host informed us, was, a few days previously, one of the most popular and esteemed citizens of the country.   He was the son of a highly respectable farmer living a short distance from Middletown, and his marriage with one of the prettiest girls of the village was to have taken place the day after Christmas.   He had received the education most of the American people obtain from our free schools, and helped his father in the management of his farm.   He used to come and spend a few hours every week, at the very inn we were then stopping at, and which was a favorite resort, especially on Saturdays, for farmers living ten miles around. He was a young man of affable disposition, frank and open in conversation, and was always welcomed by his neighbors.   The conviction that he had committed an awful crime was certainly deeply rooted in their minds ; for they were, according to our host, the very men who, taking in their own hands the vindication of the law and of society, had put George Harris—such was the name of the young man so summarily dealt with—to death. Five days before, he had gone to a small town named Gregory, about ten miles from Middletown, for the purpose of purchasing some wedding-gifts. He met there a young doctor, named Plunkett, who was then collecting his bills, as was then, and perhaps is now, the custom of country physicians, at the end of the year. The doctor had been very successful; for he had collected about one thousand dollars, nearly the whole amount due him by the country people. The two young men spent together a part of the day at Gregory, and left in the afternoon, as was stated by some witnesses, and admitted by Harris himself. But while the latter reached his home, Doctor Plunkett was doomed to see his own no more. His corpse was found about two miles from his home, the day after he had met George Harris, and at the very spot where they had separated. His horse had returned without his master, and some relatives and friends, uneasy about his absence, had gone in search of him. The poor man had been shot in the head while, doubtless, talking with the murderer. Plunder had evidently been the motive of the foul deed; for a few dollars only were found in the pockets of Plunkett's coat; while it was found, from the testimony of many persons, and a memorandum made by the doctor himself, that he had collected over one thousand dollars. When found, he was holding in his right hand a small pocket-book, which he had evidently snatched from the murderer during the struggle which, according to the relatives and friends of the doctor, had preceded his assassination. This pocket-book revealed the perpetrator of the crime; on the first page the name of George Harris was written;

and while many persons recognized at once the hand-writing of the young man, others asserted that they had seen the pocket-book in his possession on the very day the murder had been committed.

"'The county judge and the sheriff went at once to the farm of George Harris's father. George was absent; he had gone to Middletown, for the purpose of settling a few bills, and he had already paid five hundred dollars when he was arrested, in the very room of the inn in which we were standing and listening to our host. Harris was very much astonished and depressed on hearing of the violent death of Doctor Plunkett, and gave the following details concerning his acquaintance and transactions with the murdered man. According to him, he had met the doctor in the town of Gregory, on the homeward journey of the latter from his collecting trip. Harris had never seen him before, yet their acquaintance ripened, in a few hours, to such an intimacy, that the doctor lent George five hundred dollars on hearing of his lack of money to defray his wedding expenses. Plunkett had refused any written acknowledgment for his loan, declaring he would not consent to be reimbursed until his new friend should be in better circumstances. As a token of friendship, he would accept only the pocket-book which Harris had just purchased, and in which he (Harris) had written his name. Nobody was present during this transaction; and both friends, after spending a few hours together at Gregory, had returned home, separating at a branching-off of the road.

"'None among the magistrates—not even his best friends—could believe George Harris as to the way he alleged the money had come into his possession. Who could believe that a man whom he did not know the day before had loaned him such a large sum of money? The suspicions derived from the discovery of the pocket-book were on the increase, when two new facts corroborated the circumstantial evidence which pointed out Harris to be the murderer. In searching the house of George's father, the sheriff found a revolver, one barrel of which had been recently discharged; and it was stated, besides, that George, after returning home on the day of the murder, had begged one of his sisters to wash his clothes. When questioned about this circumstance, she declared that those clothes were saturated with blood; and as regards the revolver, that weapon was recognized as belonging to the doctor. In fact, only one revolver had been found in the doctor's possession, though it was well known he carried two when riding out.

"'Harris explained the above facts as follows: he asserted that Doctor Plunkett, before they separated, and as night was coming on, had lent him one of his revolvers, to protect his life in case of need; and, concerning his blood-stained garments, he related that, a few minutes after leaving the doctor, he heard the report of a gun. About the same time, a wounded deer ran by; and hoping to finish it, he had shot at the deer with the doctor's revolver, and brought it down. Then, alighting to carry off his prize, he had the disappointment to see the deer spring to its feet—nay, shaking off his assailant and covering him with blood, the beast had escaped in the woods.

"'Unfortunately for George Harris, the investigations made on the spot failed to confirm his explanation. Nowhere in the woods could be seen any trace of the struggle which he said had taken place between him and the deer. On the contrary, and as a convincing proof of Harris's guilt, near the spot where the doctor had fallen, a ball of wadding was found, which no doubt had served to load the murderer's weapon. This wadding was formed of pieces of an old country newspaper; and when the other barrels of the revolver in Harris's possession were emptied, it was stated that their wadding was composed of the same material!

" 'All these circumstances left no doubt in the magistrate's mind, and even in that of his neighbors and friends, that Harris had murdered Doctor Plunkett; and he himself but slightly persisted in denying the charges preferred against him, as proof after proof of his culpability was brought forward. He was taken to the county jail; but fearing he might escape, and for the sake of an example, the country people had burst open the doors of the jail, and, in spite of an energetic opposition from the sheriff and his assistants, they had removed the prisoner, and hung him in front of the inn at which we were stopping.

" 'Early the next day, the snow-storm had subsided; the sun rose amid a clear atmosphere, and we were soon in readiness to resume our journey. After packing up our clothes and paying our expenses, we drove off, with a feeling of relief in leaving Middletown.

" ' It is rather a singular thing,' pursued Doctor Hamill, ' but it is nevertheless true, that though I have, time and again, traveled through this village, to-day is the first time I have stopped here since the dreadful occurrence I have just related. The inn which at that time sheltered us (and in similar circumstances to those which have interrupted our journey) has disappeared; it has been replaced by a building adequate to the exigencies of the times and the increase of the town. New streets have been opened; elegant mansions have been built; every thing here now breathes of happiness and contentment; and I know of no place more

lovely in the fall than this small town, with its winding rivulet coursing down the hills, looking like a belt of silver,
and those beautiful hills themselves covered with trees of
golden foliage. But notwithstanding all these beauties, I
feel uneasy here. I fancy I again see Judge Lynch with
his terrible followers ; the red flames of the fire which lit
up the forms of the bloody men, wrapped in their cloaks
and hiding their faces, as if ashamed of their actions ; and,
lastly, that miserable wretch, swinging in the air, and who,
I imagined, cried out, "I die innocent !"'

"Doctor Hamill was here interrupted by a heart-
rending groan from an adjoining room, and at the same
time the landlord came in, and inquired whether there was
not a physician among us, who could do something for a
traveler, who had arrived the day before, and was now
suffering intense pain. The doctor instantly followed the
landlord, saying, however, that he would soon return, as
he felt anxious to play whist by the side of the bright
wood-fire—that unparalleled rare luxury to a New-Yorker.

"But it seemed to be fated that we should not play
whist that night, in the pretty village of Middletown, as
you will see ; for Dr. Hamill's visit to the patient in the
next room lasted over two hours, and we were just on the
point of retiring to our sleeping-apartments (it being now
midnight) when he reappeared among us. His face was
singularly altered, and as white as the snow which continued to pelt against the windows. He emptied, one
after the other, two glasses of the whisky-punch we had
duly appreciated while waiting for him ; and after recovering the balance of his mind—to use his own expression—
the doctor gave the following explanation of his long
absence.

"'I have always distrusted,' said he, 'the voice of the

people—irreverently assimilated to the voice of God. People may err in their judgment and acts as well as a single individual. More than that: I hold that a crowd of persons, acting under the heat of the moment, is more liable to commit errors than a single individual. They excite each other, their imagination reaches to an extravagant pitch, and, unwilling to wait for the "sober second thought" which would bring them back to reason, they instantly begin to execute extreme measures, adopted under the spur of passion, and from which any sensible man, conscious of his responsibility, would certainly recoil. In the United States, especially, with a people fickle and easily excited, great danger is to be apprehended from these verdicts of the mob, these tumultuous manifestations of public opinion, which are too often mistaken for truth and justice. The masses, obeying too sudden impulses, blinded by anger and resentment, know no control, no obstacle, to restrain them, and therefore use unmercifully an irresponsible power, to the possible detriment of reason, justice, and humanity.

"'I needed this exordium as a fit preface for the melancholy scene I have just witnessed in the next room. A man in the prime of life, and who appeared to have been once possessed of a strongly-built frame, was writhing under the most acute torture. I saw at once that his earthly career must soon end, and I gave him a few drops of a strengthening cordial. When, after much trouble and difficulty, I succeeded in obtaining from the patient some explanation respecting the locality and progress of his sufferings, I arrived at the conclusion that he was dying through starvation and exhaustion! His hollow cheeks and wild staring eyes made him a dreadful sight to behold. His bony arms, which he kept most of the time over his head, made, when in motion, the same noise as those of a skeleton, and his voice was so weak I was obliged to lean over his ghastly face to understand what he meant. I gave him another cordial, mixing with it a few drops of laudanum, and he soon experienced some relief.

"'Thanking me for my attention, "I feel," said he, "all is up with me in this world. I may have one hour to live, but no more. I will avail myself of that time to confess to you an awful crime. Remorse has long preyed upon my mind ; for fifteen years I have led a miserable life. I believe I ought not to carry with me to my grave a secret which I feel I can reveal, at the present time, without danger to myself, while my confession may be the means, perhaps, at some future day, of saving the life of a fellow-mortal from the impetuosity of a mob, misled by prejudices or a sudden thirst for blood.

""" I was hardly twenty years old when the sad event I am now about to reveal occurred. I had unhappily fallen into the company of men who possessed no scruples about the means to obtain money, and who gave full reins to their evil passions. We passed most of the day and night in gambling-houses and other places of resort for idle and corrupt persons ; and when we grew tired of that life or deemed it prudent to disappear, for a while, from town, we repaired to the woods, living on game and plunder. One day, we were (one of my boon companions and myself) lying nigh a ditch, waiting to shoot game. Thick bushes prevented the passers-by from seeing us. Night was coming on, and, tired of our long watch, we were just about giving it up, when we perceived two men on horseback coming straight in our direction. They stopped in front of us, to exchange parting words ; for the road branched off at that place, and, as their conversation led us to believe, they had to take opposite directions to get home. One of them was profuse in his thanks for a loan of five hundred dollars, and anxiously insisted on giving his friend a receipt for said loan. But the lender resolutely declined to receive it. 'Then take this pocket-book,' said the borrower, and keep it as a token of the friendship which will forever unite us.' The horseman accepted the gift; but, at the same time, drawing a revolver from his coat —'Gift for gift,' said he merrily; 'as you are now a capitalist, and as night is approaching, you want a weapon to protect your treasure. As for me,' showing another revolver, 'I have this to protect my carpet-bag, in which is the balance of my money.' At these last words, after heartily shaking hands, they separated.

"'"We had not missed one word of this conversation, and the same devilish idea flashed through our minds when we heard one of the horsemen speak of the money he had collected. We were strangers in that part of the country, and could travel one hundred miles from it before another sun had set. Hidden by the thick bushes which bordered the road, we followed the horseman about one hundred yards, and then stopped at an angle of the road which he had to cross. A few seconds after, he was in sight. 'Take charge of the man, and I will look after the deer,' whispered my companion, pointing out a stag at some distance. We fired at the same time; but while the horseman fell to the ground a corpse, the stag, though wounded, had sufficient strength to run away, tracing the course of his flight by his blood. We found five hundred dollars in the carpet-bag of the horseman, who was holding in his hand the pocket-book which his friend had presented him a few minutes before. Then, as we were hun-

gry, we searched for the wounded deer. We found it lying
in a hollow; and while we were cutting it in pieces, we made
a discovery that greatly puzzled us. Though my companion had fired only once, the beast had been hit twice·
Anyhow, we hastily left the wood and that bloody scene,
in which I had played the principal part. Twenty days
later, we reached the banks of the Mississippi, on our way,
with a thousand other adventurers, to newly discovered
gold mines. When we arrived at the borders of civilization, and were on the eve of moving into the endless solitudes of the great West, we purchased a lot of newspapers,
as is usual with pioneers, with the view of lightening the
tediousness of a long journey. In one of those papers I
read an account of the murder I had committed, and thus
learned the name of the horseman my rifle had mortally
wounded. His name was Plunkett, and he was a physician. I read in another newspaper that his supposed murderer—a young man named George Harris, the same who
had given the pocket-book, as a token of friendship, to the
physician—had been hanged. This George Harris, fifteen
years ago to-day, was taken out of jail by an infuriated mob, and put to death for a crime I alone had committed! Since this discovery, that crime has heavily
weighed on my conscience, and my life has been one of
continual suffering. I vainly tried to procure by hard work
a respite from the remorse that was fast consuming my
strength. Even the sight of gold (and I found large nug-
gets almost without any trouble, while my companions
could find but small bits of the precious metal) had the
effect to increase my grief and suffering; for I had become
a murderer for the possession of it! My mind gradually gave way; every night I had terrible dreams, in
which I saw a violent mob hang the unfortunate Harris,

while he was protesting his innocence. Soon after, it
seemed to be my turn to become the object of the mob's
fury.   Laboring under a frightful hallucination, I felt the
executioners, with their rough hands, pass the fatal noose
around my neck, and drawing it closer and closer, until,
my breath, leaving my body, I fell a corpse from the post!
What is truly horrible and unaccountable is, that, after
those dreadful nights, and while the song of birds and the
splendors of the rising sun and the morning's perfumed
breezes seemed to invite mankind to renewed life and happiness, this awful hallucination still clung to me !   Wide
awake as I was, I imagined I still felt the rope gradually
pressing against my neck ; I became almost suffocated ;
my throat seemed to grow narrower, and in spite of all
my efforts I could not swallow food !

" " You now understand how I thus gradually became
lean and shrunken up like a skeleton, and why all remedies are powerless to prolong my life !"

" ' After this frightful confession, the unfortunate man
sank back on his bed, his pulse rapidly decreased, and I
found it was useless to give him any more of the cordial
I had previously administered.   I had scarcely time to
perform another important duty. Tearing out a blank leaf
from my diary, I hastily wrote the following declaration,
taken from the lips of the dying man :

" ' " At this solemn moment, and soon to appear before
my God, I declare that, on the twentieth day of December,
18—, I murdered Doctor Plunkett, and am the sole author
of the crime for which George Harris was hung by the
people."

" ' " Sign," said I, holding the murderer's hand, after
reading him the few lines I had written.   " If George
Harris's parents are alive, your declaration may cheer their

remaining days, and you will leave this wörld more contented in mind by offering to the victim of a fatal error the only reparation that now lies in your power."

"' He signed with a bold hand, and whispered a few words of satisfaction at what he had done. Then he closed his eyes—stretched out his arms—the death-rattle appeared, and a slight spasm told me that Doctor Plunkett's murderer was no more!'

"After pronouncing these last words, Doctor Hamill took from his pocket-book a small sheet of paper on which was written the murderer's confession. After we had examined the document and satisfied our curiosity, the doctor put it back in his pocket-book.

"' I will carry it with me,' said he, ' as long as I live. Who can say I shall never again witness Judge Lynch's nocturnal revels ? or that I shall never sit as a juror ? In the first place, that declaration will go far to calm a popular outburst, and to secure, as the murderer himself hoped it would, to any man charged with a capital offense, the protection of the law ; and, in the second place, it will help me to demonstrate to my brother jurors that, when the life of a fellow-creature is at stake, something more than a chain of circumstantial evidence is needed to authorize society to take away his life.' "

The ferry-boat had reached the New-York side at the very moment Asmodeus terminated this impressive narrative.

" Every body should read this dreadful story," said I. " On seeing how very possible it is to make mistakes, the Americans should be less hasty in depriving a mah of the benefits of the law."

" Undoubtedly," answered Asmodeus ; " still, in the sparsely populated cities of the Far West, the terror inspired by Judge Lynch is, to some extent, salutary. I even believe the same summary practice would be productive of much good were it resorted to, from time to time, in some of our large cities; as, perhaps, there is no other means to relieve them of the many scoundrels and rogues who infest them, and whose political connections secure them from the stringency of the law. Indeed, I would not have objected to the hanging of that bar-keeper, who is guilty of the most atrocious crime, and whose avariciousness has caused the untimely death of a score of poor people. All the charges brought against him by the mob were true to the letter, and he was indeed fortunate in having his life spared, through the interference of a pompous lawyer. But lawyers are meddlesome fellows; they are forever poking their noses into every affair. To-day, you shall see those of New-York at work; for I propose to show you, after you have taken a little rest, how justice is administered in the United States."

CHAPTER VII.

 HAD, indeed, great need of rest: I was ex-
ceedingly tired, both in body and mind, which
unpleasant state may be readily imagined from
my excursion with Asmodeus and the terri-
ble scenes through which we had passed. Still, I could
enjoy but little repose, so busy was my mind with
the many incidents of that excursion. Most assuredly, thought I, in many respects the morals of the Americans are strange. We find here a society which is not as
yet firmly seated—a premature civilization, which, like a
plant in a conservatory, has had no time to ripen in conformity with natural laws. But pure gold, I doubt not,
is largely mingled with scoria. The Americans' love of
money is very great; but does not Asmodeus himself admit that the evil is corrected, to a certain extent, by their
love of luxury and by a liberality which seems inexhaustible? And I recollected, in this respect, that no people,
in the hour of want, had ever vainly appealed to the
Americans. According to Asmodeus, wealth is the cri-
terion for public estimation, and the standard of merit in
the United States. But is it not so in every other
country? Here, every body is more or less engaged in
business; and as there is no nobility, no class distinctions,
wealth or success in some calling is about the sole thing

that can create distinction. Then, the observations of Asmodeus concerning marriages in the United States impressed me favorably. I felt pleased to know that women were left free to choose their own husbands—heiress-hunters being almost unknown and always despised in America. Paternal power is weak, it is true ; but this is the result and consequence of democratic institutions. It is well to be taught, from youth, to rely on one's self. What progress could a people, providentially designed to settle a continent like America, make, were they trammeled by the many prejudices, timid laws, and obnoxious restraints by which the masses of Europe are shackled? And I concluded it were wise not to disapprove too hastily of either the habits or institutions which permit the American people to make such gigantic strides in the career of progress and power.

A burst of laughter here interrupted my meditations. I turned and perceived Asmodeus standing beside me, fanning himself with his handkerchief, and in a very merry humor.

" I have just met," said he, after recovering himself, " in the hall of this hotel, a very queer personage—something like an apparition—a ghost—a spirit ; and while you dress yourself, I will relate to you his adventures. But I must candidly warn you that the conclusions you may deduce from my narrative will not, perhaps, be in conformity with the optimismal reflections that pervaded your mind when I interrupted you."

D. D. MERRYMAN'S HISTORY.

"About two years ago, the city of Omega, situated in the State of New-York, was thrown into much consternation, in consequence of a sad accident. The good people of that lovely town were startled one morning, on learning that their beloved minister, D. D. Merryman, had been drowned the day before, while on a fishing excursion with his children. As the minister's clothes had been found on the banks of the river, and his children had declared they saw their father, after swimming for a time, sink beneath the waves, no one doubted the awful catastrophe. The coroner held an inquest, and half-a-dozen wise men of Omega returned a verdict of accidental death. In consequence of this sad calamity, a New-York life insurance company paid the minister's widow the sum of twenty thousand dollars, for which the divine had insured his life a few months before.

"At the time of this occurrence, Dr. Merryman was a great favorite with the Omega ladies. Handsome and good-hearted, he had been consecrated when twenty-three years old, after devoting, for a time, his theological talent to Erastus Braggart's notorious agency. This Erastus Braggart had long been connected with periodicals, when, one day, he published the following advertisement:

"'INTELLECTUAL BUREAU.—Tired of newspaper falsehoods and humbugs, and anxious to benefit my countrymen, from this day I place the intellectual faculties I have been blessed with, as well as the large experience of the world I have acquired, at their disposition. Henceforth, the *Intellectual Bureau* I have just started will furnish (orders executed at twenty-four hours' notice) epistolary masterpieces for lovers of either sex ; eloquent speeches for congressmen and politicians ; sermons of the highest evangelical standard for ministers of the Gospel ; circulars for merchants ; sensation novels for publishers ; dramas of assured success for authors ; and, for aspiring poets of the United States, poetic works, compared to which, those of

Homer and Milton will sink into insignificance. From
this date, to attain either distinction or a fortune, or even
both, churchmen, statesmen, tradesmen, men of science,
of means, of large imagination, etc., etc., have but to apply
to my Intellectual Bureau, where other information, if required, may be obtained.'

" This singular undertaking, it is said, brought large
sums of money to Erastus Braggart, who kept in his employ many talented young men. There were in the agency
a theological department, in which were written sermons
for ministers of the Gospel ; a political department, whose
business it was to keep ever ready, on every topic, thrilling
speeches for congressmen and politicians ; an academical,
or belles-lettres department ; and a few others of less importance.

" As secrecy was a well-understood condition of this undertaking, those among our congressmen, ministers, and
authors, who dealt with Braggart's agency, were not
known to the outside world. But, though the mystery concerning it was never cleared up, it is, nevertheless, a well-
authenticated fact that the pulpit and forum had their
palmiest days during the agency's existence.

" Merryman, after being consecrated, to charm the Chris-
tians of the town of Omega, where he had been sent to exercise his vocation, with his eloquence, had but to open
his portfolio to find it replete with sermons on every conceivable text, duly elaborated, while in the theological department of the agency, for Braggart's clients ; and, as
Omega's faithful people were left in blissful ignorance that
others had previously enjoyed their pastor's rhetoric, they
lauded his learning and eloquence to the skies.

" However, as his annual salary amounted to hardly
eight hundred dollars, on account of the scanty contribu-

tions of the members of his church, Merryman, in the second year of his ministry, devised, as a means to increase it, a very sagacious plan. He put up at auction the pews of his church, and, owing to a preconcerted understanding with some friends, the biddings were exceedingly spirited, and the result highly gratifying. Pews near the pulpit were knocked down to some ambitious people of Omega at a large premium ; and, through this auction, Merryman carried his income up to fifteen hundred dollars. As soon as it became known, this bold stroke of his genius found imitators throughout the States. Ministers of the Gospel became speculators, and, instead of humbly begging from the faithful, they sold them the privilege of listening to their sermons. In that way they created for themselves a pleasant independence, while, at the same time, largely increasing their salaries. The letting of church-pews has now become a very extensive practice, some of them yielding, though the fact seems hardly credible, twenty-five thousand dollars per annum, and even more ; and such are the inducements they present to capitalists, that churches are often built for the sole purpose of selling their pews !

" Having so remarkably improved his prospects, D. D. Merryman decided to marry. He had favorably noticed among the female members of his church, Cora Cackling, the daughter of a well-to-do farmer. She was not actually beautiful, but she had a very pleasant disposition, and Merryman thought her quite fitted to enliven his parsonage. Before the third year of his pastorate had expired, he fairly entered upon his honeymoon, which, it is said, sometimes lasts the whole year in the United States.

" Such, perchance, would have been the case with Merryman and his wife, but for Erastus Braggart's accidental visit, a few months after their marriage. The 'Intellectual Bureau' still continued in existence, supplying, as usual, the pulpit, bar, and stage, with its masterpieces. But Braggart now aspired to play a still more conspicuous part. He was ambitious to enlighten not only a few classes, but the whole of mankind ; and he was busily engaged in establishing a new religion, when, returning from a trip for that especial purpose, he made a short stay at Omega.

"It is certainly strange that spiritualism, or the pretended intercourse with the spirits of an invisible world, should have made its appearance in the United States at about the time Swedenborg's doctrines (foretold by himself) were in the ascendant. When, at the point of death, he was asked by one of his friends whether he persisted in his belief and assertions, as contained in his works, the Swedish philosopher answered affirmatively ; adding, that nobody would, a hundred years hence, doubt the soundness and truth of his spiritual teachings. It may be that Braggart had read this incident in one of Swedenborg's numerous biographies; and, learning, one day, that two or three young girls, living in a northern county of the State of New York, fell, from time to time, into magnetic trances, during which they pretended to communicate with spirits, he believed the era predicted by Swedenborg had arrived. He went to the village where the young girls lived, for the purpose of hearing their revelations ; and, satisfied with the experiment, he was on his way back to New-York, when he met his former employee, Merryman.

"The minister, proud to entertain such a noteworthy personage as Erastus Braggart, took him to his parsonage, where he was not slow to notice the fine figure and intelligent countenance of the minister's wife. She was no longer the homely country girl the minister had married. Hymen had polished a rough marble and fashioned a charming statue out of it. Her auburn hair fell in massy curls over her finely rounded shoulders, her blue eyes were brilliant with the soft light of love, and a sort of poetical halo seemed to surround her, by which bystanders were involuntarily entranced.

"It may be doubted whether Merryman was conscious of the great change that matrimony had wrought in his wife, and of her actual beauty and wit. But Braggart saw, at the first glance, that she was the very woman he was in search of, to help him in his forthcoming revelations to the world of a new religious system. Under some pretense, he lengthened his visit to Omega, and before taking his departure for New-York, he had come to a thorough understanding with Mrs. Merryman regarding their future operations. The small town of Omega, it seems, had become tiresome to her ; and when Braggart pointed out the notoriety in store for her, she became willing to play a conspicuous part in the spiritual exhibitions he had in view— that of intermediary, or medium, between the dead and living. So, every thing prepared, one evening, she hastened to New-York, to meet Erastus ; and Merryman, on returning to his parsonage, found it deserted.

"The minister learned of her whereabouts from that very notoriety Braggart had promised her. Cora had commenced a series of lectures, or revelations she pretended to have received from the spiritual world, and upon which a new religious system was to be based. People fond of new sensations flocked to her lectures and applauded the fair lecturer. They were moved to enthusiasm by her sympathetic voice and facility of expressing startling theories. Cora, with an imperturbable coolness, described per-

sons who had been dead many years, and repeated con-
versations she said she had held with their spirits.   Many
illustrious men of modern, and even of ancient, times, were
the objects of her so-called supernatural power ; and her intercourse with the invisible world continued several months,
until interrupted by the medium's mysterious disappearance.
Among the persons converted to spiritualism, a wealthy
merchant had early shown himself as one of the most enthusiastic, and he finally prevailed upon Cora to confer on
him alone, to the exclusion of the public, the benefit of her
intercourse with the world of spirits.

" In the mean while, D. D. Merryman had taught himself
to look philosophically at his conjugal misfortune.   Cora's
lectures in New-York had created such a sensation that he
could not think of ever taking her back to his parsonage—
even admitting that she might be willing to resume her former quiet and decent life.   As her notoriety increased,
owing to her extravagant style of living, and the great display she made after her acquaintance with the wealthy
merchant, the minister concluded that a divorce was now
the only issue forced upon him ; and so, after she had been
absent over a year from his roof, Merryman obtained a divorce from Cora Cackling.   But, shortly after, he married
again.

"With few exceptions, ministers of the Gospel do not
remain in celibacy.   The feelings of Protestant communities regarding this matter are altogether different from those
of Roman Catholics.   A Protestant minister must marry,
if he wishes to enjoy the full confidence of his flock ; though
he can not in that blessed condition obviously entertain for it
such inexhaustible devotedness as the Catholic priest, who
belongs entirely to his flock.   It has been contended that
the imagination is not as fervid with people of the Protes-

tant persuasion as with Catholics ; and also, that they are
less kindly of heart and less disinterested in mind.   If so,
Protestant communities must not expect from their ministers qualities with which they are only moderately endowed.
But, if public opinion approved D. D. Merryman's second
marriage, it was for him the occasion of many unpleasant
trials—like those that conquered Peter's opposition to a
Castilian Hidalgo.*   Merryman's second wife was afflicted
with that troublesome mania, jealousy, and in its most unpleasant form—*retrospective* jealousy.   She forever fancied
that her husband still loved his first wife, and more than once
caused Merryman to regret that he had married again.
However, maternal duties soon absorbed the thoughts of
the minister's wife and brought some relief to her husband.
Those duties were almost constantly required for six years ;
for after the lapse of that time, the minister had a family
of two boys and two girls—an evident dispensation of Heaven's bounty, in the opinion of the old ladies of Omega.

"Large families, in fact, are far from being considered
a burden by country people.   The corruption that has invaded large cities is, as yet, unknown in most country-
places, and Malthus's theories and charlatan practices do
not obtain among them.   They feel no uneasiness in bringing up their children, nor any anxiety for their prospects.
They are aware that when boys arrive at the age of fifteen,
they will make money enough to meet their own expenses ;
and, as regards the girls, if they are pretty and modest,
husbands will not be wanting.   Consequently, the increase

---

* An allusion by Asmodeus to the following legend: Peter declined to allow an
Hidalgo to enter Paradise.   "Go through purgatory's probation first," said he.
"I have been twice married," replied the disappointed Castilian.   "That is another
affair," gently rejoined Peter ; "a second marriage is equivalent to purgatory's probation.   Come into Paradise !"

of his family gave no uneasiness to D. D. Merryman. But an occurrence took place about eight years after his second marriage which was destined to work a considerable change in his prospects. He was obliged to go, from time to time, to New-York, to confer with some brethren of his church ; and on one of these trips he met, on her way to the metropolis, a friendless young girl in search of a situation. The doctor felt a profound compassion for this young lady, thrown upon the cold charity of the world. He recommended her to some friends, gave her money, and returned to Omega, well satisfied with his day's work.

"In this affair, the minister had been guided by pure motives of Christian charity; but the devil delights, as you know, to turn aside the best intentions, and he resorts especially to very wicked means when he wants to overcome a servant of God and plunge him into sin. It appears that D. D. Merryman visited this young lady, whom he had made his ward, several times. She had become a teacher in one of our public schools. At the time the minister chanced to meet Angela, she was hardly twenty years old, while Mrs. Merryman was nearly thirty-five, being of the same age as her husband ; and the latter could not help contrasting the beauty and loveliness of the young teacher with the fading charms and morose disposition of his wife.

" No matter to which persuasion he belongs, in spite of his layman's dress, the countenance always betrays the Roman Catholic priest or the Protestant minister. Angela was, therefore, well aware, from the beginning of her acquaintance with Merryman, of his sacred character, and she displayed all the arts of female coquetry to lead her protector astray. It may be supposed he became a too willing victim to the snares laid by the fascinating Angela ;

for a few months after meeting her, Merryman, besides his home in Omega, had fitted up a temporary one in New-York., This establishment proved a costly luxury, and Merryman was far from being wealthy. To complicate the difficulties of his situation, his now frequent visits to New-York awoke in the bosom of his legitimate wife the slumbering fires of jealousy ; while the old ladies of Omega began to gossip among themselves of the repeated absences of their pastor. Merryman was not slow to realize the dangers of his situation—dangers that were every day increasing ; and he was gradually led to devise some means to extricate himself from the embarrassing situation in which he was placed. The shortest and surest one, perhaps, was to leave Angela to her fate, and never to see her again. But the minister had it not in his heart to abandon the young teacher ; because, besides being passionately enamored of her, he was fearful she might expose him, in case he should determine to put an end to all further intercourse with her. Scandal is the very thing the Americans, in every station of life, are most afraid of. As, in general, they make a parade of virtue, they inevitably lose public esteem when they turn aside from its paths. If traders, they no longer find countenance with banks and bankers, and ruin befalls them. If ministers of the Gospel, the result is the same ; and Merryman knew too well that his church would be deserted and his pews unsalable, if his intrigue with Angela became known.

"After duly considering every side of the case, he determined to elope with Angela. But, as he had imbibed casuistic principles from his theological studies, he took care to reconcile his duties as a father with his love for the teacher. To that effect, he insured his life for a sum of twenty thousand dollars, payable, in case of his death, to his wife and children; and to procure the means he needed to carry out his plan, he sold two houses purchased out of his savings. A few months after these transactions, the inhabitants of Omega, as I related in the beginning of this veracious narrative, were startled to hear that their beloved minister had been drowned."

Here Asmodeus again gave way to a fit of laughter, and then resumed his narrative.

"Think of my amazement on meeting, a few minutes ago, that same D. D. Merryman, whose untimely end the Omega community has long lamented! I met him in the hall as I was coming here to take you out to show you, according to my promise, how the judicial institutions of the United States are operated. I recognized him at first sight, skillfully disguised as he was; for," added Asmodeus, in a vainglorious manner, "it is not an easy matter to deceive a little devil who has seen much of the world!

"'My dear doctor,' said I, 'how glad I am to see you, and looking, too, as young and handsome as ever.'

"'Sir,' he angrily replied, moving off, 'you mistake me for another.'

"'Oh! no; my name is Asmodeus, as true as yours is Merryman, who was, a few years ago, the beloved pastor of Omega. If you have forgotten me, I have not you, for the very reason that I chanced to meet you on a memorable occasion of my life. I had just broken my leg for the second time, and a country physician had so badly adjusted it, that an accident of no consequence, if properly attended to, put my life in jeopardy. A few old ladies at that time called you to my bedside, to reconcile me with heaven and prepare me for that country "from whose bourne no traveler returns." But I got out of the scrape in spite of the ignorant country doctor, but with the unpleasant result of limping a little more than before. You now understand, my dear doctor, that a man snatched from the brink of the grave can hardly forget those whose business it is to gently push him into it. But, at the time of the occurrence I allude to, your face was as smooth as that of an infant; to-day, you wear both mustache and whiskers. Again, your hair was at that time of a sandy color, and now it is as black as ebony. Please, tell me, my dear Mr. Merryman, the meaning of this wonderful and no doubt successful transformation.'

"'I will confide all to you, on condition that you will not again call me by my real name,' said the minister, looking anxiously around. 'There is no use, I see, to dissemble with you. Let us go to some secluded place, and I will unvail the mystery to which you seem to attach so much importance.

"'I had resolved,' he began, 'to leave my family forever, but, at the same time, to secure to them the means of subsistence in case the plan I had matured should succeed. I arranged, in consequence, a fishing-party with two of my children. We accordingly enjoyed ourselves all day, boating and fishing, about two miles from the town. When night came on, saying I would take a swim, I undressed myself and told the children to quietly wait for my return. After swimming about awhile, I dived under the water and swam toward the opposite bank, which I reached in safety. Nobody was in the vicinity, and so I landed unseen. I had, a few days previously, concealed a few clothes in a clump of bushes; and after putting them on, I waited to mark what effect my manœuvre would have upon the children. I perceived from my hiding-place, they felt uneasy concerning my absence, and perhaps also about themselves, as it was now growing dark. Soon they commenced crying aloud, and attracted the attention of some country people who were passing by. The latter, after learning the cause of the little ones' trouble, began at once to search for me. Relieved now of all anxiety concerning the children, and having nothing further to do in that vicinity, I rapidly walked away. The night was very dark, and I would have experienced much difficulty in traveling but for my knowledge of the country. I walked till the dawn of day, and then took a little rest in a wood near by. When I awoke, I cut off my light hair, covered my head with a black wig, adorned my lips with a thick mustache, and my face with heavy whiskers; and when I looked in a pocket-mirror I had with me, I could hardly recognize myself. Satisfied my identity could not be easily discovered, I took my course toward the nearest railway station. I arrived, in a few hours' time, at a small town in Canada, where it was agreed, before I left her, Angela should meet me. I waited there for her a whole week. At last she came, bringing with her several newspapers, in which was an account of the sad accident that had deprived the Omega community of its pastor; and we instantly made preparations to sail for Europe.

"'With so restless a people as the Americans, who are so fond of traveling, we could not think of settling in the vicinity of the States. I was artfully disguised, it is true—so much so that Angela hardly recognized me when we met; still, I thought somebody might have the same perspicacity you have just exhibited—though several years have elapsed since we have met; and therefore, impelled by a sense of safety, we took passage on board the first vessel that sailed for Europe.

"'I had provided myself with twenty thousand dollars, and expected, on arriving in England, to increase my resources by means of some occupation. But Angela would not listen to any project of that sort. She wanted to see the world ; so I unwillingly submitted to her desire, and said no more about it.

"'I loved her more passionately than ever ; and besides, I soon perceived she had discovered a secret that placed me entirely in her power. The newspapers she had brought me contained editorials respecting the contract of insurance I had made for the benefit of my family ; my foresight was highly praised, and presented as a commendable example to the public in general, and ministers of the Gospel in particular. One word from Angela would arouse the company's suspicions, provoke fresh inquiry respecting my sudden departure, and finally deprive my wife and children of the fruits of my insurance. In consequence, I thought it advisable to blindly follow Angela's whims and fancies, for fear of exciting her resentment.

"'To tell you the truth, the two years I spent with her in Europe gave me a foretaste of hell's torments—that is, if such a place as hell exists—a matter concerning which you know, perhaps, more than myself. Sometimes she wished me to marry her, as she could no longer tolerate, she said, her degraded existence. As I had assumed, on leaving America, the name of Samuel Elope, she desired me to resume that of Merryman. I resisted, of course, because I could not condescend to commit an act of bigamy, and also because it would prove a dangerous experiment to resuscitate Dr. Merryman of Omega. Sometimes she found fault with my beard, and objected to my dyeing it and my hair—the safest way, undoubtedly, to conceal my identity. She declared she had fallen in love with me, when I used to shave and had light hair ; that she could never have loved the bearded mulatto into which I had transformed myself. In short, not a day, not even an hour passed that was not marked by some quarrel instigated by this devilish woman, which inevitably ended in her threatening to divulge the trick I had devised, as she said, to bleed a life insurance company. More than once, I confess, I regretted having left my home, in spite of every circumstance that once tended to make it irksome.

" I found that only traveling would make our association endurable, and soften Angela's bitter temper. So we successively visited Scotland, Ireland, and England ; then France, Spain, Italy, and a part of Germany. But our traveling expenses were rapidly exhausting the money I had brought with me ; and one day I made the sad discovery that only one thousand dollars remained in my pocket-book.

" ' Now is the time to return to America,' said Angela. ' There, if they do not always make fortunes, smart, energetic men easily find a means of subsistence. Besides, I am disgusted with the Old World. All European countries, when compared with the United States, seem backward by at least a century. I feel distressed, and my republican feelings are hurt by seeing everywhere females working like cattle, and society divided into classes and castes, as it was in the time of the Pharaohs or the days of the Crusades. And what an amount of misery these country people endure, living in thatched shanties, with not even a window to ventilate them ! Their very costume is painful to contemplate—wearing, as they do, a loose frock, and walking barefooted—except the better classes among them, who wear wooden shoes. I long to see again the pretty cottages of New-England, and their decently-dressed women ; I long to travel on American railways, in those spacious cars in which people move and breathe freely ;

in short, I long to return to a country where all men are gentlemen, all women ladies !"

"' While relieving herself of this harangue, Angela packed up her things ; and notwithstanding my objections, the next day she paid for her passage on board a German steamer bound for America. I was weak enough to follow her, and we arrived here five days ago. I have already met some former acquaintances ; but though they did not recognize me, I do not feel secure, and think it best to leave this great metropolis at once.'

"' And Angela,' I ventured to ask the minister ; ' what has become of her ? '

"' When on board,' answered Merryman, sighing and visibly depressed, ' I deemed it prudent to shut myself up, most of the time, in our cabin. Angela, who had no reason to keep herself secluded, was constantly promenading the deck or singing in the saloons. It appears she made the acquaintance of a wealthy Californian, who was also on his way to the States. The day after we arrived, while looking for her through the hotel at which we put up, a messenger handed me the following letter :

"' " MY DEAR DOCTOR : We have, indeed, had a pleasant time together—spending, in our tour from one place to another, about twenty thousand dollars, which is considered a large sum on the other side of the water. Unfortunately, by living in such fine style, I gained a taste for luxury ; and as you are no longer in a situation to satisfy it, I have accepted the gracious offer of a wealthy Californian to become his housekeeper. The Morning Star is just steaming up ; and when you receive these few lines, I shall be on my way to the Pacific coast. So, farewell, reverend sir.

Do not become excited; and above all things, do not
weep for me, lest your grief find an echo at Omega.

" ANGELA."

" ' Now,' concluded Merryman, after reading this letter,
'mindful in my conscience of what I owe that poor, erring
girl, I myself intend to sail to-morrow for California.   I
will endeavor to bring that stray lamb back to the path of
virtue.   But, with or without her, I am determined to settle in that wonderful State, and to forget, by hard work,
the faults, errors, and deceptions of a misspent life ! ' "

CHAPTER VIII.

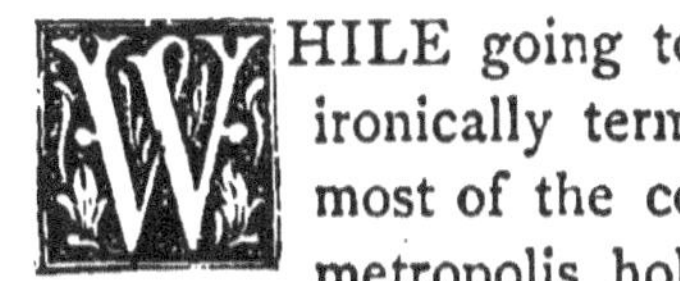HILE going to Justice's temple, as Asmodeus ironically termed the spacious building where most of the courts of justice in the American metropolis hold their sittings, I did not cease admiring the handsome edifices which line the commercial thoroughfare of the city. Many of the warehouses, where all the products of the world find room, have a very imposing appearance, most of them being built of white marble and in the most tasteful style. And what bustle everywhere—what activity—what confusion! The city of New-York is built upon an island called Manhattan, whose area does not exceed fourteen thousand acres ; and when it is considered that the capital of France contains within its present limits eighteen thousand miles, there can be no wonder that the value of real estate has, within but a few years, so rapidly increased. At the same time, the shape of the island renders circulation a matter of great difficulty to the million and a half of individuals living within the limits of the city or in neighboring towns, the inhabitants of the latter coming every morning to transact business in New-York. Broadway, the principal thoroughfare, is often beset with fearful dangers—wagons, drays, and carriages of

every description choking it up for blocks, as well as many
by-streets and avenues. Foot-passengers have often to
wait very long before they can cross from street to street—
unless they belong to the fair sex, in which case they are
soon escorted safely over, as polite policemen seem to
make it their principal business to open a way for the
ladies.

I noticed that very few of what we term old people are
met with. Every body looks young ; old men walk with an
elastic step, and seem to carry easily and comfortably the
burden of many years.

" People here have no time to grow old," said my companion, guessing my thoughts. "Their business, the
bracing air they breathe, the general activity pervading all
things, make men forget the encroachment of years, and
hence they grow old unconsciously. Contrary to the
custom of European merchants, none here thinks of retiring from business, even after accumulating wealth. Men
of eighty years, and over, go regularly every morning to
their office, and wonderfully withstand the ravages of
time. Repose seems unbearable in the United States.
Millionaires themselves keep ever busy, until death
snatches them from their labors. To the inhabitant of the
New World may be quite properly applied that well-known
sentence : ' In the grave only there is rest for man.'

"With such a people, and considering the favorable
situation of New-York, with its two rivers, navigable for
the largest ships ; with a harbor in which all the navies of
the world might safely ride at anchor ; with an admirable
net-work of railways, it is impossible to predict any limit
to the development of that great metropolis. To-day, it is
the commercial and monetary market of North-America.
Before a quarter of a century has elapsed, when railways

shall connect the Pacific with the Atlantic Ocean, it will become the mercantile and financial centre of the world. Its population, with its steady increase, will before the end of the present century exceed that of London."

By this time, we had arrived at the court-house, and we entered one of the rooms where a case was in progress. This room was lined with green hangings, and an iron railing separated the magistrates and lawyers from the public. It looked like one of the halls for the administration of justice in Europe. The presiding judge was assisted by two others. At his right, a little further off, twelve jurymen were seated, and on his left were the district-attorney and the clerk of the court, behind whom could be seen many newspaper reporters. Opposite was a wooden bar, behind which seats were disposed for the lawyers ; and in the middle of the room stood a bench for persons whose testimony was to be received. There were no soldiers present—not even a single policeman—in a word, not the slightest sign of brutal force, or of what is termed "authority" in the Old World.

A young girl was on trial for the supposed murder of her mistress ; and no one but one of the keepers of the prison where she was detained was standing by her. Neither the presiding judge, his assistants, the state-attorney, nor the prisoner's counsel—in short, nobody in the room—wore a costume distinct from that of the public. The red or black gown, worn by magistrates in Europe ; the ponderous wig of English judges and lawyers ; the square cap and white band of French advocates, are unknown in the United States ; and it does not appear that the administration of law is less dignified, because of the repudiation of the staid ideas of past ages.

According to Asmodeus, the Americans are, as a

general rule, a good-natured people. They are cool, not over-fond of heated debate, and good breeding seems to be quite common. Writers who have burlesqued American habits and reproached the inhabitants of the United States with gross improprieties, have done so either for speculative purposes or to revenge some supposed personal slight.

The trial was indeed conducted with perfect decorum; and the audience, refraining from expressing either approbation or disapprobation, exhibited much respect for law and justice. I was struck by another peculiarity—namely, the slowness of the proceedings. I learned that the case now going on had commenced ten days previously, and that five days more would be required to bring it to a conclusion. I readily believed it on seeing the wranglings and chicanery resorted to, every moment, by the prisoner's counsel; and I could understand, in consequence of an incident I will relate, how trials which would terminate within a day or two in Europe, last a fortnight and even more in the United States.

According to the state-attorney, the young girl had been induced to kill her mistress in the hope of marrying the victim's husband. The murder had been committed in broad daylight, while the lady was alone. On their side, the girl's counsel contended that robbers, stealing into the house, had been surprised by the poor woman, whom they assassinated to get rid of her resistance and testimony. Suddenly, one of the counsel rose to propound what seemed to me a nonsensical question—that of ascertaining at what time the moon had shown on the night previous to the day the murder had been committed. The discussion on this point lasted two hours. The counsel of the accused asked leave to produce an almanac, which demand the state-attorney strenuously opposed, as being contrary to the law.   After a long rejoinder from one of the prisoner's defenders, the court ordered that the almanac be produced. The triumphant lawyer then drew from his pocket an almanac published, it appears, by a gentleman belonging to his own political party.   The state-attorney, who belonged to another party, objected to the production of the almanac, as coming from a suspicious source ; and then both delivered themselves of a wearisome argument on the merits of their respective parties, the court-room all the time resembling a political arena.   The fight over, the presiding judge decided that only an official almanac should be produced — the one published by the Smithsonian Institute of Washington.   Nobody in the court-room had this impartial document in his possession ; it was even surmised by some malicious persons that such a document never existed.   To clear up this point, an order was given to one of the ushers to go to some stationer's and procure the Smithsonian Institute's Almanac.   In consequence of this incident, the court adjourned, and Asmodeus availed himself of the adjournment to give me some information respecting a few 'limbs of the law,' as he facetiously called members of the bar ; and, also of the judicial institutions of the United States.

"That stout gentleman," said he, "whose red face and whiskers unmistakably proclaim him to be an Englishman, arrived, a few years ago, from the United Kingdom, leaving behind him many debts and a not very enviable reputation.   He was welcomed here by every body as a victim of the aristocratic institutions of Europe.   An Irish widow, who had just inherited a large fortune from her husband, took a fancy to this merry son of Albion, who undertook to solace her widowhood by marrying her. Within two or three years he squandered his wife's fortune, and then recovered his freedom, after a somewhat scandalous divorce suit. This late member of the English bar lacks neither talent nor energy, and as he is a jovial man, is quite popular among his friends of the legal profession, and also with people who are bankrupt. When he pleads for a bankrupt, he displays such warmth, such earnestness, one would think he pleads his own cause.

"That gentleman by his side, whose hair is white as snow, was long looked upon as one of our best speakers. He well knows how to move his hearers to tears. His pantomime, especially, is singularly expressive. Many years ago, when yet a young lawyer, he was intrusted with the defense of a poor fellow charged with having murdered an old miser. The latter's son was present in the Court of Oyer and Terminer while the trial was in progress. The young lawyer depicted all the circumstances of the murder with such wondrous skill that every hearer was moved to tears ; he ended by hurling the curse of the accused on the real culprit's head—'A wretch,' said he, 'who has tried to add to one horrible crime another as great—that of causing the death of an innocent being.' On hearing the lawyer's curse, the miser's son threw himself at the feet of the judge, and confessed that he was the real murderer !

"But this remarkable mimic, this powerful orator, lacks decency and honesty. I heard him, one day, on his leaving the court-room, only a few minutes after obtaining the acquittal of a prisoner, say that he would not venture to employ him for his cook. He is one of those lawyers who have introduced the practice of engaging in suits upon speculation—that is, for a part of what they expect to recover —and also, to buy up claims. An agreement with a client for a compensation, at a different rate from what is prescribed in the fee-bill, has for its result to lower the profession in public estimation. A very serious case being confided to the care of the lawyer I speak of, a few years ago, he stipulated that his fee should be one thousand dollars only in case of conviction, and three thousand in case of acquittal. He earned the latter sum.

"Among the four thousand lawyers in New-York who practice, or are supposed to practice, law, all nationalities are represented. The number of Irish lawyers, especially, is very great. The sons of the Emerald Isle seem to be born with the gift of eloquence; and what remarkable coolness or audacity is always exhibited by these countrymen of O'Connell! One would think, from their conversation, that America belongs to their race. They no sooner arrive here than they aspire to public offices—the most important even in the gift of the people. Irishmen fill all branches of the federal, state, and municipal government. I am willing to wager, at any time, that out of twenty politicians, a dozen have emigrated from Ireland.

"If I am not mistaken, the state-attorney is an Irishman. He came to this country shortly after one of those political disturbances so frequent in Ireland—believing it the safest plan to place the ocean between himself and the queen's officers. Like all his countrymen, he immediately connected himself with a political organization, and soon his worldly prospects improved. None knows better than he how to make, at a political convention or national commemoration, an impressive and grandiloquent eulogy on some great man of the Union, living or dead—especially the former.

"That lawyer in front of us settled in New-York a few years ago. He was born in one of the New-England States, and his noble countenance, eloquent eyes, and high forehead can not fail to attract attention everywhere.

He is one of the best debaters in New-York, and is all the more worthy of praise because he had to struggle hard to obtain his present exalted position, being born of poor parents. In politics he is a formidable antagonist to his opponents; but his own party can not appreciate his indomitable pride and domineering propensities. At the present time, he ranks among the most indefatigable lawyers in the United States. Though his appearance might lead one to think otherwise, he is exceedingly fond of money. It is related of him that, in a cause in which important interests were at stake, (a physician being charged with poisoning a friend who had bequeathed him his fortune,) he displayed an exasperation, an animosity, unknown before in the States. He was the attorney of the poisoned man's family; and when the physician, whose doom he had sealed by his eloquence, was hanged, he was the most conspicuous individual among the spectators, as though he was not sure of earning his fee until he saw the poisoner swinging in the air!

"That old gentleman conversing with him still retains the fires of his youth, and our actresses have no more ardent admirer than he. It may be that he acquired from the footlights that taste for emphasis and theatrical effect which he always displays. Pleading one day against a man possessed of a large fortune, and prosecuted for an indecent assault upon a young lady—'Gentlemen,' said he, looking imploringly at the jury, 'you are fathers!' It was all he said; but the effect was magical. He sank overcome upon his seat; and after deliberating a few minutes, the jury returned a verdict of conviction.

"As is the case in all countries where representative governments exist, lawyers abound in the National Congress and State Legislatures. Two thirds of the members of the legislative bodies are lawyers, which fact shows how great their influence is in the United States—though that *esprit de corps* which distinguishes the legal profession in Europe is but little developed here. They have no superiors among them ; the equality which exists everywhere is to be found also among members of the bar. It may be even suspected that they are more impatient of governmental control than the rest of the population.

" Of course, it is from among the legal profession that politicians mainly spring ; and the growing influence of lawyers is well illustrated by the fact that they have occupied the presidential chair since the time of General Jackson. According to the official census, thirty-five thousand persons belong to the legal profession in the United States—a number equal to that of mantua-makers and milliners, and also to that of ministers of all denominations. Out of thirty-five thousand lawyers, two thousand were not born in the United States ; they came here from all parts of the world, which fact seems to demonstrate that if lawyers experience hard times in Europe, they enjoy a better and easier life in this land of freedom.

" In fact, in no other country has chicanery more free and lively scope : not because the Americans are a quarrelsome people—few have more peaceable and tolerant dispositions ; but while the national character has nothing to do with lawsuits and judicial difficulties, which cost the people, every year, on an average, fifty millions of dollars, it is not so as regards the law. And here it is necessary to give a general idea of the Federal Government and of its relations with the several States.

" There is a national or central government, having under its exclusive control all affairs of a general character, and principally treaty relations with foreign countries.

But there is also a separate and distinct government for every State of the Union, composed of an executive power and legislative bodies, like the national government. These particular governments attend to the internal affairs of their respective States ; but they are not permitted to coin money, to make treaties with foreign nations, or to regulate the general trade of the land, which prerogatives devolve upon the federal power. But, aside from these prerogatives, the field, as regards the internal administration of the States and the relations existing between their inhabitants, is large enough to reap a perfect harvest of fresh laws at every session of the local legislatures. Their members, you may be sure, legislate to their hearts' content. Every representative arrives at the capitol of his State with a law-project of some kind in his pocket, as a means whereby to play the man of importance ; and besides, as all law-makers receive a compensation for their labor, they feel bound to earn it.

" It is really impossible to calculate, even by approximation, the number of laws passed by all the States since the American Union first sprang into existence—the mania for legislation, for the reasons I have stated, being cotemporary with the republic. To the innumerable laws in force in the States, we must add those passed by every Congress since the days of Washington—laws often conflicting with those emanating from local legislatures. Of course, the latter are in force in their respective States only, and great discrepancies sometimes exist between the laws of neighboring States. For instance, divorce may be granted for some causes in the State of New-York, while these causes are deemed insufficient in a neighboring State ; civil rights may be acquired under certain conditions in some States, but not in others ; and perhaps a similar law concerning persons and property does not exist in two States of the Union. Now, you can comprehend how such a chaos as this favors the legal profession, and also why the United States are a sort of Eldorado, a golden land for lawyers ; and thus it will be for a long time to come.

"The fees that lawyers exact from the unfortunates who must solicit their services are, in general, considerable ; as I have said before, they exceed the fee-bill in almost every case, owing to private and previous agreements. Lawyers in the Old World are, proverbially, a greedy set ; and though it is safe to be on friendly terms with those of the United States, truth compels me to say they are no better, in this respect, than European barristers. Most assuredly, there are lawyers who, for their talent as well as honesty, are an honor to their profession. But the number of such men is small. As there is no senior or superior, no committee among them, as in Europe, to whom, in case of ill-behavior, they must account, they are too often unrestrained in their dealings ; and I think that foreigners are right when they reproach the legal profession with having fallen to the level of a trade. Some go so far as to try to drum up clients in the newspapers, in the same strain as do patent-medicine venders and other charlatans. I see a few around us who make divorce cases a specialty, and who daily advertise that, through their agency, absolute divorces may be legally obtained in New-York and other States, without publicity, and without charge until the business is definitively settled. In the West, it appears, there is published a price-current for such proceedings, the fees varying according to the difficulty of the case, the social standing of the parties, and the time they have been married. Nothing there seems to be easier than to break a marriage contract. On reading his morning paper, a husband learns he is free to marry again, and his wife packs up her things and quietly departs.

" With few exceptions, laws are not codified in the States, and the reports of judicial decisions, published in some of them, are insufficient to establish a common law; even the law of precedents would be quite powerless in a democratic country, where the caprice of the hour rules every thing.

" In general, in American courts of justice, when a case is new or offers serious difficulties, magistrates have recourse to the principles established by English jurisprudence.   But as the judiciary depends on popular suffrage, it often happens that judges are replaced by new favorites of the people, at the very moment they have become well posted in their business.   Hence, there can be no wonder that judicial decisions often lack breadth and ability, and even reveal gross ignorance of the general principles of law; neither need one feel surprise at the dilatory and languishing proceedings in the administration of justice, to the detriment of the litigants.

" Unity of law—that is, uniform laws for a country—is possible only where political centralization exists.   In the United States, the political fabric rests on federal ideas and principles; and as it is probable that the preservation of free institutions and of liberty, as understood in America, depends on the prevalence of those ideas and principles, unity of law is a social blessing not to be very soon realized here.

" The Americans, aware of the multiplicity and confusion of their laws, never transact any business of importance without the help of a legal adviser.   In Europe, families in good circumstances employ a physician with a fixed salary; here they indulge in the indispensable luxury of a lawyer, yearly salaried.

"As regards the judicial system of the United States, it is really a labyrinth, where only people well posted in chi-canery may safely pick their way. Besides the Supreme Court of the United States, composed of judges appointed by the President, with the approbation of the Senate, there are Supreme Courts and Courts of Appeals in every State; Courts of Common Pleas, whose judgments may be sub-mitted to appeals, except in such cases as provided by law; and, finally, District Courts. These organizations would be simple enough, were the judicial circumscriptions and ascriptions of the different courts well defined. But this is far from being the case.

"To speak only of the State of New-York, the officers of the judiciary are eight judges of the Court of Appeals and thirty-three justices of the Supreme Court. The State is divided into two federal judicial districts, in each of which is held a district court. These courts have nearly concurrent original jurisdiction in all matters in which the United States is a party, and in offenses against the fede-ral laws. The Court of Appeals is composed of eight judges, six of whom constitute a quorum. It has power to correct and reverse all proceedings of the Supreme Court. The Supreme Court has general jurisdiction in law and equity, and power to review the judgments of County Courts. The judges of the Court of Appeals are also independent in their respective circumscriptions. Hence the frequent conflicts, in which all justice is lost sight of, under the ridiculous squabblings and controver-sies which occur. The judges are all elected by the peo-ple. In the County Courts, held by the county judge, as-sisted by two justices of the peace, the judge performs the duties of surrogate, except in counties having a population of over forty thousand.

"There is, in the United States, no court to which commercial litigation is exclusively and specially confined—a deficiency somewhat strange, and hardly conceivable in a country so much given up to trade. Upon the jury rest a very large proportion of the burdens of every trial ; that is, jurymen are called upon to give verdicts not only in criminal, but in civil causes. The institution of the jury is justly respected by the Anglo-Saxon race ; but it is surrounded by many inconveniences, as are all institutions by which nations endeavor to secure their freedom. Those inconveniences are such that many observers have not hesitated to prefer the prompt method of judging adopted by countries ruled by despotic governments. Nowhere are trials by jury free from criticism, and their defects are nowhere more apparent than in the United States. However, the institution of the jury in civil causes (as regards criminal causes, the judgment by jury is considered necessary) could not be abolished without giving birth to even more serious abuses than now obtain. For judges, being elected by the popular vote, would be clothed with a dangerous power, were they allowed to decide in civil causes, and corruption would soon, openly and remorselessly, invade the judiciary. As it is, these elections lead to frequent abuses ; the judges seldom forget they belong to a political party, and when one of their adherents is engaged in a civil lawsuit, or is criminally prosecuted, they can hardly conceal their sympathy ; and in case of a criminal offense, if they are obliged to apply a penalty, they will reduce it to the smallest punishment possible, and then, even, not without regret.

"If you had been present at the opening of the present

case, you might have formed an idea of the difficulties attending trials by jury in the United States. The clerk of the court called successively three hundred names, from which, to use a law phrase, to impanel a jury, that is, to single out twelve impartial and free men to sit as jurors in the case. But, as every body reads newspapers, it happened that out of these three hundred persons whose names were called, only two or three had formed no opinion upon the case at issue; the others were excluded from service for want of an impartial disposition of mind. So three hundred new names had to be again called to complete the required number of jurymen. You can not conceive of the reluctance felt by citizens in every station of life, to serve as jurors. With a people so active as the Americans, it is a serious affair to be absent from one's business during several weeks. Jurymen being drawn from the list of voters, many persons prefer to give up their franchise privilege rather than be compelled to serve on a jury. And you may be assured that many of our merchants, when they are notified that their names have been drawn, and receive a summons to attend court at an appointed time, at once repair to their lawyers and procure their aid to have them excluded from serving on the jury. If their lawyers fail, they procure from their physicians a certificate of incapacity, which sometimes has the desired effect. You now understand the general causes that make the impaneling of a jury an herculean labor. It may, perhaps, be necessary, some day, to establish a sworn body of salaried jurymen, if the American people persist in having juries for both civil and criminal cases.

"The difficulty of obtaining a jury, added to other dilatory causes inherent in lawsuits, resembles the task of Penelope. Among other causes, there is one peculiar to

the institution of the jury, which deserves a passing notice: the law—or rather the custom, for the law is silent
in this respect—requires a mutual agreement of the twelve
jurymen. There have often been doubts whether the advantages of this rule are sufficient to compensate for the
mischief which sometimes results from it. For instance,
an offender often escapes from the law, because one among
the twelve jurors could not be convinced or has been bribed.
It has been several times vainly tried to change the law,
or the custom, and to provide that, in certain specified
cases, a verdict founded upon a certain majority should be
sufficient. But the proposed change has not as yet found
favor, and the unanimity of the jury will be wanted for a
long time to come.

"There is, in the United States, a state-attorney, who,
in criminal cases, represents the people. But it would be
a mistake to confound that officer with the magistrate who
represents the government in some countries of Europe.
His office is, principally, to conduct all lawsuits in which
the state is concerned, and to give his advice and opinion
upon questions of law. As regards criminal cases, if we
except a few circumstances defined by special laws, he is
deprived of the prosecuting power. He can not, of course,
order any arrests, and when he prosecutes, it is only on
the complaint of certain parties, at their risk and peril,
and after a grand-jury has found a bill of indictment.
The grand-jury, so called because its number is larger
than the petit-jury, must not be confounded with the latter, to which all that has been previously said relates. It
tries no question and finds no verdict. No one is present
during its deliberations but the officer of the state. That
officer brings before the grand-jury cases of supposed
crimes or wrongs, with bills of indictment, and the evidence on the subject. If the jury does not think the evi-

dence sufficient, it ignores the bill, and no indictment is presented. If the evidence be deemed sufficient, it approves or finds the bill, and presents the accused to the court.

" The jurors are exclusive judges of the weight and force of the testimony offered to them. In a country where personal liberty is protected by the prerogatives of the *habeas corpus*, any attempt to overthrow that liberty would be scarcely possible. He is so bound by the law, that any magistrate is sure to abide by it, when he orders an arrest and signs a warrant to that effect. Without speaking of legal penalties, he well knows his real and personal property is at stake, in case of an error or undue precipitation. Almost any judge, whether of the Supreme Court, of the Court of Appeals, or even of the Common Pleas, has the right to admit any prisoner to bail ; and if it happens, therefore, that bail has been refused to any offender, it may be inferred the crime he has committed does not deserve leniency in the opinion of the magistrates."

Asmodeus had reached this point in his observations respecting the judicial institutions in the United States, when the court and jurors resumed their seats. The usher who had been sent for the Smithsonian Institute Almanac had just returned with that document, and deposited it triumphantly on the presiding judge's desk. The magistrate, after looking over it a few moments, announced that the moon had risen at nine o'clock, twenty-five minutes, and seven seconds, on the night previous to the day the murder had been committed. We believed that question was now thoroughly settled to the satisfaction of all concerned, and the trial would smoothly resume its course. But we were doomed to disappointment ; for one of the prisoner's counsel, to our dismay, begged leave to call as a witness the director of the Washington Observatory, where, it ap-

pears, notes are taken, every minute, of the motions of the
stars, and where the moon's behavior, according to the
learned counsel, is the object of special attention. This
request was the signal for an animated debate between
him and the state-attorney, the latter charging his opponents with prolonging the trial beyond all endurance, and
with an attempt to tire the jury, whose verdict they were
afraid of. To these attacks and recriminations the prisoner's counsel retaliated with a sharp rejoinder, asserting
that notices or observations made by almanacs deserved
no confidence; that "lying like an almanac" was a popular saying; that it was far from being proved, because an
astronomer said the moon rose at such and such a time in
the night, that the heavenly orb had obeyed the summons;
that the sky might have been cloudy at the time specified,
thus preventing that satellite from illuminating our planet.
He concluded by stating as his candid conviction that the
jury would run the risk of shedding an innocent creature's
blood, were it to return a verdict without hearing the testimony of the director of the Washington Observatory. It
was evident these last words produced a deep impression on the mind of the jury; and it was in vain the state-
attorney declared that the moon, in reality, had nothing to
do with the pending trial, since it was conceded by all parties the murder had been committed in broad daylight.
Though the jurors could not possibly understand the aim
of the counsel for the prisoner, it was apparent they were
anxious to hear the testimony of the director of the Washington Observatory, a celebrity of the times. So the presiding judge, thinking, as he said, it was always desirable
to throw as much light as possible upon every dark subject, decided that the director's testimony should be received, and the crier adjourning the court, every one withdrew.

CHAPTER IX.

"WE are near the chamber where the Common Council of the city meets," said Asmodeus. "Let us enter, and devote a few minutes to seeing in operation the municipal institutions of a city whose income exceeds that of many a European kingdom. The 'city fathers' are now sitting; and if, as a philosopher has contended, people enjoy the government they deserve, you will see that New-Yorkers have no grounds to be proud of that they are now enjoying."

We entered a spacious room, nicely furnished. Desks were arranged in the form of a hemicycle, and upon them were scattered books, newspapers, pens, inkstands, paper, and documents of every sort. On the floor, near each councilman, was a spittoon. The attitudes of the councilmen lacked dignity and decency. Many had their legs reposing upon the desks, with their boot-soles pointing toward the presiding officer—the latter occupying a more elevated seat than the other members. Many placed in their mouths, from time to time, something which they took from a small, square, silver-papered package, which Asmodeus informed me contained tobacco ; and the black spittle they frequently ejected into the spittoons confirmed the correctness of his statement.

The sittings of the councilmen, I was informed, are not public—newspaper reporters only being admitted ; and so, not to attract attention, we mingled among them. But if this chamber was closed to the public, it was not so of an opening or passage, leading to the hall of civic legislation, and which has received the name of lobby. This was crowded with anxious people, and almost every minute some councilman would leave the room to confer with members of the lobby, as if in quest of important information. This going to and fro at once ceased on the transmission of a note to the president ; and immediately a discussion commenced on the privilege of granting some gas company, recently formed, the right to lay gas-pipes in the streets of the city. A member said that, in his opinion, the new company offered such advantages to consumers, by the superior quality and cheapness of its gas, that the privilege ought to be granted at once. Should they refuse it, they would no longer be the watchful guardians of the public interests, but, on the contrary, be suspected of favoring the monopoly of existing companies. The speaker was not allowed to proceed further ; for the president, urged by the majority to put the privilege to a vote, closed the discussion, and the privilege was unanimously voted.

" The most amusing part of this comedy, enacted in the name of the public good," said Asmodeus, " consists in this fact : The councilmen declined to take up the petition of the Hygienic Gas Company until they received some perquisites ; and the note, which one of them has just sent to the president, inclosed a certificate for a thousand shares of the gas company, to be divided, of course, among the members of the Council, and also a check for twenty thousand dollars. So, you see, in case the Hygienic Gas Company does not succeed in raising a working capital, and consequently its shares not be worth the paper they are printed upon, the check would be a compensation for their trouble ; and at all events, as their number is twenty-four, their vote will bring to each of the city fathers a little over eight hundred dollars."

When the excitement of the vote was over, and the councilmen had congratulated each other upon the advantages to be derived by the imperial city (a name its inhabitants are pleased to give New-York) from the future gas company, the project to sell a public square came next in order. A speculator, anxious to establish a depot, on a public square in the populous portion of the city, for a railroad company, of which he was one of the heaviest stock holders, offered to purchase that square for one hundred thousand dollars. "It is a very large sum," said one of the councilmen—"a princely offer ; and, considering the precarious condition of the city's treasury, it would be folly to reject it." The majority coincided in this opinion, and the sale of the square to the capitalist who wanted it for his railroad was unanimously approved.

"Here we have," said Asmodeus, when the president announced the result of the vote, "a shameful desecration of the city's most sacred interests. Public squares are, in reality, the lungs of all densely populated districts, and we have so few in New-York, that the reduction of their number would be a blow to public health. But these councilmen do not care much about considerations of this nature ; they mean to make a good thing out of their vote, and in the following manner : The owners of houses fronting the square will receive, according to the bill, ten thousand dollars each as a compensation for the damage their property will suffer. The capitalist's proposition has been kept secret, in order to give time to the councilmen to purchase, through intermediaries, all the houses fronting the square, and they will cash the indemnity to be paid to their owners. The result will be that they will become proprietors of fine dwellings at a low cost ; and the capitalist, on his side, will realize a handsome profit ; for the square is worth one million dollars, and as the compensation he will pay to actual owners, and his purchase-price, will not exceed five hundred thousand dollars, his own part of the profit in the operation will amount to half a million."

Asmodeus was here interrupted by the reading of a report from a committee, stating that the owners of several houses on one of the most fashionable avenues had transgressed the building-law, the spacious stoops of their mansions encroaching on the public way, and it concluded by offering a plan for an ordinance to compel the owners to remove the obnoxious stoops.

"That report," said Asmodeus, "will fall like a bombshell among the nabobs of New-York. They are proud of those large stoops, which give a princely appearance to their residences ; and, to retain them, they will make any sacrifice. The members of the Council well know this, and the report you have just heard read is but a means to bleed the nabobs. The latter will raise money among themselves ; and when the councilmen have it in their pockets, they will discover that the so-called infringement on the building-law is covered by limitation, and will carefully frame another report to demonstrate that the city has lost all right to demand the destruction of those elegant stoops."

In the mean while, the walking to and fro of the city
fathers and the members of the lobby had again commenced. The lobby-men, Asmodeus informed me, are, in
general, brokers, bankers, and members of the legislature,
interested in speculations the success of which depends on
some privilege or authorization to be granted by the city
councilmen. We were on the point of retiring, when the
president, energetically hammering on his desk, urged the
members to silence, as they had to deliberate on a pro-
jected railroad through one of the great thoroughfares of
the city. He then explained, in a somewhat long but lucid
speech, that, owing to the steady increase of the population, and also of house-rents, a number of families were
compelled to remove to the country, and consequently
that many business men were obliged to lose much precious time on their way to and from their offices. A railroad company had offered to lay rails to the very centre
of the city, so as to connect it with the surburbs ; and in
view of the grave interests involved, he had believed it his
duty to speak to the councilmen of this project and submit
it to their consideration. " The capital stock of this company," he continued, " is twenty millions of dollars, in
shares of one hundred dollars each ; the market price of
these shares is actually twenty-five dollars. But it can be
demonstrated that they will go up to par and probably
over, if the privilege now solicited is granted by the city
council. In expectation of that advance in the price of
their stock, the directors of the railroad company will place
at our disposal, and at the actual price, ten thousand
shares. All the necessary papers have been intrusted to
me. You will not fail to perceive that the railroad company's proposition presents such immediate advantages to
the public, that it deserves approbation ; and therefore

I do not deem it necessary to make any further explanation."

"Let us vote ! vote ! vote !" shouted the councilmen, as the president ended his speech.

They had already made a calculation that every one of them would have about thirty thousand dollars for his share of the operation, in case the stock of the company should rise, as expected ; and in their hurry to vote, they left their seats, and, standing by the president, did not cease shouting until he declared the right to lay rails was granted to the railroad company, according to the conditions and stipulations annexed to the authorization.

"The city fathers," said Asmodeus, taking me aside, "are brazen-faced rogues ; their love of gain is equal to their hypocrisy ; and I wonder how they dare to cover their intense greed with the pretense that all they do is for the public good.   But, like professional robbers, who fight among themselves for the spoils, I believe, upon my soul, our city fathers are coming to blows."

In fact, the president, as far as we could understand, was endeavoring to secure for himself the lion's part in the division of the shares placed at his disposal, which, now worth twenty-five dollars, their actual market price, would be, within twenty-four hours, worth perhaps one hundred.   A few councilmen sided with the president ; while the others hurled at them most insulting epithets. An indescribable scene of confusion followed, and soon they began throwing at each other books and inkstands. One of the councilmen was unfortunately hit by one of the latter articles ; and, exasperated at seeing the black liquid spotting his shirt and clothes, he pulled a revolver from his pocket, declaring that he would shoot his assailant. His example was instantly imitated by others ; and with-

out caring to know what would be the result of the skir-
mish, we hastened from the room.

"A stray ball," said Asmodeus, as he hurried me out
with him, "might hit one of us ; and when an individual
is provided with but one sound leg, as is unfortunately my
own case, he must take care lest some awkward fellow
break it."

When we were safely in the street, we could not refrain
from laughing heartily at the strange wind-up to the councilmen's deliberations.

After he had resumed his wonted seriousness — "All
this," said Asmodeus, "is the direct product of universal
suffrage, as understood and practiced in this first city of
the Union. Verily, if he be not the most stupid, man is
the most wicked animal of creation. He finds means to
pervert and degrade, after he has put them in operation,
the most rational theories and soundest principles. Is
there, for instance, a more rational and sound principle
than that all power must come from the free consent of
the people? Still, see the result in practice of that political truth, proclaimed by the founders of American independence. Though New-York City is governed by men
elected by popular suffrage, there is not a hamlet among
the Hottentots which can not boast of a better government."

"What has caused such a state of things?"

"It would take too long a time to explain it. Be satisfied, for the present, to know that any person of age, after
a year of actual residence in the State of New-York, (and
it is so in nearly all other States,) is clothed with the right
to vote for the officers of the municipal administration. In
large cities, the majority is on the side of the most ignorant classes of the people, and the councilmen are, as a
matter of course, elected from its ranks. In New-York City,

men of quiet habits dislike the noise attending elections, and the riotous manner in which they are often conducted, and, as they are sometimes conscious their vote would not possibly influence the final result, they do not go to the polls. Neither care they themselves to be candidates for any public office, because, though large salaries are in general attached to some of them, the profits of their business are still larger — that is, unless public officers determine to swell their legitimate salaries by peculation. Again, government officers in this great metropolis, when their term of office expires, do not stand very high in the estimation of their fellow-citizens — a prospect hardly to be coveted by any man who can find, in another sphere of action, honest and remunerative employment for his activity or talent. If you read the morning papers, you will perceive that the City Hall is designated as the Cave of the Forty Thieves, from a tale bearing that title in the Arabian Nights ; and you can readily comprehend how every honest merchant, naturally enough, shrinks from associating himself with such company.

" Elections being conducted by the people, and for the profit of demagogues, neither talent nor honesty can be reasonably expected from successful candidates. Again, jealousy—that vice of democratic societies—is strikingly exhibited, not only at presidential, but also at local elections. Democracy dislikes (as if it were afraid of it) any social superiority, resulting either from capability or wealth.

"The Athenians proscribed Aristides ; and Calhoun, Clay, Webster, and General Scott could never be elected president of the United States. You comprehend the simile.

" According to reliable statements, there are in New-

York forty thousand voters, whose votes belong to any unscrupulous party that has money enough to purchase them. Those forty thousand voters are almost sure to win the day, and vote to a man for the candidate who pays them for their services. But to marshal ·this large force, leaders are necessary. Those leaders, after providing for themselves, stipulate, in order to assist their friends, to obtain the many small offices in the gift of elected candidates; and the bleeding of the public treasury begins as soon as the fight is over. Some time ago, a lawsuit revealed to the public the extent of this evil, and the consequent corruption of public morals. An officer of the municipal government, as soon as the term of a certain mayor had expired, demanded the return of the ten thousand dollars which he had to pay to the first magistrate of the city to obtain his situation. That mayor, to secure a majority of voters, had spent, it was asserted, over one hundred thousand dollars ; and to again obtain that amount, he began selling all the offices in his gift; he even created new ones, which he sold to any corporation or person willing to pay for them.

" All elected functionaries are anxious, of course, to keep themselves in office ; and on the eve of every election, they make up a common fund, to which they contribute, as do also the clerks in their employ. In that way, they are enabled to meet the heavy expenses attending all elections ; such as renting rooms for the headquarters of their party ; fees for speakers at public meetings, and for bribing voters. Finally, from the pockets of the people comes all the money thus lavished to corrupt them and vitiate elections. With such a sad state of affairs, the city expenditures have fearfully grown, from year to year. They amounted to about five millions of dollars when there were five hundred thousand inhabitants. The latter do not, certainly, exceed one million to-day; while the former reach nearly twenty-five millions.

"One may see, every hour in the day, in the fashionable places in New-York, a crowd of well-dressed, idle people, having no regular occupation, no known means of support. They are electioneering agents, stump-speakers, and wire-pullers, who marshaled an army of voters at the last election for the benefit of their patrons. The latter, and the political party to which they belong, afford them the means to live in idleness. The privates have been disbanded; but the chiefs are kept in service, at half-pay, to be again actively employed at the next election.

"The legislature of the State of New-York, the majority of which is composed of members returned by rural districts, has tried, time and again, to put the administration of the most important city of America on a sound and honest basis; but it has not yet succeeded in cleaning out its Augean stables. These good intentions, and the bills to effect reform, have proved fruitless, either on account of objections from the judiciary, or the opposition of the political organizations, grounded on popular suffrage itself. A few years ago, the number of councilmen was sixty; but they were reduced to twenty-four, in the hope that the reform would curtail the evils of corruption. The mode of choosing heads of departments was changed, in several instances, from an election to an appointment by the mayor and aldermen, with the supposition that they would appoint only men of integrity and capacity. Still further changes were introduced into the original charter of the city, granted by James II., in 1686; amended by Queen Anne in 1708; further enlarged by George II., in 1730; and specially affirmed, after the Revolution, by the State legislators. But the safeguards enacted against reckless expense and abuse proved of little avail; and the city fathers, whether few or many in number, seem equally powerless to administer it properly. On the other hand, the appointment by the legislature of special commissions, and the taking of some departments from the mayor's control, have created much confusion in the working of the administration ; and corruption, perhaps, has finally been the gainer by the change.

"Corruption has thoroughly wormed itself into the institutions of the United States. It may be found everywhere, in the highest as well as the lowest offices. In fact, all public offices are looked upon by many as a means of promptly enriching their possessors; and for this reason extravagant sums of money are spent to obtain them. Convictions and principles have little to do with party strifes : the fight is for the spoils, as the Americans term it ; and the great interests of the land are sacrificed to private ends.

" You have seen how New-York councilmen discharge their duty. Go to the State capital, and you will witness the same spectacle ; you will also see it at Washington, the Federal capital of the Union. Most of the laws are enacted to promote private interest. Lobbymen, with their poisonous influence, block up the doors of local legislatures and the halls of Congress. For fear even that corruption may be exposed, there is a law on the statute-book of the State of New-York, the leading State of the Union, to the effect that any witness shall be sent to prison who shall testify against members of the legislature accused of bribery."

" But, then, with institutions so distorted by corrupting influences, how can you explain the continued progress of the United States ?"

"The problem is easily solved by comparing the New

with the Old World.   The area of the United States is as great as that of all Europe, and contains a population of only thirty-six millions of inhabitants, who have the privilege of working and turning to advantage the untold and unexplored wealth of this whole continent. Suppose it to be inhabited by three hundred millions of men, as in Europe, the struggle for a living would be as great as it is in the Old World—even greater, in consequence of the prodigal habits of all classes of society here. Besides, there is here a principle which paralyzes, to a great extent, abuses resulting from the working of political institutions, and which spreads its beneficent influence everywhere ; that principle is liberty, upon which the political and social fabric of America rests. Liberty is the very life of the people ; it is as necessary to them as the air they breathe. They are conscious that the working of republican institutions is often neither regular nor satisfactory, but they attach little importance to it. In Europe, public functionaries form a distinct class, a sort of aristocratic body. Every one of these considers himself of importance, is prone to exaggerate the authority with which he is clothed, and is constantly disposed to make others feel it. Here it is just the reverse. The Federal government and the local administrations are nothing— the people is every thing ; and office-holders, whether in high or low positions, are only the public's servants. Hence, as authority or power does not generally reside in the latter, they cautiously keep themselves in the background, instead of assuming an overbearing importance. They do little work, following the example of the general government, which has reminded the people more than once that the least government possible is the very essence and fundamental principle of the Constitution.

" It follows, from all this, that, as the Americans are unrestrained, and nowhere and in no way impeded in the

pursuit of their well-being and happiness, they feel uncon-
cerned about abuses which in Europe would prove insufferable, and soon bring on the destruction of empires. They
are so industrious, their life is so actively employed, they
pay little attention to any thing that does not particularly
affect their interests. They leave a clear field to rogues
and intriguers who trade in politics, because their country,
in the mean while, in the rapid development of its resources, engrosses their attention to the exclusion of every
thing else. As long as this state of things exists, they will
lose none of their time in helping to reform abuses which,
in their opinion, have very little to do with the general
prosperity and prospect of the country.

" You may often hear not a few assert that corruption is
a natural and necessary element of democratic institutions.
According to these theorists, these institutions would
perish should the American people at any time become indifferent to political rights. The means to keep them alive
to the importance of those rights and to bring them to the
polls, is to show them that all offices, in every branch of
the government, lead to wealth and influence. On the
other hand, as popular suffrage, in all the States, is frequently resorted to, almost all office-holders, when their
term of service expires, make every endeavor to be re-
elected, and for that purpose solicit the influence of their
friends and partisans. The same is also done by their
competitors and adversaries ; and it follows that political
excitement is permanent in the country. Now, this political excitement is the best safeguard of democratic institutions, and the very life of healthy societies. Undoubtedly politics, everywhere in the United States, invades
every home, engrosses every mind ; but it powerfully contributes to keep the passions of the American people and
their indomitable energy alive.

" No good whatever is free from evil, in this world.
But be convinced that the abuses which do not escape the
observation of foreigners sink into insignificance, when
compared with the mighty results derived from institutions
which generate those very abuses.   Look at the American
people: among the multitude of men passing in the streets,
you can not distinguish a poor man from a millionaire.
Every body is well-dressed ; and you seldom see women
applying themselves to occupations for which nature has
not fitted them.   Under the sway of democratic institutions, every body fully realizes his own worth and dignity ;
every body here enjoys a freeman's rights ; and no class of
the population is kept in tutelage.   Every body treats his
neighbor with civility and kindness, because he expects a
like treatment ; and while he is conscious of his importance
in society, of the part he plays in the working out of his
country's destiny, brighter becomes his mind and nobler
his heart.   With such fruitful and mighty results, democratic institutions may be safely compared to those resting
on opposite principles. "

While Asmodeus was explaining, in this lofty strain, the
workings of the institutions of the United States, we had
arrived at a public square situated in the centre of the city.
It was now night ; and I noticed many dwellings brilliantly
lighted in every story.

"These are gambling-houses," said Asmodeus.   " They
seem deserted during the day, for every thing is quiet
inside.   Night is the time for their operations, as for some
birds of prey—the time to awake to life again.   Let us
enter one of them ; but bear in mind that self-control is
necessary in the place we are going to.   In the United
States, as everywhere else, it is often the part of wisdom to
keep one's eyes shut, and turn a deaf ear to every thing."

CHAPTER X.

ASMODEUS nodded to a servant standing in the hall, and we were allowed to enter. We went through an elegantly furnished parlor, in which were many frequenters of the house, either conversing or reading newspapers. We next entered a large room lighted by numerous gas-jets. In the centre of this apartment was a long table, covered with green cloth. This room was crowded with persons busily engaged in gambling. Different games of chance, Asmodeus informed me, are in vogue in the United States; but the favorite game of European gamblers, roulette, was not tolerated in the establishment we were then visiting. In almost all the States, games of chance, for money, no matter what its amount, are prohibited, and gambling-houses, being considered as contrary to good morals, are forbidden. Gambling for money was not, therefore, ostensibly carried on. The stakes consisted of counters or checks, provided by the establishment. The gamblers settled their losses by means of these checks or counters, representing an understood value. In this manner, it appears, the letter, if not the spirit of the law was satisfied.

In case of a sudden descent from the police, it was impossible to prove that the persons engaged in the games were playing for money, as no money, in fact, was apparent.

"There is no people," said Asmodeus, in the course of his explanations, "that exhibits more respect for the law than the Americans ; but none understands so well how to eschew it when it interferes with its own interests."

My companion also informed me that no one can recover money lost in gambling, because gambling itself is illegal. But debts of that nature are as secure as any other, especially among professional gamblers, and they are seldom repudiated.

"All those counters and checks," said he, "are as good as gold, and, in this respect, no difficulty can arise. But there are, in two or three adjoining rooms, games of different kinds conducted in private ; and the house, of course, is not responsible for the stakes. Money may be lost on parole there ; but the loser who will not or can not make good his promise generally finds himself in a dangerous predicament. For though there be a few men here who came attracted either by curiosity or because they have nothing else to do, the majority are professional gamblers, whose revolvers are always kept ready for great emergencies."

Besides the table in the centre of the room, there were half a dozen others in remote corners, and also in adjoining rooms, and which, as Asmodeus had observed, were occupied by persons engaged in some favorite game. Around the large table stood an anxious crowd. There was evidently an exciting game in operation. Near the centre of the table was seated a banker or dealer, with a large quantity of checks at his right hand, of the denomination of five, ten, twenty dollars, and upward. Thirteen cards, representing a complete pack, were affixed to the table, at convenient distances from each other, to mark distinctly the bets placed on each. Those who wished to play placed the amount they intended to stake on any particular card on the table. The dealer then producing and shuffling a pack of cards, placed them in a box, from which he caused them to slide one by one. He lost when the card equal in points to that on which the stake was set turned up on his right hand; but he won when it was on the left. He faithfully and gravely fulfilled his part, as though he were a public notary or any other officer of the law. Every one seemed satisfied with his dealings and decisions; for, during our stay in this "hell," (a name commonly given in America to all gambling-houses,) no exclamation of any sort was made by the gamblers.

I took him, at first, for the proprietor of the establishment. "You are mistaken," said Asmodeus; "the host is that stout man whose neck-tie is pinned with a large diamond, and who is playing a game of *écarté* near yonder window with a constant frequenter of his house. A few years ago, he was one of the most renowned pugilists in the United States. With the profits derived from his victories in the manly art, he purchased a fine house, in which congregated the patrons and amateurs of that art, which is more in vogue to-day in America than in England. Shortly after, he found himself, perhaps unexpectedly, the manager of a faro bank. The game of faro is now in progress at the green table. He gradually withdrew himself from the noisy companions of his younger years, and soon had the gratification to behold bankers, brokers, merchants, and men belonging to the wealthy classes flock to his establishment. As his business rapidly increased, he purchased this handsome house, situated in one of the

most fashionable streets of New-York. It has become a
favorite resort for many persons of good standing in
society, and for 'the fancy' of New-York. All transactions are above suspicion, for deception would be a dangerous experiment. The landlord is married, and very careful that every thing is carried on in an orderly manner.
Women are not admitted into the gaming-rooms, or even
into the parlors of the house. An elegant supper is served
up, every evening, to frequenters and visitors."

At this very moment a footman came and announced
supper. Most of the gamblers did not heed the invitation,
so deeply engrossed were they in the game. A few spectators, Asmodeus and myself among them, went down into
the dining-room, which was, like all the others in the establishment, handsomely furnished. Several ornamental sideboards were loaded with luxuries. Champagne of the best
brands was freely passed around ; and when supper was
over, the landlord treated his guests to the best Havana
cigars.   I expected we would have to face a pretty heavy
bill for this entertainment, and was on the point of pulling
out my portemonnaie, when Asmodeus whispered me to
do nothing of the sort. "Such a proceeding," said he,
"would be resented as an outrage by the proprietor.
Every body, whether known to him or not, may come here,
and either take part in or look at the game, as often as
may suit his fancy, and enjoy a good supper besides. The
proprietor hardly notices those visitors who come solely for
the purpose of partaking of the good things served up at
his suppers, and drinking his champagne."

"But such entertainments are expensive," said I, "and
I doubt whether the gambling-houses of Europe would be
profitable enterprises were they to treat visitors as is done
here."

"Have you not remarked that the dealer, at the gaming-table, takes away beforehand a percentage from the stakes? Admitting the percentage to be five per cent only, this seems of little importance to the gamblers; but repeated through the whole night, it sometimes amounts to five hundred dollars. Why, the proprietor of this establishment, within a few years, has become a millionaire."

"I had inferred, from your explanation, that gambling-houses were forbidden in New-York."

"And so they are," returned Asmodeus. "But police officers, throughout the States, are singularly accommodating, and never deal harshly with millionaires. This one, for instance, has among his friends many persons of influence. His house is frequented by bankers, lawyers, magistrates, legislators—occasionally, I am told, by ministers of the Gospel from neighboring localities. Think of the scandal a descent of the police would produce! For this reason police officers never disturb the *habitués* of houses like this."

We ascended again to the gambling-room, and were looking, with that fascination they exert upon even cool-headed persons, at the games of chance going on, when, all at once, the excitement became intense. A new-comer had seated himself at the principal gaming-table, and his high stakes and good fortune struck every body with astonishment. After a while the dealer, in a low tone, held a short conversation with the proprietor, who pulled out his pocket-book and gave him a bundle of bank-bills. Then the game went briskly on, as before.

"That young man whose large stakes have caused this sensation," said Asmodeus, drawing me aside, "and who has already won fifty thousand dollars, which the proprietor of the house has paid with such remarkable coolness, is a petroleum prince. Instead of pocketing his gain and leaving this place, he will play until fortune turns against him. Before daylight, he will have lost his actual profits and one hundred thousand dollars besides. Let me tell you that young man's history.

"An Irishman, thirty years ago, arrived in Philadelphia. He was a mason by trade, industrious and sober, which is not often the case with natives of the Emerald Isle. He managed to save a few hundred dollars, and then married.

"He had enjoyed the blessings of matrimony over ten years, when, on going to his work, early one morning, he found, a short distance from his house, a basket covered with a linen cloth. He carried it home, opened it, and a handsome baby appeared before his view. To the child's clothes was pinned a paper bearing a few lines, asking, in the name of the Almighty, the person into whose hands the basket might fall, to take charge of the new-born infant, for the sake of a poor fellow-creature. The Irishman and his wife, not having any children, at once adopted the little one, regarding it as a gift sent by Providence. A few years later, the Irishman, who had by his savings amassed quite a handsome sum of money, purchased a small farm in a thinly-settled county of Pennsylvania, and there lived quietly and contentedly, until, one day, in cutting down a tree, it fell upon him, and he was crushed to death beneath its weight. After this sad occurrence, his widow, with the help of the adopted child, carried on the business of the farm, often regretting she could not give the boy an education ; but they were so far from any school, she could not think of sending her son such a distance from home.

"One day a rumor circulated throughout Pennsylvania that, by boring into the earth to a moderate depth, in some parts of the State, oil was found to spring forth.

Startling as this rumor was, many persons were forced to believe it, when they saw, with their own eyes, a black liquid, giving a bright light, issuing from certain holes bored for experiment. After this, all persons began experimenting on their own property. The Irish widow imitated her neighbors, and with the help of her adopted son, bored a hole in her garden. After a few days' work, they struck oil—a flowing well rewarded their enterprise!

"Meanwhile speculators, wild with the excitement of this discovery, besieged Pennsylvania, and that State soon swarmed with them. The desire to possess a portion of those marvelous lands took possession of every mind. Throughout the States every one was affected with the new disease, denominated 'oil on the brain;' and soon the value of the oleaginous districts went up to wonderful figures. In many instances, as much as fifty thousand dollars were paid for an acre of land. And, availing herself of the general infatuation, the Irish widow sold her farm, for two millions of dollars, to a Boston company, which thought it was very cheap to give not quite seven thousand dollars per acre for petroleum land. The three hundred acres of the widow's farm had cost three hundred dollars a few years before, that is to say, one dollar an acre! Besides the two millions of dollars, the Irish widow had stipulated that one half of the flowing well in her garden should belong to her. That well yielded from five to six hundred barrels of oil per day. You may be sure the old lady doted on it. She visited it a hundred times a day, always surveying it with amazement, and ascertaining whether it was as productive as ever. Even at night she left her bed to go and view the marvelous spring. During one of these nocturnal excursions, she imprudently drew too near the well with a light—the spring fired up with lightning-like rapidity, and the poor woman, becoming wrapped in the flames, was burned to death. The coroner was summoned to hold an inquest. When it was over, the widow's neighbors, desiring to ascertain whether she had sold her farm for as large an amount as was rumored, prevailed upon the coroner to open her safe. It contained two hundred thousand dollars in gold, which, no doubt, represented the widow's profits for her reserved rights in the well; and also bonds of the United States to the amount of two millions of dollars, the said bonds registered in the name of Peter Crazy, the widow's adopted son, and only heir and legatee, according to her will, that was also found in the strong-box.

"Now, the young man, whose large stakes a few minutes ago caused such a sensation, is the same Peter Crazy, the widow's adopted son; and he came here to-night to complete his ruin. But I must now relate what became of him after becoming possessed of a princely fortune.

"At the time he came into possession of this fortune, Crazy did not know the difference between one thousand and one hundred thousand dollars. He could hardly write his name; and, unfortunately, he had nobody to warn him against the dangers that beset the youth of this world, and to make of him, instead of a spendthrift, a man useful to society.

"Suppose a philanthropist, a good-hearted, high-minded man, should suddenly come into possession of two millions of dollars, what a benefactor he might prove to his fellow-creatures! What useful and benevolent institutions he might found! What improvement might every branch of human labor receive if he chose to apply to it a portion of his wealth!

"As soon as it became known that Crazy had inherited a large fortune, many adventurers, with whom the new Eldorado swarmed, pounced upon him like birds of prey upon a carcass ; and then commenced for Crazy a life of prodigality and vice, the end of which is near at hand.

"In Philadelphia, he stopped with his cronies at one of the most elegant and spacious hotels of the city, stipulating for the exclusive use of it during their stay. He bought fine horses, carriages of the most approved pattern, and furnished a *maison de joie*, where he reveled every night. Many Philadelphians will long remember his daily freaks of extravagance. I will relate one as a sample of the others. One day, as a regiment stopped in the city on its way to the West, he presented it with one thousand baskets of champagne—one basket to each man—a piece of liberality that cost him twenty-five thousand dollars. After spending half a million dollars in the Quaker City, he came to New-York in search of new excitements.

" Here he met with persons who aroused a new feeling in his mind—that of pride. Those capitalists and speculators who drive their fancy teams in Central Park, who keep race-horses, who do their best to resuscitate the fine old times of France under the Regency, were not, he was told, as wealthy as himself. He was bound to live in style, lest he should be taken for a shoddy contractor, who does not know how to spend his money. Crazy, therefore, imitated the leaders of fashion—but in the same way European wood-cutters are imitated by Australasian savages, who, when they cut down a tree, wait for its fall until they are crushed by its weight. He kept as many as forty horses ; bet heavily at the races, and lost every time ; and hired a theatrical troupe, whom he provided with costly costumes, and who played only for himself and a few friends. One night, he was so delighted with the saltatory skill and *pirouettes* of the dancing-girls of his troupe, that he presented each of them, with a gracefulness of manner that Buckingham himself would have envied, pearls and diamonds worth over one hundred thousand dollars. In short, for a year, he indulged in all conceivable dissipations. But Providence has in store for him one of those visitations that, from time to time, startle and instruct the world.

" Crazy believes his main income can never be impaired. Besides the one hundred thousand dollars he has in his pocket—the last of the money found in the Irish widow's strong-box—he fancies he possesses inexhaustible means in the oil-well. On returning, he will learn that that source of wealth is dried up, and his only fortune consists of the fifty-two coats he has purchased inside of the past month."

" What will then become of that foolish fellow ?" said I to Asmodeus.

" Most actors, as you know, are warm-hearted. Those of them who have fattened on his extravagances the past year will feel concerned on learning of the petroleum prince's misfortune, and beg their manager to do something for him. The manager, who is also a good-hearted man, will hire Crazy to sweep his theatre."

I looked closely at the young man whose golden dreams would soon be ended. Fortune was now turning against him ; for the bank-bills he had received from the dealer were fast returning to the proprietor of the house. The petroleum prince, from his past life, had derived a remarkable coolness ; he bore his reverses with an Indian fortitude ; and when he left his seat, after losing his last dollar, he made a polite bow to the proprietor, whom he gracefully thanked for the pleasant night he had enjoyed as his guest.

"It is now over one year," said Asmodeus, "since the proprietor set his mind to gain that prize. He has patiently waited, following with never-tiring care every step of that young man in his rash career, and taking the best measures to get the last fruits of the tree, before the lightning had stricken it to the dust."

"What do you mean, Asmodeus?" said I.

"Simply this: those who keep gambling-houses take care to be regularly informed of every thing transpiring in the city that may be of interest to their business. You may have noticed, lounging around the most fashionable hotels, many well-dressed young men, who spend money freely, though they have no known means of support. They are agents for gambling-houses; their business is to track the footsteps of travelers visiting New-York, for business or pleasure. They worm themselves into the confidence of strangers; show them every thing worth seeing in the city; and finally introduce them to their employers, the gambling-house proprietors. This hunting after wealthy strangers is systematically carried on — it is a science. These agents leave nothing to chance; they never hurry up the conclusion of the transaction. When the unwary stranger is in a fit condition for the sacrifice, they take him to the gaming-table with as much indifference and coolness as butchers drive sheep to the slaughter-house. These agents have a commission on the profits realized from all customers they lead to the gaming-table, and they display such ability they seldom fail to entrap those they single out for their victims.

"Crazy had been put on his guard concerning these dangerous men; but he was powerless to-night against their enticement. Allured with the hope of again building up his fortune, he has just lost all that remained of it.

"There are in New-York one hundred and fifty hells or gambling-houses, all well known to the police, in which several millions of dollars are lost every year, by unwary persons. From time to time, police officers make a descent on the most dangerous among them, or (which is too often the case) on those whose owners have little political influence. Twenty-four hours after the descent has taken place, new gambling implements are procured in lieu of those taken away, and business is resumed as before.

"Games of chance are now in vogue all over the States, and rapidly multiplying, because the thirst for sudden fortunes is everywhere on the increase. Gambling is even practiced on board of those splendid steamers that ply up and down the rivers of the country; and more than one passenger, driven distracted by his losses at the gaming-table, has thrown himself overboard.

"As I have before remarked, no cheating is to be apprehended here, as the percentage taken beforehand out of the stakes secures handsome profits to the proprietor of the house. But fraud is frequently resorted to in many hells; and in some of them, whether he loses or wins, the visitor is sure to be plundered of his valuables before he is allowed to depart. Blood is often shed in these places, their frequenters providing themselves, against emergency, with weapons of every description. Some gambling-houses hire handsome females, and the allurements of these sirens are added to the dangers of the gaming-table. New-York keeps pace, in all these respects, with the large cities of Europe; and in many *maisons de joie*, unsuspecting persons run the risk, at any moment of the day or night, of losing their fortunes, their health, and their honor.

"The persons who frequent gambling-houses may be

divided into two classes : occasional gamblers and professional gamblers. Among the first may be placed those attracted by curiosity, and those strangers I have alluded to
who are brought in by salaried intermediaries. The second
is composed of men who gamble to retrieve their losses, or
those who try to deceive and lull their grief through the
exciting diversions that pervade these places.

" I see, for instance, to the right of the dealer, a tall
man with a well-trimmed beard ; he is a General in the
United States army, and married a young girl belonging
to one of our best families. A few years after his marriage,
his wife disappeared. As she seemed much attached to
her husband and a model of chastity, the general belief
was she had been the victim of some foul outrage. The
friends of her family and the police made active but fruitless search for her ; and the lady's disappearance remained
enveloped in mystery, until she was recognized by an American traveler, an acquaintance, in an Italian city. It appears she had removed there, after her mysterious disappearance from her native land, and lived quite comfortably
with a comrade-in-arms of her husband. The general has
been unable, up to this day, to forget his unfaithful wife ;
and he comes here, every night, to endeavor, by gambling,
to divert his mind from grief.

" Near him, that man whose fingers are loaded with
showy rings, and who affects womanish manners, is the
owner of a newspaper which delights in praising the aristocratic institutions of the Old World—a harmless pastime
in which any one can safely indulge, in a country where
there is no law against the press, and where every body
may relieve his mind of any foolish idea or fancy, without
injury to any thing but his reputation. Gambling is more
than a passion to that personage : it is his very life—as

necessary to him as the air he breathes. He has organized lotteries throughout the States, and though they are prohibited by severe laws, he has found the means to evade them all and build up a large fortune. He often plays very high, and recently nearly broke the bank. The latter met with a loss of two hundred thousand dollars.

" The gambler who is now leaving the gaming-table is a teller in one of our city banks. He long enjoyed the confidence of the directors; but a few days ago, they decided to have him watched, after office hours—a measure now resorted to by many financial institutions, on account of frequent defalcations. To-morrow morning, that teller will be requested by the board of directors to show his books and give an account of the situation and prospects of the bank. But, in spite of his proficiency in book-keeping, he will be unable to figure up and represent the seventy-five thousand dollars he has squandered away in gambling-houses since he commenced, six months ago, to frequent them.

" I also recognize at the table a lawyer who, a few years ago, married a courtesan, in whom covetousness for wealth had become, during the last years of her life, a ruling passion. A few weeks after their marriage, the courtesan died, bequeathing the lawyer all her fortune. It was surmised, at the time, she had been poisoned ; and perhaps her husband comes here to drown his remorse.

" That black-haired, rather corpulent man, whose visage is spoiled by a dishonest glance, and demeanor tarnished by an innate vulgarity, is a teacher of foreign languages. He assumes important airs, as teachers generally do ; and though affecting, in his discourse, a Puritan austerity, few men are more intensely devoted to the pursuit of gain. An adventurer, he had but one purpose in view when he settled in the United States and commenced teaching—to find an heiress. After a fruitless search among his young pupils of the fair sex, he finally fascinated and married a spinster. Her savings are nightly dwindling away at the gaming-table."

Here Asmodeus was interrupted by a quarrel between two players who, for some time, had been seated at a private table.

" Ha ! did you not know," said one of them, (a Kentuckian, Asmodeus informed me,) a man of commanding appearance, and whose face was hidden by a profuse beard— " did you not know the captain of a steamer, which, a few years ago, plied between Saint Louis and New-Orleans? At the time I speak of, I was a merchant in the former city ; and, one day, I sent my younger brother to New-Orleans with an important sum of money for one of my correspondents. That brother I never saw again——"

" Gentlemen," cried out the proprietor of the house, clenching his fist, and his eyes flashing anger, " leave my premises, if you have any difficulty to settle. I do not allow disturbances in my house !"

" Keep yourself easy on that score, my dear sir," replied the Kentuckian. " I know the habits of the persons among whom I am, and never depart from propriety and decency. I was only reminding this gentleman," he continued, pointing to the man he had been previously gambling with, " that my young brother had disappeared ; and I was unable for a long while to learn any thing positive concerning his fate. I could only ascertain he had gambled with the captain of the steamer I have mentioned, during its trip, and that, one morning, some passengers, inquiring after him, were told he had landed during the night. The truth is, the imprudent youth had been thrown overboard by the villain who had cheated him at play and robbed him of his money."

He had no time for further explanation. The man he alluded to pulled a revolver from his pocket and discharged its contents at the Kentuckian. But the latter, pouncing upon his enemy as a tiger upon his prey, flung him to the floor, plunging, at the same time, a dagger into his throat. Then he quietly arose, wiped off the blood which had spurted in his face, and coolly apologized to the proprietor for involuntarily disturbing the diversions of the assembly. "But," he added, "you must admit that what I have done is just; for I have met to-night, in your house, after a six years' fruitless search, the wretch who has just paid with his life the penalty for a foul crime, the secret of which he thought was buried in the Mississippi. I could not let slip the opportunity to avenge my unfortunate brother."

In the mean time, a few gamblers had thought proper to leave the house ; while others bitterly complained of having been disturbed in their play, and urged the dealer to have the corpse removed and resume the interrupted game.

"The game is closed for this night, gentlemen," said the proprietor, with an ugly look. "The police are already informed of the occurrence, and within ten minutes, they will make a descent on this house. The best thing you can do, under these circumstances, is to go quietly home."

He had no need to insist. On hearing the name police, a general stampede was made for the entrance-door ; and we soon found ourselves carried, hurry-skurry, into the street.

CHAPTER XI.

 COULD hardly stand up—I staggered like an inebriate. No one, I suppose, can witness, without horror, the murder of a fellow-creature; and I could not drive from my mind the awful sight of that murdered man, weltering in his blood.

"Try to calm yourself," said Asmodeus. "Whoever is determined to settle in the United States must learn to control his nerves. This country is not a fit abode for peculiarly sensitive persons; it is a place for the strong and energetic only. You can not expect the machinery of a new society to work as regularly and smoothly as in the Old World, where it has been in course of perfection for centuries by watchful governments. Indeed, every thing here is as yet in its infancy—cities, industry, institutions, civilization itself. The cities everywhere are growing in beauty and extent. Industry is ever in pursuit of those economical laws which afford adequate remuneration to both capital and labor. Political institutions themselves are, of course, far from being perfect; and until American civilization takes final shape and firmly secures individual rights and safety to all, revolvers and knives are of service to society. They correct the law's insufficiencies, and

private morals have no more efficient protector.   Owing to
the revolver, seduction, as I previously remarked, is not
a common thing, because seducers are aware that should
the law fail to fully satisfy justice, a terrible retribution
awaits them.   Dishonest persons, also, are cautious lest
they wound private interests which, failing to obtain suit-
able redress from the law, vindicate themselves by the revolver or knife of the wronged party.   In the most civilized
countries of the world, in spite of moralists and philanthropists, the duello is considered a useful auxiliary to
society, as an avenger of wrongs the law is powerless to
punish.   Here the formalities attendant upon the duello in
the Old World would only prove a loss of time, inconsis-
tent with the busy habits of the Americans.   But whoever
has grossly offended another has no need to receive the
offended party's seconds to know his life is threatened.
Quick work is made of the business."

I stared with astonishment on hearing this, and asked
Asmodeus whether he spoke seriously.

"Decidedly," he answered.   "But we have in the
United States, besides those I have alluded to, another
auxiliary to law and society, and far more efficient and
vigilant — an auxiliary that perceives every thing, renders
more service than the police, and does more service to
public morals than the thirty-five thousand ministers of the
Gospel, who, every Sunday, supply their congregations with
long and tedious sermons.

"We are now near the dwelling of one of those auxil-
iaries to law ; and it is just the time to visit it, if we wish
to see in operation one of the wonders of modern industry."

I understood, on entering the building, what Asmodeus
meant.   We were in the establishment of one of the most
important newspapers in the United States, and, probably,

in the world. From the roaring of the steam engine, we inferred that the next issue of the newspaper had gone to press, to be ready by daylight for perhaps one hundred thousand readers. I had previously noticed the elegant building in which that newspaper was printed and published. Activity and remarkable order were everywhere apparent ; and, as Asmodeus observed, one could easily fancy himself to be in a temple erected to intellectual labor.

In an immense cellar, well ventilated, and lighted by a hundred gas-jets, we saw the revolving printing-presses whose roar we had heard in the street. Their long arms, taking hold of a white sheet of paper, laid it open upon a table over which passed a cylinder with lightning-like velocity ; while others taking it back, all printed, carefully put it down on the other side of the cylinder. At each revolution, the forms upon the cylinders were passed over by a roller, incessantly providing itself with printing-ink. These giants of modern industry, according to Asmodeus, were capable of printing, every hour, twenty-five thousand copies of the newspaper we were then examining — a newspaper of large folio size, containing forty-eight columns of reading matter, and often having a twenty-four column supplement besides. In an adjoining room, many employees were busily engaged folding the sheets fresh from the press, and, after counting, handed them either to numberless boys to sell in the streets, or to messengers, whose business it was to carry them to the post-office or to newspaper dealers.

On the first floor, in a room provided with handsome desks, protected by finely wrought railings, was the advertising department. One might have mistaken it for a large banking institution. From daylight to a late hour in the evening, it is crowded by persons bringing in their advertisements and money. On the other floors, we were shown the rooms of the editors and reporters ; a well-stocked library, and even a telegraph apparatus, by means of which communication may be held with the most remote parts of the Union, and even of the civilized world. In the upper story we saw the composing-room, twenty feet high, provided with all the material requisite to give employment to three hundred compositors. An ingenious contrivance communicates with the different floors and carries the "forms" of the compositors to the press-room below. It is also used by the managers of the paper to issue orders, which are instantly executed throughout their vast domain.

"*Ab uno disce omnes,*" said Asmodeus, after we had examined every thing. " A number of newspaper establishments, in the United States, if not so elegantly, are at least as completely fitted up. For the Press, which is the fourth power of the state in some countries of Europe, is incontestably the first in America. The Press is the principal means that helps elect the Presidents of the Republic, secure their reëlection, or cause their defeat. It designates the members of their cabinet, influences the votes of the legislators, dictates the judgments of the courts of law, declares war and concludes peace. Its voice constantly resounds and its activity is untiring. There is not a hamlet where it is not welcomed ; no question it does not raise ; no problem it does not solve. It creates and destroys reputations, and breaks in pieces to-day the idol it worshiped yesterday. Fond of excitement, as sensitive as the ichneumon, as teasing as a spoiled child, impatient of control, crushing all competitors ; in short, as despotic as an Indian potentate — such is the Press in the United States.

"Almost the first thing an American does, on rising from his bed, is to peruse a morning paper, and after he has completed his day's work, he reads an evening journal. There are newspapers for women, for old men, and for children. Some are devoted to the married; some to bachelors and maidens; to the rich, to the poor; to the learned, to those who wish to learn; to every sect and religious denomination; to every system and theory, to every profession; and to every folly.

"To deprive an American of his newspaper would be equivalent to shutting him from the light of day. Newspapers are as necessary to him as the atmosphere he breathes, they are the food and recreation of his mind. He reads them while walking, talking, writing, or eating. Not satisfied with those he purchases himself, he borrows his neighbor's. While families club together in Europe, to secure a newspaper, with a view of reducing its cost, Americans often buy two dailies — one morning and one evening paper, and not a few purchase half a dozen dailies — so great is the eagerness for news; so general the desire of being posted on the events and things of the day.

"After returning from church, the American spends the remainder of the Sabbath in reading the weeklies he was careful to purchase the day before. His wife reads the periodicals devoted to her sex; and their children enjoy themselves with illustrated magazines.

"It has been said the very first thing Frenchmen do, in any country where they go and carry civilization, is to establish a coffee-house; the Americans, everywhere they settle, promote the interests of mankind and civilization by publishing a newspaper! There are scattered, in the far West, small villages in the midst of boundless forests, and in each of which, perhaps, fifty families dwell. Each village contains a church, which is used, at the same time, for school purposes; and in the only street, invariably called Broadway, over the door of a frame building, situated near the post-office, a large sign informs travelers that the new town is already provided with a newspaper and a printing-office.

"It is ascertained, from official sources and the census statistics of the United States, that many villages, whose population does not exceed two thousand, sustain two semi-weekly newspapers.   The United States, politically speaking, being usually divided into two parties, each of these must have its own organ.   New political organizations, which soon disappear after elections, must have theirs also.   A newspaper is their birth-register.

"All nationalities are represented by the Press in the United States.   Without speaking of those printed in English—which is, if not the national, at least the most commonly spoken language—there are newspapers printed in German, in French, in Italian, in Spanish, in Hebrew— even in the Chinese vernacular, for the Celestials in California.   These are of all sizes: some are as large as front-doors, and others nearly as small as a prayer-book. As regards the color of paper used to print upon, it is varied to suit the publisher's fancy—yellow, blue, pink, purple— without speaking of white; and that paper is made of every conceivable material, from cotton down to straw.

"Twenty dailies are published in New-York alone; Philadelphia boasts of a dozen; Boston, Baltimore, Cincinnati, Louisville, Saint Louis, New-Orleans, and Chicago, nearly as many; and less important cities sustain half a dozen dailies, either morning or evening papers.

"The subscription system is seldom resorted to, especially in large cities.   Newspapers are sold, by wholesale,

to agents or dealers, who retail them to the public. By
this means, the expenses incident to a complicated sub-
scription-list are avoided. Any responsibility at all, were
the subscription system in use, would be impossible with
some New-York and Philadelphia newspaper-houses, which
issue sixty thousand copies daily, and sometimes even
more.

"With a people so fond of reading, a printing-machine
whose powers of rapidity would be adequate to the public
wants was a great desideratum. As a matter of course
an American conceived the project of, and invented, the
cylinder printing-press we have just seen in operation.

"Concerning the unrivaled influence newspapers exert
in the United States, I must confess they deserve it. Nowhere else are they so complete and so well conceived.
They are not dull chroniclers of passing events, but rather
encyclopædias, where all interesting questions are discussed, and which abound with information on matters of
great concern to mankind. American newspapers are indefatigable expositors of truth and beauty in religion, literature, the fine arts, politics, and science, and one is struck
with astonishment at seeing the varied knowledge and real
talent these intellectual monitors exhibit every day.

"Statesmen and public functionaries are taught by newspapers ; and in deliberative bodies, the most statesmanlike
views, the most sensible opinions, the most profound dis-
sertations, emanate from former journalists ; and it is
owing to the cheapness of magazines and newspapers, that
the United States are mainly indebted for their material
and intellectual development.

"Public schools are, indeed, numerous, and answer, as
near as possible, the elementary wants of the people. But
the press completes their work, by spreading among the

masses useful and practical knowledge. Every body feels
concerned about public affairs, because every body reads
newspapers ; and the power of the Press is nearly boundless, because it represents an enlightened public opinion—
an opinion formed by all classes of society, and not, as in
Europe, by a few privileged castes only.

"From the comprehensive census published, every ten
years, by the Federal administration, it appears that, in
1850, the number of periodicals and dailies, political and
non-political, published in the United States, was 2526.
In 1860, that number had reached 4051. According to
the census of 1850, the number of copies, annually printed,
was about 500,000,000. Ten years later, it had nearly
doubled, being 927,951,548, on an average, thirty-five
copies for every citizen of the republic !

"Statisticians assert that the Press is the most important aid to their researches, and deserving their most serious attention, because no other data can afford so much
information respecting the status of society and the habits
of the people. On the other hand, an eminent thinker has
contended that the diameter of the Press is the diameter
of civilization itself. Hence the importance and bearings
of the above figures can escape no impartial mind, taking
into consideration the number of papers and periodicals
published in the United States, which actually equals that
of those printed in Europe, with its population eight times
larger than that of the American Republic !

"The American newspaper reviews every morning, in
its columns, all the countries of the world. Those columns
resemble a mirror, in which are reflected all the events
which interest or affect the different people of both hemispheres. In them may be found correspondence from all
important centres of the world ; for the American Press

employs everywhere, at an immense cost, special correspondents, not a few of whom are men of great talent and distinguished writers.

" Even advertisements in the American newspapers are attractive—more so than those in papers of other countries. Methodically arranged, they cover all branches of human activity, and apply, in turn, to financiers, lawyers, physicians, merchants, and business men ; to those in want of a situation, as to those who want help; and they forget neither our pleasures nor our pains ; neither births nor deaths. Persons in pursuit of matrimonial mates also advertise ; and though foreigners wonder at the most important transaction of life being conducted through the columns of a daily, it has not, as yet, been demonstrated that marriages contracted under the auspices of the Press are less happy than others.

" Contrary to what is observed in many other countries, magistrates and policemen admire the press, and extend to it their sympathy on every possible occasion. They regard it as the best detective at their command—the most reliable and efficient agent against evil-doers. When any offense or crime is committed, newspapers give such minute details, such complete information respecting its circumstances and supposed authors, that the latter are soon traced and discovered by the aid of a people whose suspicions and watchfulness have been thus aroused. Though the passport system does not exist in the United States, and in spite of the republic's extensive domains, offenders seldom escape. The Press, with its Argus eyes, soon ferrets them out of their hiding-places, and notwithstanding their disguises.

" Every body, you are aware, is at liberty, in this country, to choose the business or profession for which he thinks

himself qualified ; all careers are open, without reservation
or distinction. The art of printing is, consequently, un-
trammeled, like every other avocation or business ; and it
is, perhaps, useless to say that no law for or against the
Press exists. ·Whoever desires to become an editor or
journalist, starts a newspaper at the sole risk of his purse.
He needs no previous authorization from State or Federal
government ; he has no money to deposit in the public
treasury, as a pledge of his good behavior ; he is not
bound, before going to press, to submit a copy of his
paper to the scrutiny of any officer of the law ; and he has
no fear of warnings from the government. Prosecutions
against newspapers by public authorities are unknown ;
still, and because the freedom of the Press has no limit,
slander is severely punished. But lawsuits, even for slander, are not common. True, newspapers are not slow to
assail public functionaries ; but the latter, in relinquishing
their private life to serve their country, are resigned beforehand to the attacks of the Press. The organs of the
party to which they belong take their part, and public
opinion is finally the supreme judge.

"Another result, derived from the right possessed by
every body to publish without fear what he thinks concerning public affairs, must be noticed. The political police, that insufferable nuisance in the Old World, does not
exist here, because it is utterly useless. What plot could
a political police discover? what conspiracy? At the same
time, secret societies are not tolerated. Their usefulness,
questionable everywhere, can not, in any case, be acknowledged in the United States.

"Without hunting after scandals in private life, the
American Press claims the right to expose whomsoever
violates morals or public decency. Vainly such a privi-

lege is denounced as a dangerous one—as undermining the social fabric. It is an undeniable fact that the fear of newspaper comment is a salutary restraint which, perhaps, prevents many an offense ; but the inconveniences of such a prerogative of the Press are compensated by the multitudinous advantages it procures to society. If corruption has not entirely subverted political institutions ; if public morals are not yet irretrievably lost, assailed as they are by a universal and intense love of money, the American Press may boast of this result. Wicked people are afraid of it—more, perhaps, than of the law.

" For all these reasons, sensible Americans consider the Press as the keystone of their social and political organizations. Freedom of thought is, in their opinion, not less indispensable than freedom of speech, to arrive at all truths in religion, in morals, in politics, in science.

" It may be affirmed that newspapers are the true literature of the United States. They constitute, in fact, the most important branch of literature with democratic societies. When one thinks of the army of compositors whom the four thousand and more newspapers published in the United States employ, of the time required to set in type the matter contained in their thousands and thousands of columns, the efforts prosecuted with such indomitable energy by the Americans to apply steam to type-setting are readily understood. If such a problem is ever satisfactorily solved, the world will doubtless be indebted to America for it; and the steam compositor, or type-setter, will be a worthy companion to the revolving printing-machine, invented by an American."

" But how," said I to Asmodeus, " can the proprietors of American newspapers afford to keep, in every part of the globe, those correspondents you have alluded to ?

Whence are derived their resources to pay so numerous a staff of writers and reporters? And how are they enabled, with such heavy expenditures, to sell their issues to the public at so cheap a rate?"

"In the first place, no Congress has ever been so foolhardy as to subject newspapers to a stamp duty—a duty the consumer, or reader, has, in reality, to pay. Monopolies are always dangerous things, but they are exceedingly so as regards the press. If its freedom was restricted or impeded, that freedom would soon be controlled by capitalists, and the benefits of the institution cease to be within the reach of the masses.

"Well, the masses want cheap newspapers, and consequently stamp duties have not been, up to this day, thought of. For the same reasons, postage rates for newspapers are moderate. Besides these causes, which explain why American newspapers are sold at a low price, their proprietors derive extensive sums of money from advertisements. While advertising is seldom resorted to in Europe, it is here a general rule with business people. No merchant expects to succeed unless he makes repeated appeals to the public for custom through the columns of newspapers; and it is impossible to form an approximation of the amount of money yearly spent for advertising purposes. The receipts of the principal dailies of New-York sometimes amount to four thousand dollars per day, solely for advertisements to be inserted in their next issues. To these profits add those produced from the sale of a considerable number of copies, and you will comprehend that the income of some newspaper proprietors in New-York and Philadelphia, and some other large cities, is equal to that of the wealthiest manufacturers of England.

"The development of the American Press has kept pace

with that of the country. I remember the first number of the newspaper whose wonderful facilities we have just examined. It was a penny paper, printed on a sheet about one foot square, containing in all sixteen columns. The office of publication was situated in a dark basement of a modest house in a quiet street. That first number contained some startling facts concerning the status of New-York City at that time, which was in the year 1835. The editor, who had a great liking for statistics, informed his readers that New-York had, with its suburbs, a population of 260,000 inhabitants. 'The *New-York Directory*,' he added, 'gives 31,150 names, and 2000 immigrants land on our shores every year.' Well, the population of New-York and its suburbs, to-day, amounts to nearly one million and a half; the *Directory* contains 500,000 names; and instead of receiving 2000 immigrants yearly, that number of foreigners often arrive in a single day. That little quarto sheet has now become a large paper, containing every morning seventy-two columns of reading-matter!

"While profiting by the development of the country, the Press has contributed to it to a great extent. It is but just to admire the enterprise, sagacity, and love of progress of American journalists. At the same time, it is to be regretted that they believe it necessary to constantly praise the people and flatter their prejudices and passions, for the sake of retaining an influence over them. Flattery does not lose its name because it is addressed to many, instead of a few, and the flatterers of a people are no less despicable than the courtiers of a king. Because of the hyperbolic praises which four thousand newspapers lavish on the American people, the countrymen of the good and modest Washington are often exposed to the sneers of foreigners, on account of their overbearing and overweening conceit.

Constantly praise a dwarf for his high stature, and he will soon believe himself a giant."

I could not help laughing at this last freak of Asmodeus's mind, as we issued forth from the great newspaper establishment.

"If I can believe my optics," said my companion jocularly, "the stars are beginning to disappear from the canopy of heaven: it is time to seek repose. Farewell, till to-morrow."

CHAPTER XII.

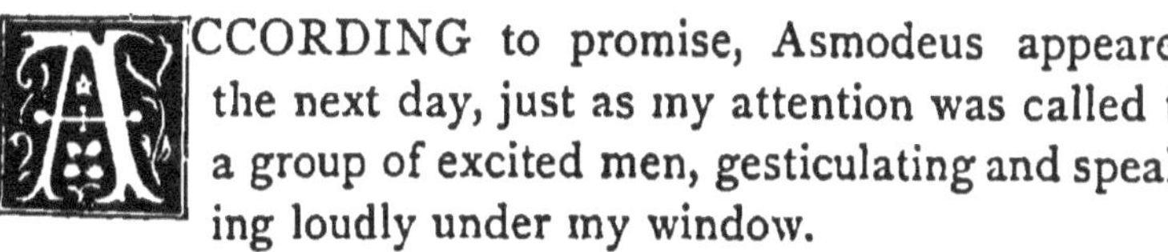

CCORDING to promise, Asmodeus appeared the next day, just as my attention was called to a group of excited men, gesticulating and speaking loudly under my window.

"It is a shameful thing," said they; "here is a poor man breathing his last, and no whisky can be procured to afford him relief!"

While advancing near the group to hear and see better, I asked Asmodeus whether he knew the cause of their concern. "Of course I do," said he, " and here it is: an intoxicated man, laboring under *delirium tremens*, has fallen on the side-walk. Many believe that only spirituous liquors can relieve sufferers of that awful disease; but as this is election-day, all bar-rooms are closed, and no liquors can be obtained. That is the cause of the indignation of these fellows. They would gladly profit by the occasion to give the slip to the law. But let us see the unfortunate man."

He was struggling and writhing in dreadful convulsions, and a red froth oozed from his mouth. Whoever has not seen the terrible effects of this disease, produced by the abuse of spirituous liquors, can not realize them.

"Thousands and thousands of people," said Asmodeus,

" die every year from the effects of intemperance ; and
you can perceive how the sight of the miseries produced
by the vice of intoxication has given birth to the temperance party, whose influence is rapidly gaining ground,
and which perhaps will finally prevail upon Congress to
enact laws prohibiting the distillation and sale of spirituous
liquors in the United States. The American people are
not very partial to wine ; the country produces but a small
quantity of it, and its quality is questionable. Whisky is the
national drink ; half of the corn crop is used for distilling
purposes.   Many physicians assert that few liquors are
more hurtful than whisky—delirium tremens being, most
generally, the result of whisky-drinking. It is a noticeable fact that, in countries where the taste for fermented
liquors predominates, the vice of intoxication is less extensive than where distilled drinks are indulged in.   The
Americans, who go to extremes in every thing, when they
once commence to drink, seldom stop until they are intoxicated.   It is contended that the country's dry atmosphere contributes to develop among them a liking for
strong potations ; and in fact, nowhere else does one need
so often to quench his thirst.

" To satisfy their appetite for liquors, the American
people import gin from Holland, rum and tafia from the
West-Indies, whisky from Scotland and Ireland, heavy
colored wines from Spain, and brandies and champagne
from France.   More champagne is consumed in the United States than in any other part of the world ; and the
demand for that sparkling beverage is ten times greater
here than in France itself.   Drinking is not a mere incident among the diversions of a more refined nature.   It is
often the concealed, if not the ostensible and paramount,
object of parties and festivals.

"As for this wretched victim of a fatal habit, now in the pangs of death, nothing can be done for him ; and death, besides, is a blessing the poor fellow has long prayed for.

" But, by the way," added Asmodeus, after a short silence, "this occurrence reminds me that I have to tell you the sequel of the history of the songstress. I will relate it while we are on our way to the political club where I purpose to take you, after seeing how elections are conducted in the great city of New-York."

HELENA RONFORT'S HISTORY.

SECOND AND LAST CHAPTER.

" IF we acknowledge marriage to be a sacred institution —the keystone of all society built upon a Christian basis, we must admit, as a necessary consequence, that adultery is the most atrocious of all crimes. It can hardly be conceived how, in some countries of Europe, the relinquishment of conjugal duties is looked upon as a venial sin. Indeed, adultery is a favorite theme with authors and poets ; and persons frequenting theatres are almost invariably entertained with deceptions practiced upon husbands. If the theatre is a school for morals, the worship of virtue is there taught in a very singular manner ; and modern dramatists have a queer way of keeping in honor an institution, considered from the church fathers down to the philosophers of our age, as the most important of society.

" The United States have not as yet attained that degree of refined civilization which openly sets at defiance principles of morality and virtue, and corrupts the frivolous under pretense of amusing them. The masses are sound here, and would hardly permit the institution of marriage to be derided in the public theatres. Vainly a sickly literature has striven to invade the book-trade, and illustrated weeklies to offend the sense of propriety and decency. The theatre has been comparatively free up to this day, of demoralizing sensation and influence. But it does not follow, because the institution is as yet the object of public veneration, no home is ever defiled. The violation of conjugal faith is not, unfortunately, an unknown fact. But here the seducer is an object of contempt and aversion, instead of being looked upon as a hero, and the insulted husband is sure of public sympathy; while, in Europe, he would be sneeringly pitied.

" When Edward Ronfort wrote he was about to return from the West, his wife Helena and his brother Robert, it may be remembered, were struck with consternation. They had, indeed, ample cause to be so. Helena shared the passion she had kindled in Robert's heart, and a criminal intimacy had sprung up between them. In her case, the violation of conjugal faith was all the more odious in that she was the mother of two children, and the sister-in-law of her paramour.

" The predicament in which the lovers were placed was awful indeed; though they had sought to conceal their intrigue, an unavoidable circumstance was sure to soon divulge it. Helena was pregnant when Edward, after an absence at the West, returned to his home; and one can imagine the perplexity of the lovers. But Robert began to look more coolly at the case, and tried to bring Helena over to his views. 'You can not,' said he, 'insult your husband's presence. In case he should kill you, nobody would blame him for thus avenging the ruin of his honor and happiness. Leave with me forever the United States; for I am determined not to await his return. Even were I to stay, it would be for the purpose of begging my brother's pardon, and asking him as a favor to take my life. Whatever be the extent of my fault, circumstances impose upon me duties respecting both you and the innocent being to whom you will shortly give birth, from which I will not shrink. You deplore what has taken place, but it is now too late. It remains only for us to accept the responsibility of our indiscretion, and hie away to some distant clime where our fault shall not be known. It is the only safe way to escape the resentment of your outraged husband.'

" In fact, their flight would have been, perhaps, for both Helena and Robert, the most desirable and rational thing they could have devised. But Helena would not listen to her paramour's advice, because the guilty mother declined to separate from her children ; and to take them along in case of their flight, was a thing neither Helena nor Robert could think of doing, as the abduction of the little ones would have filled up the measure of their infamy, besides aiding Edward to find their hiding-place. Anyhow, no time was to be lost, and some resolution had to be at once taken ; for in a few hours Edward would arrive. Extraordinary as her determination may appear, Helena decided to confront her husband, and to confess to him her fault, depending on his love for forgiveness. There are, no doubt, circumstances which may mitigate a wife's guilt, and impel her husband to pardon ; but such was the aggravation of the outrage in Helena's case, that the hope of forgiveness was a mere delusion. She reckoned too much on human weakness, on her influence over her husband, when she expected it an easy thing to soothe his resentment ; she did not know the most unmerciful and inexorable of men are those who have been deceived by the objects of their love.

" Such was Edward. When he arrived at the paternal
mansion, he found there only his mother. The old lady
was unable to give him any explanation in respect to the
absence of his wife ; neither could she tell what had become of Robert. The disappearance of both his brother
and Helena at the same time, was arousing the most painful suspicions in Edward's mind, when a servant handed
him two letters, left by Robert before going away. One of
them, from Robert himself, was addressed to his mother.
In a few lines, he apprised the old lady that he had enlisted in one of the regiments, in the course of formation
for the defense of the Union ; hoping in serving his country,
he said, to end a life that had become to him an insufferable burden, and begging his mother's blessing. The
other letter was from Helena. She informed her husband
she had retired to her father's house, declaring she would
give him further explanation respecting her strange absence, if he would call on her.

" Anatomists of the human heart have often discussed
whether the feeling of honor and self-respect is as intense
and acute with women as with men. While refraining
from giving an opinion on that interesting point, I may
state it seems conclusive that, in many cases where honor
is at stake, woman shows a less acute sensibility than man.
She is unable to understand at once the gravity of some
situations—such, for instance, as that in which a question
of honor impels two courageous men to meet in deadly
combat ; and owing to which, in spite of law, the pulpit,
and philosophy, dueling—the remains, if you please, of
a barbarous but at the same time chivalrous period—could
not be eradicated from the habits of the most refined
societies.

" In the middle ages, up to a time near our own generation, Europe contained many retreats, in which men and women sought a refuge from the world, burying with them in their cloisters terrible secrets or inconsolable sorrows. Our civilization, which carries light everywhere, can hardly reconcile itself with those asylums, the necessity of which, however, in many circumstances, some sound minds have admitted. Perhaps, had convents been in existence in our midst, Helena would have determined to shut up her miserable life forever within one of them, thus striving to redeem her fault by repentance. For want of that refuge, and after deciding not to follow Robert to a strange land, she had only one course to follow: that she took, when, the day after his return, Edward called on her at her father's house. The latter was present at the interview; and before that old man, Helena related all the circumstances attending her fall. The astonishment which followed this confession may be more easily imagined than described. The despair of Edward passed all limits. Perhaps, when Helena had completed her confession, and named her seducer, he would even have realized his brother's predictions and killed his wife, but for the interference of her father.

"Edward, almost frantic, left the house, swearing he would take his brother's life; and a fratricide would have probably startled the community at that time, and revealed to the public this scandal, had not the regiment of volunteers in which Robert enlisted already departed for the seat of war. But his children's love and his old mother's comforting words—above all, time, the soother of all sorrows—soon brought some tranquillity to Edward's mind. After a few days he was able to ponder upon the sad events which had marred his prospects in life, and he came to the conclusion that the only means left him was a dissolution of the matrimonial bonds. But, in the State of New-York, adultery of either party after marriage is the sole cause for which an absolute divorce can be granted. To obtain this divorce, Edward Ronfort would in consequence be compelled to divulge a tale of shame and misery; the names of two respectable families would be dishonored; and again, two innocent children, issue of his marriage with Helena, would be involved in lasting disgrace, and some day, perhaps, reproach their father for his revenge. Besides, Edward's mother was constantly imploring him to cover this awful secret by silence and forgiveness, and Helena's father earnestly joined in these entreaties. He appealed to Edward Ronfort's clemency, not only for the sake of his innocent children, but for the reputation of their name. Could he be so inconsiderate as to make known to the world that the best American families are not free from immorality; that corruption even invades the wealthiest classes of society; that in fine, the Old World does not monopolize domestic scandals? Certainly, were he so rash as not to sacrifice a personal grief to the general interests of society, Edward Ronfort would prove himself a bad citizen, and deserve public scorn!

These, and many similar reasons, were duly weighed by Edward; but, admitting their importance, he could see no means other than a divorce to extricate himself from the dilemma into which his wife's unfaithfulness had involved him. If the solution afforded by a divorce was set aside, what else could be done? He had to take back to his bosom a dishonored wife! At this suggestion, timidly made by his father-in-law, Edward Ronfort boiled with rage. Still, he could not fail to perceive that, to put a stop to the comments and surmises of the public, and prevent the ventilation of this terrible secret, Helena had to leave her father's house and return to her husband. Though he could not bear the idea of having his children brought up by an unworthy mother, Edward was compelled to admit he had either to take her back at once, or apply to the New-York courts for an absolute divorce— that is, to commence a law-suit that would bring in its train unparalleled scandal. In this perplexing extremity, Edward Ronfort determined upon a savage course of proceeding, the consequences of which might have been dreadful for him from man's justice, but which will be attended, at all events, by a severe judgment from a higher tribunal. He made known to his father-in-law his readiness to take Helena back on condition that she should have removed, before its coming to maturity, the fruit of her criminal intercourse with his brother. And barbarous as was such a condition, calculated to imperil his daughter's life, Helena's father accepted it. Pride silenced the voice of humanity in his heart!

"It was for such a purpose that Helena, belonging to one of the wealthiest and most respectable families in New-York, became a temporary inmate in Mrs. Killer's house. The latter practiced her homicidal art upon Edward Ronfort's wife, who was thus led from the crime of adultery to that of infanticide; and, after staying four weeks under the abortionist's roof, broken down with shame and suffering, she was allowed to again reside with her husband. But the inhuman sacrifice, resorted to for the purpose of protecting the honor of two proud families, did not conduce to the wished-for result. As soon as (to save appearances only, for they had separate rooms) Edward and his wife again dwelt under the same roof, a life full of anger, hatred, and anxiety commenced for them.

They had agreed to meet each other at meals only. Even so brief an intercourse was more than Edward could bear. He regarded as an outrage and defilement every caress Helena bestowed on their children. Soon the hatred he felt for his wife, Helena returned with interest. Inconceivable mystery of the human heart! She, since he had imposed upon her, with the view of an apparent reconciliation, the dreadful alternative she had complied with, considered him a murderer, and he had become to her an object of abhorrence and detestation.

"After one month of such a life, both became disgusted with it, and they gave up all further attempt to live together under the same roof. Helena returned to her father's house, and Edward immediately commenced an action to obtain an absolute divorce. The lawsuit lasted a long time, as is customary with all lawsuits in the United States. Numberless witnesses were called by both parties; for three weeks the morning and evening papers served up to an eager and curious public the most disgusting details concerning this family scandal. The lawyers, as usual, increased, by the sharpness and acrimony of their attacks, the violence of the passions such a lawsuit was sure to arouse on both sides. It had hardly commenced before it became a desperate contest between two families, both influential by their wealth and relations. Helena was represented by her lawyers as a victim whose virtue had been, during the absence of her husband, violently outraged by Robert ; and they almost applauded as an act of heroism the bloody transaction she had submitted to at the hands of Mrs. Killer.

"Most assuredly, the necessity to grant a divorce was never more apparent than in this case. Law should be made so clear in every country, as to secure a divorce to every husband who submits unequivocal proofs of his wife's adultery. But results of the most astounding character may always be expected when the solution of legal points, or even plain facts, depends on the unanimity of jurors. His demand for a dissolution of his matrimonial bonds was not granted to Edward Ronfort, because his wife succeeded, either in winning the sympathy, or bribing the conscience, of one of the jurymen.

"Thus it appears that, in the State of New-York, as in some countries of Europe, an honest man, after giving his name to a woman, does not always succeed in taking it back—even when he furnishes undeniable proofs of his wife's guilty intercourse with a paramour. If a unanimous verdict from jurors is not returned, the divorce is not granted. The adulterous wife may continue to use her husband's name; may bear children to her paramour, and they may also use that very name; and, however young her husband may be, he will be prevented from bringing up a family of legitimate children.

"Whatever be the soundness of these comments, Helena Ronfort has gone the way invariably followed by women who forget a mother's duty, and whose very fault gains for them an unwholesome notoriety. After leading, for a time, a retired life, she has again shown herself to the world—shaking off, as it were, all remembrance of the past. You may often see her in the Park, followed by many admirers; and her attendance at Mrs. Killer's party, where her voice and beauty created so marked a sensation, indicates that she will pursue the career of dissipation she has entered. She will be the belle of the next season, will lead the fashion in New-York—in short, will be one of the 'bright particular stars' that attract the idle and wealthy in search of adventures.

"Edward Ronfort, the day after meeting Helena at Mrs. Killer's, where one of his friends had induced him to go, took passage, with his children, for Texas, on board of a coastwise steamship. He will stay there one year; after which, according to the laws of that State, he will obtain a divorce, and thus recover his freedom to marry again if he feels so disposed."

"What has become of Robert?" I inquired, after Asmodeus had ended this narrative.

"Robert is dead; but he did not die in the manner he desired. His life was invariably spared in every battle for the Union in which he participated, though accomplishing prodigies of valor and praying for the enemy's bullets to end his life. Have you not guessed that Robert is that poor wretch we saw, a short time ago, struggling in the last agonies of delirium tremens? At the restoration of peace, his regiment was disbanded, and he then donated all his fortune to benevolent institutions, save only a sum of money sufficient to enable him to commit suicide after the American fashion. And he promptly carried his determination to a successful issue, as you have seen."

"What do you mean by a suicide after the American fashion?"

"When a merchant happens to fail in his speculations, and despairs of ever again rising in the world—when a husband or a lover, through some unexpected cause, loses the object of his love, they not unfrequently decide to get rid of their life; and to carry out their purpose, they resort to drink, absorbing, every day, a quantity of either gin, whisky, or brandy, according to taste. They gradually increase the deadly beverage—some succeeding in swallowing as much as one gallon a day of the liquor they have selected to drown their thoughts. They very soon fall into frequent fits of delirium tremens, and predict with an astonishing accuracy the day they will be through with their job! I can show you, in my memorandum-book, the names of one hundred and seventeen friends of mine, who have gone out of this world holding the fatal cup in their hands!"

CHAPTER XIII.

IN WHICH, ·AFTER "PITCHING INTO" POLITICIANS, ENG-
LISHMEN, AND INDIANS, ASMODEUS RELATES THE AD-
VENTURES OF BLANCHE RIVINGSTON.

AS Asmodeus had remarked in the morning when we set out on our rambles, it was election-day. The people, in the exercise of their sovereignty, had to elect a governor and a lieutenant-governor of the State, State representatives and legislators to the Federal Congress, Supreme Court judges, a State treasurer, a canal commissioner, and many other officers, in the different branches of public administration.

According to Asmodeus, when the popular suffrage dwindles down to such an extent, instead of confining its operations to the election of a few high functionaries, it is in a fair way to lose its *prestige*, to open wide a door to corruption, and finally, to degenerate into a farce.

All bar-rooms or drinking-saloons were closed, as the sovereigns, in the exercise of their right, must have a clear mind and full control of themselves. Hotels even, and restaurants, are not allowed to sell spirituous liquors while voting is in progress, that is, from sunrise to sunset. But, as in the course of the day we met many of these sovereigns who were somewhat unsteady of gait, the conclusion was forced upon us they had found the means to quench their thirst with a stronger beverage than the water of public fountains. However, the election was progressing everywhere, and with an order most remarkable. In streets devoted to trade, and at the wharves and piers of the great city, there was as much bustle and activity as on other days. Stations for voters had been provided, at short distances from each other, in every district. There, delegates from the two parties contending for the victory received from voters slips of paper, on which were printed the names of the candidates, and deposited them in sealed boxes. There was nowhere any appearance of brutal force. The people would not believe in their freedom if the military were stationed in their midst, or any functionary empowered, either by the Federal or State administration, to watch over the ballot. The public weal was represented at each station by a solitary policeman, whose business it was to see that all liquor-saloons were closed, and to maintain order.

The American people, Asmodeus informed me, profess such respect for freedom in election matters that, during voting hours, any force of the regular army must be removed from the polls at a distance fixed by law. The slightest suspicion that any brutal force has influenced the votes of the people on election-day, would suffice to annul the results of the ballot. The Federal and State constitutions determine the time when the election for president and vice-president of the United States, and also for members of Congress, must be held. The day for the election of State governors, members of local legislatures, and of the many functionaries who derive their power direct from the people, is also determined by the State constitutions. In that way, every person knows the day when he has to assemble to exercise his elective franchise. Thus, no false manœuvres, no party intrigues, can deprive the Americans from enjoying the right to vote—no previous notice being necessary to summon them to the polls.

The voters repaired to the ballot-boxes, either singly or in groups. The latter were manifestly under the control of a few leaders; and Asmodeus surmised that many of these sovereigns had received beforehand the price of their vote.

After all, the sight of an American election might be favorably contrasted with that offered, under similar circumstances, by European populations. No singing nor shouting could be heard; no disturbance of any sort could be seen. The day before, processions, formed of thousands of persons, belonging to political organizations, carrying banners on which were inscribed divers appropriate mottoes, marched through the streets; bands of music were heard everywhere; and in every electoral district meetings were holden in the open air. On the previous night even, long political processions passed through the streets, and, with their numberless Chinese lanterns and transparencies, resembled monstrous fiery serpents. Now the hour for voting had come, all speech-making was over; no band of music could be heard; every American was seriously discharging a duty, the responsibility of which he seemed thoroughly to understand.

"All that is very fine," said Asmodeus; "it is a pretty sight, and would be a magnificent triumph of popular sovereignty, in its most important manifestation, were not many of the electors mere tools in the hands of intriguers, who make a trade of politics; and were not the ballots manipulated beforehand by conventions or assemblies, which contrive to nominate candidates seldom known to the mass of voters, but with whom delegates to those assemblies or conventions have bargained beforehand for their personal advancement.

"As the rotation system is strictly adhered to, after each election—that is, as clerks and other employees, in every branch of public administration, are discharged, to make room for friends and partisans of elected candidates —delegates to conventions obtain, as a reward for their services, all the offices to be vacated, and which themselves or friends will, in their turn, occupy. The voice of the people, thus caught in the toils of corruption, is not really heard. It is stifled in eight cases out of ten.

"As regards, for instance, the presidential election, if the United States, since President Jackson, and excepting the lamented Lincoln, have had for first magistrates men whose minds were not above the common level, the result is attributable to the system of preliminary conventions. Candidates to the presidential chair are obliged to accept beforehand all the greedy stipulations of delegates to those conventions ; and also a series of principles, either good or bad, embodied in a programme, called, in American parlance, a platform. What man, endowed with real talent and possessing self-respect, would consent to be stretched on such a Procrustean bed ? It does not often happen that the people are ruled by men of real genius ; still, as long as American democracy was faithful to the principle of absolute freedom in selecting representatives, and scorned the dictates of conventions, presidents proved to be men of superior attainments ; such as, for instance, Jefferson, the two Adamses, Madison, and Monroe. Now we see, led and controlled in their choice by envious partisans or corrupt political organizations, the American people intrusting the first office in their gift to men comparatively unknown and of ordinary talent."

While Asmodeus was discoursing in this strain concerning the institutions of the United States, and I was contemplating the people in the exercise of their sovereignty, two groups of pedestrians attracted my attention.   In front of us walked half a dozen young men ; and their dress was so different from that of other persons I had met in New-York, it was impossible not to notice it.   They wore hats of every conceivable shape and description— square, round, and sharp-pointed, white, blue, and yellow, and so dirty and worn out, one would have thought they had been trampled upon before turned to their present use. The trowsers of these men were made of deer-skin, or some thick yellow stuff, and half-hidden by riding-boots. Their coats were conspicuous for their varied and grotesque shapes—some being very short, without tails ; while, with others, that appendage was immeasurably long, after the French fashion under the Directory.   I asked Asmodeus what this masquerade meant.   "It is not a masquerade," said he, " in the opinion, at least, of those travelers—for such are the men who are walking by us.   They belong to the most aristocratic families of old England.   Perhaps you are not aware that Englishmen, when traveling through the United States, do not take the trouble to dress decently, as the American democracy, they imagine, does not deserve it.   As for their riding-boots, they are intended to protect their owners' legs against the bite of rattlesnakes.   Englishmen firmly believe every thing written on the United States by their countrymen ; and as a few writers have seriously affirmed that rattlesnakes are plentiful in New-York, these young men have provided themselves against the danger of stumbling upon one of those reptiles.

" Montesquieu, a shrewd observer, remarked, more than

a century ago, that very few Englishmen could be found in his time, whose minds were not slightly deranged; and from the demeanor of those dust-covered sons of Albion, I apprehend there is no remedying the mental condition of Englishmen when abroad."

The other group of pedestrians was followed by a few children, who regarded the strangers with feelings of curiosity, not unmingled with fear. Their majestic countenances and fantastical costumes unmistakably showed them to be the representatives and the remnants of that race which, when the Dutch and English settled in America, was the possessor of the immense country over which now floats the star-spangled banner. The Indians, who, in a somewhat gloomy mood, thus perambulated the streets of New-York, were on their way back to the Far West, after visiting, at Washington, the Father of the Indians, as they call the President of the United States. Tall and straight as arrows, and shod with moccasins—that is, a sort of covering for the feet, made of deer-skin, without a sole, and highly ornamented on the upper side—some wore small round hats, while the long black hair of others was braided and adorned with eagles' feathers, or those of some less illustrious birds. Some of their faces were painted red, yellow, and blue; and they had evidently taken much pains to disfigure what, in our pride, we fancy to be the finest part of man. I did not perceive, hanging at their sides, the traditional tomahawk. Most of these Indians were wrapped in blankets, and smoked tobacco— not in the calumet spoken of by novelists, but in a common pipe, the bowl of which was made of a corn-cob, and the tube of a long reed. I must add, as a conscientious historian, that, if the children following them looked somewhat afraid of these inhabitants of the western wilds, the

Indians, on their side, appeared quite as uneasy among a crowd of pale faces, though every body seemed to express much sympathy for them.

" Here are the Red Skins," said I to Asmodeus ; "here pass before us those sons of the forest, whose deeds have been woven into the verse and prose of poets and novelists."

" Alas ! you are right," replied my companion ; "here are the descendants of those warriors whom James Fenimore Cooper loved to portray, and whose romantic names are familiar to every body. Cooper's heroes in reality had no more attractions than the dusky specimens of mankind we now behold. Perhaps they were a little more ferocious and wild, which enhances all the more the American novelist's works.

" Fortunately, civilization proceeds with the different races of men as culture does with plants ; culture improves the latter by rejecting and destroying those of an inferior quality ; and civilization, in its ever-advancing march, crushes out all races unwilling to be improved ; and generation after generation of strong and progressive men comes forward to till the land and turn to usefulness the solitudes in which ferocious beasts, and men no less ferocious, lived up to that time."

Asmodeus was just concluding this severe sentence, when the chief of the Indian warriors drew near my companion and saluted him, after the Indian fashion—that is, by putting his right hand on his breast. Asmodeus uttered a few words in the Indian dialect, and on the chief's nodding, he took him, with the other warriors, to a restaurant near by. Refreshments were at once ordered, which the Red Men seemed to highly appreciate. With the exception of their chief, none of them could speak English.

"Thousands and thousands of moons have vanished," said he, after indulging in the good things ordered by Asmodeus, "since three children of the Great Spirit, in pursuit of game, came in sight of a large river. On the opposite bank, they perceived an enchanter, who beckoned them to come over, showing them several gifts lying at his feet. One of the Great Spirit's sons, without hesitation, threw himself into the stream, and swam rapidly over. The second imitated the undaunted swimmer; but only after seeing him reach the middle of the river in safety. The third waited before throwing himself into the water, until he saw his two brothers safely standing by the enchanter. The stream had gradually become more and more turbid by the exertions of each of the swimmers; and when the three, standing together on the opposite shore, shook the water from their bodies, they saw with astonishment that, while the skin of the first swimmer was as white as before, that of the second had become red, or of a copper color, and that of the third black as ebony.

"'Here are the gifts I promised you,' then spoke the enchanter; 'take your choice.'

"The white man picked up a small package pointed out to him. In it were paper, pens, and ink—that is, intellectual power and supremacy over material creation. The red man discovered in his package a bow and arrows. The black man, when he opened the package allotted to him, found agricultural implements.

"During hundreds and hundreds of years," the chief continued, "my kinsmen have used bows and arrows; they were forbidden to make use of the other gifts dispensed by the enchanter. To-day, our arrows have grown blunt, and the strength which used so easily to bend our bows is fast decaying. Buffaloes and deer, startled by the screaming of your fire-horses, run away toward the frozen regions, and ourselves are slowly following them, marking the track with our bones. The Great Spirit, however, does not forsake his children. He has promised to give them, in the next life, more lovely forests than those our fore-fathers possessed, and hunting-grounds ever replete with antelopes and buffaloes ; and thus we rejoice to die."

We now separated from the Indians, and were moved to pity at the last words of their chief. But we had hardly advanced a few steps, when we observed two men carrying away in their arms, a young lady, and, in spite of her screams, shut her up in a carriage that was waiting for them. A crowd congregated in an instant—seemingly disposed to take the part of the lady ; when one of the two men, speaking from the carriage-window, exclaimed :

" Gentlemen, this lady has escaped from an insane asylum, and we are taking her back. Make room if you please."

Every body immediately moved off, seemingly satisfied with this explanation ; and the carriage was rapidly driven toward the upper part of the city.

" Contradictions abound in the American character," said Asmodeus ; " individual liberty is held in the greatest respect ; the Federal Constitution itself provides that the *habeas corpus* shall not be suspended unless, in case of rebellion or invasion, the public safety may require it. Nearly all the State constitutions contain a similar safe-guard ; and the dogma concerning the inviolability of in-dividual liberty has been so well respected at all times, that the history of the Union presents very few cases in-deed of arbitrary arrests. Even evil-doers often escape deserved punishment, because the police are afraid to en-croach on the law, and thus incur a fearful responsibility, by arresting them. Notwithstanding all this, there is in that carriage, driven as fast as two strong horses can go, a victim of arbitrary arrest. Three words—'she is insane'— have sufficed to quiet the crowd, to satisfy the minds of those republicans, so proud of the prerogatives attached to the *habeas corpus.* Those same words, written on a physician's certificate, had previously been sufficient to cause that unfortunate lady to be imprisoned in a madhouse."

" But is she not really insane? and has the crowd been imposed upon?"

" As a general rule none of us is sure of possessing a sound mind ; but I am satisfied that the lady you allude to is possessed, to an ordinary degree, of that attribute which, according to benevolent philosophers, distinguishes our species from that of monkeys and other four-footed animals."

" Then why is she thus hurried away to an insane asylum ?"

" Ah ! you believe, because men are ruled by republican institutions, instead of living under the sway of a king, they are not subjected to evil passions, such as pride, covetousness, revenge ! An act of a domestic drama has just been enacted in our presence, I assure you, because I am conversant with the facts."

" Then why did you not at once disclose the facts of this shocking violence, since you are acquainted with the circumstances of the case ?"

" Sir, one day I was good-natured enough to interfere between two furious fellows, who were tearing each other in a fearful manner. Well, what happened ? They at once assailed me and broke my leg—an accident of small import, you may perhaps think, but which left with me a very stubborn and troublesome reminder of the circumstance. From that time, I gave up all Quixotic redresses, and let mankind settle its own quarrels. But I observe the time has not yet come to go to the club where I propose to take you; so we will visit the asylum in which the young lady, in whom you seem interested, has been confined. You will be at liberty, I suppose, to see her—even to try and liberate her, if you wish to constitute yourself her knight, after hearing her adventures.

BLANCHE RIVINGSTON'S HISTORY.

"BLANCHE RIVINGSTON's father is a Mississippi planter. The pride of Southern families before the civil war was something that exceeded all belief. According to their idea, mankind is divided into three categories: first, the aristocracy, which embraces the crowned heads and nobility of Europe and the chivalry of the Southern States; second, the working-class, to which belong the operatives in Europe and the whole population of the Northern States of the Union; and third, the negroes. I will not warrant that such and similar notions have become obsolete since the severe trials the Southern States have undergone.

"At the time slavery existed, Blanche's father owned many slaves, and enjoyed a princely income. His daughter was reared in luxury, while his sons grew up with the idea that they were far removed from social laws, and that the type or model of a gentleman is a man who does not do any thing. This absurd conceit prevailed to a great extent among Southerners at the period I speak of, and brutal force was the only power they acknowledged.

"At eighteen years of age, Blanche married a Louisiana planter, and during several years no misfortune disturbed their happiness. But three years ago, she was afflicted with a very troublesome if not dangerous disease—deafness, and all the country physicians she applied to failed to cure her. Mr. Dalton (such is the name of her husband) then decided to take her to New-York. But the physicians of this city also failed to relieve the lady, and finally gave it as their opinion that the European climate, with the aid of Parisian doctors, might restore her to health. In conformity with this advice, Mr. Dalton and his wife determined to spend a few months, perhaps years, in the gay capital of France ; and so sailed for Europe.

"They had resided three months in Paris, and Blanche was under the care of a medical celebrity, when Mr. Dalton received from an agent he had left in Louisiana a letter, the contents of which were such as to necessitate his immediate return to the United States. After renting a furnished apartment for his wife in the St. Germain suburb, he took his departure, promising to promptly settle his business and immediately return to France.

"At this time Blanche's health had improved rapidly, and her deafness was fast disappearing. The attending physician had assured her that no trace of it would be left in a year's time, provided she continued to follow the treatment he had prescribed. Under these circumstances, Mr. Dalton could not think of taking his wife with him, as by so doing he would compromise the good results already obtained ; and though deeply affected at their separation, they were compelled to submit to this dire necessity.

"For several weeks Mrs. Dalton shut herself up in her apartment, receiving no other visitor than the physician who attended her. The doctor, a medical celebrity, as I have said, and withal a kind and honest man, considered it his duty to increase his attendance on Blanche during her husband's absence. In consequence, as he was unable

to see her every day, most of his time being absorbed by
other patients, or by lectures at the medical college, he
determined, when thus prevented himself, to send a young
graduate to visit Mrs. Dalton; and it so happened that
this well-meant attention proved decidedly detrimental to
Blanche's happiness. This young graduate had come to
Paris several years before, to complete his medical studies.
He was an American by birth, and had been selected,
among other graduates and former pupils of the physician,
because he was a countryman of Mrs. Dalton. But Lewis
Gambler (the name of this graduate) saw in the trust
confided to him but an occasion to gratify his evil passions.

"The Roman Catholic priest enjoys, from his confes-
sional, an influence often unrivaled over weak minds; but
it may be affirmed a physician exerts a more dangerous
one over his patients, permitted, as he is, to enter their
chambers at every hour of the day and night. In remote
times old men only had the privilege to practice medicine.
It was denied to young men; and such prohibition demon-
strates that the ancients were perhaps better acquainted
with the human heart than the moderns. Even admitting
a young physician is sincerely devoted to his profession
and thoroughly conversant with its duties, still he will
sometimes find himself in most critical positions, such as
may make him forget, for the time, his love of science
and honesty. The physician will disappear; the man alone
will remain, with his passions, and unable to control them.
Now, if a medical practitioner be a corrupt man, a liber-
tine, the happiness of many a family is, as a matter of
course, in his hands.

"The freedom allowed to the disciples of Esculapius, in
virtue of the real or supposed exigencies of their profession, has brought, and brings every day, many a virtuous

woman to ruin. In such a way Blanche gradually, and quite unconsciously, was led to forget her duties to her husband and to herself. As her physician and country-man, Lewis Gambler was doubly entitled to her confidence. No sooner had he obtained the charge of visiting her in his medical capacity, than he began to display artifice after artifice to seduce her. And Blanche fell, and was not slow to perceive to what a depth of shame and misery.

"There are discreet men who scorn to abuse the love they have inspired, to compromise the reputation of their paramours; who do not hesitate to give up all the claims of a lover when they discover that they please no longer, or that their presence might endanger the objects of their love. Such was not Gambler; he became a tyrannic master over Blanche, and a life of indescribable suffering commenced for his victim as soon as he had conquered her resistance to his lust.

"Lewis Gambler was addicted to a vice which soon extinguishes all generous feelings in the human heart; he was passionately fond of games of chance. Now, according to an English philosopher, gamblers are the worst species among the class called lovers. They sacrifice all to the gaming-table; the latter absorbs every thought of their mind, every feeling of their heart—in short, entirely possesses them. Gambler's passion for gambling suffered no abatement from his intrigue with Mrs. Dalton. In no instance could the entreaties of the latter retain him by her side in the evening; he would always repair to some gaming-house; and soon he borrowed from Blanche dollar after dollar—one day under this pretense, and the next under that—the six thousand dollars Mr. Dalton had deposited, for her use, with a Parisian banker before leaving for the United States. With the view to save money,

she soon left the *Saint Germain* suburb, and rented a
small room in the *Quartier Latin;* but her trials had but
just commenced. One by one her jewels and dresses were
stolen by Gambler, and pawned. Not even her linen was
left her; and more than once this daughter of a wealthy
planter was obliged to borrow money from some of her
own countrymen or friends whose acquaintance she had
made since her residence in Paris, to prevent her dying
through starvation.

"Mr. Dalton had been six months separated from his
wife, when he was able, at last, to leave the United States,
and return to France. Astonished at the state of destitu-
tion and distress in which he found his wife, he was nevertheless unable to discover the causes which had produced
it. Gambler had thought it advisable to cease for a while
his visits to Blanche, after her husband's return; and the
latter, happy by the side of his wife, attributed to her
inexperience of life and prodigal habits the expenses
she had incurred, and the straitened circumstances in
which she had therefore found herself during his absence.
He removed her to a convenient apartment, in a fashionable district, and made every preparation to spend, in a manner adequate to his standing in society and fortune, the few
months yet to be devoted to the complete cure of his wife.

"After a while, Gambler recommenced his visits to Mrs.
Dalton. At the same time, and at every opportunity, he
always begged for loans. So repeated and exacting were
his demands for money, that Blanche threatened to disclose his obsessions to her husband, were she even forced,
by so doing, to expose her shame to him. Gambler coolly
listened to her, answering that he knew too well the human
heart, and consequently attached no importance to her
threats. He added that if Mr. Dalton ever became acquaint-

ed with the priceless favors he (Gambler) had received at her hands, it would not be through the agency of his wife, but through that of her lover. 'The day,' said he, in giving her this warning, 'you refuse to give me money, I will apply to your husband, and get a few thousand dollars from his pocket, by selling him the letters you wrote me during his absence.' When Gambler spoke in this threatening manner, he had already borrowed two thousand dollars since the return of Mr. Dalton—that is, within two months ; and, though liberal with his wife, and fondly loving her, Mr. Dalton could hardly believe she spent for charitable purposes the large sums of money he was constantly asked for.

"One day, Blanche begged her husband so earnestly to shorten their stay in France, and to return to the United States, that Mr. Dalton could not resist her entreaty. Blanche asserted that her deafness had nearly disappeared ; she felt, she said, that the old life on the plantation would completely restore her health, while, far from America, it was fast dwindling away ; and the fact is, Gambler's repeated obsessions and the anguish that filled her mind had commenced to tell on her health. Her nights were sleepless, her cheerfulness was gone, and her beauty rapidly fading. She somewhat recovered her wonted gayety when her husband told her, one day, to pack up her things, and prepare to leave the French capital. According to her desire, he had paid for their passage on board of an English steamer which would leave in four weeks for America. But as Mr. Dalton had some business to transact in England, they left Paris a few days after this welcome news to Blanche. They spent three weeks in London ; after which they went to Liverpool.

"At last Blanche embarked on board the English steam-

er, hoping in her heart she would never see Gambler
again.   The steamer left her dock ; Blanche mingled with
the passengers on the deck, and the very first person she
saw was her tormentor.   Horror-struck, she vainly tried to
conceal her emotions from her husband ; she trembled
from head to foot ; and though he did not understand the
cause of the aversion Gambler inspired in his wife, when
he bowed to the former, Mr. Dalton informed him that his
medical attendance would not be required on their way to
America.   Gambler, however, while Mr. Dalton was in the
smoking-room, or walking on deck, several times availed
himself of the opportunity to speak to Blanche.   When
that opportunity failed him, he sent her notes through a
servant ; and it was always the same thing he demanded
from her — money to gratify his passion for gambling.
Gambling, in fact, was carried on among the passengers,
to render the trip less tedious ; and ill-luck persistently
marred Gambler's expectations.   After a few days, poor
Blanche had given him her last dollar — though her husband had filled her portemonnaie with gold and bank-bills.
Before even the shores of America were reached, the unfortunate woman had been driven to rob her husband.   While
Mr. Dalton was asleep, she took from his pocket-book two
hundred dollars, which she handed to Gambler, who was
anxiously waiting for them.

" At last they arrived at New-York ; and Blanche, hoping
her husband would take her at once to the South, fancied
she was now secure.   But her hope was again deceived.
Her father and two of her brothers had just arrived in
New-York.   It was the summer season, and her relatives,
as is usual with wealthy Southerners, had come to the
North on a visit.   At their request, Blanche and her husband decided to stay a week with them.   So they stopped

at the same hotel as Mr. Rivingston and his sons. Surrounded by her father and brothers, Blanche believed she was released from any further importunities from Gambler. She was well aware he would have no difficulty in discovering her stopping-place, but she thought he would not be bold enough to try to see her again. But she did not yet know that heartless villain. Gambler, a few hours after landing, hastened to a gaming-house, and, as usual, met with ill-luck. Two days after, Blanche became satisfied she was not liberated from her tormentor; she saw him in the parlors of the hotel, and learned he was actually stopping there. Several times he tried to speak to her, and his attempts having proved fruitless, he sent her a note, in which he asked for an interview. No answer being given, another was handed to Blanche, the next day, by one of the waiters. In it, the poor woman was coolly informed that in case she did not send five hundred dollars before night, Gambler would come himself for it, at the risk of meeting Mr. Dalton. In this extremity Blanche came to a desperate determination. Gambler had been the recipient, on board the steamer, up to the last dollar, of all the money her husband had given her, previous to their leaving England; and she could not think of borrowing five hundred dollars from either her father or brothers, lest they should reproach her husband for his parsimony toward his wife. To ask her husband for money was out of the question; for she would have been obliged to confess she had already squandered the important sum she had received from him a few days previous; and withal she could not think without terror and remorse of the two hundred dollars she had taken from his portemonnaie during their passage to America. She finally decided to beg the youngest of her brothers to remain by her side all that day; and, opening to him her heart, she told him of the indignities she had been subjected to from one of the physicians who had attended her, and who had followed her to America, and that her own happiness and that of her family required, at once, a stop to be put to his degrading importunities.

"After dinner, Mr. Rivingston, his oldest son, and Mr. Dalton went to the theatre. Blanche, under pretense of indisposition, had declined to be one of their party, and her young brother declared he would keep her company. Shortly after, Gambler knocked at the door of Blanche's room. Young Rivingston was ready for him. He dryly informed him his sister was not at home to any body, and especially to her late physician, Lewis Gambler. Exasperated, and threatening revenge, Gambler withdrew, and, unluckily for Blanche, he was true to his threat.

When Mr. Dalton returned from the theatre, a waiter handed him a letter from Gambler, in which was inclosed a few lines to him (Gambler) in the handwriting of Blanche —lines that left no doubt as to the intimate character of the relations that had existed between Gambler and Mrs. Dalton during her husband's absence from Paris. As to the letter Gambler had written to Mr. Dalton, it was for the purpose of acquainting the latter that the former was the owner of ten letters of the same style and nature as that sent as a specimen; and the planter was coolly informed that he could prevent their circulation by depositing five thousand dollars with a friend whose address was given. The cause of Blanche's distress in the French capital, and her anxiety since she had left it, was thus revealed to her husband. He now understood why she had desired to return to America before the completion of the treatment prescribed for her by the Parisian physicians;

the terror she had more than once manifested during the sea-trip, and since their arrival in the metropolis ; and also the use that had been made of the money he had lavished on her. The unfortunate woman had been the victim and tool of a most contemptible villain ; but though pitying her from the depths of his heart, Mr. Dalton came to the conclusion that all further life with her was at an end. She could not possibly be the mother of children he longed for, and he was forced, by the necessity of releasing himself from his matrimonial bonds, to plunge into grief a family to which he was sincerely attached, and who gloried in an unspotted name.

"The next day Mr. Dalton asked to have an interview with his father and brothers-in-law, and heart-broken and with trembling lips, he deposited in their hands the lines written by Blanche to Gambler, and the letter the villain had sent to him. After reading these proofs of his daughter's guilt, 'Sir,' said Mr. Rivingston, 'I have loved and treated you like one of my own children ; but I now understand that family connections between us must be severed. So far as my consent goes, you are at liberty to take another wife in place of the woman who can no longer be my daughter. To-day she must retire forever from a society she has proved herself unworthy to further associate with, by betraying your honor, and defiling her family's good name. Here,' added he, addressing his sons, 'take five thousand dollars out of my drawer and carry them to the person named by the wretch who has ruined your sister ; and if ever you chance to meet him, shoot him down like a dog.'

"A few hours later, Mr. Rivingston, accompanied by a physician, entered his daughter's room.

"'Madam,' said the proud planter, showing her a bundle of letters, 'here are evident proofs that your mind is deranged, and this gentleman, according to law, will swear to it. A woman who belongs to one of the oldest and most respected Southern families, and who so far forgets herself as to trample upon the sacred laws of chastity, is undoubtedly mad. You must, therefore, to-day, enter an asylum ; and if it depends upon your father's will, you shall never come out of it.'

" That evening, Blanche, thoroughly overcome by terror and remorse, and in a state of insensibility, was taken by her father and brothers to Doctor Greedy's institution."

CHAPTER XIV.

IN WHICH ASMODEUS TAKES THE READER TO AN INSANE ASYLUM; THEN TO A POLITICAL CLUB, WHICH IS BUT "ONE REMOVE" FROM THE FORMER.

"THIS is a dreadful history," said I to Asmodeus, when he had concluded his narrative.

"Undoubtedly; and it is sad to think Blanche's sequestration is not an isolated and unfrequent case. Insane asylums, kept by private individuals, are numerous in the United States, because very excitable persons are more exposed than others to lose the equilibrium of their minds; and perhaps, in every one of them, detained in spite of all human and divine laws, may be found some victims of domestic revenge or cupidity. A husband who wants to get rid of a troublesome wife, a brother coveting his brother's or sister's fortune, a son who thinks his old father is clinging too long to life, have but to procure a physician's certificate, to be enabled to keep for any length of time, perhaps forever, within the walls of an asylum, the victims of their rapacious passions. And when thus incarcerated, how many varied interests will be at work to prevent their liberation!

"But we are arrived at Doctor Greedy's; let us go in. We shall very likely find many a subject that will interest us."

The doctor kindly bade us welcome, thanking us for visiting his establishment.

" It is somewhat removed," said he, " from the populated districts of the city. But you know, the health and welfare of our patients are of paramount importance. I suppose it did not escape your observation that the house is built upon a hill, and in an unrivaled locality as regards the beauty of the surrounding scenery. You will perceive there are fine, large gardens attached, with charming walks where our patients may ramble about and take healthful exercise. Such advantages can be procured only in an establishment removed from the city. These advantages and the profound quietness our patients enjoy in this beautiful solitude, are an absolute necessity for the improvement of their health."

Extensive as were the grounds, they were fenced in by a wooden wall, of such height as to prevent any one outside from seeing inside, and the inmates from escaping. Much order, method, and regularity were everywhere apparent. One might have readily fancied himself in a young ladies' boarding-school, but for the fact that, from time to time, a startling shriek reminded him he was in an insane asylum, and that some unfortunate creatures were confined in lonely cells for prudential reasons. But most of the inmates were in the full enjoyment of their freedom ; that is, within the limits of the establishment. They could be seen in the gardens, the parlors, and even in the kitchens. There were two separate buildings—one for the males—the other for the female patients ; and assuredly, if all other asylums in the United States are as well managed as this one, the American people are ahead, in this respect, of many European nations.

"Do not deceive yourself," said Asmodeus to me, when Doctor Greedy had left us, to receive new visitors ; "you are in one of the most fashionable establishments of the kind. Common patients are not received here ; one must pay, and that dearly, to be allowed a resident's privilege. Asylums kept by private individuals must be distinguished from those every State maintains for the wants of poor persons. You would certainly not find in the latter all the comforts you here perceive. But, at the same time, it must be admitted that individuals of sound mind are never confined in public mad-houses. The victims of error or violence would soon discover a means to gain their liberty, as neither the directors nor keepers have the slightest interest in confining them.

"It is not so with private enterprises. A French proverb says that a priest must fatten on the proceeds of the altar ; by the same rule, the proprietors of establishments for the insane must gain a living from their business. Of course, that business is not in a prosperous condition when many cells are unoccupied ; and for this reason it sometimes happens they are occupied by persons of sane minds."

At that moment, we were accosted by a well-dressed gentleman, of easy and courteous manners ; and, as we had occasion to notice, of refined education.

Until undeceived by Doctor Greedy, I took him for one of his patients happily recovered. He offered to escort us through the establishment, "whose every corner I know well," said he, "for I have been an inmate here for the past six months. But, thanks to the assiduous attentions of that excellent man, Dr. Greedy, I am now myself again, and my health is as good as it has ever been. I have heard," he went on to say, "that patients do not suffer when their mind gives way. It is a great error, gentlemen! I speak with a perfect knowledge of the case; for when I became mad, I experienced such sufferings, that I shudder at their very recollection. I was conscious my reason was gradually leaving me; and I could not hold it back. Anyhow, I expect to leave this house to-morrow; and my joy at being cured is not unmingled with regret, I assure you, gentlemen; for the patients are here the objects of really paternal care."

This obliging person then conducted us through the vast establishment of Doctor Greedy.

We saw, first, in the vegetable-garden, a number of patients, busily gardening.

"One of the means," observed our cicerone, " most successfully employed to calm an over-excited brain. The nearer to nature a man keeps himself, the better. On seeing the plants whose seeds they have sown, little by little sprouting forth, insane persons take interest in their work, and that interest sometimes becomes so powerful as to gradually drive from their mind the fancies by which it was disturbed, whether from ambition or love, disappointment or pecuniary reverses. Music, also, is a successful remedy, and the ancients were right when they elevated its inventor to the rank of a god. We have here many examples of infuriated patients to whom music's harmonious strains have restored calm and reason. But let us enter the concert-hall, and you will see."

We followed our guide into the concert-hall, where were assembled about one dozen performers. We were introduced to them with the accustomed formality, after which, at the request of Asmodeus, they performed the celebrated overture to *Robert the Devil*, and with such expression, such *brio*, that we heartily applauded. We thanked them for their kindness, when we were taken to see the library. It contained at least six thousand volumes. It is free to both the male and female inmates, some of whom, as we inferred from the voluminous books they consulted, seemed to be intensely absorbed in patient study and research. Others were reading reviews or works of light literature, and others, again, writing letters to their friends, and even articles for the press.

"You can not imagine," said our guide, "the number of very talented persons we have here. That lady, for instance, who is so tastefully dressed, whose beautiful ringlets, really her own, fall so abundantly over her well-shaped shoulders, is no other than Mrs. Blooming, who has written, under a well-known *nom de plume*, one of the most attractive novels of the day. She will remain here until an action, brought against her by her brothers, is terminated. You have doubtless heard that she inherited one hundred thousand dollars from her father, to the exclusion of those brothers. The latter are trying hard to have the will annulled, and whether they succeed or not, they have, in the mean time, succeeded in having their sister confined in this asylum, under pretense that she is insane."

"You may add to these details, which are perfectly correct," interrupted Asmodeus, "that the court, when it declined to give the brothers of Mrs. Blooming the administration of her fortune, stated that, were the author of so many charming works incarcerated in a mad asylum, her numberless readers should keep her company; and that, notwithstanding that opinion, her brothers have sufficient influence to prolong her captivity, and will keep her here until they have lost their lawsuit, without possibility of appeal, or until they are unable to pay Dr. Greedy's monthly bills."

"Those two lads," resumed our guide, "who are so busily examining engravings, became mad in consequence of over-working their brain. Their father, a man without judgment, though a teacher in one of our academies, wanted them to commit to memory Webster's unabridged dictionary. When they arrived at the second letter of the alphabet, their brains cracked.

"That lean personage, whose oval face reminds one of Francis I., has been one of the most successful financiers of New-York. He betrayed his best friend, who, to drown his grief because of his wife's infidelity, took to drink, and shortly after committed suicide. The financier, on the death of his friend—perhaps to lull his conscience—also conceived a fancy for spirituous liquors ; but, less fortunate than the betrayed husband, he did not find in the poisoned cup the death he sought, but madness only.

"The patient he is now speaking to was one of the wealthiest real-estate owners in the State of New-York. He, with the view of spreading abroad the belief that a certain locality was exposed to epizoöty, poisoned his neighbors' cattle. Discouraged and terrified, the farmers sold out for a mere song, and the cattle-poisoner purchased their lands. From that time the locality became surprisingly free from epizoöty, and real estate resumed its former value. This man had thus accumulated a large fortune, when one of his children unconsciously revealed the means resorted to by his father to become rich. Prosecuted by the farmers he had swindled, wearied with the countless lawsuits in which they involved him, his mind soon broke down.

"That bald man, wearing spectacles, and who is absorbed in reading an old book, is one of the best journalists of New-York, and one of the most distinguished publicists of the United States. Nobody can better treat of the rights of nations, and the secretary of the Federal States often avails himself of his profound views. Whenever he delays furnishing articles to the newspaper he is connected with, its proprietors are in distress; for they do not sell so many copies. The public is far from suspecting that one of the first journalists of the day resides in a mad-house; and, what is really singular, the mind of this man loses its brilliancy as soon as he leaves Dr. Greedy's establishment. His style becomes dull, his ideas are no longer profound and genuine; in short, he becomes driveling, and is quickly obliged to come back here, to strengthen and refresh his brain."

I smiled at these words; but Asmodeus seriously assured me nothing was more true, and that every body in New-York at all conversant with the literary world could confirm the statement of our cicerone, strange as it might appear.

" After all," he added, " there is more than one instance of this fact, in and out of the United States. It was in an insane asylum a European musician composed his most celebrated works; and because they are not written within the walls of a mad-house, the editorials of some European newspapers are not always conspicuous for common sense."

Next we visited the gaming-room, where several tables were occupied by whist players; while other patients were playing chess; and from the noise of colliding balls coming from an adjoining room, we inferred that some were playing billiards.

"Billiard-playing," said our guide, "is becoming more

and more appreciated by the inmates of the house. Some have acquired a wonderful degree of proficiency. Last month, a few Canadian and New-England professors accepted a challenge from three of our billiard-players; and they were beaten like children. But this is not the only triumph the annals of the house may boast of. It is notorious that one of the best chess-players in the United States is one of the inmates of this place; and you can see him, at this very moment, beating his adversary, who is no other than the president of the oldest chess-club of New-York.

" I will now show you the kitchens of the establishment; after which I shall be compelled to leave you; for I have to make preparations for my departure."

We were accordingly led to the basement, and saw many patients engaged in culinary occupations.

" One of the principal rules of the house," said our cicerone, " is to allow every patient to choose and follow the vocation most preferred—the directors only requiring them to keep always busy. In consequence, they select the kind of occupation for which they have been either trained or toward which they feel attracted by a natural taste. Here is applied the great theory of Fourier concerning callings or vocations. Every man, no matter how little he has studied the human organization, well knows that idleness, or, as the Italians say, *far niente,* is unwholesome and always deteriorating, even to the strongest minds. An active occupation, therefore, is the very first remedy intelligent physicians should apply to insane persons; and I am ready to prove, by statistics and figures, that a cure is certain, in seven cases out of ten, when the patient's mind is kept active. The more we advance in the path of civilization, the more will men appreciate manual labor, and all prejudices against it must die away. Work performed by hand is as noble as intellectual labor ; and as regards the United States, the gradual and steady increase of wages is highly satisfactory. It is a favorable sign of the times ; for, in the estimation of most men, high wages contribute to elevate manual labor, as well as all grades of mankind.

" It seems to me that every patient, on entering this house, should leave all pride at its threshold ; for alas ! if absolute equality exists anywhere, it is in death ! And madness is nothing but the death of the intellect, the chief power of man. But the directors of this asylum have encountered many difficulties in getting patients to attend in the culinary department. Many objected, because it requires manual labor ; and it was found necessary to demonstrate to them the great part the culinary art has played in the history of civilization. The French system of cooking, for instance, has been praised and practiced in all countries of the world. Well, when they set to work in earnest, the inmates here performed wonders, and speedily improved upon the American art of cooking.

" A few years ago, any American who had traveled abroad was ashamed to compare the fare of our hotels with that of European restaurants, and the courses or meals in private families with those of the Old World. But to-day American cookery may bear comparison with that of any country. The Puritan receipts for preparing victuals for the table, brought over by the followers of Cromwell, are justly discarded. Dishes as delicate as those prepared in Europe are now daily served up on our tables ; and I doubt not we eat many better things than are to be found on the other side of the Atlantic, because there is abundance here of fruits, vegetables, game, and fish. I have always suspected that France is indebted for her fine cookery to her reputation of being the most polite nation on earth. But we will beat her on that very ground ; for you have only to partake of one of our dinners, to be agreeably astonished at the luxury, variety, profuseness, and perfection of its courses ; and you will realize how much a good repast softens the heart and exercises a wholesome influence over the brain."

After this peroration our guide politely took leave of us, and, at the same instant, Dr. Greedy again made his appearance.

" Accept my congratulations, doctor," said I, " for so complete a cure as I see wrought in the gentleman who has just left us. It would have been, indeed, a great loss for society to be forever deprived of a man in the full strength of his years and gifted with such intelligence !"

At these words, the doctor and Asmodeus could not refrain from laughing.

" That ' man in the full strength of his years and gifted with such intelligence,' " said the former, " and who has been so kind as to show you through this establishment, is an inveterate fool ! Twenty times I thought him radically cured, and as many times have delivered him over to his family's care. Hardly out of this house, he indulged in such follies that it was found necessary to speedily restore him to his cell. The worship of gold, that deadly passion of our age, has upset his mind. He has speculated considerably in real estate, and lost his wealth, and finally his reason. When he has his freedom, he believes himself to be the owner of all New-York ; and while laboring under that delusion, he commits the most unheard-of and ridiculous enormities. The last time we opened to him the doors of this asylum, he availed himself of his liberty to send an injunction to the three or four hundred hotel-owners or keepers in

New-York, to leave their premises with their guests within twenty-four hours ; and that freak cost his family, for revenue-stamps alone, three thousand dollars. At the same time, he had sent an order to Rio de Janeiro for two thousand monkeys ; probably intending to put those strange creatures as guests in the vacated hotels. When the cargo of monkeys arrived, the Federal administration was in doubt whether to permit the landing of such a nuisance. But finally, the monkeys were landed, were soon sold at auction, and as a few hundred Italian organ-grinders had also just arrived, this commercial venture unexpectedly turned out better than anticipated. But sad to say, that amiable man, who, in your opinion, enjoys his reason, has but a few weeks to live. This morning I perceived a few silvery streaks amid his black hair. It is a bad sign— generally the forerunner of death."

" But what is insanity, doctor ?" inquired Asmodeus.

" Ah ! sir, you know as much on that subject as myself," answered the doctor, " though you are not a professor in a medical college. I once wrote a book on madness, and, as a reward for my researches and observations, I was appointed professor of pathology. At the same time, the French Scientific Academy elected me as one of its corresponding members. Well, between you and me, with all my studies, I confess I do not know what cause determines madness, the locality of the disease, and, least of all, the remedy for it. I have dissected more than five hundred bodies of madmen ; and I did not find in two of them similar signs of internal perturbation ; even when the external symptoms of the disease—that is, the objects of the patients' infatuation—had been identical. What do you think of science, after that ? "

" This is candor, doctor," replied Asmodeus ; " but tell

me, what do you intend to do with that interesting creature, Blanche Rivingston, who was brought back this morning to your house ?"

"To keep her, forsooth ! What good use could she make of her liberty ? She escaped from here, one week ago, to meet again the man who had ruined her, and who had succeeded in discovering her retreat. Fortunately, we traced and recaught her, and shall henceforth watch her more closely. You can see her, if you desire ; she is in the infirmary. Until she is entirely deprived of her reason, she plays the part that suits her—that of a sister of charity."

We here took leave of Dr. Greedy ; and while sauntering along, Asmodeus made sundry weighty observations.

"Good and benevolent as a man may be," said he, "that law is wrong which clothes him with an absolute power over his fellow-creatures — a power angels themselves would hardly fail to abuse. The oily and affable manner in which madhouse proprietors receive visitors is changed into brutal indifference toward those patients who endeavor either to recover their liberty or are rebellious to the house regulations. Their power over those within their control is unbounded, and ever kept alive and active, on account of their covetousness. Nothing is easier for them than to prevent a patient, either really insane or simply affected with a nervous disease, from communicating with his relatives and friends, or strangers. Their power to recapture, everywhere, escaped patients—to demand, in case of need, the aid of the police, is absolutely dreadful, and necessarily tends to many abuses. For instance, any citizen on the strength of a simple certificate from the proprietor of the establishment we have just visited, may be arrested, and the protection of the law will be denied him

under the pretense that he is mad. And what is fearful
to think of is this—the less insane a person is, the smaller
are his chances to escape from a lunatic asylum ; because
he is the object of more interested and attentive watchfulness. Crimes without number have thus been, and are
still committed, in a country which boasts of her kind and
tolerant habits.

" An evil-doer, sentenced to a term of imprisonment,
knows when his captivity must end ; while a citizen, abducted into an insane asylum, has not even the consolation
of knowing when his incarceration will cease. Undoubtedly,
all private establishments of that kind need strict watching ;
it is imperatively demanded by the most important considerations. Officers delegated by the State governments,
and committees from benevolent institutions, should frequently visit them, kindly interrogate all patients, and
observe whether their mental condition is such as to justify
their confinement. But, above all, a certificate, no matter
whether signed by one or two physicians, should be insufficient to authorize a family to confine in an asylum one of
its obnoxious members. Why, the intervention of a jury
should be necessary in every case where individual liberty
is threatened in consequence of an alleged derangement
of the mental organs. Bastiles, distinguished under the
name of villas, are none the less Bastiles ; and the certificate of a doctor, whose honesty may have been overpowered or conscience bribed, serves, oftener than the
public imagines, under the democratic institutions of this
country, as fearful ends as once did orders under a king's
signet."

It was now evening, and the election was over. At sunset, all the bar-rooms in the city had been thrown open ;
and the sovereigns rushing into them, and their outbursts

of happiness, was a sight worth witnessing. One would have thought they had not quenched their thirst for a fortnight past; and I easily believed the consumption of liquors is greater, on election-day, than at any other time of the year, though liquor saloons are opened in the evening only.

We went to the club where congregates one of the oldest political societies in the United States.

The right to hold public meetings, Asmodeus informed me, is recognized by the constitution, without limitation or reserve. The citizens meet where, when, and in such numbers as they choose, for political, religious, literary, or benevolent purposes; and the government has no power to intervene. There are clubs, or political associations, everywhere, in the smallest localities as in large cities. It even sometimes happens that two clubs or associations, re-representing different political opinions, hold simultaneously their sittings in the same building; and such is the respect for the right of meeting, that disturbances seldom happen.

When we entered, the club-room was crowded with members, anxiously waiting for the result of the ballot; as the operation of counting the votes was going on in every district. Messengers were arriving at every moment, reporting the progress of the operation and the prospect of the election. Suddenly, one of them entered, panting and in great heat, shouting, "Victory!" He had no time to say more; enthusiastic hurrahs shook the hall; and when that tumultuous demonstration had subsided, one member, then two, five, twenty ascended the platform. All began speaking at the same time, and every one was anxious to be heard. For if there is a people ever ready to discourse on any and every topic, as Asmodeus previously observed, it is the American. The president of the meeting, by dint of much hammering, succeeded in restoring order ; and he availed himself of it to make a speech.

"The American people," said he, with majestic emphasis, his eyes flashing with pride, "the greatest on the face of the earth ; the great demonstrators of universal democracy ; the standard-bearers of civilization ; the sovereigns of a land toward which oppressed nations turn their longing eyes ; have shown themselves to-day in all their wonted power! They have spoken in thunder-tones ; and the vandals who now possess the capital of the nation, the evil-doers who have crept into public offices, the villains and traitors who have disgraced the American name, will soon disappear from public view, never to rise again. The electors are the nation, and the men chosen are the depositaries of its will and power, without appeal. We are, emphatically, the most intelligent people in the world! Our institutions are models of perfection, the greatest work of the mind of man since the organization of society! Our populations, educated in free schools, and thus enabled to exercise, in a satisfactory manner, their political rights, exhibit a power of judgment and understanding which commands the admiration of every impartial observer. Heaven smiles upon us, and ostensibly favors our national development. As a proof of it, we enjoy an unbounded material prosperity, such as could not be prevented even by the infamous party which the popular verdict has just consigned to its grave."

The speaker was interrupted in his dithyrambic peroration by a messenger, bringing in an almost complete report concerning the results of the election. Amid the shouts, clapping of hands, and stamping of feet of the

members, the officers of the club examined this report;
and it soon became apparent, from their dejected looks
and angry exclamations, that the news they had to impart
to their political brethren was far from being satisfactory.
The president hardly needed to ask the members to keep
quiet; the result of the election had been guessed by
those of them sitting near his desk; and through these,
every one in the hall soon became aware that most of the
club's candidates had failed to obtain a majority of votes.
The members were overwhelmed with disappointment and
consternation.   At last, the president rose and said:

"Friends and fellow-citizens: I feel sick at heart; for
this day is an ill-omened one in the history of the republic!   Our hymns and shouts of rejoicing must be changed
into lamentations!   Corruption has won the day!   We
have been beaten in almost every district!   Fabulous
sums of money have been spent by our opponents to bribe
voters and to pervert the expression of the national will.
But the intriguers, the unworthy men who have just been
elected, know too well how to get back all this outlay of
money from the pockets of tax payers. . . . We must have
the manliness to confess it—we blow, we brag too much.
We are a degenerate people, unworthy to live under democratic institutions, as we do not know how to turn them to
good account.   Behold our present situation!   We have
lost all *prestige* abroad; we have become the laughing-
stock of foreigners, since the principal offices in the gift
of the people are held by our political opponents.   The
misery of our country is fearful to contemplate; for we are
crushed by enormous taxes, while the general commerce
and industry of the land are paralyzed by revenue laws,
voted for the profit of the few to the detriment of the
many.   The judiciary is degraded, the officers of the law

making it subservient to their personal aggrandizement; and, to complete this fearful state of things, the crops have failed, and want threatens the nation; for Heaven has, in disgust, withdrawn its protection from a stupid country that knows not how to protect itself!"

After this mournful strain, the president left the platform, visibly depressed and almost moved to tears. Many other speakers addressed the assembly, every one making still darker the sad picture which had been wrought of the nation, uniformly winding up their harangues by violent threats against the Federal government, the State governor—in short, all the public functionaries who had just obtained the majority of votes. One would have thought that terrible events were in store for the Republic—that the country was on the eve of a revolution. But Asmodeus assured me all these noisy demonstrations had no importance whatever.

"In fact," said he, "they are windy, empty words, 'full of sound and fury, signifying nothing.' To-morrow no trace will remain of this tumultuous ebullition of party rancor; and all these now exasperated men, like sensible persons, will quietly accept the result of the election. For, above all controversies and wranglings, there is a common ground for all parties—it is the universal assent to the majority's verdict. Silence will reign in this hall until the next election."

We were just on the point of withdrawing when the street resounded with shouts, and soon after we saw entering, nearly carried in the arms of their friends, the proprietor of the gambling-house where we had spent the evening before, and the elegant personage Asmodeus had described as the promoter of the many lotteries which are in operation throughout the States in spite of law. Both of these individuals announced, with cheerful and serene countenances, that they had been, unquestionably, elected representatives of the people, agreeably to the notice they had previously sent through a messenger—the same who was not allowed, because of the enthusiasm of the members of the club, to explain his errand. The newly-elected representatives were then surrounded by the members, who had become intoxicated with joy. Hurrah after hurrah reverberated through the hall, and an incredible scene of confusion ensued. All began speaking at the same time, giving extraordinary proportions to an accidental triumph of their party. They whistled, they sang, they embraced each other; and a few even performed an Irish jig—as the victory of the candidates was chiefly due to the votes of the Irish population. The excitement was at its height, when messengers brought in the news that most of the districts had elected for judges candidates of the club.

"Now," exclaimed an enthusiastic member, "they can make as many laws as they please in Congress or elsewhere! I do not care a dime about it, as the courts will finally have to determine all obscure points of law; and when those laws do not suit us, our judges will discover many flaws in them, such as to render their application next to impossible."

"That Macchiavelli," said Asmodeus, leading me out of the hall, "has just developed, in a few words, the history of many laws in the United States. The wisest legisla tion remains a dead letter, when the feelings, prejudices, or interests of the people are opposed to it. Judges, for fear of its resentment, obey the dictates of the populace. Their reëlection is the reward of their servility."

CHAPTER XV.

"THERE is," said Asmodeus, when I saw him again the next day, "a camp-meeting a short distance from New-York. Let us visit it. We were deep in politics yesterday; and to-day I want to breathe the pure air of the country."

On our way to the ferry-boat which carries passengers over the beautiful river that washes the shores of New-York, we saw a large market, where produce from all parts of the world was piled up and scattered about promiscuously. Wagons, loaded with oranges, lemons, bananas, pine-apples, and cocoa-nuts, lined several streets, and obstructed the way of passengers. Policemen were busy making a passage for persons going to or from the market. Fruits and vegetables of every description were heaped up on the side-walks; while barrels of salt-fish and meat crowded a number of stores.

"The Americans," said Asmodeus, "are really a people of Gargantuas. See yonder ships at anchor; they bring to this great metropolis produce from the remotest parts of the Union, and also from the West-Indies and Europe. I see around us breadstuffs and provisions in sufficient quantity to supply, for several months, the standing armies of the Old World.   The markets of London and Paris can hardly give an idea of the abundance to be found here. Look at those tables loaded with dishes of every description, and at which workingmen are seated.   In what other country can people afford to supply themselves with such abundance ?   Many of those laborers have eaten, I doubt not, three meals since the dawn of day.   Large consumers as they are, it is fortunate for the Americans that they live in a country whose fertility is without a rival.   But for that special favor of Providence, they would often be in extreme want."

While crossing the Hudson, we saw, either arriving or at anchor, steamers and sailing-vessels loaded with immigrants.

"Here," exclaimed Asmodeus, pointing them out, "here is America's strength !   Here is the most important source of her prosperity.   Immigration is constantly infusing a new life into the veins of the American people, thus keeping up their surprising vitality.   What would the United States be to-day, but for immigrants?   They have populated many a Western State; built splendid cities; constructed railroads; dug canals; and, but for them, the American Union would be a small nation, instead of one of the first powers on earth, by its numbers and wealth. Statisticians have, time and again, demonstrated that the population of the United States, had it followed the laws of natural increase, would be twelve millions to-day, including four millions of blacks.   Thanks to the influx of Europeans, since the beginning of this century, it exceeds thirty-six millions, and will amount, perhaps, to one hundred millions before its close.

"It is, therefore, an indisputable fact that the population of America is, two thirds of it, composed of immigrants and their children.   From 1850 to 1860, five millions of

Europeans, mostly Irish and Germans, have settled in the United States, a number superior to the whole population of the Republic when she assumed her rank among other nations.

"The United States offer to-day a great and wonderful spectacle—one highly suggestive as regards the destinies of mankind. A population of over thirty-six millions exists in conditions of perfect equality, is devoted to the same laws and institutions, in spite of its different origins and habits, even the hostility of its traditions.

" America is a meeting-ground for all nationalities, and, at the same time, it is their grave. Though every people finds here its own language, faith, festivities, national costume, even its flags, all these diversities disappear in a powerful unity ; and, instead of a chaotic nationality, one observes with astonishment a nation of freemen, whose hearts beat with the same impulse from the Atlantic to the Pacific ocean ; whose love of progress and the well-being of mankind is the same everywhere ; whose devotion to liberty is as intense on the borders of Canada as on the summit of the Rocky Mountains ; and the marvelous amalgamating process of the different elements which compose the population is carried on with a no less marvelous rapidity.

"After settling a few years in the United States, foreigners become proud of their adopted country, though retaining a pious remembrance of the land of their ancestors. Even after they have realized all their golden dreams, and become rich, they seldom think of going back to the Old World. Those who try the experiment are not slow to return to the United States. They become disgusted with the prejudices and narrow ideas of Europe, and hasten to breathe again the bracing air of a continent, providentially discovered by Columbus, it seems, to become the home of a race of men sprung from all races, and establishing a society on an entirely new basis—on principles which are like a pole-star to the oppressed nations of the Old World!

" That freedom, enjoyed by the people and protected by institutions which the masses respect as they do their religion, looked upon with admiration and envy by the population of Europe, is, no doubt, the magnet that attracts, every year, hundreds of thousands of immigrants to these shores. And poor persons are not the only ones who emigrate to America: many wealthy farmers leave Europe to settle among us. It has been ascertained that every immigrant on landing is, on an average, possessed of one hundred dollars; and you may figure up the yearly increase to our metallic circulation from three hundred thousand immigrants.

" Among the foreigners daily arriving in the United States there are some, no doubt, of depraved habits. But their number is insignificant, not worth speaking of, compared with the large number of honest farmers and sturdy operatives who come here to better their condition. May we not think, besides, that many of the former class have left Europe with the hope and desire of reforming themselves, and working out their regeneration on American soil?

" It is an undoubted fact that foreigners on landing here feel regenerated and possessed of a new strength. The European immigrant shakes off the old man, as it were, and throws aside the many prejudices with which his mind was imbued. Like all Americans, he will not bear control. On the other side of the Atlantic, despotic governments play with submissive populations the part attributed by poets to God—'*Deus ex machina.*' And whether in want or in prosperity, those populations look to their rulers as a guiding star, a second Providence. Nothing of this kind is to be seen here; and any help or protection, if proffered or imposed by the government, would be scornfully rejected. The masses consider every government as a necessary evil; and therefore the less of it the better."

I listened to Asmodeus with the attention his keenness of insight and observations concerning the United States had provoked. He continued as follows:

"The American Republic could not escape the organic law of great nationalities. History teaches us it is through long sufferings and mighty convulsions they achieve their unity and conquer their power. Civil war is their touchstone—the ordeal they have to undergo in order to get rid of the heterogeneous elements which impeded their advance toward a higher state of civilization.

"America was but yesterday a confederacy of small sovereignties, slightly bound to each other; but sectional antagonism and the feudal theory of State sovereignty have expired in the blood of a million of men. The rapid communications established by railroads and electricity; the daily and multitudinous relations of commerce; the equality of races; the uniformity of political laws and free labor everywhere, will maintain, after having hastened it, the great work of assimilating the many elements of this great republic. All differences which formerly existed between the Northern and Southern States, between the mighty West and the Middle and New-England States, have melted away beneath the fires of one hundred battles; after fusing in a bloody crucible, pure metal has freed itself from the *scoria.*

"The immigrant," concluded Asmodeus, at the moment the ferry-boat reached her wharf, "chooses the profession or trade he feels inclined to, and applies to it his faculties without restraint from any suspicious law. He soon perceives that fortune will reward his energy; his mind enlarges, for he does not feel that crushing anxiety for his daily bread which paralyzes millions of men in Europe; he knows he can not be deprived, in case of reverses, of the fruits of his labor—the law granting him the exclusive use of property to the amount of five hundred dollars in some States, and even one thousand and over in others. Such property is not liable to be seized or taken by virtue of any execution or civil process whatever; and that melancholy sight, so frequent in Europe, a sale of furniture at auction by order of the sheriff, is a very rare one in the United States."

We took the railway-cars to reach the camp-meeting, which, as we learned, was pitched a few miles off. During the journey I noticed the deference paid to females from male travelers—the latter offering their seats without being asked, and often receiving no thanks for their politeness. They were thus obliged to stand up in spacious cars, which, unlike those of Europe, are not divided into separate compartments. As no distinction is recognized in America, they are free to every body; and, as a matter of course, there is a uniform rate of fare. Travelers take the seats they prefer, and are at liberty to go from car to car at pleasure. I also observed that parents are very fond of their children—strangers, likewise, take kindly to the little ones, humoring and playing with them.

Children are, obviously, more precocious here than in Europe. There is more freedom in their demeanor; and young girls, also, are conscious they live in a free country; they are never seen with downcast eyes, nun fashion, like the young ladies of good breeding in Europe.

As I was admiring the rosy cheeks and blooming complexion of most of the female travelers, Asmodeus laughed at my *naïveté*.

"Many of those pretty women," said he, "are experts in the same artifices to which, according to some morose historians, Roman ladies, during the imperial era, devoted six hours of every day. Though American ladies do not employ all the oriental perfumes used at that time, they know well how to soften the roughness of their skin—to give it the fashionable healthy hue and stylish touch. They rouge their faces and dye their hair; and were the atmosphere cruel enough to rise above temperate heat, you would see a queer intermingling of blue, white, and red pigment on more than one of those charming faces.

"The men are generally tall and lean, and seem to have borrowed their self-possessed manners from the English people. The ladies, whether rouged or not, are pretty and graceful. They are less plump and fleshy than their English cousins, and their demeanor is free from that stiffness peculiar to the Anglo-Saxon race. Dressing, with them, is a passion; and whether at home or traveling, they are always tastefully appareled."

As I had before remarked their blooming complexion, I now noticed the regularity and whiteness of their teeth. But here again Asmodeus unmercifully dampened my admiration.

"In no country of the world," said he, "are dentists more actively employed in their art than in the United States, and, in general, they are very skillful. I do not doubt that many of the ladies around us have borrowed their ivory. It is not unfrequently the case for a husband to present his wife with a set of artificial teeth for her Christmas gift. But joking is perhaps out of place here," he added thoughtfully; "indignation, and pity for future generations, should be more proper feelings. What sort of mothers will those young girls make, trained, as they doubtless are, only in the wily art of beautifying themselves? Their teeth, hair, eyebrows, complexion, and very shape are a deception and a snare. Every thing is intimately connected in human nature, and the external appearance bespeaks the inner thoughts and feelings. One can hardly believe that those pretty dolls, who resort to all conceivable subterfuges to captivate the admiration of men, will prove honest wives, dutiful and devoted mothers!

"You have noticed the deference with which men treat the fair sex; but you failed, perhaps, to remark that ladies bow first to gentlemen. It is a consequence of the general circumspection of the people. Should gentlemen venture to give first some external sign of acquaintance with a lady, annoying consequences might result. But ladies thus permitting a recognition, the inference is, they apprehend no danger from the acknowledgment.

"Americans have been reproached for exaggerated deference toward the fair sex; but there is nothing in it, at all events, that savors of the fearful corruption which, in Europe, poisons social intercourse. Here the courtesy and attentions of men are disinterested. That young man, for instance, who has just picked up a nosegay, will not try to converse with its owner, on returning it. He sets no value on a politeness which, in his opinion, is a matter of course. Women are positively worshiped in America. In many States, the law grants a wife the right to own property in her own name, and such property is exempt from marital control. You often hear men candidly admit that American ladies, intellectually speaking, are their superiors; which may be true, after all, as a girl's education is more complete than that of a boy—the latter early leaving school for the counting-house or farm. And, as a consequence of this superiority, the influence of American ladies over their husbands is all-powerful. It may often excite and keep up man's energy, but it is not less often, perhaps, the instrument of his ruin."

Judging from the external appearance of all the persons we saw, one would think that every body in the United States is in affluent circumstances. The absence of all social distinction stamps every thing—the dress, as well as the manners of the people. Mingling with millionaires and traveling in the same conveyances, the workingman wants to be decently dressed, and does not fail to be so.

"His work over," said Asmodeus, "the operative dons an unexceptionable suit of clothes, purchased, like those of many wealthy men, at a ready-made clothing store ; associates with lawyers, merchants, and ministers of the Gospel, and does not disgrace the company. Speaking of workingmen, reminds me of an observation we heard yesterday, at Dr. Greedy's, concerning manual labor and wages, and which, though emanating from a madman, exhibits a remarkable degree of acuteness and perceptive power. The average of wages, to-day, in the United States, is three dollars per diem, and the salary of servants is ten dollars per month—at least in large cities. Well, there is now so frequent an intercourse between nations, so interwoven are their relations, that wages will inevitably increase in Europe in a corresponding ratio with those of the United States. The emancipation of the popular classes consists, in reality, in a just remuneration of labor and high wages. Democratic institutions create equality in politics ; but they contribute to establish it also in social conditions. Slowly but infallibly, capital's

influence and prestige are fast disappearing in America.
It will soon become, if not subservient to labor, at most
but its equal. Workingmen deal on a footing of perfect
equality with the capitalist, who needs their labor ; and
the relations between operatives and manufacturers, servants and employers—in short, between capital and labor,
are fast bringing about a revolution whose example will
undermine the social structure of Europe. It will uproot
traditions bequeathed by barbarian ages, and transform
for the better the miserable condition of the producers—
that is, of the most numerous and interesting class in both
hemispheres."

All along the road, frame houses and cottages were
to be seen, all neatly painted, and many quite elegant
structures.

"There dwell our farmers, market-gardeners, and arti-
sans," said Asmodeus. "The American likes comfort, and
furnishes his house with proper tastefulness, because he
is conscious of his importance in the State. Sovereigns
can not live in shanties. If you enter one of those small
but clean houses, you will find every room carpeted. You
will be introduced into a well-furnished parlor—a recep-
tion-room being of paramount importance in all American
families ; you will see in it a piano—a piece of furniture
every father must provide his daughters, if he wishes a
peaceful life with them. In the far West, in those solitudes and boundless prairies but yesterday the home of the
red men, the sound of a piano is not unfrequently heard ;
and, as a consequence of the increasing demand for that
musical instrument, piano-making is an industry second to
none in the States. It is true, all, with few exceptions, are
made after the same pattern, and by steam process, but
they are none the worse for that, nor of less durability."

I had perceived the word "Academy" several times, and at different places, in the villages we were traversing, and it quite puzzled me.

"The Americans," said Asmodeus, "like to magnify trifles and apply grandiloquent words to small things. The word village is seldom employed in the United States— every town is a city, and the smallest hamlet a town; a rivulet is a river; a pedagogue who teaches grammar to little girls and boys calls his school an academy; and even the barber sometimes gives that name to his shop. You can now understand how so many signs delight in ambitious expressions."

We had now arrived at a railway station, a short distance from which was a camp-meeting—that is, an assemblage of members of a religious sect, who, during the summer months, camp far from cities, in a secluded spot, and devote themselves to religious exercises. Camp-meetings, I was informed, originated in the far West, where pioneers, too busy with the work of clearing up, had no time to build churches, and therefore congregated to worship God under the canopy of heaven. That we were visiting was pitched on a hill, in a mountainous district enjoying a bracing atmosphere. About two thousand persons of the Methodist persuasion had accompanied their pastor there, and, a few days after, an equal number of Baptists had joined them. The two sects agreed very well together; every thing was conducted harmoniously, the hours for religious exercises having been arranged to the mutual convenience of both denominations. Elegant tents had been pitched on the hill, and disposed in such a manner as to form several pathways. Each of these tents was provided with a carpet, and ornamented with wreaths of flowers and foliage. In the centre of this canvas town, a tent of very large size had been erected, where preaching and praying were to be carried on ; and further, on a plot of ground had been appropriated for the diversions of the faithful after religious exercises had been completed. The campites were just betaking themselves to that plot when we arrived, and the air soon became enlivened by the soft strains of a band engaged for the occasion. Both Methodists and Baptists, with hundreds of friends and relatives of both sexes visiting the camp, indulged in Terpsichorean exercises ; and three hundred young men and as many young ladies enjoyed the dance with an enthusiasm the band did its best to keep alive. I remarked that the waltz and polka were favorite dances ; and Asmodeus ventured to predict, on seeing lovely girls voluptuously leaning on their partners' shoulders, that more than one among them would, for several months, dream of that delightful entertainment.

At intervals, and when dancing was suspended, gentlemen availed themselves of the interruption to take ladies to saloons and restaurants, where ice-cream and other refreshments could be procured. There were about half a dozen of those establishments, well patronized by all concerned. Wines and liquors could not, at least ostensibly, be procured at any price.

"Good diversions are wanting in the United States," said Asmodeus, "and so the Americans seize every opportunity and resort to every means to amuse themselves. Camp-meetings are but a pretext, for many of them, to devote a few weeks to the pleasures and relaxations of country life during the summer months. They pray in the morning, listen to a couple of sermons in the course of the day, and wind up with an evening prayer. But, in the mean time, when praying and preaching are over, they make excursions through the mountains ; visit some natural curiosity; form singing bands, or amuse themselves with dancing. These meetings also furnish occasion for young men to meet pretty girls, with whom they fall in love: and it so happens that many weddings take place after every camp-meeting."

Though very animated, the dancing was remarkable for its decorum. I could observe among the dancers no disorderly conduct, no exaggerated gesture, no Terpsichorean audacity, such as often give to a country ball in Europe the appearance of a riotous assemblage of demented persons. A young American dancing with a girl he perhaps intends to marry treats her with becoming respect.

" And nights," I asked Asmodeus, " how are they spent ?"

"Very quietly, indeed. Wearied with the varied labor and amusements of the day, the campites sleep soundly ; and I may add, to be more explicit, ladies retire to rest in tents separated from those of the other sex. Their fathers and brothers constantly patrol the grounds and watch over the objects of their love. Husbands themselves, as long as the meeting lasts, are excluded from the tents occupied by their wives. The slightest outrage to decency would be severely punished ; but it is very seldom, indeed, that religious festivals are disturbed by scandal."

But dancing had now ended ; and the Methodists, at the sound of a bell, congregated under the large tent in the centre of the camp-ground. A great preacher had come from New-York, and a masterpiece of oratory was confidently expected. Young ladies laid aside their wreaths of flowers, and, accompanied by their partners and parents, repaired to the spot consecrated to prayer. We did like the others, and arrived at the moment when the air resounded with a hymn of rejoicing. Male and female, old and young, sang together ; and though the ear was, from time to time, offended by a discordant note, the whole was not lacking in enthusiasm and grandeur. Praying in the open air is always more impressive than in the narrow precincts of a church.

At last, the Methodist preacher ascended the platform erected for the occasion. He commenced by reviewing the history of Methodism in the United States since 1766, when a few emigrants, after adopting the doctrines of the founders of that sect—the brothers Wesley—formed a religious society, which congregated in the shop of a carpenter—Philip Embury. That shop was situated in Barrack street, near the present New-York City Hall. He then enjoined his hearers to do good of every kind, and, as far as possible, to all men, but especially to those of their own faith. All at once, he began to denounce, in fervid tones, the oppressors of mankind, the holders in slavery of their fellow-creatures ; and he proposed to open a subscription among the campites, to supply the oppressed with weapons, adding that he would himself head the list of subscribers for so holy a purpose, and give five hundred dollars for the purchase of rifles. After this unexpected explosion of Christian charity, he spoke of one living and true God, everlasting, without body or part, of infinite power, wisdom, and goodness, the Maker of all things visible and invisible ; of the Son of God, very man and very God, who truly suffered, was crucified, died, and was buried, to reconcile his Father to earth, and to be a sacrifice, not only for original guilt, but also for all the sins of men. He warmed up so much with his subject, that the congregation was soon deeply affected. Old women moaned and sobbed ; young ladies, when the minister terminated his sermon, reeled to and fro, and shrieked ; and some, after staggering awhile, fell to the ground as in a fit ; while others, violently beating themselves, and pulling their hair, raved like insane persons. A few, amid sobs, accused themselves of imaginary offenses against chastity; and others, again, under the influence of spiritual light, said they were penetrated by the Spirit of God, and were even then beholding him. One of the members of the church very properly took upon himself to sing a hymn; others joined him, and though the enraptured meeting discarded all method, their strains had the effect to end a somewhat painful scene.

We thought the services had concluded, and were on the point of leaving the tent, when an emaciated personage ascended the platform the former powerful Methodist preacher had just left. Silence was at once restored among the audience on seeing the new speaker, a well-known advocate of temperance. After reminding the Methodists that the only condition of membership was a desire to flee the wrath to come and be saved from sin, he said that when the brothers Wesley originated their society, they drew up a set of rules inspired by divine wisdom. They prohibited profane swearing, Sabbath-breaking, quarreling, fighting, brother going to law with brother, the using many words in buying or selling, wearing of gold or costly apparel, borrowing without the probability of returning, or buying goods without the certainty of paying for them. He then arrived at the most important of the rules—that which prohibits drunkenness, buying or selling spirituous liquors, or drinking them, and gave an awful picture of the results of intemperate habits, and of the crimes and miseries they entail upon society. He next expatiated on the manifold and beneficent results of his labors, and congratulated himself on the holy mission to which he had devoted his energy, his health, his very life. At that point, he quite unexpectedly rambled about the method to avert the use and abuse of spirituous liquors—saying that the latter only was pernicious, and, quaintly enough, commending brandy. "The peculiar aroma and taste of wine-brandy," he said, "make it really a delicious drink. Holy men only, in the laboratory of their silent cloisters, could discover the means to distill it from the juice of the grape ; and its qualities really afford, in many cases, instant relief to patients. I myself derive much benefit from its use—not its abuse, mind you—and through it I am enabled to sustain my enfeebled system, and pursue my holy work !"

So saying, this temperance advocate, thoroughly overcome, sank down upon the platform ; and the congregation, struck with admiration for a man thus devoting his health and very life to the propagation of temperance principles, arose and departed in various directions.

"I am often inclined to think," said Asmodeus, while we were sauntering along, that there is much hypocrisy in the American character. For instance, that temperance advocate is an inveterate drunkard ; but, like many others, he cloaks his love for alcoholic drinks under the pretense of ill-health. He candidly believes, perhaps, after repeating it so often, that they recuperate his system, while they are, in reality, the cause of his declining health. You meet many Americans who drink only water when away from home—boasting, at every opportunity, of their soberness. Their family does not even know they are addicted to the vice of drinking. Still, you can discern on their faces, every morning, the havoc which strong liquors are making, as they have undoubtedly spent a portion of the night in imbibing ; for indeed, there is in a secret corner of their house a stock of favorite liquors.

"Neither is there any doubt that outward demonstrations of religious zeal are often resorted to by many Americans for mere show, to make an impression upon the world. A member of a religious denomination has more chances to enjoy good credit than an infidel—a name sometimes applied here to those who do not externally practice any religion. And not a few merchants occupy at their church, every Sunday, the pew near that of the president of their bank, with the expectation to find the latter more accommodating the next day, when they present their notes at the discounting-desk.

"I candidly admit, however, that religious feeling is deeply rooted in the American mind ; and it is to a great majority, principally among country people, a bulwark against dishonest temptations and corrupting influences. Since the establishment of the Republic, religion has been, in the United States, a most remarkable feature of the national character, and its spirit has penetrated political as well as civil institutions. There is no national church, and the union of any church with the state was so much dreaded by the framers of the Constitution that they prohibited Congress from enacting any law respecting religious matters. Every creed is, therefore, perfectly free ; and with this freedom of conscience, all sects, all forms of worshiping God, have been established. The want of state interference in religious matters can not be considered as a symptom of indifference or lukewarmness ; for, on the contrary, statistics demonstrate, that in no part of the world is so large a portion of the people devoted to the worship of God. Nowhere are churches, too, so numerous, considering the number of inhabitants ; and in no other place are ministers of the Gospel so liberally compensated, though their salaries are derived from voluntary contributions.

"Though no religious sect is specially acknowledged and favored by the state, the Christian religion is considered, either by State legislation or by court decisions, as a part of the common law. Hence, the enforcing of a proper observance of the Sabbath, in most of the States, though it is in contradiction to the religious freedom recommended by the framers of the Constitution.

"Perhaps intolerance is a latent disease with Americans by birth of the Protestant faith. At least, to many of them there is no salvation outside the Methodist and Baptist churches. Religious truth can only be found there, and to seek for it elsewhere is equivalent, in their opinion, to an act of treason against the American cause and American interests. It may be doubted whether any creed would be tolerated whose principles were not derived from the Bible. Even those sects whose religions are based on that book, outside of the four great Protestant denominations—the Methodists, Episcopalians, Baptists, and Presbyterians—think it wise to remain quiet, for fear of exciting envy and suspicion. Roman Catholics, for many years, have also thought it prudent to keep in the back-ground, not unmindful that Americans of the Protestant faith intensely dislike them. Only a few years ago, the Republic barely escaped the scourge of a violent and practical intolerance. But for several millions of Catholic immigrants, persecution, perhaps, would have emanated from the masses, and not from the government, as in Europe, two centuries ago. Fortunately, all animosities soon subsided, and as things are at present, one can not help admiring the unprecedented spectacle of all sects, all religious denominations, all forms of worshiping God, quietly siding by each other, and developing themselves under the canopy of freedom."

At this point of Asmodeus's remarks, we observed many vast gardens. Flowers and medicinal plants of every description were cultivated with a wonderful perfection, and the atmosphere was filled with refreshing aroma. And before us was an orchard, of many acres, whose innumerable trees were overloaded with delicious fruits.

"Upon my word," exclaimed Asmodeus, "in all the United States, the Shakers only till the land with such pleasant neatness, and raise vegetables and fruits in such abundance. A friend of mine, tired of the world, recently buried himself in that retreat. I must go and shake hands with him."

I followed Asmodeus, and we entered a spacious dwelling, divided by a wide hall. Asmodeus's friend kindly welcomed us, and gave us valuable information concerning the community:

"This building," said he, " divided, as you see, into two distinct parts, is capable of accommodating one hundred and fifty inmates. The male members occupy one, and the female the other. The society possesses a considerable tract of land, averaging nearly seven acres to each member. We believe idleness to be sinful, and hence every Shaker who is able to work is employed in some labor. The culture of flowers, herbs, fruits, and vegetables, is a favorite business with us. We supply druggists and physicians of the Union with dried herbs and medicinal extracts. The brooms, so much appreciated by housekeepers, are also made in our houses. For, independently of this settlement, we have several others in the States—the number of Shakers being, to-day, at least five thousand. Though our land is always in excellent condition, every thing else is no less neat and attractive in our storehouses and buildings, adapted to mechanical and dairy purposes ; in fact, contentment everywhere reigns."

He then conducted us to those buildings and storehouses he had mentioned, where we wondered at the great variety and abundance of products they contained, arranged in the most orderly manner. We also saw a school-house for the children that Shakers adopt, which was well supplied with apparatus and books ; and finally, we were shown a meeting-house or hall.

"The temporalities of each family," said Asmodeus's friend, "are cared for by two deacons and two deaconesses. There are three classes of members—first, the novitiates, who, receiving the doctrines of the Shakers, still prefer to reside with their own families, and manage their own temporal concerns for a time. Second, the junior class, composed of persons who have become members of a Shaker community, and unite in their labors and religious exercises, but who have not relinquished their property to the society ; third, the senior class, embracing those who voluntarily consecrate themselves, their services, and all their property to the society, never to be reclaimed by them or their legal heirs. No difference is made, on account of the amount of property any individual may have contributed ; all members are amply provided for, in health, sickness, and old age ; and," Asmodeus's friend proudly remarked, in this connection, "the Shakers are the only people who have maintained, for nearly a century, a system of living the fundamental principle of which is the community of property.

"The business to which Shakers devote their lives," he added, "seems highly favorable to health, the average of longevity among them being fifty years. We do not marry, and have no sexual intercourse. We do not mind politics, are opposed to war and bloody conflict, and try to live at peace with all men.

"Respecting our religious creed, we hold that God is

dual—there being an eternal Father and Mother in the Deity, the heavenly Parents of all angelic and human beings, and that the revelation of God is progressive. We hold Christ to be also dual, male and female, a supermundane being. Mother Anne Lee, by strictly obeying the light revealed in her, became righteous, even as Jesus was righteous. She formed the same character as a spiritual woman that he did as a spiritual man—the necessity for a second appearance of Christ, in the female form, resulting from the female nature of Christ and the Deity."

The worthy Shaker was just beginning to state that they recognize four cycles of religious progress, and also four heavens and four hells—the first three being places of probation—when the bell rang for the Shakers' religious exercises.

We went to the meeting-house, and observed that their mode of worship is peculiar, as in it is combined the exercise of both soul and body. The two sexes were arranged in ranks facing each other, the front ranks about six feet apart. One of the elders delivered an address upon a doctrinal subject ; after which they sang a hymn ; then they formed in circles around a band of male and female singers, to the strains of whom they went forth, in merry dances, and manifested, in that way, their religious zeal. Soon the fervency and excitement of the Shakers became very great ; their bodily evolutions, while maintaining the order and regularity of the dance and tunes, grew inconceivably rapid, and they advanced, receded, and turned about with a vertiginous velocity.

" They begin," said Asmodeus, " to experience the immediate influence of spiritual agency, both of angels and the departed members of their own fraternity who have advanced further than those still in the body, in the work

of the resurrection, or redemption from the generative nature and order.　But let us go.　We have nothing more to
do here among these extravagant fanatics.

" All systems, all theories, all follies, have free scope in
the United States," pursued Asmodeus, after we had left
the Shaker settlement.　" Besides the hundreds of theological creeds and religious sects, which have sprung from
the various interpretations of the Bible, there are many
social systems in existence and in course of experiment.
In all ages of the world and in every civilized nation, good
or visionary men have devised, and attempted to put into
practice new schemes of social life—convinced that the
methods society has adopted for the distribution of the
bounties of heaven are deficient.　With a people so fond
of progress and novelty as the Americans, Robert Owen,
Charles Fourier, and Saint Simon could not fail to find
enthusiastic disciples.　The government does not interfere
with the plans and experiments of social regeneration.　It
wisely believes that time and a free Press are sufficient
to help consign bad ones to oblivion and secure the triumph of those which may procure to each person the fullest, or a fuller, satisfaction of his wants.　Even toward
the Mormons, who boldly acknowledge and practice the
right of a plurality of wives, the government maintains an
attitude of expectation ; though fanatical advisers have
more than once demanded the intervention of the Federal
authority to blot out the system of Brigham Young and his
followers.　Up to this day — and for all time to come, let
us hope—the government has depended on the march of
civilization for the destruction of insane or hypocritical sectarians or reformers."

"But," I asked Asmodeus, " how are these Shaker

communities recruited—marriage being forbidden among them ?

" They are exclusively recruited from accessions from without; by the children they adopt, and thoroughly educate, as my Shaker friend lately remarked; by bachelors and spinsters, tired of the turmoil of large cities. But they lead a spiritual life, free from all carnal indulgence ; they rise above the order of natural and innocent human reproduction, which, they say, may be proper enough for the children of this world ; but, as for themselves, being the children of the resurrection, they are daily dying to the generative nature ; and thus are better enabled to comprehend the mysteries of God.

" It has been more than once hinted, I know, that some young Shakers of both sexes do not wait for celestial joys, and so find means to procure those of our own planet. But evil-tongued persons are to be found everywhere ; and whether the love of Shakers for spiritual life is sincere or not, the fact remains the same. They do not marry—at least, ostensibly.

" Were it not so late in the day, I would take you to the settlement of a new sect, not very far off, and which numbers a few hundred novitiates. These sectarians, like the Shakers, give special attention to the culture of medicinal plants, fruits, and vegetables, and their preserves are well appreciated in and out of the States. Like the Shakers, also, they live in celibacy — though I am not sure they are free from lust and sexual indulgence. They do not marry, because they consider civil or religious marriage a superfluous ceremony, a barbarian custom, in violation of all human freedom. They decline, in consequence, to bind themselves by matrimonial bonds. These Free-Lovers, as they are called, have meetings every evening, in a spacious hall,

after labor hours ; and there, after expounding some doctrinal point, they confess aloud their most secret thoughts
and feelings. Their theological creed, as well as their
practices, are as yet enveloped in mystery. Enough is
known, however, to warrant the assertion that material-
ism is queerly associated, in their doctrine, with spiritual
illumination. A point of it which is clear enough is
that concerning love, which, in their judgment, must be
progressive, like every thing else. They mean that young
persons of both sexes must have an apprenticeship in love,
as in any other business. As a consequence, old men have
the charge of training young girls in love affairs, and old
ladies attend to boys who have arrived at puberty. It
would not be surprising if the new religion should rapidly
spread among lewd persons of both sexes. Concerning the
manner in which Free-Lovers of the male gender choose
their female partners, after oral confessions are over, is an
obscure point of their doctrine which the initiated keep to
themselves.

"Situated in a charming valley, the Free-Lovers' settlement was, at first, an object of uneasiness to, and of an anxious watchfulness from, the neighboring country people, slow
to understand the mysteries of progressive love. And it was
apprehended, for a time, that the new sectarians would
call down upon them their neighbors' hostility. But their
quiet demeanor, their proficiency in agriculture, the benefits they conferred on the country, soon dispelled that hostility. There are about three hundred of them living, it
appears, happy and prosperous together. In fact, the
prosperity of their original settlement has been such as to
enable them to establish branches of their society in two or
three neighboring States.

" Singularly enough, the founder of this sect was a minister of the Gospel, having several children ; and, not less singular, the first disciple converted to his doctrines was his wife. His supposed revelations and a remarkable business capacity have secured him a comfortable situation and affluence, besides the influence he enjoys among his followers—a gratifying result for any reformer, whether he be an honest theorist or simply a charlatan.

" If you closely scrutinize their motives, you will discern that, in nineteen cases out of twenty, the desire to make money is the main incentive of most modern reformers—at least in the United States.   And whether derived from the Bible or not, the most impracticable schemes, the most extravagant utopian mysticisms, the most revolting systems, are sure to find partisans and disciples in a country whose people are ever fond of new sensations, and whose laws are wise enough to allow charlatans to sell, and fools to buy, drolleries and trash of every description."

CHAPTER XVI.

T was quite dark when we reached the great metropolis of the United States. The streets devoted to trade were quite deserted, and we met only a few policemen passing up and down on their beat. New-York merchants, I was told, do not reside in the business parts of the city; they keep their offices there only. Many of them live far from New-York; hence, the great thoroughfares are crowded morning and evening by thousands and thousands of pedestrians, going down or up-town. After business hours, stores and offices are watched over by patrolmen; they do not sleep inside, as fire insurance companies prefer the buildings to be left without inmates after working hours. Clerks and other employees also reside up-town, or in neighboring localities; and Asmodeus observed that many a poor family would find decent lodgings in the upper floors of hundreds of those marble buildings, which are, to-day, the recipients of empty boxes. What comfort might not thousands of operatives, now confined with their families in damp cellars, or crowding squalid tenement-houses, find in those buildings, thus deserted during the

night. Nay, how many merchants might fit up for
themselves a nice suit of apartments within those very
buildings where they keep their goods or offices, did not
the fashion of the day demand they must reside far from
business localities.

But if the lower portion of the city looked like a solitude, it was not so with the upper part of it. Theatres,
restaurants, and hundreds of pleasure resorts were crowded
with persons. About twenty theatres, including minstrel-
halls, are opened to the public every night, and the opera
and the drama are there interpreted in divers pleasing
ways to suit all tastes. As regards drinking-saloons, their
number is beyond calculation.

"A few years ago," said Asmodeus, "the number of restaurants and liquor-saloons was rather limited; eatables
and other refreshments could be procured in public hotels
only. There were, it is true, a few eating-houses, located
in damp basements; but their dirty appearance and offen-
sive smell were not calculated to attract many guests. A
great change has taken place; bachelors now live after the
Parisian fashion; they rent furnished rooms, and take their
meals at some restaurant.

"The number of restaurants or dining-saloons is now
larger than that of the French capital; and New-York can
boast of a few which, for their luxury in every particular,
may well challenge comparison."

"What are those places we meet at almost every step,
from which issue musical strains?"

"They are concert-saloons—a new feature of the metropolis—I might say, of the country: bar-rooms, where an
orchestra delights the frequenters while enjoying some of
the one hundred and fifty beverages in vogue in the States.
We are mainly indebted to Germany for that novelty. The

custom of drinking under green arbors or umbrageous trees, was brought from that country; but with this difference—the drinkers here, instead of enjoying themselves under shady trees, are crowded in dingy, badly-ventilated basements, whose walls are sometimes highly painted to represent magnificent gardens, lawns, rocky retreats, etc. Nobody would resort to them, were liquors, or even music, their only attraction. But, as I have said, they have become a feature of New-York, and as such they deserve a passing examination."

By a long flight of steps, we entered one of those concert-saloons, which, according to the sign, promised to be a spacious and shady garden. But, as Asmodeus had said, the walls alone represented the garden in highly inflamed patches of red, green, and yellow paint. Hardly inside, we were almost suffocated with the fumes of liquor and smoke of meerschaums and cigars. To be sure, the place was handsomely fitted up, and crowded with visitors—a number of what they call "pretty waiter-girls" flitting about among the customers, and laughing and loudly talking with them. A piano-player, wildly thumping and banging upon a cracked and hideously wiry instrument, the rattling of glasses, moving of chairs and tables—all contributed to bewilder and madden me with the discordant tumult, and I was on the point of leaving that pandemonium, when Asmodeus prevailed upon me to stay.

It may be doubted whether our retreat could have been successfully effected; and Xenophon's strategy, perhaps, might itself have failed in the attempt. For, on entering, we had been surrounded and coaxed to take refreshments by a dozen "pretty waiter-girls," and they importuned us so persistently that, to get rid of them, we gave our orders. So we took our places at a table in the midst of the drinkers, and paid the female waiters the price they asked for the refreshments they served us. Whereupon, two of them sat down by our side, and presented us with their photographs, on the backs of which their addresses were written.

The whole force of female waiters was in attendance— that is, about thirty or forty young women, all busy endeavoring to quench the thirst of several hundred men; and, while executing the multitudinous orders given them, they found sufficient time to distribute their photographs, to talk, and drink with visitors. . I noticed that they consumed nearly as much as the men, and wondered how they could stand it.

"The excesses of those poor creatures," said Asmodeus, "are sure to bring their miserable lives to an untimely end. For, as the concert-saloon owners pay them an insufficient salary to live upon, the girls, for the purpose of increasing it, purchase, every morning, a certain number of drinking-tickets: for instance, a glass of ale or porter costs ten cents, if taken at the counter; the saloon-owner sells tickets for the same to the waitresses with a discount of thirty per cent, and sometimes more. If you follow their motions, you will perceive they themselves keep the money received from visitors, and pay the bar-tender with their own tickets, on obtaining from him the ordered refreshments. Now, to dispose of the largest possible number of tickets, the girls have recourse to all conceivable stratagems—the most usual being to ask the visitor to drink a toast to their beauty. Though the latter is generally faded, the visitor accedes for gallantry's sake; and as the Hebe has to keep him company while toasting her charms, he pays for two drinks instead of one. After a few months of such a life, the health of most of those female waiters—

I do not speak of their virtue—is utterly ruined. They soon become, with few exceptions, confirmed drunkards."

Hurrying from the tables to the counter, and from the counter to the tables ; carrying glasses of liquor to and fro ; talking and drinking with every body—in short, displaying a wonderful activity, they presented a queer though melancholy sight. They evidently competed for the largest sale of tickets.

"I have already sold fifty," said one. "I have but twenty out of one hundred purchased this morning," said another. "I beat you all," exclaimed a third ; "I have but ten out of one hundred !" And while exchanging these confidences, they were not the less attentive to the wants of the visitors. The activity of these Hebes was only equaled by that of half a dozen men, protected by a railing, behind which they manipulated the drinks ordered by the crowd.

"It is a business of no small importance," observed Asmodeus, "to be a bar-tender—to thoroughly understand how to properly prepare the almost infinite number of beverages appreciated by the Americans. A long apprenticeship is necessary ; and the salary of bar-tenders is sometimes as high as that of a French prefect. A bar-tender must be somewhat of a chemist ; for the number of ingredients which compose many favorite drinks, and their proper mingling, constitute almost a science. I have known impoverished noblemen, lawyers, and physicians, who, after leaving the Old World, in search of fortunes in the New, have been finally in circumstances so reduced, as to turn bar-tenders ; but they were obliged, beforehand, to learn the business, receiving no compensation, during several months, for their services.

"Most of the American drinks are made of rectified

spirits, mixed with medicinal herbs and all conceivable spices. Beer, it is true, has come into use within a few years ; but Americans by birth only occasionally drink that bitter beverage so much relished by Germans ; neither are they very fond of the juice of the grape, which gives to the Celtic race its courage and gayety."

Meanwhile there happened among the drinkers what Asmodeus called a "suspension of hostilities," and a lull of excitement. The going to and fro of visitors and female waiters was subsiding ; conversation was carried on in a subdued tone ; the drinking and toasting were slackening ; many drinkers had fallen into a happy state of drowsiness, while a few looked admiringly at the bare shoulders of the "pretty waiter-girls," and tried hard to keep some of them by their side.

"Now is the time to leave," said Asmodeus. "Bloody scenes are not uncommon in concert-saloons after these drinking revels have reached their height. Jealousy is quick to fly to the brain of a drunken man ; and most frequenters of concert-saloons carry a couple of revolvers in their pockets. We have, besides, time enough to go to a theatre near by, where a play of Shakespeare is representing ; and it is better to listen to good verses, even poorly recited, than to breathe a putrid atmosphere."

I thought so too, and heartily followed Asmodeus to the theatre, where the masterpieces of the great English poet were nightly given by a renowned company of players.

"When one thinks," said Asmodeus, "that the saloon we have just left is one of the least disreputable among some hundreds of the kind, the amount of corruption and misery they necessarily entail on the community is truly appalling. I have recognized there clerks of banking-houses, old merchants, and even officers of the municipal administration. Young and old alike frequent these schools of vice—the former to learn, the latter to teach; all, to degrade themselves. Go to any large city in the Union, and you will find like establishments, the proprietors of which admit only fallen women for waiters; or, if not lost to virtue, in a fair way soon to become so. This great metropolis, in fact, sets examples for other cities, and whether they be good or bad, they are certain to be followed. Dens of corruption, I admit, exist in all large centres of population; but it may be doubted whether vice shows itself elsewhere so impudently—it recedes from the gaze of the public and dwells in remote streets; while here it displays itself on the most favorite thoroughfare of New-York, one which is a sort of Parisian Boulevard for New-Yorkers, and, at the same time, the pride of commercial men. I have heard health-officers state that over five hundred young girls employed in concert-saloons die every year of drunkenness and other nameless vices—thus filling an early grave. Between these unfortunate creatures and unwary young men spring up relations fruitful of many dreadful evils. From what you have seen, you may form an estimate of what is transpiring in saloons removed from the gaze of the police. The least disreputable of those resorts are schools for licentiousness; the others, nurseries of crime. In the latter the waiter-girls are prostitutes, connected with professional thieves and assassins; and woe betide the stranger who falls into the snares of those dangerous sirens! More than one has found his grave in the Hudson, dragged there in the darkness of the night, after being drugged by poisonous liquors and robbed of his valuables!

"The State Legislature has more than once tried to suppress concert-saloons in New-York. Its attempts have

been invariably defeated by the confederated efforts of dis-
tillers, proprietors of restaurants, bar-keepers, concert-saloon owners, and liquor-merchants—finding a willing help
in the judiciary. The spirit of the law has been perverted,
and its effects paralyzed by magistrates elected by these
confederates.

"I consider concert-saloons are now a definitive institution of New-York—notwithstanding young men spending
their evenings in these vile places gradually debase their
manners and minds by low associations. In any country,
ruled either by despotism or free institutions, law is powerless to eradicate an evil when it once becomes rooted in
the habits of the people ; the latter must be amended first."

We now entered the theatre. The play that night was
Julius Cæsar, a work in which the great poet has shown
such a wonderful knowledge of the human heart and popular passions. The house was crowded. Small, but handsome and elegantly decorated, there was, however, in its
shape and dispositions an irremediable defect : the stage
was too near the spectators, and thus spoiled the effects of
illusion. We took our seats at the moment Julius Cæsar,
drawing Antonius aside, says :

> " Let me have men about me that are fat ;
> Sleek-headed men, and such as sleep o' nights :
> Yond' Cassius has a lean and hungry look ;
> He thinks too much : such men are dangerous."

The actor who personated Cæsar was not wanting in
dignity, and his mien was quite appropriate to the situation. But the performers who represented the three Romans who became Triumvirs after Cæsar's assassination
were miserably deficient in a knowledge of the men among
whom, and times in which, they were supposed to be mov-

ing. And the terrible scene in which Cæsar is stabbed by
Casca, then by several other conspirators, and finally by
Marcus Brutus, and pronounces his despairing farewell to
life, "*Et tu, Brute!*—then fall, Cæsar!" looked more like
a street-riot than the dramatic catastrophe so admirably
delineated by the poet. As for the actresses who represented Calphurnia and Portia, they seemed more intent
on ogling the audience than anxious for their husbands.
Finally, when, in the fourth act, the ghost of Cæsar enters
and tells Brutus he shall see him again at Philippi, the
actor who personated the ghost did it in so ridiculous a
manner that the house could not refrain from laughing.

"It is certainly very difficult," said Asmodeus, during an
intermission in the performance, "to properly interpret the
great bard of Avon. One can hardly expect an actor to be
possessed of such historical knowledge as to successfully
represent all of Shakespeare's varied characters—to be, in
turn, Macbeth and Richard II.; then Henry IV., Henry
V., Henry VI., Richard III., Henry VIII., and, again,
King Lear and Julius Cæsar. One must be endowed
with natural genius to interpret men of genius, and, in
particular, so great a thinker and sagacious an observer as
the prince of tragic authors. But if actors lack superior
talent, a proper sense of decency, as regards history, is to
be expected from them. The costumes on this occasion
are simply ridiculous, and the scenery which purports to
represent a Roman city, during a great part of the play,
would serve as well for any town of Europe or America.
I am, above all, irritated at the absence of truth and reality in the players, who are advertised as an unparalleled
cast of stars in the dramatic firmament. Exaggerated
gesture and furious utterance weaken, instead of adding
strength to Shakespeare's poetry. For instance, the actor

who plays the part of Antonius, is unquestionably unacquainted with history and classical literature ; for he gives to the character the cant and mien of a Puritan preacher."

The curtain, which rose for the fifth act, here interrupted the discourse of Asmodeus, and we silently assisted at the peripetie of the battle of Philippi.

When Cato, the son of Marcus Cato, after heroically charging the enemy, is overpowered and falls, a great excitement among the actors became noticeable ; then they suddenly ceased playing, and somebody in the house shouted out that it was on fire! Instantly a scene of indescribable terror and confusion ensued ; ladies fainted, and men, in a state of frenzy, rushed to the door—the excitement being the more intense when the very insufficient means of egress became fully known to the audience.

"Whether there be a fire or not," coolly said Asmodeus, "let us keep quiet. It is the best means to protect our lives. We should be crushed and trampled to death by those mad people were we unwise enough to try to go out. The theatres in the United States are built after so defective a plan, and the means of egress are so scanty, that, in case of a fire during a performance, the loss of life would be frightful. Previous to going to a theatre, every man of common sense and discretion ought to set his house in order and make his will. This theatre, which will contain about two thousand persons, has but one entrance-way. In case of fire, the audience would be burnt alive, as were, a few years ago, hundreds of unfortunate beings who had been shut up in a church until the holy mass was over.

"Most fortunately; there is no real danger. Smoke, issuing from a defective flue, is the cause of the alarm ;

and the performance will soon proceed—though, it may be, but few spectators will resume their seats."

In fact, the manager at that moment stepped to the footlights, and, after quieting the fears of those who had not yet left the theatre, announced that the actors would immediately resume the play. "The cry of fire," said he, "was raised by some evil-disposed person—the tool, probably, of a rival company, by whom all means are resorted to with a view to destroy the unprecedented success of this *troupe*, so enthusiastically welcomed every night by the *élite* of New-York society!" After this speech, the actors resumed their parts and the play went on; but, as predicted by Asmodeus, before an almost empty house.

"You may now form an idea," said Asmodeus while we were going home, "of the American theatre, and the manner in which Shakespeare's masterpieces are interpreted. The company we have seen is one of the best and most complete to be found in America. But whether they interpret classical authors or the modern drama, the defects you have noticed are none the less shocking—namely, want of truth and reality, exaggerated gestures, insufficiency of study, and ridiculous conceit of their proficiency and merit. Independently of natural disposition, much study and labor are required to become a good actor; and few American actors are fond of these requisites—believing their art may dispense with them; and, as a consequence, the majority is but a crowd of brainless braggarts and ridiculous swells.

"Concerning the plays in vogue, if we except a few from Shakespeare, they are, in general, translated from the worst French dramas, and arranged to suit the taste of the American public. If this taste has not as yet become entirely corrupted, it is not for want of opportunities; as theatre managers and playwrights, instead of making of theatrical representations a school for morals, convert them into a sort of arena, where highwaymen and other low characters delight the crowd with their adroitness and audacity—to the confusion, of course, of the law, police, decency, and common sense.

"No," continued Asmodeus, "theatrical art does not exist in the United States, and never will, so long as honest critics are snubbed by dramatic authors and actors. To-day, a critic who should dare to censure an actor, and, least of all, an actress, would be certainly exposed to the resentment of the parties he had censured and that of their friends. No newspaper is bold enough to doubt the excellency of the American people in the scenic art, as in every thing else. That self-admiration so universally practiced in this country, is especially pushed to extreme limits in every thing pertaining to the theatrical world.

"But it is not there only that the want of labor and patient study produces almost negative results. It is the same with the arts, the sciences, and literature.

"The American people do every thing in a hurry; but masterpieces can not be the fruit of sudden inspiration, and any intellectual effort to challenge lasting admiration requires long meditation and careful elaboration. Many American writers lose sight of the art itself, when they make books or plays—they think only of the money they will reap from them; literature with them is, as with the publishers for whom they work, but a mercantile business.

"No wonder, then, so many works lauded to the skies by a complacent press are short-lived! But, as I said before, the true literature of democratic societies is their press; and the Americans, in this respect, are without a rival.

"James Fenimore Cooper is, and will be for a long time to come, the author whose works deserve unqualified admiration, as regards talent for narrative, truth of description, and originality of character. But Cooper is not popular among his countrymen, because of his *critique* of American manners and institutions. People, as well as kings, love flattery, and do not easily forgive those who teach them virtue.

"However, I am ready to admit that the Americans will succeed in the fields of literature, arts, and sciences, when they shall display there the spirit of enterprise and perseverance they have so conspicuously exhibited in mercantile affairs. They are a people to whom every thing seems possible; and I should not be surprised were they some day to produce in the arts of painting and sculpture, for instance, masterpieces that all Europe will envy, though those arts have flourished, up to our time, in old communities only, and among classes that enjoy leisure—a thing unknown, as yet, in the United States.

"Every thing in America being undertaken and carried on in the interest of the million, Photography was sure to be welcomed. It is now a national art, practiced in every town, in every hamlet, and inundating the country with multitudinous productions, sometimes of very superior make. Not a few Americans carry a stock of their own photographs in their pockets, giving them away among friends and acquaintances. Some even add to the gift a short biography—a practice that has recently contributed to make biography-writing a branch of literature much in vogue, and more remunerating, I suspect, than many others.

"And no wonder this is so. Candidates to public offices, from the would-be President of the Republic down to the village alderman, are evidently marked out for great men—inasmuch as a Boston professor has lately demonstrated that the face of the Yankee bears a striking resemblance to that of the illustrious Romans, as transmitted to us by sculpture or numismatics. Bound, then, for immortality, candidates must have their own biographies written and printed on the eve of election ; and hundreds of thousands of them are distributed among the community delighted to possess so many great men.

" Apart from their achievements in the photographic art, the United States have, in reality, made little progress in purely industrial arts, as compared with the rapid advance of other countries. The explanation of this undeniable fact is again found in insufficiency of study, and the habit of doing every thing too hastily. The Americans blindly adopt the inventions of the Europeans ; but while the latter incessantly improve on these, science is wanted here to follow in the same track. The country possesses very few machinists really learned and skilled in the theory of their art.

" A good system of industrial education is certainly needed ; and until they have one, the Americans will be enabled to boast of but few specialties. Nowhere else is more money spent for primary educational purposes— almost every body being able to read and write ; but that education is about the only one within the reach of the people ; and though admiring the advantages and results derived from it, it is time the masses were enabled to increase the superficial knowledge they obtain in the public schools."

Asmodeus was thus discoursing about theatres, arts, and literature in the United States, when repeated hurras broke upon the stillness of the night, and crowds of people issued from neighboring streets.

" They are coming ! here they are !" exclaimed a number of voices, amid increasing confusion.

" Some Ambassadors from an Asiatic nation have just arrived," said Asmodeus. " They were expected at three o'clock in the afternoon ; but they could reach New-York at midnight only, because they had to stop at every railway station, during their journey, and exhibit themselves to the thousands of people flocking there from miles around. To-morrow they will have a public reception, thus affording you an opportunity to see that ceremony as managed by the city officials and a people always in pursuit of new sensations. But the clamor is becoming more stunning, and—here are the Ambassadors ! Let us stop, for to walk amid such a crowd is really impossible."

Asmodeus had hardly concluded these words, when we were jostled in contrary directions, by men either intoxicated or who feigned to be so ; and before I was aware of it, I found myself abruptly separated from my companion.

"Beware of pickpockets !" cried he, while being pushed forward by the swelling tide of the populace. Heeding his advice, I hastily felt in my fob. My watch was gone !

CHAPTER XVII.

THUS learned, to my cost, of the world-renowned skill of American pickpockets; and I went home all the more irritated at the occurrence because the stolen watch was endeared to me by family recollections. I could hardly sleep that night, and rose early to go to police-headquarters, and make known the theft of which I had been made the victim.

"An antiquated idea, sir—an obsolete notion, which you had better at once banish from your mind," said Asmodeus, appearing at the very moment I was leaving my room. "Leave to the Old World such proceedings, which would have for their only result to make you a laughing-stock to the police. Do as every sensible man does in similar and all other circumstances—that is, depend on yourself alone, either to succeed in any enterprise or to get out of a scrape. Believe me, you will again possess your watch by simply resorting to means used in cases of this kind, and which are certainly less expensive than would be the intervention of meddlesome lawyers and policemen. They could detect, perhaps, the pickpocket, and even find your watch. But in no case would the latter be restored to you. Valuable goods are never returned to their owners, sir, in this country; they are kept, as evidence, by the lawyers and police. Your antiquated notion would only serve to add to the loss of your watch a fruitless outlay."

Agreeably to his advice, I followed Asmodeus to a newspaper office, and there my companion handed in for the next issue the following advertisement:

" Yesterday, during the arrival of the Asiatic Ambassadors, a gentlemen was relieved of his watch (a genuine Breguet) by some artistic manipulator, possessed of a skill and cunning really wonderful. Desiring to give to the artist a testimony of his admiration, the owner of the chronometer will pay him fifty dollars for his trouble, if he will condescend to return it to-morrow at nine o'clock A.M."

The advertisement concluded by giving my name and address.

" Now," said Asmodeus, after paying two dollars to the cashier at the desk, " I will guarantee that you will recover your chronometer at the time stated in the advertisement, and thus be compelled to admit that this course of proceeding, compared to the rough, blunt way of the police, savors of a courtesy and good breeding which mark an advance in civilization."

At that moment, several regiments of the State militia marched through the street to inspiriting strains of martial music, and we mingled with the lookers-on.

" The taste for music," said Asmodeus, " has considerably increased throughout the States, owing, in a great measure, to the many Germans who have settled in America. Everywhere piano-playing is indulged in ; and, in large cities, Odd Fellows, firemen, target-companies, benevolent societies, and workingmen's associations, delight in parading through the streets with bands of music. In time of war, regiments of one thousand men each, when complete, keep a musical band at a heavy expense to the public treasury. The number of musicians alone would form a respectable army."

The regiments we met on coming out of the newspaper office, were parading, Asmodeus informed me, in honor of the Orientals who had arrived the day before, and to whom a public reception was actually tendered. Regiment after regiment went by, with artillery and cavalry, composing a really formidable army. It was the first time I had seen a military display in the United States—not even a single uniform had I seen before.

" New-York alone," said Asmodeus, " could raise an army of one hundred thousand men. The State militia is organized throughout the Union with such efficiency that soldiers are never wanting in the hour of peril.

" This country, though devoted to the useful arts and much given to the pursuit of gain, is not deprived of warlike spirit. Far from it; and the old nations of Europe will act sensibly in leaving the United States to quietly fulfill their destiny. It really seems, in case of emergency, that innumerable armies spring, as it were, from the American soil, and, judging from the past, this country might keep, without apparent uneasiness, a standing army of one million men.

" Not less worthy of notice, next to its wonderful power of raising armies, is the facility the American Union possesses for disbanding them. One can but wonder at the rapidity with which soldiers, fresh from camp-life, return, and settle down to the labors of the farm and factory. The country is so vast, the field of labor so extensive, that a million men can find employment at once, and the confusion which everywhere else would attend the disbandment of numerous armies is here quite unknown. In time of war, the Americans are proud of their soldiers, and of their fighting qualities. They are the objects of an unrelaxing solicitude from the government. As soon as the bloody work is over, feelings of an opposite nature prevail among the people: the sight of a uniform makes every American nervous, and soldiers become hardly tolerated. The heroes of the day before are now looked upon as lazy fellows and parasites on society. Hence the prevailing opinion that a standing army ought to be as small as possible ; and even the necessity for it has been often questioned. Such is the public antipathy for military service, that heavy bounties sometimes have to be granted to recruit the ranks. Nay, more, as trade and industry offer more inducements to Americans than the army, its ranks, in time of peace, are mainly filled up by foreigners. Militia regiments themselves would soon lose their prestige and popularity were they to parade too often in the streets. The American is singularly proud and suspicious of his freedom, and he takes umbrage very easily at the sight of brute force."

In the mean while, regiment after regiment of volunteers was filing by. Their uniforms were quite varied ; some reminded one of German troopers ; others, those worn by French or English soldiers. As regards the regular army, Asmodeus informed me, there is but one kind of uniform for the infantry ; the cavalry regiments also have all the same uniform. By this means, a great saving is realized by the public treasury for the clothing of the soldiers ; and, on the other hand, as the uniform is not often changed, as in other countries, dishonest bargains between contractors and army officers are not to be apprehended. The uniform for the standing army is very simple and costs little ; the epaulet is unknown, some staff-officers only wearing it. Not only many of the regiments of volunteers filing by wore the uniform of foreign countries, but I also noticed they carried the flags of those countries.

" The flags of all peoples living in the world," said Asmodeus, " are welcome here. They are soon merged in the broad folds of the Star-Spangled Banner. America is a neutral ground for all the human race—a common inheritance for all men who want to be free ; and the Americans do not find fault with foreigners for their keeping a pious remembrance of their native land. In their turn, foreigners, in a national emergency, flock to the flag of the Union, which represents a government emanating from their own will ; and if that Government displays an irresistible power, it is because a whole people is interested in its preservation."

The crowd waiting on the sidewalks for a sight of the Asiatic Ambassadors was enormous, rendering walking almost impossible. However, remarkable order prevailed, though no extraordinary measures had been taken to protect the public peace. The number of policemen on duty was no larger than usual. A population of free men is undoubtedly an intelligent one ; and there is, among the American masses, a deep and sincere love for public order —statements to the contrary, notwithstanding.

At last the long-expected *cortége* appeared, with a platoon of policemen in front ; then followed many regiments of infantry and cavalry ; carriages, containing the city councilmen and their friends, came next ; then a magnificent vehicle, drawn by six horses decorated with ribbons and feathers, disclosed to the gaze of the spectators the Orientals, wearing their national gowns. All along the route they were welcomed with enthusiastic shouts, and they seemed quite astonished at the sympathetic demonstrations they everywhere met. Finally, several regiments of volunteers completed the procession, which extended several miles.

"These poor fellows," said Asmodeus, "will be exhibited in this way for six hours at least; they will be taken up and down New-York's principal avenues and streets; and after satiating the puerile curiosity of the people, they will stop a couple of hours at the City Hall, during which time a general shaking of hands will take place. This habit of hand-shaking with the populace, which is imposed upon distinguished guests honored with a public reception, is often a positive martyrdom. Some have passed the fearful ordeal with their shoulders unhinged; for, among every crowd, facetious Irishmen are never wanting, who, to show their strength, squeeze, as in a vice, the guest's proffered hand. Imagine, then, what a punishment is in store for those effeminate Orientals. The trials which encompass them will not end with the shaking of hands. The city fathers will not cease to persecute them till a late hour of the night. When the public reception is over, the Orientals will be treated to a magnificent dinner, the cost of which will be, of course, borne by tax-payers. The councilmen never miss any occasion to treat themselves and friends in this cheap manner; and the city treasurer has to disburse, every year, many thousand dollars for such festivities. In the New as in the Old World, the people have to pay for the diversions their rulers grant them."

At this point of the conversation we passed a street, a short distance from which could be seen a granite building, whose style was similar to that of an Egyptian temple.

"What is that building, yonder?" said I to Asmodeus. "From its gloomy appearance, one might take it for one of those spacious tombs in which, in the time of the

Pharaohs, were deposited the remains of wealthy Egyptians."

"That is just the name that heavy structure has received," answered Asmodeus; "but the living, and not the dead, are buried there. It is the city prison. There evildoers are detained until they are discharged; or, in case of condemnation, taken to the State's prison. There also are imprisoned those unfortunates sentenced to be hanged, and anxiously awaiting the day they expiate their crimes."

We entered the gloomy building, every part of which was readily shown us by its polite keepers. First, we saw a small, ill-ventilated room, where a justice was sitting, who has to deal with persons guilty of slight offenses. We next entered a square building, with cells ranged on all sides. The keeper informed us these cells, though originally intended for one hundred and fifty persons, sometimes contain as many as five hundred, and yet each of them is but twelve by eight feet wide !

We saw, in another part of the prison, cells for female prisoners; and in a narrow yard, those where boys are confined. All the cells seemed very damp, and lacking ventilation.

"This prison," said Asmodeus, "was built when nobody foresaw the wonderful growth of New-York. One feels deeply aggrieved when thinking of all the miseries yearly inclosed within these walls. If you except the penitentiaries, where the solitary system is generally adopted, the other prisons of the State of New-York, and, I dare say, of the other States of the Union, are in no better condition as regards the health of the prisoners. In most of them there are no baths. The old are mingled with the young, and depraved offenders with culprits of slight offenses only ; and the prisoners' sufferings are often increased by cruel treatment from the jail-keepers.

" Undoubtedly, abuses, so frequent in Europe in cases of imprisonment before trial, are of rare occurrence in the United States ; because persons arrested for petty offenses may be discharged on giving reasonable bail. Still, when they have neither friends nor money, they run the same risk of mouldering in jail in the United States as in Europe, because magistrates do what, in their opinion, seems most needful. Well, the most needful thing to many is to have offenders who belong to the same political party as themselves, or are provided with money, promptly brought before an examining court and discharged. To other prisoners, they refuse a. writ at pleasure, or insist that it can not be issued in term-time. Of course, all court magistrates must not be involved in so serious a charge ; there are honest men everywhere, and in every station of society. It is nevertheless a fact boldly asserted by opponents to the actual system of recruiting the judiciary, that many judges, after a term of four years, retire from office with fifty thousand dollars and over, though their yearly salary does not exceed four thousand.

" Committees from benevolent institutions, besides inspectors from the Federal and State government, should visit all prisons, as well as insane asylums, once a month at least, and interrogate every person as to the cause that deprived him or her of liberty. Their reports should be published by newspapers, so as to incite magistrates to promptly discharge their duty, secure a wise discrimination in the appointment of wardens and keepers, and compel the latter to treat prisoners with a proper regard for their condition.

" The kind, humane disposition of Americans, fortunately, often corrects many abuses, arising from the want of an efficient control, as regards both the execution of the law and prison management and discipline.

"Convicts are generally sentenced to an imprisonment of comparatively short duration. Again, the American peo ple, as I have said, one of the most benevolent on earth, have invented the most terrible punishment—solitary confinement. But, at the same time, they have discovered that strict confinement ought to be limited to the shortest period possible. The Auburn system is now adopted, with more or less rigor in the enforcement of silence, in the State's prisons of most of the States, and in the principal penitentaries. But the term for which convicts are imprisoned is often diminished in case their deportment is exemplary, and also through the intervention of relatives and friends. Offenders are seldom sentenced to a term of imprisonment exceeding five years, unless they have been convicted of serious crimes, and do not deserve any mercy at the hands of magistrates. The latter never abuse or torment the accused, and they are generally careful to keep the prosecution on a level with the defense. They know that society has a right to punish, but, even when so doing, that it does not forget that the offenders belong to it, though unfortunately led astray.

"Many foreigners often wonder at the indulgence and lenity with which offenders are treated by the community they have outraged, and the magistrates whose duty it is to sentence them when found guilty. Those foreigners pay an unconscious homage to American institutions ; for the mild and conciliatory disposition of the people is, to a great extent, attributable to these institutions."

We had examined enough to have the sad conclusion forced upon us that the city prison does not afford to its inmates what they are everywhere entitled to—pure air, wholesome and sufficient food, protection from cold and dampness, and opportunities for frequent exercise ; and also that, in consequence of too often intermingling young with old offenders, the former become tainted with the vices of the latter, and are thus liable to leave the prison thoroughly educated in crime. Philanthropists have here, as in Europe, a vast field open to their benevolent efforts.

As we were on the point of retiring, Asmodeus asked one of the keepers to show us the celebrities of the day.

"Ah sir! replied the keeper, "we have very few of them, at the present time. To speak the truth, crime is tame just now ; and were it not for the drunkards, too much inclined to use their knives, when in a state of intoxication, and for burglars and forgers, the house would be far from being full. As it is, however, I will show you the most notorious of our guests.

"That one, smoking fifty-cent cigars, and who has furnished his cell with the luxury you see, is the well-known Coupon. A few weeks ago, he went to a banker, and while engaging him in conversation, his confederate carried away a tin box, containing government securities to the value of about three millions of dollars. Unfortunately for Coupon, most of them were registered bonds. He was arrested and could not furnish the heavy bail fixed by the judge. But after many conferences with him, the banker has come to terms ; and in consideration of two hundred thousand dollars which Coupon is allowed to retain out of his prize, he will to-morrow return the stolen securities and recover his freedom.

"The next cell is occupied by old Tricker, who owns two or three country-seats in the State of New-York, and keeps fast horses. No country can boast of a more skillful engraver than he. Half a dozen banks have broken in consequence of the millions of counterfeit bills with which Tricker had inundated the country. Perhaps he will not get out of the scrape this time without much trouble. The Federal Government is in a rage, because Tricker has imitated the United States bonds with such perfection that the treasury clerks themselves are at a loss to distinguish the genuine from the imitations. Tricker takes it quite coolly, and gives directions from his cell for the management of his farms and race horses."

"The counterfeiting of bank-bills and federal securities of every description," interrupted Asmodeus, "is a business carried on on a large scale in the United States, and gives employment to thousands of persons in various capacities. The sale, for instance, of counterfeit bills is in itself a very important branch of the counterfeiting business. There are, in New-York alone, a dozen offices, known, it is affirmed, to the police, where any body may purchase counterfeit bills at a discount of thirty to fifty per cent, according to the quantity taken up. The Western States have been principally the object of the attentions of counterfeiters ; and many farmers are far from suspecting they have received worthless paper for their breadstuffs."

"That young man," continued the keeper, "who walks alone in the court-yard, and seems in a gloomy mood, is a precocious bigamist, who has vainly tried, from the day of his imprisonment, to be bailed, because of the enormity of his offense toward the fair sex. He married, in the West, when about eighteen years old, and two years later came to New-York, leaving behind his wife and one child. Here he fell in love with a young lady belonging to one of our most respectable families, eloped with and married her.

His first wife having ascertained his treachery, he thought it advisable to abscond. Only a few days ago, the miscreant was discovered in a boarding-school for young ladies, where, disguised, he had found a situation in the capacity of chambermaid. In consequence of this sad affair, five young ladies have been obliged to leave the school, and five families are in distress."

" 'This is the fruit," again said Asmodeus, " of marriages hastily contracted, and without previous publication ; and also of a demoralizing literature. That precocious scamp had poisoned his mind, no doubt, with those books leavened with the spirit of licentiousness, and published by authors thirsting less for reputation than for money. But," he abruptly remarked, " is not that the lawyer, Forger, I perceive yonder, walking with two other limbs of the law ?"

" You are right," replied the keeper. " Forger does his best to procure clients for those two lawyers, on the condition, of course, of getting a percentage out of the stipulated fees. In point of greediness, no offender equals those two sharks of the law. I have seen them, more than once, taking for their fees portions of stolen goods, after defending the thieves. You can hardly conceive of their tender feeling for their clients. They invariably represent them to the jurors as the most honest, the purest creatures in the world ; and they have really come to the point of considering evil-doers as victims of society, and our court magistrates as remorseless persecutors. They worship thieves, as they are indebted to them for their luxurious existence and the reputation they enjoy in the infamous resorts of the city. They will almost surely be elected representatives to the New-York State Legislature, or even to Congress, when they choose to become law-makers.

"As regards Forger, his trial will not be soon over. You perhaps know he had among his clients an old lady who was possessed of great wealth, in consequence of the growth of New-York—she owning a farm in what has since become a populated part of the city. The old lady had but one son, who had gone to California, at the outbreak of the gold-fever, and of whom she had not heard for a very long time; when, one day, a man calling himself her son made his appearance at her house. That man was no other than Forger's accomplice, who played his part so well, the old lady never suspected the imposition. She died a short time after, bequeathing all her fortune to Forger's friend. The thieves had just begun selling off her estate, and dividing the spoils, when the true son of the old lady returned from California. He was at once recognized by his many relatives and friends, and succeeded in having his identity judicially proved. He did more; he offered convincing proof that the false heir was an adventurer, who, under a dozen assumed names, had as many misunderstandings with our criminal courts. Forger and his friends were arrested, and they are deprived of their liberty because they can not furnish the required bail. They spend their time here in studying the means to escape the law, and, above all, to retain their spoils; they are assisted in their endeavors by the two lawyers you have noticed, and who do not fail to visit them daily.

"The tall man who has just stopped them is General Boisterous, who, after fighting the Indians, came home a few months ago, to recruit his health. Through some inconsiderate words of a friend, he was apprised of his wife's treachery during his absence. The general met his wife's paramour, a State senator, at the very moment he was about making a speech, and coolly shot him down, in the presence of the terrified legislators. As some among them have, perhaps, coveted their neighbors' wives, as did Boisterous' victim, they do every thing in their power to influence public opinion and our magistrates against the general, who has been unable, up to this day, to recover his freedom under bail. But somebody has called me," here observed the keeper. "It is a bank-teller, who after leading for many years an exemplary life, fell into the snares of a concert-saloon siren. His defalcations amount to one hundred thousand dollars ; and the queer part of the story is, he hardly spent the third of that large amount with the waiter-girl—the greater portion having been extorted from him by two or three scamps, under a threat of making known his intrigue to the bank officers. The subsidies they obtained in that way were almost instantly lost at the gaming-table. Fortunately for the teller, he is afflicted with consumption, induced by the dampness of this building, and is in a fair way to soon get rid of a burdensome life. Our magistrates, aware that he is beyond all hope of recovery, allow him to rest in peace."

" I am sorry," said Asmodeus, thanking the keeper for these details, "you have no time to show us a few celebrities of the fair sex."

"I have scarcely one worth seeing," replied the keeper, "with the exception of a young girl who murdered her mistress through motives of jealousy. The jury have just returned a verdict of guilty, and she will not be sentenced till to-morrow, as the judge of the court wanted twenty-four hours to prepare. a speech for the occasion. As soon as the verdict was returned, the girl confessed that she alone had assassinated her mistress ; and her counsel, who had represented her to the jury as pure and innocent as a lamb, are of course indignant at such indecorous proceedings and treachery. Females, you know, are worshiped in this country, and unless they have committed some atrocious offense, our magistrates generally dismiss with but a gentle reprimand those brought into their presence by the police."

As we left the prison, Asmodeus observed that crimes as villainous as those which European newspapers frequently relate, are seldom heard of in the United States.

"Outrages against property," said he—" I mean thefts and robberies—are certainly of less frequent occurrence here than in Europe, as also outrages against persons. Cases of intoxication and disorderly conduct fill up to a great extent the criminal·calendar and statistics. In a country where wages are high and the means of acquiring property within the reach of every energetic man, burglary and theft should be less common than in those countries where one can hardly obtain a living by his labor. On the other hand, evil-doers are not ignorant of the fact that the banks are the great depositories of the circulating medium and other values. A robber does not covet an empty portfolio, and seldom cares to break into a house, because he knows there is nothing but cumbersome furniture to be carried off. The habit of depositing their money in banks, and drawing checks for it, is so general with Americans, that very few keep at home important sums of money.

"Concerning personal security, it is as great in the United States as in any other country, and perhaps greater. Of course, in such a large city as New-York, if an imprudent man inclines to frequent places resorted to by sailors and other rough customers, I will not vouch for his safety ; dens of this kind offer the same perils everywhere. These cases excepted, I maintain that any body

may travel throughout all the States—North and South,
East and West—without incurring any more danger to his
personal safety than if he were in Normandy at the time
of the good Duke Rollo. Nay, America is the only country in the world where women may travel alone, confident
that, in case of insult, they will find ready protectors everywhere.

"I propose," continued Asmodeus, "to pursue our in-
spection of the public institutions in the city of New-York.
There is near by a hospital worth seeing; you will have
an excellent opportunity to compare it with institutions
founded in Europe for the benefit of diseased or incapacitated persons."

Asmodeus was right: the hospital we visited was
worthy, in every respect, of such a city as New-York.
Clean, well-ventilated, and kept in fine order, it offered
the unfortunates obliged to avail themselves of its hospitality conditions of comfort they seemed highly to appreciate. Unfortunately, vast as is the establishment, there
is room but for a restricted number of patients; and here,
again, the growth of the American metropolis has got the
start of public charity. That charity, however, is praise-
worthy. Nowhere, according to Asmodeus, are its works
more multiplied, its efforts more persevering, than in the
United States. There are, in New-York, asylums for
foundlings, for old persons of both sexes, and for the
blind; almshouses, small-pox hospitals, homes and asylums for colored persons, etc. Religious influence has
also been at work to erect hospitals for members of the
most important Christian denominations. In numerous
instances, wealthy persons have bequeathed a portion of
their fortune to either founding or endowing benevolent
institutions.

"But withal," said Asmodeus, "the multitudinous wants of the vast population are far from being satisfied. The mortality is very large in New-York, especially in the poor districts ; though no city in the world can boast of a more salubrious location, and consequently, life should be longer on an average here than anywhere else. But not far from those palatial residences and splendid streets that make New-York one of the most beautiful cities in the world, thousands of tenement-houses have been built. Out of a million inhabitants, more than one half dwell in those tenement-houses, which are so constructed as to be deprived of free ventilation, and in which every indispensable condition for health has been entirely overlooked. The consequence of such a state of things is a fearful increase of mortality among working-men, and principally their children. While for the wealthy classes of New-York, residing in salubrious streets, the average of life is fifty-two years, it is but seventeen in crowded districts. It has been stated that, in thousands of cases, a single room is occupied by a whole family, in which they cook, eat, and sleep—all huddled together, father, mother, and children. Often as many as three families occupy the same room. So, you see, all the miseries attending the working classes in Europe are also to be found in the New World ; for, if the wages of working-men are higher in the United States, their wants are greater than in Europe, and all seem to be addicted to an unwholesome love of expense. When we bear in mind that any man is at liberty to remove not only to the Far West and new Territories, but to many Middle and Western States, and there cultivate land that will become his own after fulfilling a few easy conditions, we can not but wonder at the persistency of large numbers of poor people in living in our overcrowded cities.

Many want the energy necessary to lead a pioneer's life ; and others are too fond of the allurements offered by vast aggregations of men. In Europe, with a crowded population and poorly remunerated labor, it is almost impossible for a man to better his condition ; but the reverse is the case in the United States ; and when Americans assert that misery should not exist in their country, that there is room for every body, and plenty to spare, they simply state a fact that can not be denied."

We noticed many young men in the hospital-yard. Some, as we were informed, were attached to the institution as helps to the physicians ; and others had come to listen to a renowned professor, who was to commence that day a course of lectures on anatomy. Asmodeus proposed we should mingle with the young men, and listen to the professor. So we entered a sort of amphitheatre, where, from a very nauseous smell that saluted our nostrils, we conjectured anatomical operations were conducted. Our surmises proved correct ; for our eyes soon fell upon an object of an oblong shape, covered with a blanket, and lying on a large marble table.

The professor, a well-proportioned, handsome man, commenced his lecture by a historical sketch of the medical art.

"In all rude nations," said he, "priests are the physicians ; they attend to the soul as well as the body. Thus it was among the Egyptians and Greeks ; and in our day, such is the case among the Indian tribes. But with a people so well endowed, intellectually, as the Athenians, medicine could not fail to become elevated to the rank of a science, and its practitioners were soon honored by their countrymen. Among the Romans, in the early days of Rome, medicine was despised, and practiced by slaves only. But a change for the better took place when the liberal arts, imported from Greece, were cultivated by the Romans. Physicians, under the first Cæsar, obtained the right of citizenship; but his successor went further—he raised to the rank of knight a physician who had cured him of a serious disease. Still many years elapsed before the law exacted from practitioners guarantees of capacity and proofs of competency. Any one calling himself a physician could exercise his profession, until it was enacted by Christian emperors that physicians, before being allowed to practice, must submit to an examination by learned practitioners. When deemed competent, they were licensed.

"After the fall of the Roman empire, medicine, as a science, disappeared; and in the middle ages, it was practiced exclusively by the clergy. But as clergymen were forbidden to shed blood, surgical operations were confided to an inferior class. In that way arose the fraternity of barber-surgeons. In France, only a few lay-surgeons, under the title of the Surgical College of Saint Damian, carried on a determined struggle with the barbers, and also with the faculty of medicine, until the year 1515, when the College of Saint Damian was united with the University. Barbers, from that time, were not allowed to practice surgery, unless examined by two surgeons of the king, and deemed competent. Surgery now rose rapidly in honor, and the surgeons' importance to the community was no longer questioned.

"In France, medicine is not separated from surgery; but in England, the two colleges of surgeons and physicians remain perfectly distinct.

"In the United States, medical institutions, like the

French universities, give a common degree of medicine and surgery."

After this sketch, the professor complained of the difficulty of acquiring, in the United States, knowledge and skill respecting surgical operations—a state of things attributable to popular prejudices and objections to analysis or dissection of dead bodies.

" It is impossible," said he, " for young men to become conversant with and skillful in the treatment of the diseases our organs are heir to, if they are ignorant of the correct place in the body of every muscle, fibre, and sinew, and their connection with each other—a knowledge that can be possessed only by a thorough examination and analysis of the body's flesh and bones ; and to acquire which, many true lovers of medical science are often obliged to go abroad."

Then he objected to the short duration of medical studies. " After two years' attendance," said he, " on lectures from physicians, more or less authorized to teach youth, our young men obtain a diploma of doctor of medicine, and forthwith commence to practice an art the very first rudiments of which they do not understand.

" We even have in our midst, many who practice without a diploma !

" Medicine must be free, of course, like other professions. But the principle of freedom that governs human labor in all its branches, in our democratic institutions, would not be imperiled were true guarantees of competency exacted from practitioners. This observation may be applied with equal force to druggists and apothecaries. No guarantee of their capacity is required from the twenty thousand individuals who prepare prescriptions throughout the States—hence the fatal errors daily recorded by newspapers. I am aware that a physician, in undertaking the treatment of a patient, assumes legal responsibilities. The law holds that he must be in possession of a reasonable amount of learning, skill, and experience; and in case of malpractice, or of gross ignorance, he is exposed to heavy damages; but leaving such instances out of consideration, I maintain that a medical man, professing to deal with human life, is in conscience bound to be possessed of competent skill, which he can only acquire by long and patient study."

The professor informed his pupils that he expected to have an abundant supply of subjects during his course of lectures, so as to illustrate and confirm his theories and teachings by a tangible examination and comparison of the human organic structure. " For," he concluded, " when the divine spirit that animates the human body has departed, nothing but clay remains; and to examine into it, in order to find out the locality of disease, and thus be enabled afterward to cure it, is a consummation that deserves the thanks instead of the disfavor of the community."

After these words, he went to the marble table upon which the subject was lying, and bade his pupils remove the blanket enveloping it. Then appeared to the gaze the remains of a young woman — tall, admirably formed, and retaining a surprising beauty in the very embrace of death. When the professor's eye fell upon the features of the corpse, he started back as though overcome with horror. Then, becoming pale and bewildered, and trembling as with a fit of ague, he looked mournfully at the body, and in broken accents, with a sobbing sigh, like a man prostrated by immense and sudden affliction, he staggered and fell heavily to the floor.

CHAPTER XVIII.

 DECLARE," said Asmodeus, while we were leaving the hall, "New-York is a queer place. One can scarcely take a step without falling upon a dramatic picture of human life. Just see that eminent professor—a worthy man, besides—how could he suspect, when he procured a dead body for the opening of his lectures, it would be just that of a former sweetheart! What singular incidents occur in this great planet of ours!"

"Why, was it the corpse of his former mistress he was about to cut with his scalpel, and whose sight so tragically ended his lecture?"

"Certainly, it was. A mistress he tenderly loved, and whose whereabouts he had been vainly trying to ascertain for three years past. Science alone could console his mind and reconcile him to his melancholy separation. It will now be more than ever the object of his devotion."

"Do you know the history of the doctor and of this unfortunate woman?"

"What a question! I had foreseen, my dear sir," coolly replied Asmodeus, "the sad occurrence which terminated the doctor's lecture, while I was taking you to the hospital. And now I will commence the doctor's history."

DOCTOR SAUNDERS'S HISTORY.

"The hero of this story is not yet thirty years old, and is already celebrated in America. He has discovered a process to cure consumptive and asthmatic persons, which consists, I believe, in the inhalation of ether; and as a lecturer, his talent is really of a superior order.

"Born of poor parents, his serious turn of mind and great desire for learning, while attending a public school, were noticed by one of the professors. This gentleman advised young Saunders's parents to confide their son to him, as he would like to complete his education. He found, soon after, to help him in his good work, a Boston merchant. The latter took charge of the boy, and placed him in one of the best Boston schools. His intention, at first, was to make a merchant of him, when of age. But he had the good sense to consult Saunders's disposition when his education was finished. The young man evinced a preference for the medical art; and in consequence, his protector sent him to New-York, where, after two years of diligent study, he obtained the degree of doctor of medicine from the medical college.

"At that time Saunders's protector was one of the most prosperous merchants of Boston. His main business consisted in shipping ice to nearly every part of the world. The ice trade was quite insignificant at the beginning of the present century, and for a long time was monopolized by two or three merchants, who had taken it into their minds to turn to account the ice of the New-England lakes. Competition soon followed, when the taste for this cheap luxury spread from the Southern and Western States to the West-Indies, South-America, even India and China; and Saunders's protector was one of the merchants who competed with this monopoly. Success had early rewarded his enterprise. He began to live in high style, and, as is customary with most Americans, he spent all his profits. Saving, as I have already observed, is an exception in this country; few merchants provide for losses and reverses, and many even spend beforehand their expected profits.

" The merchant's wife helped him, as much as she could, to squander the profits of this ice trade. When, after years of hard toil, people become prosperous, they often turn extravagant and lose control over themselves; they imagine their prosperity will never cease; and Mr. Brainless (such was the name of the Boston merchant) was fated, as will be seen, to add his name to those of many Americans who, after living in affluence and realizing large profits, end their lives in misery.

" Mr. Brainless possessed a benevolent disposition, which he strikingly exhibited toward Saunders. Not satisfied with paying for the primary education of the young man, he displayed the same generosity when Saunders went to New-York, sending him money to pay for his board and other expenses attending his medical studies. Mr. Brainless found a reward for his liberality in the praise bestowed on the young man by his professors. The progress of Saunders in medical science was, in fact, rapid and promising; and his protector, who continued to be prosperous in his trade, had come to think that Providence favored him for his giving a helping hand to the young man. The latter was looked upon by the family of Mr. Brainless as one of its members; he spent the holidays with it; and an ardent affection had sprung up between him and the eldest daughter of his protector, to the apparent satisfaction of the parents.

"Delia, and a sister two years younger, were the only children of Mr. Brainless; and his wife had early taught them her own ideas as regards American ladies—that is, that they are born to adorn the world and govern the other sex. As a consequence, they worshiped luxury, and were not tempered to undergo with fortitude the many trials of life.

"Most assuredly, many American ladies are prepared for all emergencies. Not a few follow their husbands to the Far West, and aid the bold pioneers in the good work of carrying American civilization beyond the Rocky Mountains. But, as a truthful historian, I must add that young ladies, brought up amid the luxuries and pleasures of large cities, object more and more to a dull and solitary life in remote and thinly settled parts of the country. Hence the great number of bachelors in the new States and territories, and the plethora of maidens in the Atlantic States—especially in those included in the section of country known as New-England.

"Saunders, after obtaining his degree of doctor, returned to Boston. Delia was at that time in the full bloom of her beauty, and courted by many young men. Her parents were reputed wealthy, and therefore, many a young Bostonian, beside his admiration for Miss Brainless, would have been glad to marry her, with the cherished prospect of being, at a future day, her father's partner in business. But, as I said before, the young lady loved Saunders; and they were engaged a few months after the return of the latter.

"When informed of that circumstance, Mr. Brainless did not object to the marriage of the young couple. But he wisely observed to Saunders that he thought him too young to marry then, and that his daughter, not yet eighteen years old, could wait for him a couple of years under the paternal roof. That time, he said, Saunders could devote to the study of medicine in France; and if he could succeed in getting a diploma from the Paris University, his fortune in the United States would amount to a certainty; as the public is aware that the medical education young men can procure in the United States is but superficial— hence the general preference for those physicians who have been able to perfect their medical study in Europe.

"These observations deeply impressed Saunders's mind. To complete in Paris his medical attainments was the secret desire of his heart. He loved Delia, but he loved science also; and he well knew he had acquired but the rudiments of medicine. Europe alone offered him the means to complete his education; and he was delighted to think he might be an honor to the profession, after returning to America. Would not Delia also be proud to marry a man of science and reputation?

"When he was ready to depart, Mr. Brainless put in Saunders's hand a sufficient sum of money to secure him a living in Paris during two years; and after exchanging the usual vows of eternal love with Delia, our future celebrity sailed for Europe.

"A few letters of introduction, from some Americans of high standing in science, opened to him the doors of all the learned societies of Paris. Besides, strangers are sure to be warmly welcomed in France, when they go there for the purpose of enlightening their minds—thus paying an admiring tribute to the scientific institutions of that country. Saunders had, in consequence, no trouble in getting admitted, as an assistant physician, into one of the Paris hospitals; and he devoted himself to learning with indomitable energy. He regularly wrote, concerning himself and his studies, to Mr. Brainless, who answered him with a merchant's regularity. Delia also added, from time to time, a few lines to her father's letters; and thus, divided between love and study, time passed rapidly and pleasantly with Saunders.

"But he met with an unexpected disappointment when the two years he purposed to spend in Paris were elapsed: he was obliged to prolong his stay in the French capital, as the long-desired diploma from the Paris University could be obtained only after a three years' course of study; and sorely grieved at this unlooked-for turn of affairs, he imparted the news to his protector and to Delia. While thanking Mr. Brainless for his past and present liberality, he informed him he was now able, through the salary he received from the hospital managers, to provide for himself; and he wrote to Delia to assure her of his unfailing love, begging her to wait for him a year longer. Mr. Brainless and his daughter sent him encouraging words; their feelings for him, they said, remained unchanged; and Delia, in particular, wrote him that, as she had waited two, she could easily wait one year longer, adding, in a somewhat coquettish manner, that, by that time, she would be hardly of age. But, as will be seen, serious and sad events in the Brainless family took place during the few months Saunders was obliged to prolong his stay abroad.

"Mr. Brainless had been singularly fortunate in his speculations as long as he had confined them to shipping ice. But, in an evil hour, he entered into a combination with a few capitalists, which proved disastrous. Their object was to monopolize the cotton crop, so as to determine an advance in price, and sell the article at an advantage. Many banks of Boston and New-York became interested in this scheme, and a large quantity of cotton was purchased, at a low rate, throughout the South, while none was selling in the North. The effects of the combination were soon felt in the Atlantic ports; and the difference between the purchase price of the article and its actual market value represented profits to the amount of several millions of dollars, when a financial crisis burst out in England, owing to sundry changes the Ritualists endeavored to introduce into the liturgy. Within a few days, tidings reached here that the hours for labor had been shortened in Manchester; then came news that some factories had been obliged to close; again, that the crisis was spreading over all the continent; finally, that enormous quantities of Indian cotton were shipping for Liverpool, so that there was no prospect of a demand, for several months to come, for the American textile.

"The influence of this sad news was decisive. The price of cotton, in New-York and Boston, fell rapidly; and all the efforts of the confederates to stop its depreciation were powerless. They had accumulated an immense stock, with the expectation of dictating their own conditions to foreign markets; and now the latter did not want the article at any price. At the same time, the promissory notes given in payment tc Southern planters and cotton-brokers were coming to maturity; and the confederated speculators were doomed to a dreadful catastrophe. Compared with the purchase price, cotton was now five cents lower per pound! The banks withdrew their credit, and Mr. Brainless and all his associates, being immediately subjected to unrelenting prosecutions from the very monetary establishments that had countenanced, at its inception, their monopolizing operations, were obliged to fail.

"In a few weeks, Saunders's benefactor was so far reduced as to be compelled to appeal to his friends for means to live. All his property had been either attached or sold; and when he saw the result of twenty years' hard labor swept away, as by a whirlwind, his mental faculties gave way; in a short time he became so much demented that he was confined in the State insane asylum.

"Unfortunately for Mrs. Brainless and her children, she had not imitated the foresight of many American women, who urge their husbands, as soon as their business permits them to do so, to purchase a house. The house so purchased belongs to the wife; and whatever be the vicissitudes of her husband's affairs, his creditors can not touch it, unless they prove it has been purchased out of their own money. As it was, Mr. Brainless, during his prosperity, had not thought of this prudential course; and so, when the crash came, his wife and children were actually houseless and homeless.

"Under these painful circumstances, Delia did not hesitate to write to Saunders, and inform him of the misfortunes that had befallen their family. Though she did not tell him what he should do, she did not conceal from her lover that three unfortunate women had now no one else but him in the world they could depend upon.

"Unfortunately, Saunders had left Paris when Delia's letter arrived. He was one of a committee of young physicians the French government had sent to Asia, for the purpose of investigating the causes of an epidemic disease, and had been himself affected by it, and obliged to stay several months in Constantinople. When he returned to Paris, after his recovery, and saw Delia's letter, he at once acted as became a high-toned gentleman. He immediately took leave of the numerous friends he had made among the learned society of Paris; and, handsomely rewarded by the French government for his devotedness to

the cause of mankind during his stay in Asia, he sailed
for the United States.

"As soon as he arrived, he went to Boston to see the
Brainless family ; but he learned they had left that place,
nearly one year before, with the apparent determination to
settle in New-York. He at once returned to this city, and,
after many pertinacious researches, he succeeded in ascertaining that Mrs. Brainless had kept a boarding-house in
New-York, and had, after a few months, failed in her undertaking. Furthermore he could not learn. Nevertheless, the doctor continued his search, and through the newspapers tried to obtain some information concerning the
whereabouts of the persons to whom he was so tenderly
attached. He repeatedly advertised in the West, in the
South — wherever he thought his inquiries might be successful. But all his expense and exertion proved fruitless.

"In the mean while, the fame he had acquired in Europe
rapidly spread over the United States. He had hardly arrived in New-York, when he was surrounded by enthusiastic friends ; and the door of his house was besieged with
patients as soon as it became known he would thenceforth
devote his attainments to his native land. Modest, as are all
men of real merit, affable to every body, he is very popular.
An honor to his profession, his most extravagant dreams
of fortune are realized.

"In the midst of the many cares imposed upon him by
the position he had attained, Saunders did not relinquish
his search for his benefactor's wife and daughters. He
has placed poor Brainless in Dr. Greedy's insane asylum,
and he goes there every week, spending a few hours with
the unfortunate man. Wealthy and celebrated, he knows
the debt of gratitude he owes to every member of a family
that, at the time of its prosperity, had adopted him ; be-

sides, he had kept in his heart, as intense as in his youth, his love for Delia. When, a few weeks ago, he was pursuing his investigation concerning her throughout Canada, France, and California, he was far from suspecting she was living in New-York, and but a few doors from his house. What had become of her and the other members of the family, after Mr. Brainless's bankruptcy, remains to be said.

"When an American lady, reduced in circumstances, is obliged to labor to support her existence, she promptly comes to a determination. She does not think of keeping a millinery or a hosiery store ; to turn mantua maker ; to keep a school for children ;.but her mind settles at once upon opening a boarding-house.

" American women dislike manual labor ; few are fitted to keep a store, and still less to manage female operatives, for the very reason that they have not been brought up to a trade ; and, to be able to manage others, whatever be the branch of labor, the manager must be thoroughly acquainted with it. This mischievous condition of females in the United States begins, justly, to attract the attention of philanthropists. It is all very well to assert that American women are not born for work ; that the only parts assigned to them in life, are those of wives and mothers. These assertions, pleasing as they are in theory, are not indorsed by the stern logic of fact, thousands and thousands of women being compelled to work in the United States, as well as in Europe, unless they choose to starve. For here, as in Europe, few only are born in affluence. But many occupations, within the reach of women, can afford them a living, when they choose to procure an honest means of subsistence, and when mothers learn to bring up their daughters properly, by instructing and preparing them to meet all the emergencies of life, instead of merely making of them priestesses of fashion.

"To-day, as a consequence of the education they receive, growing up amid prejudices and deceit, American women often lack fortitude in the hour of misfortune. Proud to a fault, they know how to conceal their wants. When young, they often have recourse to questionable means to release themselves from embarrassment; and, after their youth has faded, they take to keeping a boarding-house.

"Mrs. Brainless and her daughters, unwilling to keep a boarding-house in Boston, the place of their former prosperity, had come to New-York. They sold their jewels, and, adding the money thus obtained to a few hundreds loaned them by old friends, they comfortably furnished a house in a fashionable street of this city. Unfortunately, Mrs. Brainless, lacking experience in that line of business, accepted as boarders adventurous young men, who are always in quest of new establishments of that kind. They usually paid their bills by taking her daughters to theatres and other places of amusement; and she was soon perplexed with debts and other demands beyond her means of payment.

"After a few months, the dealers who supplied Mrs. Brainless with provisions, refused to longer sell on credit. This refusal was the death-blow to her enterprise. Her boarders left the house, as soon as scanty meals became the daily fare; and one evening Mrs. Brainless found herself alone in her house, with only her two daughters, and a Louisiana planter, enamoured of Delia, and who had made known his intention to share the family's fortune. A few days later, the furniture was sold at auction, and Mrs. Brainless, her daughters, and the planter, went to New-

Orleans. They had been there but a few days, when the old lady was seized with yellow fever, and died in her children's arms.

"As soon as Mrs. Brainless was buried, the Southerner took Delia and her sister to a villa he owned on the banks of Lake Pontchartrain; and one can easily imagine what became, shortly after, of Doctor Saunders's betrothed, alone as she was, without a protector, in the power of an unprincipled man. For six months she remained the planter's mistress, after which time he became tired of her. So, selling out his villa, he returned with Delia and her sister to New-Orleans, on pretext that he had business to transact there. They stopped at a house, the mysterious behavior of whose inmates soon aroused painful suspicions in the minds of the two sisters, concerning its character. One evening, their suspicions were confirmed. The planter coolly told them he was going to Texas, for the purpose of making money, and he candidly advised them not to expect him back before he had succeeded. In the mean while, they could find, he added, in the very house at which they were boarding, many admirers to provide for their wants.

"Brainless's unfortunate children at once endeavored to leave that abode of perdition; but the landlady refused to allow them to go until they had previously paid a considerable sum of money due her for their board. Failing to do so, they were forcibly compelled to succumb to a life of untold misery and shame. Obliged to submit to every outrage in the den where they were detained as prisoners, they sought to forget their degradation by indulging in noisy dissipations. Both of them, under assumed names, became the stars of the *demi-monde* during a whole winter; and, as is commonly the case with those poor creatures lost to chastity, they sank rapidly into the slough of vice and corruption.

"After leading a few months this unnatural life, Delia's sister was drowned in the Mississippi, while on a pleasure excursion with a party of profligates; and shortly after, Delia was induced by the captain of a steamer to follow him to New-York.

"Once in the great metropolis, Saunders's former sweetheart abandoned herself more than ever to the excitement of the hour.   She began to exhibit a passion for spirituous liquors—perhaps to divert her mind from her degraded position—and soon she sank so low as to become a frequenter of those infamous haunts where thieves and the worst characters of the community resort to escape the surveillance of the police.

"Eight days ago, in a lucid interval, maddened by the horror of her situation and the recollection of the past, she came to a terrible resolution.   With a few cents she had obtained from begging in the streets, she purchased some opium; and the next day her dead body was found in one of those dirty lodging-houses where beggars and vagrants obtain a night's shelter for a small remuneration.   Neither the owner of the lodging-house nor the poor wretch who had slept beside her corpse, knew Delia Brainless.   She was taken to the morgue, where she remained exposed to the public gaze for three days.   Her identity could not be established; nobody could give to the police any information respecting her; nobody came to claim that body, still so beautiful in spite of a life of such depravity, and hence it was carried to the hospital for the use of the medical students, the very day Professor Saunders commenced his course of lectures on anatomy.

"You know the sequel."

CHAPTER XIX.

IN WHICH ASMODEUS, AFTER SPEAKING OF THE WAY MANY
PEOPLE LIVE IN NEW-YORK, TAKES THE READER TO A
PYTHONESS.

"I SEE," said I to Asmodeus, "that many miseries of the Old World are to be found in the New."

"No doubt of it. Did I not tell you, when we commenced our survey of the morals and institutions of this country, that human passions are about the same everywhere—whether men reside near the tropics or the regions of perpetual snows, and whatever be their complexion? There is in the human mind a disorderly element which the best institutions are powerless to eradicate.

"A habit, which has gone far to corrupt American morals, is that adopted by many families of living in a sort of community, in family hotels—commonly called boarding-houses—and to which I alluded when relating Doctor Saunders's history. There are over two thousand such houses in New-York—the boarding expenses varying per week and per head from three to thirty dollars. Those which ask the former price are principally patronized by the poorer working classes: there the agglomeration of men and women, from all parts of the Union, and, I might say, from the world, is ill calculated to make of them abodes of morality.

"As regards boarding-houses of a higher class, there are a few where family habits and traditions are honored—and a very few only. In all of these, ladies, free from household affairs and cares, spend their lives in leisure, while their husbands attend to their respective businesses. Idleness is everywhere an ill-adviser. Dressing and otherwise adorning themselves become their all-absorbing occupation. Besides, when all the guests of the house sit at the dining-table, every lady is anxious to look well before the boarders, and, of course, strives to outshine her neighbor. Again, although most Americans are engaged in business, there are, nevertheless, a few wealthy enough to dispense with labor, that restraint upon evil passions. Boarders of the latter class avail themselves of their leisure hours to keep company with lone ladies; accompany them in their walks, and shopping—that fascinating pastime of American women. Then, who can affirm that the camel's-hair shawl hanging from the shoulders of a fair lady, or the laces and diamonds which adorn another's ball-dress, are not so many mortgages upon their virtue? I am ready to admit that there is more disinterestedness in American politeness than in French gallantry; still, it is hard to believe Americans spend their dollars for the sake of politeness only, and through a sense of admiration for the fair sex.

"Not every American married lady, living in a boarding-house, may prove a good mother; and it may be doubted also whether every husband there enjoys the happiness of a true home. Still, the difficulty of procuring good servants; the never-ceasing exactions of the latter, their high wages; above all, the bad training of young American ladies, which makes them unable to manage a house after being married—all these reasons compel many a husband to resort to boarding life; and when ladies once become accustomed to rely upon others in household affairs, it is seldom that they can be prevailed upon afterward to keep house.

"Servants are one of the most perplexing difficulties to American families. Banded together and united by a kind of free-masonry, these helps dictate their conditions to those who require their services. Are they without employment? They receive subsidies from mutual societies. Very few become attached to the family they serve. Mobility everywhere exists in the United States—in the institutions, in the morals, in the fortunes, in the feelings of the people; and servants, of course, could not escape what seems so general a law. They leave their situations on the slightest pretext—sometimes on the flimsiest expectation of bettering their condition. Some American ladies, to retain a valuable servant, have to display much forbearance; and forbearance is a virtue seldom associated with pride.

"Servant-girls are, for the most part, Irish-born; few, very few American women condescend to serve as such. The Irish servants show little sympathy for their mistresses, who, in their turn, exhibit little kindness toward them. It has even been noticed that a latent hostility exists between female servants and their mistresses. The latter look with disgust on the extravagant taste for dress displayed by Irish girls almost immediately on their landing; and this is a detail of no small importance, when the question of domesticity in America is considered. For it is obvious that the more the servant's dress resembles that of her mistress, the more the distance which ought to separate them diminishes—at least in the opinion of the former.   Hence the silly pretensions to equality, and the consequent wranglings and difficulties which take place between mistress and servant.

"The high rents and increasing cost of provisions have lately contributed to augment the number of boarding-houses.   An American who receives a fixed salary from his employers, knows the amount he can afford to spend for the support of himself and wife.   If he keeps house, he never knows where his expenses may lead him.   As I have said before, there are about two thousand boarding-houses in New-York.   In that number are not included the many hotels, open day and night to the public, and where live, during the winter season, many American families.

"If the necessity to be constantly moving in society and among strangers has developed among American ladies a taste for dress, it has, on the other hand, trained the men to decency and good manners.   As a general thing, they are well appareled.   The American of leisure is careful to go every morning to a barber, and have his beard and hair dressed.   In every large hotel there is a regiment of these useful practitioners, of black or white complexion, and one can hardly go from one street to another without seeing a barber-shop, or, as it is genteelly termed here, a ' hair-dressing saloon.'

"A number of boarding-houses are kept by merchants' widows, who have been left in indigent circumstances. Some women, aided by old bachelors or other persons, rent houses, and furnish and open them to boarders. Among this latter class of boarding-houses, not a few are in bad repute.   In these one can rent a room for a week, a day, even an hour, for the purpose of receiving paramours ; and there, elegant prostitution finds a secret and mysterious abode.

"How many women, robed in gorgeous silk and velvet dresses, seen every hour of the day stepping from ferry-boats or horse-cars, could be traced to those secret abodes of licentiousness!   How many artless girls have been led to take the 'first false step' in these gilded dens of infamy! Every thing, however, is carried on with the utmost circumspection ; and after leaving such places, the lover and his mistress will meet each other without exchanging the slightest mark of acquaintance, without looking at, without speaking with each other."

Here we found ourselves in front of a brown-stone house, conspicuous by an elegant flight of steps.   From a sign over the front-door, this magical word,

" ASTROLOGY,"

glared at us, and green shutters, tightly closed, gave the house a mysterious appearance.

"Well," said Asmodeus, while I was gazing at it; "for one dollar apiece we can enjoy the fun of seeing at work one of our modern augurs ; and if you do not object, we will beg the Pythoness who presides within, to exert her remarkable powers of divination for our benefit."

I followed my sarcastic companion into the sibyl's dwelling, and we were shown into a parlor where we found several old and young men waiting for the oracle.   Asmodeus informed me that visitors of the fair sex are taken to another room, as also persons who desire to escape the gaze of others, until admitted into the presence of the sorceress.

A liveried servant, the same who had opened the door for us, handed us a ticket marked with a number, for which we paid two dollars.   From this number, we inferred that twenty persons, at least, had preceded us in the

waiting-rooms ; and I was afraid many hours would elapse
before we could hear the oracle ; but Asmodeus dismissed
my apprehension.

"The interview," said he, "the sibyl grants any visitor
never exceeds five minutes—a rule she strictly adheres
to. If your curiosity is not satisfied after five minutes'
questioning and counter-questioning, you may enjoy five
minutes more for the trifle of another dollar. But in no
case will the sibyl allow more than ten minutes ; for fear,
perhaps, of exposing herself in too dangerous a manner,
and wasting her time in idle controversies."

I had time, while pacing the parlor, to survey every
nook of it. It was plainly furnished ; on the mantelpiece
was a clock covered with various cabalistic ornaments, and
a few tawdry paintings were hanging on the walls.

"You can not expect to find masterpieces in America,"
said Asmodeus, interrupting my meditations ; "paintings
from masters are scarce everywhere ; and the taste of the
Americans for pictures has lately so much increased, they
satisfy it with any painting they can procure. Many persons believe their parlors poorly furnished unless their
walls are hung with half a dozen paintings. Thousands
are yearly imported from Belgium, France, and Germany ;
and they all sell well—especially those whose frames are
showy. There are, perhaps, two or three galleries in the
United States worth observing ; but the number of con-
noisseurs is very limited, in spite of the infatuation for
paintings evinced by persons rapidly accumulating wealth.
Besides, taste and an unerring appreciation for works of
art are derived from comparative studies of different
schools of art ; well-stocked public museums only can
afford adequate facilities for them, and there are none in
the United States."

From different places on the walls hung ebony frames, ornamented with a gilt bead. They inclosed a show-card, elegantly printed, in English, French, German, and Spanish. I copied in my diary the intelligence thus conveyed to the world by the priestess, and which ran as follows :

"Mrs. SMART reveals most important secrets to persons of both sexes, and restores peace and happiness to those in despair, in consequence of loss of fortune, or the death of friends or relatives. She reunites separated lovers ; gives information respecting absent persons, and also property lost or stolen ; indicates the profession or trade visitors should adopt to acquire wealth ; brings about desirable marriages, and gives the name and prognosticates the character of future husbands or wives.

" From her knowledge of the effects and different aspects of the stars, she can foretell future events and reveal the whole life, from the cradle to the grave."

The show-card concluded by stating that persons residing abroad, or in the country, could obtain the astrologer's advice, by sending a lock of hair, date of birth, a likeness, and one dollar.

I had just copied this amusing notice, when we were notified the oracle of the house was awaiting us. We entered her sanctum, a small room, lined with green hangings. She was seated in a gilded chair, and in front of her was a table, whose carved legs represented Egyptian sphinxes. As far as I could judge, through the dim light of the room, the pythoness was a tall woman, about thirty years old, and quite good-looking. She was robed in black velvet ; and through the open sleeves of her dress, arms as white as Parian marble could be discerned.

"This, my dear sir," said she, approaching Asmodeus, " is quite a surprise from you, for which I feel deeply thankful. But why did you not send me your name? I would have spared you the tediousness of waiting one hour. Yet it was only through chance, while looking through yonder concealed lutherns, I perceived you in the parlor among the others there waiting."

"You are always as good as beautiful," gallantly responded Asmodeus ; "but we live in a land where equality reigns supreme, and where privileges are hardly tolerated. We would have patiently waited until entitled, by our ticket, to be ushered into your presence."

"You have not come, I suppose, to enjoy my performances?" asked the pythoness playfully. "I can not teach you, Mr. Asmodeus, concerning future events; but if you felt inclined, you could say a great deal about them. But, whatever be the object of your visit, I hope it will be a long one, for my day's work is now over."

Then, at the tap of a bell, a servant entered. Handing him a bundle of bank-bills, "Give back," said she, "this money to the persons waiting, unless they prefer to keep their tickets for to-morrow. I am tired ; and I feel," she added, looking knowingly at Asmodeus, "I am no longer under the influence of the spirit."

"If," said Asmodeus, "all our clairvoyants and astrologers were like you, they would compose, I apprehend, one of the most charming and dangerous classes of society."

"Though I do not well understand what you mean, I admit they form, if not a charming, at least a dangerous class. To levy a tribute on human credulity is, I admit, going far ; but to make a supposed science subservient to men's debauchery and woman's frailty, is, most assuredly, a detestable aggravation of the evil. You know, as well as I, that most of our astrologers are but intermediaries between persons of both sexes in quest of adventures, and that interviews are brought about in the houses of these fortune-tellers."

"And why, entertaining such an opinion of your profession, did you enter it? Nay, why do you persist in following it?"

"For an explanation of that mystery, ask those actresses who will not leave the stage after making a million of dollars, what induces them to cling to it. Necessity compels us to do something; and if we are fortunate enough to please the public, we persist, with feelings of satisfaction, in a calling at first reluctantly adopted. Besides, I have four children; and I mean to supply them with an education, and leave them enough money to enjoy the goods of this world. Through my knowledge of human, in default of celestial affairs, I have arrived at the conviction, though the confession is somewhat painful to womanly dignity, that money is equivalent to genius, to health, to honesty. For with money, almost every thing may be procured. Then my children shall prosper, if they live; and I will continue to foretell future events from the course of the stars, unless you can point out another profession which, with so little trouble, yields as much money as mine."

"Is it really a profitable one?" I asked the lady.

"You are the friend of Mr. Asmodeus," she replied; "I have therefore nothing to conceal. Every sitting lasts five minutes. When a visitor enters my sanctum, I turn up this hour-glass. As soon as five minutes have elapsed, I dismiss the visitor, and another is admitted. Not to over-task myself, I receive but eight visitors per hour, and deliver oracles during only six hours of the day. To the forty-eight dollars usually gained for these sittings, add an equal sum obtained through my correspondence; and you will know, almost as well as myself, the daily benefits derived from astrological science."

"It yields you," said Asmodeus, "an income quite as large as that of the President of the United States. But, I declare, I was far from suspecting the correspondence netted as much as the sittings."

"I will show you a proof of it: here are the letters received this morning. I have not, as yet, unsealed one of them." And so saying, she proceeded to open them, one after another, and disclosed to our view a large quantity of bank-bills.

"You can not imagine," she went on to say, "how very busy this correspondence constantly keeps me. Two clerks are constantly occupied either in copying my answers, or writing letters I dictate. A sort of subtile intimacy springs up between my correspondents and myself; and you would be much surprised were I to reveal the names of some among them. You would recognize statesmen, bankers, merchants, officers of the law, even ministers of the Gospel, without speaking of their wives and daughters. How many confidences, both pleasing and painful, have found a resting-place in those boxes piled on the top of that bookcase!"

I asked, rather inadvertently, to what causes she attributed the great notoriety she enjoyed.

"To newspaper advertisements," she replied. "Whoever entertains an implicit faith in the influence of the Press, and is able and willing to pay handsomely for that influence, will reap, soon or late, large profits from his outlay. Any adventurer bold enough to risk a fortune for the purpose of making and selling ordinary perfumes or remedies, is sure to double, or even treble, that fortune in a short time. Every day affords an instance of such strokes of good luck.

For my part, I spend twenty-five dollars per day for advertising; and you have seen the profitable returns of such an investment."

"You well know," interrupted Asmodeus, "the power of that great agent of modern times—*Publicity.* It is the drop of water that makes its way through granite. On reading each morning that Mrs. Smart can foretell every body's life from the cradle to the grave, every body decides to test the astrologer's skill. But I apprehend, in spite of your attractive conversation, my friend, who desired to see a pythoness on her tripod, will be sorely disappointed."

"God forbid," replied the lady, "I should disappoint the friend of a man I consider as the author of my fortune." And without adding another word, she touched a bell, and ordered the servant who answered it to introduce the first visitor who should call into her sanctum.

"I was saying, my dear sir," she resumed, "that I am indebted to you for my fortune. In fact, a suggestion from you instilled into me the idea to try astrology as a business —a new thing, at that time, in the United States. My husband, Colonel Smart, died, leaving no fortune to his family. He had squandered a somewhat considerable patrimony in a very singular manner — by purchasing patents. One of those boxes you see on my bookcase is full of those patents, obtained from the Federal Government, after paying a few dollars into the public treasury. Every week some new discovery engrossed the Colonel's mind, for which, of course, he had paid, and sometimes very dearly. One day, he bought a patent by means of which rails could be dispensed with, and locomotives run on common roads. The next day, he had secured the means to use, as an accessory power, the engine's smoke. At one time, he purchased a process to manage balloons;

at another, a discovery which solved the problem of a self-acting propeller. Finally, when he discovered he had squandered all his wealth for mere chimeras, grief so preyed upon his mind that he soon shortened his life by dissipation. You were among those of his friends who assisted at his funeral, and I heard you lament that he had wasted his talents and energy in scientific researches, in preference to embracing some quack profession. 'For,' you said, 'in a country of charlatans, to make money, one must become a charlatan!'

"I was struck with that observation—not very flattering, to be sure, to the American character; and when I was obliged to seek, by my own labor, a means of subsistence for myself and children, I was involuntarily reminded of your suggestion.

"I had studied, and felt a fondness for, the science which treats of the laws of the heavenly bodies, and the principles by which their motions are regulated, with their various phenomena. The term astrology was used by the ancients instead of the modern word astronomy; the etymology of both is the same; and up to the time of Galileo, no distinction was made between astronomy proper and that science which attributed to the heavenly bodies a ruling influence over the physical and moral world, and which was so unfortunately exploded by true philosophy. Astrology was practiced among the Romans; it was in high repute at the court of Catherine of Medici, and Alphonso the Wise, King of Castile and Leon, made himself more famous by his astronomical tablets than by his code of laws. Prophetic power has been in vogue at all times and in every country, and is sure to make proselytes wherever it finds a foothold.

"With these notions, and persuaded you were right respecting charlatanry in the United States, I boldly commenced the business of fortune-telling, and I succeeded beyond my most sanguine expectations. Now, you see, Mr. Asmodeus, I was right when I said I was under great obligations to you for your suggestion."

At this moment the hall-bell rang, and the servant soon after announced that a visitor was waiting. We now entered an adjoining closet, from which, through holes in the partition, which were concealed from visitors, every thing transpiring in the sanctum could be seen.

Mrs. Smart sat in the gilded arm-chair, which Asmodeus had called a tripod ; and, at a given signal, the visitor was ushered into her presence. This was a tall, thin lady, who remained closely vailed, until the priestess bade her reveal her face. This done, Mrs. Smart attentively looked at the lady, whose hands, after they had, at her request, been ungloved, she closely examined.

"How old are you ?" she then abruptly inquired.

"Twenty-eight," answered the visitor.

"I want to know your real age," rejoined the sibyl. "Because there is no registration of births in the United States, women pretend to remain always young; at least, they adopt the number of years that suits their fancy. But I will show you that those who consult my science can never succeed in deceiving me : you are forty-two years old. And now, what do you require of me !"

"I desire to know whether the man I love will marry me."

"You love nobody," sternly responded the sorceress ; "you covet the fortune of the man you want to marry, and nothing more. But, before attempting to realize your wish, be sure the husband you left in the West is not living, and let me advise you to find a less dangerous means to pay your debts than the marriage you have in view."

So saying, the pythoness, with a dignified wave of the hand, dismissed the visitor, whose uneasiness and dismay were apparent. We then reëntered the sanctum, and congratulated Mrs. Smart upon the soundness and morality of her advice.

"Chance again favored me," she answered. "I instantly recognized that woman, whose cold, studied manner and uneasy glance bode no good. We do not speak with the same freedom and boldness to all visitors, unless we are fully acquainted with some peculiarities or circumstances concerning them. For that purpose, we keep a rather expensive staff of agents in the principal hotels and large boarding-houses of the country. Through these agents we get information respecting the persons who are induced to visit us, and thus are enabled to make startling revelations. Again, through those holes in the partition, which are invisible to callers, and yonder reflecting mirrors, we can leisurely survey visitors, before admitting them into our presence, while confidential agents, always in waiting in the parlors, induce them to talk of their feelings and situation. Then those agents repair to the sanctum, through a secret passage, and impart to us the information they have thus gathered. By this means, the astrologer is thoroughly prepared to pronounce her oracles."

We laughed heartily at this candid confession of the artifices which compose the stock in trade of clairvoyants and astrologers. After which we kindly took leave of Mrs. Smart, very much pleased with our visit.

"I was far from thinking," said Asmodeus, when we reached the street, "that the business of those impostors is so profitable—which fact shows the American people's thirst for sensations. I was aware that diviners have in every society exerted much influence upon the ignorant classes. But a large part of the wealthy and educated also, if we are to believe Mrs. Smart, apply to fortune-tellers to unvail the future; and idle women, principally, are the best clients of those swindlers, with which New-York abounds. In some European countries they would not be tolerated. Here, grave, learned men do not mind them; and they offer ladies an opportunity to fritter away their time.

"The evil, after all, would not be a serious one, were not most of the sibyls, as confessed by Mrs. Smart, dangerous intermediaries, encouraging transactions of a more reprehensible character than their fallacious oracles."

Asmodeus was here interrupted by a crowd of newsboys, howling the evening papers. Every body eagerly purchased one, as the excited boys shouted that an awful calamity had taken place. We purchased a copy, and read that a number of persons had perished on board of one of the steamers plying between New-York and a neighboring island. That steamer had met another, and both had concluded to run a race. For the purpose of increasing her rapidity, the firemen of one of the boats had poured turpentine into her furnaces; and the inflammable ·liquid, spreading with lightning-like rapidity, had fired the ill-fated steamer. A number of persons had been burned to death, and others, seeing the destruction of the boat was inevitable, had jumped overboard, and sank before assistance could be procured.

"Here," coolly remarked Asmodeus, after perusing the paper, "is a calamity Mrs. Smart had not foreseen, on looking at the stars. Out of the four children she had sent to breathe the fresh sea-air, two have been drowned, and the remaining two have been so dreadfully burned their life is despaired of!"

CHAPTER XX.

THE day had arrived when, according to Asmodeus's prediction, I should recover my stolen watch. Precisely at nine o'clock in the morning, that mysterious personage walked into my room, and a few minutes after, we heard a knock at the door, when, on saying "Come in," a young man entered, whose whiskers were cut after the latest fashion, and whose aristocratic demeanor would have nowhere passed unobserved. He was by no means deficient in self-possession—rather one of those men who are at home everywhere.

"Gentlemen," said he, holding up a newspaper, "it was yesterday my good fortune to read an advertisement that places me in the pleasant situation to be of some service to you. Circumstances of no importance whatever to anybody but myself have put in my possession the time-piece you have lost, and which I am indeed fortunate to restore to you, though it is a genuine Breguet."

So saying, he pulled my watch from his fob, and handed it to Asmodeus.

"Here is a fifty-dollar bill," said my friend, "which would be, indeed, an insignificant compensation for your trouble, but which we should be exceedingly grateful to have you present to the person who found the article. Accept personally, sir, our thanks for your gentlemanlike punctuality."

So, here I beheld one of those notorious pickpockets, and assisted in one of those transactions Asmodeus represented as an advance of civilization. This pickpocket was evidently a character worth studying, and Asmodeus, who understood the curiosity of my mind, asked him how long he had been in the United States. " For," he added, " you speak more purely than many Americans by birth. I mean, you do not employ any of the slang phrases peculiar to Americans. Besides, your pronunciation stamps you as a son of Albion."

" You are right, sir," answered the pickpocket. "I was born in Old England, the land of large fortunes and great miseries, and you will be not a little surprised to learn I belong to one of the most ancient families of the United Kingdom—that of Earl Stirling's, of Stirlingshire. My childhood was spent in the Sidlaw mountains, where arise the beautiful rivers Tay, Clyde, and Forth. My father, Lord James Stirling, died a few years ago, leaving as usual, and in conformity to the grant made to his ancestors, all his fortune to my eldest brother. That fortune had been reduced by Lord Stirling's extravagant style of living, and the estate bequeathed my brother was heavily mortgaged. ' William,' said he, on our return from our father's funeral, ' I wish you to thoroughly understand my situation, and here it is in a few words : Lord Stirling's income amounted to thirty thousand pounds. But he regularly spent double that amount, as he resided in London most of the time. The estate is mortgaged for three hundred thousand pounds, and I have just signed an instrument for the be-

nefit of my creditors, in consequence of which all mortgages will be paid after twenty years. During that period,
I shall be compelled to live on an income of ten thousand
pounds—hardly sufficient to keep a dozen horses and a
pack of hounds. So, you perceive, the Earl of Stirling
will fare miserably during that period of privation, and is
sorry to say he can do nothing to help you. Consequently,
you will do well to try your fortune in any part of the
world but Scotland. You do not lack talent, and can not
fail to succeed.'

"I had never thought of the laws concerning the state
or privileges of the first-born among children—laws to
which Great Britain clings with so much tenacity. My
father had liberally provided for my expenses, and, since I
had left school, I had resided in London, in a style adequate
to my birth. My brother, on the contrary, had mostly
lived at home, among the mountains. He belonged, soul
and body, to our ancestors' domain. And I know him well
enough to be convinced he would sacrifice every thing, without speaking of brotherly affection, to liberate the patri-
monial estate. He hardly believed himself to be Earl Stirling, of Stirlingshire, when it recurred to his mind that our
father's creditors had a legal lien upon those farms and
forests he inherited. Positive I could expect nothing whatever from him, I started for London, with light baggage,
after shaking hands with the new Earl of Stirling.

"As soon as I arrived in that great commercial metropolis of the world, I ordered a suit of mourning, rented a
house in the West End, which I handsomely furnished,
and purchased a team of splendid horses and several carriages. The sons of noblemen can buy, without difficulty
—of course, on credit—any thing they desire from tradesmen, accustomed from generations to worship the aristo-

cracy. And besides, in this particular case, that interesting class of society mistook me for the eldest son of Lord Stirling, my brother having seldom appeared in London. It was not my business to undeceive them ; and therefore, during three years, I led a very pleasant life, borrowing money from my father's old friends—even from shop-keepers—and sometimes making handsome profits at the gaming-table.

" A misunderstanding which took place at one of the fashionable clubs in London, between one of the queen's ministers and myself—one evening he had been severely handled in the Parliament—shut me out of the houses and clubs I frequented. When I imparted to some friends, living, like myself, by their wits, this misunderstanding at the gaming-table, with a cabinet minister, they advised me to leave London at once.

"'Lose no time,' said they, 'to put the Channel between you and your creditors. Before forty-eight hours are elapsed, every body in London will know you have been caught cheating at play. People will inquire about you and your family ; and when it is ascertained that you are Lord Stirling's youngest son, and consequently not worth a farthing, your creditors will become infuriated ; and, mind you, the debtors' prison is, unfortunately, still frowning in White Cross street. Repair as soon as possible, to the gay capital of France."

" Their advice seemed sound enough ; inasmuch as the amount of my debts was a great deal more than my friends could suspect. They tendered me a few sovereigns, which I accepted ; and, hastening to borrow whatever I could from my father's old friends, my tailor, and a few other shop-keepers—to sell to some Jews my horses and carriages, and also my house-furniture, on condition they should remove nothing till twenty-four hours after my departure, I left the field of my first exploits.

"In Paris, I soon realized that the manners and customs of the French are entirely opposite to those of their neighbors across the Channel. The police are everywhere, and a freeman feels somewhat uneasy in moving about the city. Some of my countrymen who had also thought it advisable to wait in France for the cooling of their creditors' wrath, introduced me into some gaming-houses. One of the gamblers who frequented these houses was such a suspicious-looking individual that we could not drive from our minds the thought that he was a detective. While in London I had frequently visited James Stealer's well-known institution, and tried my skill among, and in competition with, his many pupils. Numerous manikins, dressed in every conceivable manner, are scattered though a spacious hall; and there James Stealer, with his white neck-tie, his rosy cheeks, and oily manner—in short, looking like a Cambridge professor or an Episcopalian minister—may be seen walking to and fro, and teaching young boys to abstract from those manikins any article he may point out—which article the boys must obtain without moving the other figures—without giving the bystanders a chance to notice the removal. And they perform the task while walking, running, tumbling—in fact, in every imaginable position.

"After a few weeks, perhaps a few months, devoted to such performances, the boys acquire a really wonderful proficiency in the art of relieving the manikins of numerous articles such as cloaks, umbrellas, watches, but principally portemonnaies. When thoroughly proficient, Stealer lets loose his pupils upon the world, and allows them to practice the science in which they have graduated, on the denizens of the goodly city of London. By this means, in spite of many losses from the interference of the police, the ranks of the pickpocket army are always full.

"Stealer had time and again congratulated me upon my proficiency in sleight-of-hand, and even offered me a diploma as graduate of the institution he had managed, for many years, with an incomparable efficiency. But though exceedingly flattered at this acknowledgment of my skill, the son of Lord Stirling had declined the proffered honor. I remembered the teachings of that excellent man, and decided to make use of them, after exhausting, in Paris, the liberality of her most gracious majesty the queen's ambassador, his secretaries, and even his servants. Every thing 'went on smoothly and satisfactorily for several months; though I could not help observing that the French are a parsimonious, cautious people. For instance, they keep their portemonnaies in a secret pocket, and those portemonnaies themselves generally contain very little. And, as a climax to their meanness, a double chain secures their watches to the bottom of their fobs! Such a ridiculous and antiquated habit nearly involved me, one day, in serious trouble, from which I was rescued through national pride. When they were apprised of my mishap and consequent imprisonment, her most gracious majesty the queen's ambassador, his secretaries and servants, asked for my release, pretending I was mentally deranged. The police, for fear of weakening the alliance between the two countries, set me free, on condition that I should leave France within twenty-four hours. I assented to the proposition, inasmuch as I had nothing more to do there; and, as it was not yet quite safe for me to return to the land of my birth, I sailed for the United States.

"I have resided here several years, and hardly a day passes that I do not congratulate myself on having become

a citizen of the great Republic.   What a delightful country, gentlemen !   How tolerant the people !   With a little
ingenuity and expertness, what an easy life every one may
enjoy !   On reaching this highly favored land, one feels
he is really free.   Name me another country where business is conducted on such loose and careless principles?
Look at the merchants and bankers !   Why, gentlemen,
they trust to the care of small boys bags of gold, and tin
boxes containing millions of dollars !   From my particular stand-point, this state of things is highly gratifying, and
far be it from me to object to it.   Again, in no other country can one meet, at every step, at every hour, day and
night, so many ladies whose dresses and jewels in themselves represent a fortune ; and I dare say many a man
has been tempted to run away with one of those fair creatures, if only for the sake of possessing himself of the
treasures she carries about her.   Then, every body in the
United States—man, woman, girl, and boy—must have a
time-piece, inclosed, if you please, in a case a great deal
more substantial than those used in Europe.   Among many
other oddities, the American people are conspicuous for
their want of being posted on time.   To satisfy an extraordinary demand for watches, steam is now applied to their
manufacture ; and watch-making by steam machinery is in
a fair way to soon deprive Switzerland of her monopoly of
selling cheap chronometers to the world.

" You understand, gentlemen—and the fact is so plain
I need not insist upon it—that the general habit of wearing
watches and jewels makes of the United States a really
attractive country for the light-fingered gentry—a ' promised land ' for rogues and pickpockets.   So absorbed are
the people in mercantile transactions, that the business I
devote to my leisure hours is alike profitable and pleasant.

Though operating with the utmost confidence, I have recently determined to give a part of my proceeds to car-conductors and a few police-officers. But for the aid of these associates, something might sometimes happen to baffle my skill and experience ; and you will concede it is good policy to avoid all unpleasantness by giving away a part of my profits."

With these words, the son of Lord Stirling, of Stirling-shire, after bowing in the most exquisite manner, and retaining to the last an incomparable suavity, left my room.

" That fellow," said Asmodeus, " is certainly one of the most impudent rogues I ever saw. His photograph ought to be placed in the pickpockets' gallery. But only those of poor unfortunate devils are to be found there, I am told ; and one vainly seeks for the likeness of many an elegant scamp who moves in the best society. The love of luxury, the loose way of transacting business, want of vigilance from policemen, excessive indulgence from courts of justice—every thing favors the pickpocket's business, as boldly admitted by that pretended son of an English nobleman. But it is not always, and in every case, carried on safely—even though it be true that some bad members of the police force connive with the light-fingered gentry.

" A few weeks ago, I joined a picnic-party ; a steamer had been chartered and a band engaged for the occasion. In spite of all precautions, a few pickpockets will sneak in among excursionists ; and such was the case with us, as you will see.

" While our boat was steaming up the river, I had a fancy to make a running knot, that I dropped into the pocket in which my money was deposited. Young girls and their partners were dancing on the deck, to the melodious strains of our band ; and, mingling with the excursionists, I soon became quite interested in the merry scene. Suddenly, I felt that something suspicious was going on in my pocket, and at once rapidly drew up the running knot, the end of which I was thoughtlessly holding in my hand. To my utter surprise, a pickpocket's fingers were caught as in a vice. He tried to move me by his doleful supplications. 'Let me off,' said he in a whisper, fearing the bystanders might hear him, at the same time carefully walking beside me, while I paced the deck. 'It is my very first offense, and it shall be my last, I promise upon my soul.' When I judged he had been sufficiently punished, I loosened my knot, and the pickpocket walked away. That incident had disappeared from my mind through the diversions of the day; though afterward I could not help laughing heartily, on recalling the man's piteous voice as he begged for mercy while slowly pacing the deck beside me.

"Evening approached, and, the festivities over, our boat put off on her return to New-York. While admiring the effulgent light of the setting sun upon the surrounding scenery, a disturbance at the fore part of the boat, and screams from ladies, attracted my attention. The same fellow who had vainly tried to pick my pocket in the morning, had just been caught in the very act of stealing a lady's portemonnaie. 'Overboard with the pickpocket! Overboard with the pickpocket!' exclaimed a number of excited voices. And in spite of women's prayers to spare his life, and the desperate resistance of the unfortunate man, he was thrown into the river, and consigned to a watery grave!"

CHAPTER XXI.

CONTAINS A BARBER'S AUTHENTIC HISTORY, WHICH EX-
HIBITS SOME CHARACTERISTICS OF AN OBSOLETE INSTI-
TUTION.

E went out for the purpose of assisting at the
close of the criminal case, an incident of which
we had witnessed a few days previous. The
girl, accused of having killed her mistress was
to be sentenced on that day, as one of the prison-keepers
had informed us. While on our way to the court-house,
Asmodeus stopped at a barber's shop.

"After residing a few years in any country," said he,
"foreigners begin to ape the natives ; so I get my hair
dressed every morning, as most Americans do. In case I
am detained too long, you may prevail upon the proprietor—a mulatto, whiter than many Spaniards—to tell you
his history. It is a very interesting one ; besides, it is
replete with useful information concerning an institution
now extinct, but which has left vivid impressions upon the
country."

We entered the barber's shop. It was the first time I
had seen an establishment of this kind, and I was struck
with its size and importance. We found ourselves in a
spacious hall, crowded with people, whose wants — hair-
dressing and shaving—were attended to by fifty waiters.

Order and regularity prevailed ; every new-comer received a ticket, and patiently awaited his time. Though barbers have been charged with loquacity, I declare they gave no sign here of that peculiar attribute of their class.

Asmodeus introduced me to the owner of the hair-dressing saloon, who, as soon as he was informed of my desire to know his history, gratified it in the following manner :

ALBERT'S HISTORY.

" I am a Southern State governor's son. The governor owned a large plantation on the banks of the Savannah ; and among his female slaves was one noted for her beauty. He noticed her growing charms, and soon set her free. She became his mistress, and—my mother. Such was the manner with most planters of doing business. Their legitimate wives felt no concern regarding the intercourse of their lords with female slaves. It was a means of increasing the family's wealth ; and besides, negroes being considered as only chattels, the favors enjoyed by a negro girl at the hands of a planter had no more importance, in the opinion of the legitimate wife, than the attentions shown by her husband to a handsome horse. '

" The large number of mulattoes one meets throughout the Southern States affords convincing proof that the practice to which I am indebted for my birth was extensively carried on. Though my mother was free, the children she gave birth to—two girls and myself—remained in slavery. After she had been liberated, a law was enacted which forbade the freeing of negroes, unless they were removed from the State. To obey the law and secure our services, our father kept us in slavery.

"We grew up, mingled with the colored children of the plantation and also those of the planter. From the former, only light services were exacted, such as fanning the ladies, or taking the cattle to the fields. The latter grew up in laziness. Learning to read and write was out of the question. In the first place, there was no school in the neighborhood ; the nearest one being thirty miles off ; and, besides only the children of white people were admitted to the few schools then existing in the South. The law prohibited the teaching of reading and writing to negroes ; and though I was the son of a white man, I was nevertheless involved in that intellectual ostracism.

" I was my mother's youngest child. When my sisters were about sixteen, they were given away by the planter to his daughters, when the latter married. They thus became the slaves of their own sisters.

" About that time, my father began to exhibit a great liking for me. Through a freak of nature, it was noticed I had very little black blood in my veins ; and I was said to resemble my father very much. He had no son by his legitimate wife ; and so, in every circumstance, he gave me proof of his regard and kindly feelings. When his wife died, those feelings seemed to increase. He allowed me to sleep in his own room, and to go with him everywhere.

" Besides keeping him company, I was charged with many important transactions, and also with overseeing the slaves of the plantation. Neither was I ever in want of money ; and though a slave legally, in reality I was in possession of my freedom.

" My father was addicted to that terrible vice, gambling ; and, as I seldom left him, I noticed that fortune was not often in his favor. I had soon a sad proof of this fact.

"We had gone to New-Orleans, for the purpose of selling our cotton crop; and, once there, my father spent day and night at the gaming-table with other planters and cotton-dealers. One evening, he came home, visibly depressed.

"'I am severely punished,' said he, 'for an evil passion. I have lost at the gaming-table our entire cotton crop; and, besides,' he added, in a sorrowful tone, 'been obliged to pledge you in order to secure the payment of my debt. To-morrow morning, a planter will take you away; and you will belong to him until I can pay the one thousand dollars I owe him. He has promised to treat you kindly. I hope you will not have to stay long with him. As soon as I reach the plantation, I will raise the money necessary for your liberation, and will return myself to take you away.'

"I could hardly sleep that night. The planter alluded to came for me early in the morning, and I was soon separated from my father, who could not help shedding tears as he embraced me. I never saw him again.

"My new master was a man about forty-five years old—good-natured and kind to every body. He assured me I would have no time to get weary on his plantation, and advised me to do my best to please his two sons. We left New-Orleans the next day, and in the evening reached my new master's home—situated about sixty miles from that city.

"He had not deceived me when he said I would have no time to be weary. As soon as we arrived, and after being informed of the rules of the plantation, I was sent to the fields with the other negroes. At the dawn of day, one of the planter's sons blew a horn, to wake up the slaves; within twenty minutes they had to dress themselves, harness their mules, and go to work in the fields. At nine o'clock in the morning, children brought us our breakfast, which had to be over within ten minutes. At noon, the horn again was sounded, which was the signal to repair to our cabins. There we partook of a meal invariably composed of corn-bread, bacon, and a little molasses. At one o'clock, we returned to the fields, and worked until sunset. Two sons of our master, the oldest of six children—strong, tall young men, about twenty and twenty-two years of age respectively—were incessantly, with whip in hand, watching the negroes at work ; and their whips unerringly fell upon the shoulders of any one, either man or woman, who, overcome with fatigue, happened to cease work for a moment to take rest.

"From what I saw and heard concerning the neighboring plantations, I soon perceived that negroes were generally ill-treated—dealing kindly with them, as at my father's farm, being the exception. I must say, however, my master's sons never ill-treated me ; because, doing as much as I could, I never gave occasion to incur their resentment ; and also because they had been commanded by their father to treat me well, as I was not yet their sole property. As it was probable my father would soon come for me, it was perhaps thought best I should be favorably impressed with my temporary masters. Men do not disdain the opinion of others, whether the latter are free or in bondage, white or black.

"Notwithstanding this passable treatment of me, my desire to be released from these strangers was increasing every day. The planter's oldest sons, who had charge of the plantation, as I have said, were rude and violent, and could hardly control themselves, when their father was absent, which was often the case.

"Negroes have been often reproached with licentiousness; but when slavery was in existence, that very licentiousness was taught them and encouraged by the whites themselves. Marriages were not solemnized among negroes; as that would have weakened the planter's power over his slaves, and prevented the separation of husband from wife, of mother from children. Such separations were of frequent occurrence, children being the object of a brisk traffic. When either of my young masters took a fancy to a likely negress, he whispered in her ear some imperative command, and the slave had to obey, no matter whether she loved any negro or was connected with him by one of those temporary bonds tolerated by planters; and in case any negro exhibited resentment, his fate was sealed—he was immediately sold to some trader.

"One day, one of those negro-traders came to the plantation with a gang of unfortunates, of both sexes. Among these was a young girl, as black as ebony, yet really beautiful. She attracted the attention of the planter's eldest son; and, after a few words with the trader concerning her price, he purchased her. The fate that was in store for her was a mystery to nobody; and she had been the favorite slave of the planter's eldest son for some weeks, when a horseman, accompanied by the county sheriff, stopped, one morning, at the planter's house. He claimed the negro girl as his own; and I then learned, for the first time, that the slave-trade gave birth to many frauds and frightful crimes. Negro-stealing was practiced in every Southern State, extending even to the free ones. In the latter, white; in the former, mulatto or black children were frequently abducted, during the night, and borne away to remote places, to be sold when the robbers believed they could without danger get rid of their plunder. Certifi-

cates of ownership, skillfully forged, facilitated these frauds
—all the more easily perpetrated because the Southerners
were, in general, people of scanty education ; and though
numbers of traders had been hung for negro-stealing, such
were the profits of the business that it greatly flourished in
most Southern States.

"The sheriff acquainted my young master with his errand, and exhibited documents showing beyond doubt that
the young girl had been stolen from her lawful owner, the
horseman, who had secured the officer's services. My
master's son suggesting that some mistake concerning the
stolen negro girl might be possible, all the plantation
slaves, at the sheriff's request, were assembled in front
of the house. The horseman at once, and without hesitation, pointed out, among the group, the young girl he
claimed ; and she herself seemed quite glad in recogniz-
ing her former master. The latter was on the point of
taking her away, when the planter's son offered to buy
again the handsome slave. I did not hear the horseman's answer. But, anyhow, high words were soon ex-
changed between him and my master's son. Each had a
rifle in his hand. We saw them go to a field near by, and
coolly measure a short distance. Then we heard the sim-
ultaneous report of their rifles, and saw the planter's son
fall dead to the ground.

" A few days after, my master, who had been several
weeks absent, returned ; and his grief was intense on
learning the sad event that had deprived him of a beloved
son. From that day he took to drink, and soon the plantation became a hot place for the negroes.

" My master's disposition now completely changed. He
was ever angry, and became as cruel as before he was
gentle and kind-hearted. For the most insignificant mis-

take or fault, he unmercifully flogged his slaves—men, women, and children. The strict but humane rules which existed previously were replaced by the most rigorous measures. But, at the same time, the negroes resorted to such retaliations as to convince the planter he was rushing on to his own ruin. Those retaliations were conducted with a method and skill which I could not understand till a long time had elapsed.

"One day the best milch cows disappeared, and all search for them proved fruitless, though the negroes, sent miles around, seemed to take especial pains in endeavoring to find them. A week after, a swarm of buzzards, flying over an adjacent wood, was noticed by the planter to settle in a particular spot. He went to the wood, and there found all that remained of the cows, which undoubtedly had been poisoned, and with which the buzzards were now gorging themselves.

"From that time the negro cabins were strictly watched by the planter and his second son. Both of them locked us in every day at sunset, and several times during the night they stealthily entered the cabins to ascertain whether their inmates were sleeping. But in spite of all precautions, the negroes carried on their revengeful work in a sure and determined manner.

"One morning, while we were picking cotton, we heard the planter and his son shouting and swearing with great vehemence, as in a fit of rage. We soon learned the cause. The corn was then half grown; and in a field near by, all the stalks, as by enchantment, had been nearly cut through, about two feet from their roots. The crop was evidently ruined. In dismay, the planter sent a dozen negroes to other fields, to ascertain whether the corn there had been also damaged. They soon reported it as injured in the same manner, a few whole stalks only standing up. Completely overpowered by this new disaster, the planter tried every means in his power, employing threats as well as entreaties, to discover its authors. The negroes contended they could give no information respecting this outrage, as they were locked up every night in their cabins. Some even gave vent to much indignation, and threatened the evil-doers who had so utterly ruined the prospects of a promising crop. But the planter was not deceived by this feigned indignation of his slaves, and their pretended ignorance of the authors of this mischief.

"'They did it,' he said to me in the evening, while giving me an insignificant order. 'I know I live among enemies with whom I can never become reconciled. This is the fate of all white people in the Southern States—the result of a cursed institution we can not get rid of. And now that I have opened to you my heart, I shall depend upon you to help me in tracing and finding out the plotters who aim at my ruin. You have very little black blood in your veins, and you ought to serve the interests of the whites. I will take care to properly reward you, if you show yourself faithful and devoted. You must now consider me as your real master, as there is no probability you will ever be redeemed ; indeed, any claim to that effect would now come too late, as it would not be countenanced by the law.'

" More than six months had passed since I was separated from my father. I had never heard of him, and what my master had said I found to be but too true. I had been left as security for my father's gaming debt for the space of six months ; after that time, and this debt still unpaid, he could lay no claim to me.

"As regarded the planter's inducement for me to play the spy over my fellow-slaves, it quite perplexed my mind.

Admitting I might by chance discover his enemies and the destroyers of his fortune, I could not be so base as to disclose the fact. At the same time, if I failed to serve him after receiving his confidence, I was well aware I should find in him a bitter, inexorable foe.

"When night came on, I repaired to my cabin without imparting to any body my conversation with the planter; and, after thinking awhile over my situation and the incidents of the day, I fell asleep, when a slight noise awakened me. An old negro was standing by my side, having crept into my cabin in some unaccountable manner. Putting his finger to his lips, as though to preclude any question:

"'We know,' said he, 'what took place between our master and yourself; and we shall soon discover whether you are a traitor or not to the negro race. The one hundred and fifty slaves who toil on this plantation have vested me with an absolute power over them, and so have the negroes of the neighboring plantations. We punish cruel masters by ruining them or taking away the objects of their care or affection. For those who show any kindly feeling toward their fellow-creatures, we apparently do every thing in our power. But we never go so far as to help enrich them; for, just so soon as planters are convinced that negro labor is no longer profitable, and that slavery entails untold miseries upon society without increasing private wealth, the institution will be doomed. The whites are quick to understand every argument that tells on their purse. And now heed my last words: be always ready to obey.'

"The mysterious old man disappeared before I had time to recover from my surprise. The next day I vainly tried to discover, among the other negroes, my nocturnal visitor, whose face I had distinctly perceived in the resplendent moonlight that came through my cabin window.

"A few weeks later, the planter's second son married the daughter of one of his neighbors. Great festivities took place at the plantation, and a day of rest was granted us for the occasion. The slaves indulged in every kind of diversion; they danced during a portion of the night, while dancing was also carried on in our master's mansion. Numerous slaves from neighboring plantations had joined our party; and on seeing the general contentment, the signs of happiness exhibited by both races, no observer would have suspected there existed between them an intense and inextinguishable hatred. We had a striking proof of it a few months after that wedding.

"Among the house servants was a girl whom the newly-married young man had kept as a mistress for several years. She had become the mother of a couple of children, and was sent to work in the fields soon after our young master's wedding, old female slaves being intrusted with the care of her children. The neglected girl became the object of many a bitter joke from the male and female slaves of the plantation. She seemed to bear patiently her new situation, but was intent on having revenge, as soon afterward appeared.

"One night we were awakened by frightful clamors from the planter and his household. They hurriedly entered our cabins, and we saw, from the glare of volumes of flames at a distance, the cause of their fright. A barn, where ginned cotton was deposited previous to pressing, was on fire, and all our endeavors to subdue the flames were of no avail. A considerable portion of the cotton crop was destroyed in an instant. The cause of the fire

could not be ascertained. The planter visited every
evening all the outbuildings, which he locked up himself;
and the authors of this new disaster remained unknown.
But, when conversing about it the next day, with the former
mistress of the planter's son, and seeing her eyes sparkle
as though with feelings of joy and exultation, I was con
vinced she was the offender.

"But her resentment did not stop there. We learned,
one morning, that the planter's family had narrowly escaped
being poisoned. A doctor, returning from an early excursion, had been invited to breakfast. The peculiar aroma
of the coffee arousing his suspicions, he forbade the family
to drink it. The coffee was analyzed that very day by the
physician, who found it impregnated with arsenic. The
woman's children had the privilege, with others of the
plantation, to enter at pleasure the kitchen of the house.
When questioned by the planter, the eldest, a little boy,
five or six years old, confessed he had placed in the coffee-
pot a white powder he had received for that purpose from
his mother, who had enjoined him not to taste it. That
revelation clearly pointed out the author of the crime. The
planter immediately stripped his son's former mistress,
tied her to a stake in the yard, and flogged her until her
body was thoroughly lacerated. When her wounds were
healed, the planter's son took her to Virginia, then the
great slave-mart, and sold her.

"This last proceeding may serve to explain why crimes
seemed, from statistics published by the government, comparatively less frequent in Southern than in Northern
States. Offenses committed by blacks were seldom exposed; as, by publishing them, the institution of slavery
would have been depreciated. The law in the Southern
States enacted, it is true, that, in case a planter should be

deprived of his slave's services in consequence of an offense, he would be entitled to a compensation from the State. But few planters availed themselves of that law, preferring to sell a dangerous negro rather than to apply to the State for an indemnity, often meagre and always obtained after much delay. In that way, the true condition of negroes and their relations with the whites were kept from the knowledge of the public, and statisticians themselves deceived in their statements and conclusions.

"Anyhow, the separation of the young negro woman from her children had been exceedingly painful; and it was a sight well calculated to destroy that carefully entertained notion among white people that maternal love is a feeling unknown among negroes.

"Repeated losses obliged the planter to successively sell off a dozen negroes, thus separating them from the objects of their affection; and their parting was invariably followed by many gloomy days among the remaining negroes— thus becoming more and more impressed with their unfortunate condition.

"The planter now was almost constantly in a state of intoxication, and his fits of passion were frightful. One evening, we were busy weighing the cotton we had picked in the course of the day, when our master detected a sickly negro who had not picked the quantity exacted from every one. The slave's enfeebled health was not taken into consideration by the planter, who reproached him with laziness; and, after abusing, commenced to whip him severely. The poor fellow tried to escape his infuriated master, when the latter, grasping an ax, and before the bystanders could prevent him, split open the slave's head. The frightened negroes began running away in every direction, when an old slave, whom I at once recog-

nized as the man who, a few months before, had come
during the night into my cabin, called them back, with a
commanding voice.

" 'Lift up,' said he, with a dignified air that surprised all,
'one of your brethren, whose misery is just ended ! Carry him to his cabin, and cover him with wreaths of flowers !
We will, on Sunday next, attend his funeral.'

"It was, in fact, only on Sundays that negro funerals
took place, before the abolition of slavery. By choosing
the great day of rest for such solemnities, the blacks had
sufficient time to decently bury their own kin. And their
masters could not object, as the week's work was not interfered with.

"When Sunday arrived, hundreds of slaves from adjacent plantations came, to pay a last tribute of regard in this
world to our master's victim—a victim whose death was
not avenged, as a jury, selected among neighboring planters, declared the murder was justifiable, as the negro had
tried to resist a deserved punishment. All the slaves
attending the funeral uncovered their heads, and passed
in front of the dead body, whose eyes were concealed by
silver pieces—the negroes, perhaps, ignoring the process
by which eyelids are closed ; and then we carried our dead
companion to a graveyard, situated a few miles off, and
where negroes were buried. The leader of the procession
was the mysterious old man—the oldest slave, I was told,
on the plantation. He acted as gardener for the family of
our master, and was a member of the Methodist Church.
He was even acknowledged as a minister of the Gospel by
those of our race. A few negroes dug a grave, and after
the coffin was lowered into it, all the attendants, one after
another, threw a shovelful of earth into it. When it was
filled, at a sign from the old man, who acted as minister,

every one knelt.   Then he recited a prayer, spoke in glow-
ing terms of the deceased, and concluded by dwelling on
the sufferings of the black race.   •

"'Those sufferings,' he concluded, 'are fast coming to
an end.   The day is near, when proud masters, amid dire
lamentations, will acknowledge we are their equals—the
children of the same God ; and Heaven, to compensate
our people for the oppression of many centuries, will allot
it the finest countries in the world, suffused, all the year
round, by the rays of a genial sun.'

" After this speech, the negroes arose and returned to
the plantation.   The men, in couples, led the march, and
the women and children followed.   Every one in the ranks
was silent, and when we had reached a thick wood, at a
bend of the road, the minister clapped his hands ; then
five negroes, the best laborers of the plantation, immediately left the lines, and disappeared in the woods.

" The old negro himself gave notice to the planter that
five slaves had run away.   The latter, in a fit of rage, rode
immediately in search of them, accompanied by his son
and a few neighbors.   But the dogs they took with them
could not track the runaway negroes, who had strewn
pepper along the path they had taken—an infallible means
to deceive and put bloodhounds off the scent.

"When night approached, our master and his friends
returned home, after a fruitless search for the negroes—
without obtaining even the slightest information respecting
their hiding-place or the direction they had taken.

" But the planter's trials were not yet ended ; for after
many losses of money, he was destined to suffer in his
feelings as a father and as a man.

" The excitement which followed the flight of the best
laborers of the plantation was subsiding ; the advertise-

ments inserted in the newspapers, giving a description of the runaway slaves, and promising large rewards to those who could catch them, had been fruitless; and the planter was beginning to feel resigned to his loss, when, one evening, the old man, who had absolute control over the negroes of the plantation, ordered me to inform our master I had perceived the runaway negroes, basking in the sun in a wood in the vicinity of which we had been at work during the course of the day. I did as directed, little suspecting I was, by so doing, endangering my own life.

"Without losing time, the planter locked up the slaves in their cabins, and started immediately with his son in the direction of the wood. Of course, his search after the runaway negroes resulted in nothing. But when he returned home, about midnight, a terrible surprise awaited him.

" His remaining five children consisted of two sons and three daughters. The youngest of the latter, named Nellie, about six years old, was the object of her parents' most tender love. The child slept in the planter's room; and when, on that eventful night, he went to her cot to kiss her as usual, he discovered with dismay that it was empty. His wife was aroused by the clamorous inquiries of the planter; and both hurriedly questioned the other children. But they could only grieve with their parents at the disappearance of their sister—entirely unable as they were, to give any information respecting this awful mystery. The shutters of the house had been bolted by the family from the inside, and as the entrance-door had been opened by the planter himself with his latch-key on his return from his fruitless journey, it was really impossible to conceive how and when the abduction of the little girl had been accomplished.

"The members of that unfortunate family made search everywhere—in the outbuildings, in the neighboring fields and woods—all the while vainly calling aloud the name of the object of their pursuit. All at once, the planter remembered the intelligence I had given him, and owing to which he had left his house on his nocturnal hunt. That circumstance, he thought, clearly pointed me out as one of the conspirators who had deprived him of his child; so rushing to the cabin where I was sleeping in entire ignorance of the calamity which had befallen him and his family, he roughly pulled me from my bed, beat me unmercifully, and dragged me to the yard, in the centre of which was a stake, to which negroes were fastened previously to being flogged.

"'Do you see that stake?' said he, 'I am about to tie you to it with my own hands, keep you there and watch you myself; and if my child is not found at dawn of day, I will burn you alive!'

"I vainly protested I knew nothing about the child, as I had learned of her disappearance through himself; but I could move him no more than if I had spoken to a rock. He fastened me to the stake, tying my legs and arms, and, with revolver in hand, sat down to wait for morning.

"It was not long before the stars commenced to disappear from the heaven, and birds to welcome the return of daylight. Then the planter's son blew the horn, and the slaves' cabins were opened. In a few minutes, every one of them knew of the event of the night and the frightful death with which I was threatened. The planter ordered them to remain a short distance from the post; then he sent his children for wood and turpentine, and himself heaped the fuel around me, sprinkling it with the turpentine.

"Whether bond or free, life is still sweet to a man not yet twenty-two years old; and I was terrified at sight of the torture in preparation for me, and implored the slaves, and especially the old Methodist minister, to restore to the planter his child, if they knew what had become of her. But all of them remained silent. I then begged for mercy from the planter himself—his wife, his children. I warned them that the blood of an innocent man would fall upon their heads. To all my protestations and prayers the planter made this invariable answer: 'Tell me where my child is; and not only will I spare your life, but I will even set you free.'

"He now sent one of the slaves for a firebrand; and, after adjuring me, for the last time, to give him the information which was entirely out of my power, he fired the pile. The ascending smoke commenced to suffocate me; I grew faint and dizzy, and was just about addressing a last prayer to God, when it seemed to me, from the confused hum of unfamiliar voices, that strangers were pulling down and scattering the burning pile. I soon recovered the use of my senses, and could then understand what was going on.

"Between the planter, surrounded by his family, and the stake to which I was fastened, six men were standing. One of these, a gray-haired gentleman, seemed the father of the others; all were tall, and carried rifles in their hands. At a short distance on the road, four or five wagons, covered with white canvas, each drawn by four mules, could be seen. Some young ladies, neatly dressed, were sitting in front of the foremost of these wagons; while others, strolling on the road, threw to the breeze the burden of a song. They were a family of Yankees, who, as I learned afterward, were emigrating from New-England to the Far West.

"'I will not stand idly by,' said the old gentleman, after ascertaining my life was out of danger, 'and see the American name about to be disgraced by an infamous outrage to mankind!'

"And as the planter, in a frenzy, bade his motionless slaves to drive away the intruders:

"'There are six of us here, and each provided with an unerring rifle,' continued the Yankee; 'and you are but two. So the best thing you can do is to keep quiet and answer my questions.'

"Then, with a serene but dignified look, he asked the planter what offense I was guilty of. When he learned I was suspected of having abducted a child, but that no satisfactory proof, no evidence of my culpability could be procured, he said to the planter:

"'You may thank God that I have arrived in time to prevent you from committing a frightful crime—one of those outrages to mankind newspapers sometimes relate; but which I had attributed to party spirit, for the welfare of my country's good name. And you,' he pursued, while untying my arms and legs, 'tell us, I adjure you, in the name of the Almighty, the Master of all men, where is the abducted child?'

"'If I knew,' I answered, 'I would have long ago put an end to my master's anxiety; for I have no feeling of hatred or revenge against him.'

"'You are indebted to me for your life,' continued the Yankee; 'had it not been for me, your earthly frame would be now only ashes; but I shall consider myself amply paid

for my service if you will give me the means to restore
their child to those miserable people.'

"It was utterly impossible for me to satisfy the Yankee's
desire, and I perceived he began to question my feelings
of gratitude and sincerity, and perhaps to regret his intervention.   He took aside two of his sons, and after conversing a few minutes with them, asked my master:

"'How much is that negro worth?'

"'One thousand dollars,' answered the latter.

"'Here is the money,' said the man who had saved my
life, handing a bundle of bank-bills to the planter. ·'This
slave henceforth belongs to me.   Having interfered with
your affairs, justly or unjustly, I can not leave that young
man in your hands to be exposed to your resentment; and
it is better for you to take that money than to become
guilty of a heinous crime.   Besides, if he knows any thing
concerning the circumstances which have deprived.you of
your child, he will speak out when relieved of all fear of
you or his fellow-slaves.   Perhaps the bargain I propose
to you is the only means to recover your lost child.'

"The planter agreed to the proposition, and ordered
some slaves to bring me a few garments.   Then the Yankee beckoned me to follow him; and, a few minutes after,
the heavy wagons of the Northerners were again on their
way toward the Far West, with one more emigrant.   Those
wagons were a sort of migratory town, offering all the
conveniences of life.   Two of them contained food for the
cattle; the others, provisions for the family and household
implements.   In one of them a sleeping and dressing-room
had been provided for the ladies.   The men walked; and,
when tired, which was seldom the case, rode on their
mules.

"When evening came on, the Yankees stopped near the

banks of a river, and made preparations for the night. One of the young men cut wood and kindled a fire; another attended to the cattle; another pitched the tents; while the Yankee's wife and their three daughters prepared supper. This meal over, and after a prayer, the members of the family separated—the ladies repairing to the wagons, and a portion of the men to the tents, while the others posted themselves here and there to keep watch during the night.

"After traveling in this way many weeks, we arrived in Western Texas, where the Yankee had originally intended to settle; but the sight of the miseries we met at every step, while going through the slave States, had gradually shaken his purpose; and when we believed our journey was at an end, he made known his resolution, to the intense joy of his wife and children, of going to the coast of the Pacific Ocean and of settling in the free State of California. We consequently resumed our journey, and traveled over almost the entire breadth of the Mexican republic—often amid dangers which only the prudence and energy of the Yankee successfully overcame.

"When he perceived the star-spangled banner—that revered flag which he had not seen for many a weary month—the Yankee knelt down and thanked God for having protected him through so perilous an enterprise. Then, turning to me, 'You now tread,' said he, 'on American soil, where every man is his own master; consequently you are free, and can do what you please. The best investment I ever made in my life was when I gave one thousand dollars to release you from bondage; for you have amply paid me for it up to this day by your devotedness.'

"I asked the gentleman, as a favor, to permit me to stay with him a few years, until I had made enough money under his advice and direction, to redeem my two sisters from slavery. He readily assented; and a few weeks after, two of his sons and myself set out for the gold regions, while the Yankee and the remainder of his family settled on a farm, situated a few miles from San Francisco.

"We had hard times at the diggings, though favored with better luck than many other miners. After a year spent there, we went to San Francisco, and sold for about four thousand dollars the gold-dust we had gathered. I now refunded to my benefactor, though he long declined to accept it, the one thousand dollars he had paid for me; and I left in his hands, besides, five hundred dollars when, after a few weeks' rest at the farm, I returned with his two sons to the diggings. We again toiled there a little more than two years, returning each year for a short time to the farm, where I was always welcomed as one of the family.

"When I was possessed of over five thousand dollars, I determined to buy my sisters' freedom. The Yankee and his family approved of my resolution; so, after taking leave of those good people, with heart-felt grief, I took passage on board of one of the San Francisco and New-York line of steamers. I was then far from believing I had to again undergo many and painful trials.

"While working at the gold mines with my benefactor's sons, and during the long winter evenings, they had taught me to read and write. I had also learned a little of arithmetic and geography; and, living with freemen, I had lost the slave's cautious habits and bashful demeanor. I was, besides, worth five thousand dollars, and I knew enough of the world to be fully aware that money overcomes many difficulties.

"After spending a few days in New-York, I set out for

the South, taking with me three thousand dollars, and depositing the remainder of my money in the hands of a banker.   I had no trouble to find the place where I had spent my early years ; and my mother's and sisters' joy was unbounded when they recognized me, though they did not conceal their apprehension concerning my safety.   I learned through them that my father, before dying, had begged one of his sons-in-law to go for me to New-Orleans.   He had made a solemn promise to do so, though probably intending never to keep it.   My father, a few days after his return, had been thrown from his carriage ; and after languishing a few weeks, had died broken-hearted, speaking of me till death closed his eyes.

" I decided to see my father's son-in-law, and carry out the purpose of my journey, which was the liberation of my sisters.   The planter exhibited great satisfaction on seeing me alive, and asserted there was no difficulty in coming to an understanding.   A few days later he agreed to take three thousand dollars for my two sisters, the price of slaves having considerably increased in consequence of the extension of the cotton culture.   A girl twenty years old was then worth fifteen hundred dollars and upward, and strong male laborers three thousand dollars apiece. The planter estimated I was worth the last amount.   Consequently, I paid him three thousand dollars for my sisters' ransom ; drew on the New-York banker for the two thousand dollars deposited with him ; and, as soon as received, I hastened with them to the planter, offering him, to perfect the payment of my own freedom, a note for one thousand dollars, payable after six months—fully convinced I should receive, in the mean time, that amount from my Californian friends, to whom I had already written several letters.

"On hearing my proposition, the planter burst out laughing. 'Boy,' said he, 'a negro is not a person, according to the law. He can hold no property; he can make no will; he can not go to law; he can not be even a witness; he has no more rights than cattle; every thing he is possessed of belongs to his master; hence the note you proffer me would be perfectly worthless. I have countenanced, up to this day, a farce that must be ended at once. You are my slave; your sisters have never ceased to be so, in spite of the three thousand dollars you gave me for their liberation. All the money you have brought from California belongs to me, and I consider it as a fair compensation for the labor I have been robbed of by your absence. I advise you to become reconciled with your situation, without either grumbling or again alluding to the freedom you have enjoyed. I repeat you are my slave, and no power on earth can snatch you from me.'

"My mother's and sisters' misgivings were thus realized, and I again found myself in slavery. The next day I was sent with the other negroes to the fields. But I remained a few weeks only with my family. The planter seemed uneasy whenever he met me, as though his mind were preyed upon by fear and remorse. So he sold me, for two thousand dollars, to a trader who was on his way to Tennessee. After this negotiation, I started with the trader, and we arrived at Memphis on the eve of a presidential election, and in the midst of a violent party strife that boded no good for the peace of the country and the preservation of the Union. Here the trader sold me, for two thousand five hundred dollars, to the proprietor of one of the largest hotels in that city; and as I could both read and write, I was charged to keep the books in the hair-dressing saloon attached to the hotel. There were in the saloon about fifteen waiters—all slaves, of course, and busy day and night. I was fortunate enough to discharge my trust to the satisfaction of my master and, I dare say, of the public.

" My situation would have been pleasant enough but for the want of freedom, without which the finest occupation in the world is insufferable. Besides, my anxiety respecting my beloved relatives ; the recollection of the swindle through which I had lost the fruits of several years' labor ; the uncertainty of my prospects—all these causes filled my mind with distress. I had found means to write to my California friends, and impart to them the misfortunes I had met, owing to my excessive incautiousness. But my letters were not answered, or rather, the answers of my friends did not reach me, on account of circumstances I will now relate.

" As I said before, when I arrived at Memphis, political passions were in a violent state of fermentation. The presidential election took place shortly after, and the Republican, or Abolitionist, candidate was elected. And now a revolution became imminent. The Southern States immediately took up arms, and soon war fiercely raged between the two great sections of the land. All communication between States faithful to the Constitution and those who repudiated it was interrupted ; and thus it happened that letters from California could not reach me.

" From that moment commenced an era of fearful trials, in the South, for the negro race. The war had for its object—if not ostensibly acknowledged, at least generally understood — the maintenance of slavery. While many planters blindly depended on the devotedness of their slaves, the majority mistrusted them, and believed the secret sympathies of the negroes were with the North.

The majority was right, as fully shown by subsequent
events.   Anyhow, as soon as hostilities began, it was
deemed prudent throughout the South, to watch more
closely the slaves, and tighter draw their chains.   They
were often treated with the utmost severity; and when
a portion of the Southern States was laid waste by the
Northern armies, the planters could hardly control their
hatred for a race which, though it was the innocent cause
of the war, had brought upon the South untold miseries.

" With the reverses of the Southern armies, ill-treatment
of and cruelties to the slaves increased; and more than once
I wondered at the patience of the blacks, though I was not
less surprised at the imprudence of the slaveholders, talking as they did, without restraint, in the presence of their
slaves.   That imprudence I had previously noticed, when
I was one of the working hands on a Mississippi plantation.   There, while struck with the perspicacity of the
slaves, with their knowledge of the political questions of
the day, I was no less astonished to hear their masters
discussing with utter freedom those same questions in
their presence—perhaps because they did not believe in
the intelligence of the negro.   At any rate, they were un-
intentionally giving a political education to their slaves;
and now, in the midst of a desperate war, the whites exhibited the same incautiousness.   They constantly talked
of the belligerents' pretensions; of the threats of negro
emancipation, repeatedly made by the North; of the military projects of Southern generals; of their successes and
defeats—as if they had only friends among their negro
hearers, while many of them, undoubtedly, were irrecon-
cilable enemies, and not a few, perhaps, spies.

" The colored people, I must say, behaved during that
period of adversity, with consummate discretion.   That

discretion had been recommended them through secret emissaries, before the war, and after hostilities had actually commenced. Negroes were especially instructed to respect persons and property; being warned that they would lose the sympathy of the North were they insane enough to commit such excesses as the blacks had been guilty of in other countries. And you can now understand why the slaves refrained, during the civil war, from any violence or retaliation, even in those localities where they had been quartered in large numbers, and among women and children deprived of their natural protectors, who were fighting under the Confederate flag.

" The negroes had been successively removed from the States exposed to the incursions of the Federals, to the interior of those which were supposed to be safe from invasion. And this was the case when Memphis was threatened by the Northern fleet. All the slaves—men, women, and children — were taken to a neighboring State — or rather, driven like cattle, by cavalrymen, sword in hand, and often in a state of beastly intoxication.

" I was among those unfortunate victims of the war. We were hurried to a locality where half the plantations were uncultivated, for.want of hands and mules—the latter having been turned over to the Confederate army. Almost naked, living on corn-bread only, we there spent several months. The whites, I must admit, had also to endure frightful privations; for the consequences of the war were felt everywhere and by every body.

" One day we heard a hollow sound, at a distance, like that of a clap of thunder. The sun was shining in a cloudless sky, and we could not explain the mysterious noise. Suddenly we saw a number of frightened white persons running in every direction, carrying bundles of clothes in their hands, and shouting to us to take to our heels and provide for our safety. Soon we heard the martial strains of a band of music, and, as if inspired with one impulse, we ran to meet the strangers. They were Northern men; and we beheld with joy the star-spangled banner which carried our freedom in its folds!

"I enlisted in one of the colored regiments, then raising for the purpose of helping the work of regenerating our race, and during two years, fought by the side of my deliverers.

"One day my regiment was designated for one of those incursions the object of which was to destroy the resources of the insurgents. On our march, we chanced to pass a short distance from the plantation where, many years previous, the Yankees had rescued me from death. We were allowed to rest here awhile, and I was not slow to perceive that the plantation had previously been ransacked and laid waste by the Federals. All the fruit-trees had been cut down; only the walls of the mansion were standing; and snakes were hissing and sporting amid the thick, high grasses of this once flourishing place. A few negroes, among whom I recognized the old Methodist minister, were the only human beings to be seen on that desolate spot. The minister, it appears, employed his time in singing alleluias; and it was with great difficulty I obtained from him some information respecting the former owners of the plantation. Shortly after I had left the country, dissipation had brought to an untimely end the planter who had attempted to burn me alive at the stake. His sons had perished in the ranks of the Confederate army, and his widow and daughters had fled a few months before, at the approach of the Federals, while all the negroes had followed the invaders.

" 'And Nelly, the abducted child,' said I, when the old man had given me this information, ' what of her ? Was she ever found ? '

" 'Never,' answered the preacher. ' Transported during the night from plantation to plantation, to the extreme borders of Arkansas, she was there sold to an Indian tribe, and since that time, I have not troubled myself about her fate.'

" Consequently Nelly was very likely kept in slavery by the red men ; for, strange as it may seem, those wild sons of the forest, supported by the liberality of the Federal government, possessed slaves, and it was to retain the institution of slavery among them, that many tribes embraced the Confederate cause.

" A few months later that cause was definitively lost, and the victorious armies of the Republic disbanded. Possessed of a large sum of money, saved from the pay I had received from the Federal government, I again set out for the plantation where I had been brought up—this time without fear that my father's heirs might use a power they had lost forever ; and besides, I had letters of introduction to the military commanders, the country being then under martial law. . The planter who had again plunged me into servitude had enlisted, I was told, in the Confederate army, and had been killed at the beginning of the war. The plantation had been deserted by all valid negroes, and desolation reigned on the banks of the Savannah as on those of the Mississippi. After vainly trying to take away with me my mother and sisters, I left the South forever. Such is the love of negroes for their native land, that they leave it on compulsion only ; they prefer to lead in it a miserable life to living in affluence in another country, where they would be separated from early associations, and also from the recollection of their past miseries.

"Leaving my family ample means, I decided to go to California. The prosperity of the Yankee's family had rapidly increased—many acres had been added to his farm; and I was welcomed with feelings of the most sincere friendship. Two of his sons were married; the other three were on the eve of starting for the Atlantic States, with the view of obtaining wives there, to bring back to the farm.

"'It was our intention,' they said, 'during our travels, to search for you; for after you wrote us you had been swindled out of your freedom, we ceased to hear from you.'

"I related to them my adventures after that time, and the Yankee patriarch fondly took me in his arms, when he heard I had fought for the preservation of the American Union.

"'You pleased me the first time I saw you,' said he, "and now I love you as much as if you were one of my children.'

"Meanwhile, the three young men were ready to start. They had decided to go North by the overland route; and though their father desired me to settle in California, I decided to return with his sons to the Atlantic States. At that time mining was very dull, and besides, I felt no disposition to work alone in the mines.

"When my Yankee friend saw I could not be prevailed upon to settle in California, he gave me a draft on a New-York banker for five thousand dollars.

"'Dispose of that sum,' said he, 'to the best of your judgment. Whatever be the business you engage in, it is better to commence it with a few thousands. You may pay me at your convenience, and I am sure, unless you die, the money I lend you will not be lost.'

" To secure the excellent man against such an event, I obtained an insurance on my life for his benefit; and that transaction over, the three young men and myself started on our overland journey. We traversed the recently admitted State of Nevada, and examined on our route some exceedingly rich silver mines. Soon, we reached Salt Lake City, in Utah, the capital of American Mussulmans. We spent a few days among the industrious Mormons, whose faith is but a cloak for sensualism, and were on the eve of resuming our journey, when we learned that some Indian tribes had commenced war against the pale faces.

" Fortunately, a cavalry regiment was dispatched, a few days after, to protect the California mails, and we joined it to cross the plains. Almost at every step, traces of the red men's ferocity could be seen. All along the road were scattered the dead bodies of emigrants, dreadfully mangled. Surprised by the Indians, they had been mercilessly slaughtered. They were pierced by hundreds of arrows, and their scalped heads eloquently warned us of our fate, should we lack courage and vigilance. The three brothers and myself, carrying repeating-rifles, never separated during the journey, and when camping, two of us kept watch, while the other indulged in a short nap. We had noticed that the precautions required by the dangers to which we were exposed were not taken by the Regulars, as though they despised our enemies ; and soon had cause to congratulate ourselves on our determination to watch on our own account.

" One night, two of my traveling companions caught an Indian just as he was creeping into the inclosure where our horses were kept. The purpose of the red skin was, no doubt, to frighten and drive them into the plain. The struggle was short, ending by the Indian losing his life. But, short as it had been, its noise aroused the Regulars from their sleep, and this perhaps was the means of saving our lives ; for a few minutes had hardly elapsed, when the Indians assaulted our camp from every side. But we were well prepared for them ; and after vainly waiting for the confusion and disorder they had expected when they commenced their attack, they beat a hasty retreat.

"As the sun was now rising, we vigorously pursued the Indian warriors. We killed many, and some we made prisoners ; then, intoxicated with our success, we determined to set fire to a village, a few miles off, to which some Regulars, who were acquainted with the country, guided us. After accomplishing our purpose, we returned to camp, bringing with us a few Indian women and children whom we had found in their huts, before burning them. Among our female prisoners was a young girl of remarkable beauty ; and when it was known she could speak English, she became an object of general sympathy and interest. When I saw her, I was struck with her resemblance to the planter's child whom his slaves had abducted years before. I spoke to her, and her answers left no doubt in my mind that the stolen Nelly stood before me ; and when I pronounced that name, which she had not heard for so long a time, she wept and sobbed bitterly. Recollections of her childhood came back fresh to her mind, and she seemed even to remember having seen me at her father's plantation. I gave her an account of the many events that had occurred since her abduction, and which had liberated an oppressed race, but, at the same time, had brought ruin on her family, and taken from this world most of her relatives. A friendship soon sprang up between us ; and after we had crossed the plains, Nelly decided to come to New-York with me. She is my wife to-day.

" The remainder of my adventures may now be summed up in a few words.

" I purchased, two years ago, this establishment, which was far from being as important as it is to-day. I sent for the colored boys who were employed with myself in the hair-dressing saloon at Memphis ; and they are not the least smart among the hair-dressers and barbers, fifty in all, I keep in my employ. From eight o'clock in the morning till eight in the evening, as many as one thousand persons come here to have their faces shaved or hair dressed. I have been able to repay to my Yankee benefactor his loan ; and only a few days ago, I asked his advice concerning the project I have formed to start, in San Francisco, an establishment of this kind and on as large a scale. San Francisco will be, at no very distant day, as important a financial and commercial centre for the Pacific coast as New-York is to-day for the Atlantic States. And besides, when success and fortune favor an American, he can not but make the most of them."

CHAPTER XXII.

TAKES THE READER TO A PLACE WHERE THE GODDESS FORTUNE IS DAILY WORSHIPED, AND, AFTER ASSISTING AT A CORONER'S INQUEST, TO THE HOUSE OF AN ARISTOCRATIC FAMILY.

LBERT concluded the story of his adventures just as Asmodeus was released from the barber's hand. We then resumed our way to the court-house, and arrived long before the sitting of the court.

"We have time to go," said Asmodeus, "to the place where they worship the goddess Fortune in New-York—I mean the Stock Exchange. From the society of a pickpocket to that of a stock-gambler, the transition is quite natural and the change of company imperceptible."

So we started. In a short time we entered a large white marble building of somewhat elaborate workmanship. Its elevation seemed to me too great, and out of proportion with the size of the whole structure. It is situated in one of the widest streets of New-York, and stands on a line with other edifices in its neighborhood. There are many handsome buildings in New-York, which the passer-by fails to observe because they are either mingled with others of common appearance, or because the point of view is obstructed by more pretentious edifices. The ancient Greeks, who understood architecture and perspective so well, never failed to erect their temples and monuments on hills or elevated sites, and apart from other structures. The churches in New-York, some very elegant, are, with few exceptions, erected on the same line as dwelling-houses, which gives to these temples of God a very commonplace appearance.

Such was the case with the building we had finally entered, after elbowing our way through a crowd of speculators, who, amid frantic cries and gesticulations, were buying and selling stock—in short, speculating in that commodity, on the sidewalk. An immense hall, reaching from street to street, was crowded with operators, who were constantly sending orders to stock exchange brokers, sitting in a room, in the upper floor, where the public was not admitted. The noise and confusion were indescribable, as the demands and offers of excited speculators were echoed in every part of the hall.

"Independently of this Stock Exchange Board," said Asmodeus, "there is another near by, a rival board, where speculations in public funds and other securities are conducted, and where the public is admitted, thus being able to have their orders executed in their presence. On the floor above, there is a board, where mining, petroleum, and insurance company stocks are dealt in ; and there is, finally, in the next building, the Gold Room, where brokers congregate to sell or purchase the precious metal ; for gold is now a merchandise, the value of which fluctuates like that of other goods. On seeing the many places where stock-jobbers assemble, one would believe speculation to be the general calling of the people ; and in fact, thousands of persons, from ten o'clock in the morning to a late hour in the evening, devote their thoughts, their energy, their very existence to stock-gambling. When, at five o'clock in the

afternoon, the speculators with whom this hall and the
street swarm go to their homes, their day's work is not
ended.   While digesting their dinner, they gamble up to
midnight, in the rooms of our fashionable hotels.   The
Gold Room is a favorite resort for Jews, who flocked to
New York from every part of the United States, as soon as
the Gold Exchange was in operation ; for the patriotism of
the Jews in the New as in the Old World dwells only in their
pocket, and their country is that place where they can make
the most money.   They have been often suspected of
having done their best to destroy the credit of the Federal
treasury ;   and they often use the transatlantic telegraph
with dangerous ability.   News transmitted by them to the
public has ruined many a gullible operator.

"Concerning these men around us, speculators or stock-
brokers, going to and fro, not a few among them never
shrink from the most villainous *ruses* to draw into their
pockets the money of the public.

"That young fellow, for instance, so elegantly dressed,
and who, with his light curly hair, rosy cheeks, and pleasant
smile, looks like an ingenuous girl, is possessed of several
houses in New-York, and drives a fine team in Central
Park every Saturday.   He has built up his fortune on the
ruin of many a family.   He was among those who, a few
years ago, called public attention to the gold mines of
Nova Scotia.   He organized a company for the purpose of
working one of those mines ;   and, after a few weeks' existence, the company commenced distributing large dividends.   There were, in its office, a dozen gold bars,
bearing the stamp of the Nova Scotia mint, and purporting
to be a part of the mining proceeds ; and as dividends were
paid regularly, several months in succession, every body
believed in the richness of the mine and the soundness of

the enterprise. Under that impression, fifty thousand shares, of ten dollars each, were sold out in a few weeks. And now, the scheme having succeeded, the company stopped paying dividends. Some shareholders who had lost heavily made inquiry respecting this unexpected collapse, and ascertained that the mine and its fabulous wealth, also the gold bars, were all mere fabrications. A lot of American eagles had been sent to Halifax, the capital of Nova Scotia, melted there into bars, and returned to New-York, bearing the stamp of the mint of Nova Scotia. The fraud was so well devised, it was really difficult to detect it. The money distributed as dividends had been advanced by some confederates, who made a good thing out of their loan, the swindle having produced, it is said, a net profit of over three hundred thousand dollars."

"And the originator and accomplices of that swindle, did they escape punishment?"

"Yes. Any action against wealthy swindlers requires a large outlay; and generally, victimized stockholders pause before adding fees for greedy lawyers to their losses. However, the success of the Nova Scotia company was so tempting, it found numerous imitators; one of whom I notice in that stock-broker, wearing a diamond pin worth a few thousand dollars, and who is now shaking hands with another sharper. About two years ago, he purchased twenty acres of land in a Western State, and commenced boring, with the expectation of finding oil. They had gone to the depth of two hundred feet, and, to the dismay of the shareholders, there was not the slightest indication of petroleum, when, all at once, it was rumored oil had been struck. A meeting of shareholders was immediately convened, and a committee appointed to go to the West and report. After a few weeks, the committee made known the result of its investigation. It proved to be most gratifying. The company's well yielded in abundance a lubricating oil, specimens of which, taken out by the committee itself, were triumphantly exhibited in the company's office. Its shares went up immediately—everybody wanted to purchase so promising a stock. Even Irish servants and laborers withdrew their money from savings-banks, to invest it in the great lubricating oil concern. The excitement had hardly subsided, when a rumor began to spread that all further traces of oil had disappeared. And such was the case : the well had dried up. In reality, oil had been purchased in Pennsylvania, carried secretly to the West, and poured into the well by discreet agents. The operation yielded considerable sums of money to the master-spirit of it—yonder broker—as well as his confederates of the shareholders' committee.

"An operation quite in vogue among stock-jobbers is what they call a 'corner.' It consists in secretly holding, either through purchase or trust, a considerable portion of a company's stock, and then purchasing all the shares offered for sale. Some inexperienced or incautious speculators sell, on time and at the buyer's option, more stock than they possess, and then they are pushed into a 'corner;' for the clique makes a sudden call for the stock it has purchased, and compels the parties, who sold it 'short,' or without owning it, to buy of it at a high price, in order to deliver the stock, previously sold at a low figure. The operation is attended with multitudinous risks ; and millions of dollars are lost and won in that way every year, the losers being designated, in the parlance of brokers, as 'lame ducks.' "

At that moment, several boys began shouting, and distributing throughout the hall the prospectus of a new enterprise.   Brokers and operators eagerly seized a copy.   I did like the others, and read the following:

"Wonders never cease ! ! !   We possess gold mines rich enough to pay, within a few years, the debts of all existing governments, including that of the United States.   The Rocky Mountains contain in their mighty recesses silver enough to supply with argentiferous rails the road now building from the Atlantic to the Pacific coasts ! !   We work out, by the healthful light of the sun, inexhaustible mountains of coal, unrivaled in quality ; while the miserable nations of Europe are compelled to extract their fuel from the bowels of the earth, at a depth of several thousand feet—even below the bed of the ocean.   To supply with a most beautiful and economical light our cities and dwellings, we had but to bore a few holes in the soil of two or three States ; and behold ! we to-day announce to the whole world a discovery that exceeds the most extravagant dreams of modern novelists and the most wonderful fancies of the Arabian Nights' tales.

"In the State of Humbuggia, while cutting through a hill, which the railroad connecting Humbuggia with the other stars of the American constellation will traverse, some workmen struck a never-failing spring of milk, of exquisite flavor and taste.   This phenomenon was explained when the workmen, cutting still deeper, arrived at immense deposits of petrified butter and honey.   These products, buried to a great depth, no doubt for centuries, have retained their original flavor and resume a golden hue after being exposed to the air a few moments.   The celebrated Professor Sillyman has just completed a report on this prodigious discovery, which report is approved by a committee of geologists and other learned gentlemen, who have flocked to Humbuggia from every part of the

Union ; and in which it is demonstrated beyond cavil that those inexhaustible deposits of butter and honey have been heaped up (in prevision of events, the real character of which, at this distant date, can not be safely ascertained) by a race of men of stupendous strength, probably giants, who lived before the flood. The great bankers, Gullying and Company, whose name is a tower of strength, after examining all the particulars of the enterprise, have read-ily. assented to place forty thousand shares, of fifty.dollars each, of the company, (organized under the State laws,) for the purpose of working out these deposits of incalcu-lable wealth, whose discovery, at this time, must be attri-buted to an ever-benevolent Providence ! The subscription to the capital stock of the Condensed Milk, Honey, and Butter Company will be opened to-day, at noon, at the office of the afore-mentioned eminent firm."

As the time for the opening of the subscription had nearly arrived, the crowd, after reading this astounding prospectus, hurried out of the hall. We followed, and saw it hastening to the great banking-house of Messrs. Gullying and Company.

"Come on ! come on !" vociferated one of the clerks, standing on the stoop of the building. "Come on ! twenty thousand shares have been already taken up by our friends ! The proprietors of the deposits could have form-ed three companies out of them—one for the milk, one for the honey, and the other for the butter. But they aspire to be benefactors to their countrymen, and sacrifice their own interest to the public welfare ! Hurry up ! hurry up ! Within ten minutes all the stock will be disposed of, and you will lose an opportunity to make a fortune at a bound !"

"I will take one hundred shares !" exclaimed one of

the bystanders. "I will take two hundred!" said another. "Three hundred!" "Five hundred!" vociferated others. The would-be stockholders crowded around the office, where two persons only were admitted at once, to avoid disorder. As they emerged from it, after depositing their money, they held up in a triumphant manner a slip of paper.

"Do not believe," said Asmodeus, "that these men who seem so eager to subscribe to the stock have the slightest confidence in the success of the enterprise. None considers he has made a sound investment, and most of them will get rid of their certificates of stock before night. The last holder of those worthless bits of paper is infallibly the loser; and the great point, in the emission of such fictitious values, is not to be the last holder."

Asmodeus's observation was justified by the event. As soon as the clerk, who kept up the enthusiasm, notified the crowd that the forty thousand shares had been taken up and the subscription-book was closed, a tremendous excitement at once occurred among the stock-gamblers standing in front of Messrs. Gullying and Co.'s office.

"I will sell at ten per cent premium!" said one. "Sold!" exclaimed another. "At fifteen per cent premium!" "Sold! sold!" rejoined the same purchaser. The biddings warmed up; and before we went away, the stock of the Condensed Milk, Honey, and Butter Company was at fifty per cent premium!

We now retraced our steps to the court-house. The case of the young girl had not yet come on, and a solitary judge was rendering a decision on wills and legacies.

"The American," said Asmodeus, "generally makes his own will. The principle of liberty, which stamps itself on every thing in the United States, could not fail to

exert its wonted influence in the grave matter of inheritance and succession. Disposing, while living, of his property as he pleases, the American believes he has the
right to dispose of it in case of his death. His free will
as a monument of the immortality of his soul, survives him
after he leaves this world. The validity of his testament
and the last manifestation of his free will are seldom
questioned, except in case of insanity.

."The law neither ascribes an equal portion nor a reservation to children ; and a father leaves them such shares
of his fortune as he deems proper. A New-York merchant
worth seven millions of dollars, died a few years ago, leaving several children, among whom was a daughter, who
had married contrary to her father's desire. He deprived
her of any inheritance ; and though the victim of a resentment which the approach of death could not appease
was the object of general sympathy, her father's testament
was not questioned.

"In fact, the right of making one's own will being admitted, no limit, as a logical sequence, can be put to it.
From another point of view, it is obvious the power vested
in fathers to dispose of their property, without limitation
or reservation, strengthens family ties instead of weakening them. Children behave well toward parents, and
cheerfully perform the duties nature requires of them, because they are aware their father might punish their ill-
behavior by excluding them from his inheritance. Fortune and succession hunting, though a thing not absolutely
unknown in the United States, is far from being as common as in Europe.

"Wealthy persons often bequeath a portion of their
money to benevolent institutions ; and their natural heirs
do not complain, as it is a general creed that a man who

has accumulated a fortune has the right to dispose of it as he likes. Another thing is worth observing : sons do not selfishly long for the death of their fathers, as the law does not allow them a reserved portion ; and instead of awaiting a fortune from an inheritance, they strive to make one themselves. Besides, the fluctuations of life are so frequent in the United States, that any dependence upon a millionaire's succession would often prove delusive. The American enjoys no rest until he breathes his last, and never thinks of retiring from business. Then, what a folly to wait to build a fortune upon the inheritance of a man who perhaps may die penniless !

" Successions and legacies are, in Europe, the source of many a base transaction, and, perhaps, of many a crime. Unprejudiced minds have regarded the portion allowed by law to children as an outrage on paternal right and morality. And in the matter of succession, as in that of marriage and marriage portions, the American democracy teaches the Old World some valuable lessons. Young men who have not desecrated the solemn compact of marriage by making of it a mercantile transaction, do not wait in shameful idleness for the death of their parents. Thus labor becomes a wholesome necessity for every body —for wealthy as well as for poor people's sons. As a consequence, in the Northern States, labor is held in such high esteem that men feel uneasy when they have no regular business to employ their minds. Public opinion is so strong in that respect, that they rent an office, even when they have no business to transact, for fear of showing, by their idleness, a bad example to their children, and being charged with wasting in leisure a useless life."

Asmodeus was here interrupted by the court magistrates and jurors entering the room. And now the criminal case was called up. The young girl to be sentenced was brought in by one of the prison-keepers ; and in the midst of a solemn silence, the presiding judge began a lengthy speech. He minutely summed up all the incidents of the case, and concluded by saying that, the jurors having returned a verdict of guilty, a painful duty devolved upon him—that of sentencing to death the convicted prisoner. The speech, which lasted nearly an hour, ended amid sobs and every demonstration of genuine grief.

I asked Asmodeus whether it was customary to deliver so prolix a harangue to prisoners before sentencing them. Asmodeus answered affirmatively, adding :

" The passion for speech-making and playing the orator is so general, the Americans seize upon every occasion, even a solemn one, to gratify that immoderate passion. Most of the officers of the law being politicians, they de-' light, on every convenient occasion, to show the public they have lost none of their eloquence since they commenced to administer justice and decide controversies. But it may be doubted whether the custom of addressing prisoners enhances the prestige and majesty of the law. The taste and sense of the orators, on these solemn occasions, are not always above criticism ; and it would often be praise-worthy were magistrates to confine themselves simply to applying the law."

When the keeper was on the point of removing the sentenced girl to prison, I noticed that many persons presented her with books, newspapers, linen, flowers, and dainties. "The Americans are emphatically a good-hearted people," said Asmodeus. "Those persons wish to comfort as much as possible that unfortunate girl, who will not be in need of any thing while detained in custody. There is little probability, however, of the death-sentence being carried into effect. Not half-a-dozen women have been hanged since the beginning of this century, and the State governor will certainly commute her sentence."

We left the court-room, expecting to have nothing more to do that day with the judiciary ; but hardly had we stepped into the street, when we jostled against a corpulent man, with a ruddy face, who seemed to be in a hurry.

" Halloo ! Coroner Sharp, where are you going in such haste ?" said Asmodeus, who positively knows every body in town. " To hold an inquest on Dr. Clever, who was found dead this morning in his office," replied the officer of the law ; "and, if you say so, I will take you along with me, to serve on the jury."

My companion assenting, I followed him, and we soon arrived at a house situated in a fashionable street of the city. Friends of the doctor and persons attracted by a morbid curiosity were standing in front of the dwelling, and made way for us, when the coroner's business was known. We went into a room situated on the first floor— it was Dr. Clever's office. The shutters were so tightly closed that I could hardly discern the dead body of the doctor, which was lying on a sofa in a corner of the room. A lady was kneeling beside it, weeping and sobbing. When a servant, at the coroner's command, opened the shutters, and daylight dispelled the darkness of the room, I recognized in the kneeling woman the visitor who had asked Mrs. Smart, the day before, her advice and prognostications concerning her intended marriage, and whose ill-looks, according to the pythoness, boded no good. The coroner now went out on the stoop, and inquired whether there were among the crowd any persons qualified to serve as jurors. Eleven of them having answered affirmatively— for Asmodeus made up the required twelve—"Come in, then," said the officer of the law; "we will at once commence our inquest into the causes of the doctor's death."

While servants stripped the dead body, and a physician, among the persons present, volunteered to make a post-mortem examination, the coroner took the testimony of several persons. The first heard was the woman, who continued sobbing near the sofa. She declared her business was that of keeping a boarding-house; that Dr. Clever had boarded with her but a few months; that wondering why he did not come down at his usual time for breakfast, she had gone up to his room, and, to her utter consternation and horror, found him lying in a pool of blood and already a corpse. Alarmed at this discovery, she had aroused the other inmates of the house, and sent immediately for the coroner. The latter heard successively all the boarders. But none gave any information concerning either the circumstances or the authors of the murder, which looked very like a domestic drama, when the physician, having examined the victim's body, stated that Dr. Clever had been stabbed in twenty-two different places, the said stabs and consequent loss of blood having caused his death.

"That murder is a woman's work," sternly remarked Asmodeus, who was, as I have said, one of the jury. "A man stabs once or twice, and the bloody work is done; but a woman mangles her victim—she strikes at random —especially if she be infuriated and blinded by passion. Is not this your opinion, Mrs. Cunning?" he added, turning to the boarding-house keeper.

But the coroner silenced Asmodeus, observing that the right to ask questions devolved upon himself alone. Then the boarders having stated that each of them had a latch-key, and consequently could come in and go out at any hour of the day or night, the coroner remarked that nearly all New-York dwelling-houses are built upon the same plan, and externally resemble each other.

"One day," said he, " or rather, one night, after partaking of a dinner, given me by my political friends, to celebrate my election, I mistook another door for mine, and opened with my latch-key that of the next house. I discovered my mistake just as I was on the point of gliding into the bed of my neighbor, who slept soundly by the side of his wife."

At these last words, the company burst out laughing, in spite of the solemn occasion and the proximity of Dr. Clever's mangled body. Then the coroner requested the jury to withdraw into one of the parlors, and to return a verdict. One of the juryman asked whether it would not be proper to adjourn the inquest to the next day.

" No need of it," answered the coroner. " You have heard the testimony of all the inmates of the house ; and there is not the slightest possibility on earth we shall obtain any further information concerning this mysterious murder."

Thereupon the jurors retired, and, after a few minutes' deliberation, brought in a verdict, by which they declared that Dr. Clever had died, according to the best of their knowledge and belief, from wounds inflicted by a sharp weapon, either a knife or dagger, and that the author or authors of the bloody deed were unknown to the jury. The coroner thanked them for the remarkable sagacity and high sense of duty they had exhibited, and discharged them from further attendance. Mrs. Cunning, who had fainted several times during the inquest, then made known her intention to have her unfortunate boarder decently buried ; and every body left the house.

" This is a queer way," said I to Asmodeus, " to conduct an inquest and investigate a case of murder."

" Do you not remember I once told you that many officers of the law, though their salary amounts to only four thousand dollars per annum, and sometimes even less, find means, notwithstanding, to have a bank account of fifty thousand dollars, when, after four years, their term of office expires ?   Mrs. Cunning belongs to a family of good standing, and as she found in the doctor's desk a quantity of bank-bills, many of them, I apprehend, are actually in the pocket of the jolly coroner, whose inquest would have been carried on differently had the murder been committed by a poor girl, without money or friends, like the one sentenced this morning to be hanged."

Night had approached, and Asmodeus remembered he was invited to a *soirée*, to take place that very evening, at the house of one of the most aristocratic families of New-York—a family of Bourbons, as he facetiously remarked.

" Let us go and spend a few hours there," said he. " We have need to move in a less gloomy atmosphere than that of the house we have just left ; though, to tell you the truth, the persons to whom I shall introduce you are not conspicuous for the sprightliness and witty turn of their minds."

We soon reached the house, and were inducted into a spacious parlor of oblong shape, in which were, as yet, but a few guests. The furniture was not as stylish as that seen nowadays among the rich.

" The New-York ladies," said Asmodeus, " want new furniture every five years. As a consequence, it is made in a hurry, of showy materials, and lacks durability. The same is true of New-York dwellings—they are built exclusively according to the taste and conveniencies of the day. The American does not think of erecting a dwelling for future generations, as in Europe. He builds it for himself, and according to his own fancy. The plan he has adopted and the internal arrangements of his mansion, which suit him, might perhaps displease his children ; yet, by building a house with strong and lasting materials, he would, in a measure, encroach on their liberty. In fact, many sons often rebuild the paternal mansion to fit it agreeably to the prevailing fashion ; and that love of change and improvement, coupled with the necessity of erecting new edifices in place of those destroyed by fire, explains why our streets are generally topsy-turvy and their circulation impeded by piles of dirt."

Meanwhile, the parlors were fast filling, most of the guests being officers of the army and navy, high functionaries of the Federal administration, and some distinguished foreigners. With the exception of a few steamship and railroad directors, commerce and industry had few representatives—though the grandfather of the lady of the house, according to Asmodeus, had accumulated much money in mercantile pursuits. In fact, hanging in one of the parlors, could be seen the portrait of an old gentleman, wearing a wig, as was the fashion in the last century. At the foot of the picture was the following inscription :

" Van Oldscamp, Member of the Chamber of Commerce, New-York, 1770."

"There is incontestably," said Asmodeus, " among the countrymen of Washington, a morbid taste for distinction— a craving for aristocratic titles. If you listen to the guests, you will notice they call each other either general, colonel, or commodore. The truth is, that among the officers of the army and navy actually here, few, very few hold those ranks. As they belong to some yachting-club or militia regiment in which high-sounding titles abound, they glory in these glittering distinctions, which, after all, open to them many a house in Europe, where such deceits of American vanity are little suspected. Perhaps you have also noticed that public functionaries form an important part of the assemblage. In Europe, the aristocracy, especially during the past fifty years, has monopolized public offices. Hence the reason, to some extent, of that reverence shown by the masses for government officers. Here they do not, as yet, form a distinct class, and have not the influence they enjoy in the Old World. The main reason of the difference is, there is no permanency or stability in the condition of public officers. Every new President removes all those he finds in office, and appoints his friends and partisans in their stead. Still, that ' clean sweep,' as the operation is termed, does not include the officers of the army and navy, who have been educated, in general, at the Government's expense. They retain their situation and military rank, notwithstanding all presidential changes ; and thus form the only class in the country that may boast of some stability. Besides, they are men of more refined education than the majority of their countrymen. Hence the aristocratic pretensions not a few assume, and their undisguised contempt for the mass of the people. Though devoted to their country, I suspect the army and navy do not entertain an unbounded enthusiasm for democratic institutions. Some officers offered the crown to the modest Washington, which offer he resented as an insult. But should the standing army of the United States at any time become more numerous than it is to-day, I draw this conclusion from that recollection of the past—democratic institutions would find in it, as in Europe, a dangerous enemy.

" There, for instance, is an admiral, whose name has been made illustrious by his grandfather, who was an admiral in the Revolutionary War ; his father was also an admiral ; in short, this dignity is transmitted from father to son in that family, and consequently its aristocratic aspirations increase from generation to generation. That general who is conversing with him has written his name on the scroll of fame. He is possessed of the rare gift of reticence, or of uttering words, when condescending to speak, which have little meaning ; hence his reputation for being a profound statesman no less than a good general. He is a graduate of West-Point, a military school where young men are submitted to a discipline somewhat at variance with the general habits and tendencies of the people.

" The gentleman who is now shaking hands with the general, and who will, undoubtedly, try to 'pump' him concerning his political opinions, is one of the few merchants and bankers admitted into this aristocratic society, and he is indebted for that privilege to his wealth, which is large, though but recently accumulated. He acquired it through stock-gambling, and is one of those financiers who, when the Federal Government wanted to borrow money for the maintenance of its large armies, proclaimed, through the thousand organs of the Press, that the more a nation increases her debt, the richer she becomes ! That new principle of political economy was not certainly a sophism, so far as concerns the banker. He has just constructed a palatial residence, where over five hundred guests may find comfortable accommodation. There is in that residence an ancestors' gallery, consisting of about one hundred and fifty portraits in oil, purchased at random in Paris and London. Our stock-jobber has so often paraded these paintings as family portraits, that he is now firmly convinced every one of them represents one of his ancestors—though they are, for the most part, old Dutch burgomasters."

We now made our way to the lady of the house, to whom Asmodeus introduced me.

" How happy you must be," said she, after the usual ceremonies, " to have resided in *la belle France!* When I visit that country, I can not help admiring the respect the people entertain for their rulers.   Here it is just the contrary.   Respect for services rendered to the country, for traditions, for our standing in society, exists nowhere. There is no distinction, no caste—in short, to speak to the point, no common people at all.   Every body dresses alike, and I may not be distinguished from my cook when, her work over, she takes a promenade through the streets. Ah! how many times have I wished that the United States contained such a class of rustics as that to be met with in France, and whose dress and habits are to-day exactly as they were eighteen hundred years ago!   How quaint, how charming are the country women, with their caps of so many and whimsical shapes!   And the men, wearing blouses and wooden shoes!   How prompt they are to guess our rank, and to bow respectfully as we pass by! Alas! there is nothing of that kind here.   During my last visit to Europe," pursued the lady, " I spent eight days at the country-seat of the Countess of Strass.   At church, we sat in a separate pew ; the priest offered us holy water, and young girls and little children, on our leaving the sanctuary, kissed our hands.   In England, at the manor of my friend, the Marchioness of Fairrags, I was the object of the same reverence and homage from the country folks.   When I travel in Europe, I feel loth to confess I am a native of America—a country where public offices are within the reach of every body; where a mechanic may become the supreme magistrate of the land—in short, a country of upstarts."

"I admit," said Asmodeus, "that the United States are, in many respects, the antipodes of Europe. We enjoy, in the fall, a temperature experienced there in the spring; east winds bring with them rain and dampness, instead of dryness, to the atmosphere, as in Europe. The sky here is never so lovely as in winter, and the snowy season is one of carnival and pleasure to the inhabitants of both city and country. The States' heaviest expenditure is for educational purposes; while in Europe, it is for the maintenance of large armies. We appreciate self-made men more than scions of ancient and wealthy families. All our women are queens—at least they have an undisputed sway over men, whom they try to convince that extravagance in dress is conducive to general prosperity. I do not pretend to say that commerce and industry would languish and all progress cease, should notions of economy prevail here as in Europe; still, I would rather see our women decked in silks and velvets than in coarse cloths, and their husbands wearing well-cut coats than the Celt's smock-frock !"

"Ah sir !" said the lady, "I had been told, but could not believe it, that you were a warm friend to and admirer of the United States !"

"Madame," answered my companion, "I am far from admiring every thing; for I find fault with many things. But, on calm consideration, whoever has traveled throughout the world must agree with me that man is better fed here, better clothed, better housed, and better paid than in any other country. Whatever be the cause of this—

whether the disposition and habits of the Americans, their
institutions, or the rich continent they inhabit—it is an
undeniable fact, sufficient to justify my preference for the
United States. And the greatest compliment you ever
paid it was when you pointed out this favored land as a
country of upstarts. Every one of us· strives to rise to
wealth, power, and distinction ; and when we have succeeded in our endeavors, is it just to stigmatize a country
where the energy of its men is more surely and promptly
rewarded than in any other ?"

"Give me your hand, my dear sir," said the lady, at
the last words of Asmodeus. "You know well our weak
points. We Americans are apt to find fault with every
thing pertaining to our country, our morals, our institutions. When foreigners do the same, we impatiently bear
their criticism. But we are always grateful for their eulo-
gies—even when they contradict our notions and ideas."

While Asmodeus was conversing with the lady, some
· young officers had drawn near and listened attentively.

"Then you believe," said one of these to my friend, "in
the destinies of the American Republic?"

"Unless blind," answered Asmodeus, "or unable to
understand the great events which have occurred in the
history of this country since the beginning of this century,
we must admit a mighty mission has devolved upon the
American people—that of expanding throughout the vast
continent of North-America the institutions of an enlightened society, of religion, charity, art, and education—in
short, all the blessings of an advanced civilization—of
carrying them, ere long, even to the West-Indies, and the
group of islands scattered throughout the Pacific Ocean.
As one of the most gifted sons of Massachusetts said, a
few years ago, ' The pioneers are already on their march,

and who can tell how rapid it will be ; where and when their onward course will stop?   Who would dare to lift the curtain which conceals the varied events of future centuries? The Turkish empire, pitched for four hundred years on the borders of Europe, and the Chinese monarchy, cotemporaneous with David and Solomon, are crumbling into dust.   Europe is exhausting her vitality and strength in mean rivalries ; and the political life of the world seems really to advance toward a new hemisphere.   The business and duty of the American Republic will be to settle the future condition of existence of that hemisphere's millions and millions of inhabitants ; and the world will behold, at a no distant day, a confederacy of free states, more powerful than ever was the Roman empire !"

The auditors could not refrain from warmly applauding Asmodeus, who politely bowed at the compliment ; and shortly after, we took our departure.   When in the street, and while I was congratulating my companion on his brilliant sketch of America's destiny, a beggar approached and asked us for alms.

" This time, Marquis," said Asmodeus, " I catch you *in flagrante delicto;* and to punish you, I shall relate your history to one of your countrymen."

CHAPTER XXIII.

"IN every community, based either upon monarchical or democratic principles, there is a class of persons that depends on public charity for a living. Pauperism was not unknown among the Athenians. Their legislator, Solon, directed that the republic should adopt the widows and children of those who had been killed while fighting for their country. It existed also among the Romans. The laws of that iron-hearted people plainly declared it to be better to let beggars starve than to support them in their idleness. During the mediæval period, pauperism spread to a frightful extent; and in our own age, when commerce and industry have made such wonderful progress, the scourge does not seem to abate. As concerns the United States, pauperism would be unknown if the vice of intoxication, idleness, and some other evil practices could be eradicated from human society; because the means of acquiring wealth is within the reach of every body, and also, because the remuneration of labor affords to men of economical habits easy ways of living. Pauperism, however, especially in large cities, is fearfully on the increase. Hundreds of mechanics are daily met with in New-York in quest of work. Propose to give them employment, on condition that they remove to some State—for instance, to the fertile West—and they will scorn the proposition ; they will decline to leave the metropolis, where they wallow in misery and vice. Furthermore, many immigrants to this country refuse to work when the salary offered them is below the expectation they cherished on leaving Europe, and will perhaps finally join the ranks of those professional mendicants who have crossed the ocean to practice here their calling.

"It is even highly probable that pauperism would have more rapidly increased, had not the Federal administration objected to the sending here, by some European governments, of their paupers and vagabonds ; and its threat to prevent the further landing of immigrants of that class was the only means to stop this growing evil.

"The man who asked us for alms was brought over, a few years ago, by a ship chartered by a foreign government for the purpose of transferring its surplus paupers and vagrants to the care of the United States. He belongs to one of the most ancient families of France, and is, in reality, a marquis—the title, you will remember, by which I addressed him. You will doubtless be surprised to learn that the marquis's wife has again married, notwithstanding her lord is still living ; and his own children have inherited his fortune in the same way as though he were really dead. There are in France, as well as in other countries, very singular laws ; and you will understand, from the sequel, how that nobleman became a mendicant in the streets of New-York.

"In 1832, two years after the overthrow of the Bourbons from the throne of France, an insurrection broke out in some western provinces of that country. Noblemen, and especially the poor country squires, rose in arms against

a government repugnant to their feelings and prejudices.
Well acquainted with a country intersected with cross-
roads, hedges, and woods, through which the regulars
did not dare to move, the insurgents resorted to a par-
tisan warfare. They did not shrink from even committing many a highway robbery; until the people, coming to
the government's assistance, put an end to the insurrection.

"One of the noblemen, who had, with the aid of his
servants and farmers, attacked the tax-collectors and *gen-
darmes*, stopped public conveyances, and robbed the travelers, was a young man whose father had lost his patrimony at the time of the first French revolution. That
young man, the Marquis of Limbaudieres, is the beggar
whose history I am now relating.

"It is useless to enter into details concerning the Vendean insurrection. Suffice it to say, the royalist chiefs
could not come to an understanding; and the Duchess
of Berry, the mother of the Pretender, after a short stay
among her partisans, and many a romantic adventure,
took refuge in a devoted friend's house; but only to be
soon betrayed by a German Jew, and delivered over to the
French government.

"When peace was restored in the western provinces,
the duchess's partisans—principally those who had resorted to plunder—were unmercifully prosecuted. Among
these was the young Marquis of Limbaudieres; and as it
was proved he had committed many a deed of pillage,
such as civil warfare itself could not excuse, he was sentenced to hard labor for life.

"According to French law the consequences of such a
condemnation are terrible. The man who has incurred
it is divested of all his property, which at once devolves

upon his natural heirs, in the same manner as though he were dead; and if he be married, his marriage is annulled —his wife being at liberty to enter again the matrimonial state.

"When the Vendean insurrection took place, the Marquis of Limbaudieres was married and the father of two children. As he had no fortune, he condescended to ask in marriage the daughter of a lawyer, a man of considerable wealth. Though the lawyer's daughter was reputed to be in love with one of her father's clerks, she had to submit, and had been the marquis's wife three years, when he was sentenced to hard labor for life.

"The marchioness, though she had borne her husband two children, had never loved him; and in the sudden bereavement that had come upon her, she thought proper to take the advice of her father's former clerk, now himself a promising lawyer. The lawyer informed her she was free to marry again, as, according to the laws of France, her husband was dead, so far as regarded his status in society; furthermore, that the administration of the marquis's large fortune had devolved upon her. This advice led the marchioness to seriously reflect on her future prospects, and the result of her reflections was, that, after a few months, she threw off her title of nobility and became her former lover's wife.

"Fifteen years elapsed. During that period, the Marquis vainly tried, from his jail, to obtain intelligence of his wife and children, and the latter had just become inheritors of a large fortune from distant relatives of their father, when he unexpectedly recovered his liberty.

"Another revolution, that of 1848, had broken out in France; and the new government granted a general pardon to all political offenders sentenced under the last *régime.* The marquis availed himself of his freedom to repair at once to his former home; and there he ascertained he had neither family nor property now on earth. As regards his children, they were squandering the fortune they had just inherited from their father's relatives; and, under the pretense he had disgraced the family name, they declined to see or have aught to do with him.

"Amid these discomfitures, the poor marquis was threatened with starvation. He had no profession; his education had been such that he could attend to no mercantile business; and to fill the measure of his misery, he could not claim an alimony from his children or from his former wife; for, as he was lawfully dead, he had no power to institute an action before any tribunal. Maddened by despair, the marquis resolved that, as a barbarous law had reduced him to beggary, he would in reality become a beggar. And hence he commenced to beg—not only to keep him from starvation, but also, by the daily exhibition of his misery, to humble and punish his ungrateful relatives. He asked the passers-by for alms in the very street in which his former wife and children resided; gloomy and resigned, he imparted to nobody the sorrow of his heart nor his resentment; but every body pitied him, and knew his distress and misery were a reproach to society, to cruel and antiquated laws, to a wealthy and unnatural family.

"The marquis led this life three years; after which, his children, urged by the clamor of public opinion and their father's former friends, offered him an annuity of one thousand dollars, provided he would leave the country. The marquis accepted it, because he had fully chastised a heartless family, and also because he knew he should lose public sympathy were he to beg again, now that his wants

were provided for. So he left the country and went to
Paris.

"Here begins a period, in the marquis's life, which
would be really unaccountable were not the human heart
an unfathomable abyss of contradictions and mysteries.
This man, who had actually a competency—this nobleman
by birth, education, and feelings—asked alms in the streets
of Paris as he had done in a French province. He had
there formed the habit of begging, and now he could not
rid himself of it. One could meet him almost any day, at
the French capital's fashionable resorts, elegantly dressed
and attracting the attention of every one by his easy deportment and gentlemanlike appearance. The same man,
at night, donning a smock-frock, and wearing a greasy,
slouched hat, begged for alms of passers-by, whom he
tried to move to pity by relating his mournful adventures.
Arrested, time and again, by the police, and several times
put in prison as an inveterate mendicant, he left France in
disgust, and went to Belgium. Beggars abound in that
small kingdom, and the public authorities—a fact the
marquis was not aware of—sometimes deal harshly with
that unfortunate class of the population. One day, they
arrested in the streets of Brussels several hundred of
these beggars and hurried them off to Antwerp, where
they were embarked on board a sailing vessel chartered
for the occasion. Those not very desirable immigrants
arrived here previously to the determination of the government to prevent the further landing of foreigners of that
description, who can be but a burden to the country ; and
thus it happened the marquis is now treading the soil of
the great Republic.

"He had hardly landed, when he began to indulge his
propensity—now an incurable mania—for begging. The

police know him well ; but as he is always supplied with
money when arrested, and has satisfactorily proved that he
has an annuity of one thousand dollars, the officers of the law
do not feel justified in dealing with him as they do with
common beggars and vagabonds. They give him a gentle reprimand, exact from him a promise that he will relinquish his degrading business, and then discharge him.
The next day, the marquis has, of course, forgotten his
promise, and begs in the streets as soon as night comes
on ; for this habit of begging is as strong now with him as
nature itself.

"This instance of a disordered reason suggests an observation, which I now venture to make as a conclusion.
I firmly believe posterity will look with contempt upon our
penal legislation, our classing of crimes and offenses, and
the severe penalties inflicted on offenders in certain circumstances. In many a dubious case, in many an in-
fraction of penal laws, society ought to require the physician's intervention rather than that of a judge applying
severe laws, which are, most of the time, of no scientific
value. We must acknowledge the United States have
been quick to understand that many crimes are brought
on by mental perturbation, and consequently criminal law
has nothing to do with them ; that many offenders are but
diseased persons and need medical examination—in short,
that physicians must point out, as often as criminal judges,
the proper remedies for all deviations from the right path."

CHAPTER XXIV.

SMODEUS has left New-York, and never, perhaps, shall I see him again! While awaiting his usual morning call, a messenger brought me the following letter:

"After leaving you yesterday, I decided to go to China, and I now write on board of one of the steamers of the Pacific Mail Steamship Company, which carries travelers to the Isthmus of Panama, thence to San Francisco, and from San Francisco to the extreme Orient. I said, last night, at the mansion of the friend of the Marchioness of Fairrags, while delineating the destinies of America, that the Chinese empire was falling to decay, and I want to ascertain whether such an assertion be correct; for, on reflection, I can hardly believe an empire founded over three thousand years ago is actually tottering—especially when we take into consideration that such was the powerful influence the Chinese exerted over intruding nations, they never failed to absorb and subjugate them to their own manners and institutions. At all events, we must acknowledge the Chinese monarchy, cotemporaneous with the Egyptian Pharaohs, was made up of wonderful materials. What a tremendous noise will such an edifice make when it falls! I want to assist at so magnificent a sight. Hence my sudden departure.

"When I visited China years ago, Europeans had hardly a foothold there. To-day, almost all the seaports of the great Chinese empire are open to the Caucasian race, and it remains to be seen whether the contact of the latter will prove as destructive to the descendants of Confucius as it has to the Indians of America—as it will, perhaps, to the blacks, now emerging to citizenship and enjoying equal rights with the whites in the great Republic. Withal, to cross the Pacific Ocean on board of one of those steamers Americans are so justly proud of, afforded such a tempting inducement to gratify my traveling propensity, I could not resist it. When, in a few years, I return to America, I may find increased by twenty and perhaps more new States—stretching from the Rocky Mountains to the Pacific coast and up to Behring's Strait and the Aleutian Islands—this already mighty Union. It will then confound the institutions of the Old World and their effete governments. For the Americans are the pioneers of the great doctrine that it is the right of the living to enjoy the good things of the earth, as much as it is their duty to create wealth for those who come after; and the great spectacle of millions and millions of people, living prosperous and happy under the protecting shade of democratic liberty will open a new era to mankind. Who can foretell the many changes such an increase of power and *prestige* will work in American manners and habits?

"I do not believe, however, the principal features of the national character will experience any marked change for a long time to come. Americans will retain, for centuries perhaps, their restlessness and spirit of enterprise, their fickleness and love of progress, in a word, their good and bad qualities, until they have redeemed from a wilderness and turned over to civilization the vast continent of North-

America. And do not apprehend they will fail to carry out this providential mission, through political strifes and divisions. The homogeneity of the American nation and the integrity of the Republic are now secure, notwithstan·ing the vast territory her flag floats over. The American carries everywhere the same manners and feelings ; and one wonders at the uniformity of language, of aspiration, of ideas, existing from Canada to the Gulf of Mexico ; from the Alleghanies to the argentiferous mountains of Nevada. And such marvelous uniformity appears in every thing, under every shape : it exists in the buildings, in the mechanic processes, in the customs of the people, in their hatreds, in their sympathies. The reason of this is obvious : the American is forever traveling ; he carries everywhere the ideas and habits with which he was nurtured, and thus he feels at home everywhere throughout the vast area of the northern continent.

"Foreigners, to correctly understand the workings of American society, should always bear in mind that the government is the people and the people the government in the American Union. Minds lacking that comprehension, or sullen and morose, predict the disruption of the Republic, and foretell that several hostile communities will arise from its fragments. The varied and antagonistic interests which, as a matter of course, exist on so extensive a territory, will peacefully adjust themselves. Steam and electricity have annihilated time and distance, and every day more firmly unite the different portions of a country in which men feel no extravagant love for the narrow locality where they were born. The patriotism of the Americans is as broad as the continent they inhabit. They are, in reality, more attached to their institutions than to the soil of their birth. Citizens of an immense country, they are strangers in no part of it, and they are as much at home on the banks of the Mississippi as on those of the Hudson; in the perfumed groves of Florida, as on the hills of Vermont.

"That unmistakable tendency of the whole nation to annex and absorb her neighbors is, to an equal extent, noticeable with individuals. Be always on your guard when trading or transacting business with an American. He has the peculiar faculty of elbowing every one out of the way, and making room for himself alone. Having a natural turn for business, he is often unwittingly led from the path of right, by the astuteness it develops in his mind. A great borrower, he will borrow with his pockets full of money, and never decline a proffered loan. As a consequence, he is the greatest maker of fiduciary paper in the world. Were such a thing possible, he would, without hesitation, purchase all the kingdoms on earth, offering his note in payment; and, if accepted, little trouble himself about it until it was due.

"As he relies upon himself to a wonderful extent for every thing, and in every circumstance, he admits of no superiority, and thinks himself equal to any body; competent for any work, any enterprise, and any station in society. Kind-hearted and good-natured, he exhibits in conversation an insufferable conceit of himself; still, such are the fairness and candor of his assertions, his hearers do not attach to them much importance, and feel no more inclined to contradict him than they would the harmless prattle of children.

"We could have visited what is termed the background of civilization—that is, the dens of misery, corruption, and crime. But what enlightenment could we have gained, as regards American manners, and the peculiar features of

American society? Some evils disgrace every community, and seem the inevitable accompaniment of society. And political institutions, as near to perfection as we fancy them, have been, as yet, powerless to eradicate thóse evils, and to establish such social relations as will give to each person the fullest satisfaction of his wants.

"If you settle in the United States, do not believe every thing that glitters is pure gold. The great wealth that many persons boast of is, in most cases, but imaginary. Americans are wonderfully predisposed to exaggeration and bombast, and though they are kind-hearted, such is often their fickleness and levity, that foreigners have charged them with selfishness and want of feeling.

"The boasted wealth of many individuals is not the only thing that is fictitious in the United States. The same is often true of science, of religion, of religious freedom, of public and private morals. Individualism, or attachment to the interests of individuals, in preference to the common interests of society, is at the bottom of every thing—political institutions, civil laws, and morals ; and consequently, to the American the world is himself.

"Hence it follows that discretion and caution are indispensable requisites for foreigners settling among such a people. If they have brought money from Europe, let them keep it, and refrain from investing it in any enterprise, until they have acquired a perfect knowledge of the country; and, to get a satisfactory knowledge of it, of the Americans' ways of doing business, of their character and morals, not a few weeks, nor a few months, but several years are required.

"It is fair to conjecture that men of refined education— such as artists and person sattached to aristocratic traditions of older forms of society—do not thoroughly enjoy themselves in, and so dislike, the United States. They have certainly little chance to succeed, whatever be the field of labor they choose to work in ; and many a disappointment, many a delusion is in store for them, whether they finally succeed or not.

"On the contrary, mechanics and operatives—those who are conversant with the useful and industrial arts—immigrants skillful in some handicraft, have no excuse for not achieving success and acquiring a competency. But whatever be the sphere they move in, the profession they adopt, or the business they engage in, they ought ever to bear in mind the advice Mentor gave Telemachus, on the eve of leaving his pupil :

' " LISTEN TO EVERY BODY, AND TRUST BUT A FEW !'

" ASMODEUS."

www.ingramcontent.com/pod-product-compliance
Lightning Source LLC
Chambersburg PA
CBHW051213120726
47905CB00004B/1096